SUMMER

At

Skylark

Farm

Also by Heidi Swain

The Cherry Tree Café

HEIDI SWAIN

SUMMER

At
Skylark
Farm

SIMON &
SCHUSTER

London · New York · Sydney · Toronto · New Delhi

A CBS COMPANY

First published in Great Britain by Simon & Schuster UK Ltd, 2016
A CBS company

5 7 9 10 8 6 4

Simon & Schuster UK Ltd
1st Floor
222 Gray's Inn Road
London WC1X 8HB

www.simonandschuster.co.uk

Simon & Schuster Australia, Sydney
Simon & Schuster India, New Delhi

A CIP catalogue record for this book is available from the British Library

Paperback ISBN: 978-1-4711-5783-7
eBook ISBN: 978-1-4711-5009-8

Typeset by Hewer Text UK Ltd, Edinburgh
Printed and bound in Great Britain by CPI Group (UK) Ltd, Croydon, CR0 4YY

Simon & Schuster UK Ltd are committed to sourcing paper that is made
from wood grown in sustainable forests and support the Forest Stewardship
Council, the leading international forest certification organisation. Our
books displaying the FSC logo are printed on FSC certified paper.

To
Mary Anne Lewis
The bravest lady I know

Prologue

At precisely 11.57 p.m., on Friday the 13th of March, I fumbled to answer my mobile phone yet again and in that moment, that much anticipated moment, when I was leaning in for my first longed-for kiss of the day and it was denied me, I knew I had reached a point in my life when something simply had to change. There was no work/life balance any more; no spontaneity, no fun, and I'd had enough.

Of course I didn't remember the blinding flash of enlightenment, the Bridget Jones 'that was the moment' freeze frame revelation as soon as I scrambled out of bed some time before six the following morning, but it did come back to haunt me. I can now say without a shadow of a doubt, that that was indeed the moment everything began to change.

Chapter 1

Friday 13 March, 11.57 p.m.

'No, no, no, don't go,' I whispered, quickly stretching across the bed as Jake sat up and began pulling his T-shirt back over his head. 'I'll only be a minute.'

'It's fine,' he whispered back, the faintest glimmer of a smile playing around his lips, but not quite making it as far as his eyes. 'I'm used to it.'

He leant over, kissed my forehead and headed for the door with his pillows and the throw from the chair tucked under his arm.

'Sorry,' I mouthed as he took one last look at me before slipping quietly out to take up his increasingly familiar Friday night spot on the sofa.

'I'm used to it,' he'd said. How tragic was that? How awful that he was resigned to the fact that our Friday Night

3

Special would, at some point, be interrupted and that he'd be relegated to sleep on the sofa on the assumption that I would be working into the wee small hours. And to make matters worse, I was about to discover that this time the interruption was actually all my own fault.

It hadn't been my fault when my boss, Simon Hamilton, had called on the commute home, then during supper and then again in the middle of the very first episode of *Gardeners' World* (which, according to Jake, was the *only* way to start the weekend from March onwards), but this time it most definitely was.

So exhausted from yet another full-on work week, I'd signed for the eagerly anticipated concert tickets a client had been clamouring for, grabbed my coat and bag and headed for the door. No one in their right mind wanted to be chained to the office at seven o'clock on a Friday night and I was completely unaware that I'd stuffed the tickets in my bag, along with my diary and half-eaten lunch when I scrambled to get out the door and run for the bus.

'Amber? Are you there?'

'Yes,' I said, stifling a yawn, 'yes, I'm here.'

'So, have you got them?' Simon asked. He was beginning to sound unusually impatient. 'I think you must have because I've searched high and low this end.'

'Sorry,' I apologised again, as I heard him slamming drawers and dropping papers, 'just give me a second and I'll have another look through my bag.'

'And if you have got them,' I heard him say before I put the phone on the bed and began another search, 'shall I send a courier or can you deliver them yourself in the morning?'

I rifled fruitlessly through the array of interior pockets for a few seconds then gave up and tipped everything out on the bed. My heart sank as I spotted the envelope amongst the detritus, now unattractively flecked with low-fat salad dressing courtesy of my lunch container, which had parted company with its lid.

'Oh God, Simon, I'm so sorry,' I winced, biting my lip as I picked the phone back up. 'Yes, yes, they are here. I'll deliver them first thing in the morning.'

'OK, no worries,' he breathed, sounding far happier. 'That's fine then. Don't worry about it, Amber. I know it's been a hell of a week. It could've happened to anyone. I'll expect you at the office around nine.'

He hung up before I had a chance to apologise for causing him such a late night and, having scribbled myself a note to remember to deliver the tickets first thing in the morning, I repacked my bag, snuggled back down in the bed and drank in the still warm scent of my now absent other half. I ached to join him on the sofa and tempt him back to bed but my head was still too full of work stuff to relax properly and it was hardly fair to disturb him now.

I thumped my pillows into a more sleep-inducing shape, reminded myself that I loved my job and tried to ignore the little voice in my head that seemed determined to remind me that I *used* to love my job. For almost as long as I could remember my career had been my life, the whole of my life. Since graduating I had worked tirelessly to claw my way up the ladder and was currently considered *the* go-to girl in the company if you were struggling to secure tickets for, or gain access to, any sought-after or sold-out event.

Top shelf corporate hospitality was my speciality and I was riding high on my success, but God only knows I'd worked hard for it. The only problem was that now I'd fought my way to the top, I wasn't actually sure I wanted to stay there. Did I really want to be the go-to girl? Suddenly it didn't seem like the be all and end all any more.

I hadn't taken a holiday in the three years since I'd joined the company or a single sick day, and the increasingly continuous night time and weekend interruptions were getting beyond a joke. Somewhere along the line, my life had definitely gone awry. Just six months ago I wouldn't have made such a silly mistake with those tickets, or anything else for that matter, but now everything was beginning to feel different and I couldn't help thinking that perhaps I didn't care about it all quite as much as I should.

I used to roll my eyes at colleagues who bemoaned the fact that their work/life balance was suffering and that they'd missed yet another school play or family function. Work was my life, no balancing act required. So what if I missed another family christening or my mum's annual summer barbecue? I could send enough stork-shaped nappy bundles and elaborate floral bouquets to make up for my absence.

Or I could until Jake Somerville landed the other side of my desk eighteen months ago and unwittingly set about pricking my subconscious into questioning my priorities. It had been a long and slow process I admit, but suddenly it was beginning to feel like there was no way back, and to be completely honest I didn't want one. I was ready for a change, as long as it was a change for the better, of course.

'Amber, let me introduce you to my little brother.'

I recalled how I had swung round in my seat, a scowl firmly etched across my face. I really didn't have time that morning for Dan Somerville, the office Lothario and all round Golden Boy. I had a fast approaching deadline and still no car to meet one of our most influential European clients whose plane was just about to touch down at Heathrow.

'Jake, this is Amber,' Dan grinned, 'Amber, this is Jake.'

'Hi,' smiled Jake, offering me his hand.

'Hello,' I breathed as I stole a quick glance and struggled to ignore the unexpected eruption of butterflies in my stomach as a result.

After a near miss at my first Christmas office party I'd sworn off the whole attraction, dating and romance thing. I really didn't need that kind of distraction in my life, but in that moment I just knew my pupils had widened beyond all

reason and the whole career driven ice queen act was traitor-
ously legging it for the door.

I quickly shook Jake's hand out of politeness, momentarily turned back to Dan and then began distractedly flicking
through the pages of my contacts book.

'You didn't tell me you had a brother,' I mumbled, looking back up, but purposefully avoiding eye contact with
either of them.

'Now why does that not surprise me?' Jake laughed.

'Well,' said Dan, adjusting his tie and running a hand
through his obedient dark hair, his tone bearing his trademark hint of sarcasm, 'to tell you the truth, we rarely mention
him outside the family. He's the black sheep. Everyone has
that one family member who refuses to toe the line, don't
they?'

Jake shook his head good-naturedly and I looked between
the two for some kind of family resemblance but couldn't
find anything to link one with the other. Dan was dishy and
dark, whereas Jake was dishevelled and decidedly lighter in
every sense.

'Well, if he won't toe the line,' I smiled, addressing Dan
but daring to risk another, longer look at Jake, 'then what's
he doing here?'

'Temporary contract,' Jake explained, fixing me with his
amused hazel flecked stare, 'arranged by my kind and helpful
brother, to see how I like the idea of earning a decent city

wage doing a job that suits his idea of what I should be doing with my life.'

'What he means,' Dan cut in, 'is that he needs the money because bumming around has left him stony broke and he's simply thrilled with the prospect of working as my assistant for the next few months.'

'Yes,' Jake agreed with an apologetic smile, 'that is of course exactly what I meant.'

'Well, I'm delighted to welcome you aboard,' I smiled, ignoring Dan's sarcasm and wondering exactly what it was that Jake thought he should be doing with his life. 'If there's anything you need help with, anything at all, just give me a shout.'

'Thank you,' Jake smiled again as Dan quickly steered him away, 'I will.'

In the weeks that followed that initial introduction, it turned out there were lots of things Jake needed help with. Initially he needed a tour guide, then a dinner date for numerous Friday nights, followed by someone to take ownership of the extra cinema or concert ticket he always seemed to have about his person and in less than six months he decided he needed someone to spend his entire weekends with. We'd been a couple for about a year now and I was beginning to forget what my life had been like before Jake landed in it.

Dan readily feigned both annoyance and disappointment that I had so willingly fulfilled the needs of his slightly scruffy, but nonetheless effortlessly stylish, brother when I had been turning down his altogether more sleek and sophisticated advances for practically as long as we had known one another.

'If I'd known you were going to fall for my baby brother,' he moaned one day as we ate lunch while working at his desk, 'then I would never have suggested he came to work here. It's very hard for me, you know, seeing the two of you together all the time.'

'What can I tell you?' I quipped, knowing he was nowhere near as heartbroken as he liked to make out. 'The heart wants what the heart wants. And besides, you only think you want me because I won't let you have me.'

During the next few days the 'freeze frame, I want to get off the treadmill moment', was pushed to the furthermost reaches of my mind, but it wasn't completely forgotten. However, my work diary was beyond manic and required my undivided attention and therefore my loyalties were still very much focused on my job, even though my heart had begun to yearn for a break. I was becoming increasingly aware that it was looking less and less likely that I was ever going to secure myself a day's holiday, let alone share one with someone else, and the acknowledgement troubled me far more than it ever had before.

Truth be told, I couldn't help feeling a little jealous of Jake who had the good sense to book the time off he was entitled to. He was staying with his spinster aunt and helping out at Skylark Farm for a few days, so I knew he would come back refreshed and ready to face whatever life threw at him, whereas I was slowly going under.

The constant pressure and last minute changes to my so-called 'free time' plans, which more often than not meant they were abandoned completely, were really beginning to take their toll. I knew something would have to give soon and Jake's absence from both the office and the flat did nothing to improve my mood.

I was used to him spending one weekend a month at the farm, but the fact that he had given up asking if I would like to go with him set alarm bells ringing in my heart. I realised that if I wasn't careful, I was in danger of losing a lot more than my perspective. I was one half of what had been a very happy relationship and it was time to find a way to tip the scales back in my favour.

Chapter 2

The kitchen in my little London flat was my favourite room in the whole place. One entire wall was covered by a seamless, smooth sheet of white high-sheen units, softly rounded corners and a contrasting spotless hob that had never heated so much as a tin of beans. The whole area was an urbanite chef's dream and I knew that should I ever decide to sell my abode the unblemished, sophisticated space would be the crowning glory on the estate agent's details.

Even though Jake and I spent practically all our nights together at my place I always insisted we ate out or ordered in. Consequently, the smell and noise that woke me the following Saturday, which was obviously coming from the aforementioned unblemished kitchen, sent a shiver down my spine and had me sprinting across the flat in a time that could have rivalled Usain Bolt himself.

'What the hell are you doing?' I shouted above the noise of the radio. 'Jake!'

I twisted the dial from tinnitus level to off and gazed, open mouthed, upon the carnage. Eggshells, mushroom stalks, discarded bacon packets and a variety of abandoned tins adorned the formerly unsullied surfaces.

'I take it you've never heard of a splatter guard?' I frowned.

'Oh, you're awake,' Jake beamed, leaving his greasy station and enveloping me in a hug. 'I wanted to surprise you.'

'You have,' I mumbled, disentangling myself and venturing a little closer. 'Why didn't you ring and tell me you were back?' I frowned, irritated to feel so annoyed that the thrill of seeing him was tainted by the mess he'd made. 'I knew you were coming back at some point this weekend, but it would have been nice to have known when exactly.'

'Sorry,' Jake shrugged, pulling out a chair. 'Like I said, I wanted it to be a surprise.'

It was a lovely gesture, but I still didn't feel ready to forgive him for the disarray.

'Come and sit down,' he coaxed. 'Let me finish cooking breakfast and I'll tell you all about what's been going on.'

'I didn't realise anything in particular *had* been going on,' I pouted, refusing to sit. 'Other than the fact that you've been on holiday, and you've come back to transform my beloved kitchen into a greasy spoon, of course!'

13

'Oh Amber,' Jake teased, tearing the cellophane off my brand new set of stainless steel utensils with his teeth, 'stop being so precious and put the kettle on if you won't sit down. I'll have tea, two sugars instead of one, please; I need a little extra after all my hard work on the farm!'

Once he had finished cooking and proudly presented me with what looked like a plate of grease, I could only pick at the food and purposefully sat with my back to the mess. I'd insisted on toast rather than fried bread and opened the window in a vain attempt to disperse at least some of the smell. Jake heartily loaded his fork with one hand and squeezed my wrist with the other. Just as I had predicted, he looked incredibly cheerful and rested.

'So,' he said eventually, 'how's work been? I hope my brother hasn't been chasing you around the desk in my absence?'

'No of course not,' I tutted, 'and as far as work is concerned, it's been . . .'

'What?'

I let out a long breath and began crumbling the remains of my toast over my beans.

'Here, don't waste that,' Jake frowned, pulling my plate nearer to him.

I picked the few stray crumbs from my pyjama bottoms and sat back in my chair searching for the right words to describe my working week.

'It's been,' I sighed, 'pretty awful actually.'

Had I not been so surprised by the admission I would have laughed at Jake sitting there with his fork frozen in mid-air and his mouth wide open, but as it was I felt heavy tears pricking the back of my eyes and shook my head dismissively.

'In what way awful?' Jake eventually asked. He sounded as shocked as I felt.

'Oh, I don't know,' I shrugged dismissively. 'I'm probably making it sound far worse than it's been. It was just odd, not having you around. I guess I've got used to having you in my life. '

Jake laid his knife and fork on his plate, pushed it away and reached for my other hand.

'I bet you got loads more done, though, didn't you?' he smiled encouragingly, no doubt trying to make me feel better. 'I bet you wondered how you've managed for so long with me under your feet all the time. Well, that won't be an issue for much longer.'

'To tell you the truth,' I sighed, his words not quite hitting their mark for the moment, 'it felt like it did before you came and I realised . . .' I swallowed. 'I realised I didn't actually like it any more. I think I've had enough of my job and the endless hours and relentless pressure. I think it's about time I started looking for something a little less, you know, full on.'

We sat in silence for a minute. In the seconds before I had fallen asleep during the last week, the only real private moments I'd had, I had been mulling it all over and I'd come to the conclusion that there was actually no way I could tip the scales back in my favour in my current work position.

There was no getting away from the fact that the role required uncompromised commitment; however, until that very moment, when I said the words out loud, I hadn't really thought I'd be brave enough to do anything about it. I had thought I'd probably just bury it away and soldier on.

'What do you mean "it won't be an issue much longer"?' I suddenly demanded as Jake's words filtered through and yanked me out of my life-changing reverie. 'Where the hell are you going?'

The whole point of me taking a step back and looking at my life was to fathom out a way to factor Jake back into it. My relationship with him, and my fear of destroying it, was the sole reason behind the soul searching and potential changes. That and a fear of burning myself out. My stomach lurched as I realised I may very well have misread how much Jake valued our relationship.

'I'm moving to Skylark Farm,' he said sheepishly. 'I've been thinking about it for some time and now something has happened that's forced my hand a bit. It's the only place that's ever really felt like home to me, so I've decided to move there for good.'

'But I don't understand,' I gaped. 'I thought your weekend there once a month was going to be it. I thought you and Annie could manage the place between you like that.'

'Not any more,' Jake continued, completely oblivious to my shock. 'Things have changed. Annie's getting old and even though she won't admit it, she needs more help, proper help, on a full-time basis. This was supposed to be a little clue,' he said, rolling his eyes and pointing at the plates. 'You know, a good old-fashioned full English farmhouse breakfast, but I've kind of messed it up. In fact, this isn't how I meant to tell you at all.'

Jake had told me all about his beloved spinster Aunt Annie and Skylark Farm in the flat Fenlands of East Anglia. In fact, after every weekend he spent there, he came back absolutely buzzing with news about crop yields and hens' eggs.

As a child he'd spent his school holidays with her, feeding the chickens and picking apples, and he'd never made any secret of the fact that one day he dreamt of moving there for good. That, I had discovered, was what he really wanted to be doing with his life and what Dan so heartily disapproved of, but I never realised that there was a possibility of him heading off quite so soon.

Interestingly, Dan had never spent so much as a single night on the farm. Apparently he preferred more refined and sedate holidays to getting his hands dirty and shovelling . . . well, you get the idea.

'And is this what you've been planning while you've been away?' I asked.

'Yes,' Jake nodded. 'Annie took a bit of a tumble while I was there, nothing serious, but the doctor sent her into a tailspin by asking if she'd thought about selling up and moving to town. By the time he left she was in a blind panic and I told her it was time she had help. She won't let on that she needs the support, of course, but she's terrified of losing the place and knows I'd never let that happen. It just seemed like the natural conclusion for me to suggest moving in.'

'So you're definitely going then? There isn't anyone else she can ask?'

'No,' Jake said simply, 'there isn't.'

'Oh,' I said, 'I see.'

'She's always known how much I love the place and has never made any secret of the fact that one day it will be mine. I don't want her to have to move out so this is the perfect solution, and truth be told I've had enough of taking orders from my brother.'

'Oh,' I said again, 'right.'

I could understand that Jake had had enough of his job and that for him and his aunt this was a totally logical progression, but I couldn't help wondering exactly where it left me. If Jake really was moving so far away then I might as well just wave him goodbye and carry on with my job because I couldn't possibly imagine how our relationship could survive such gargantuan change. I opened my mouth to say just that, but Jake cut me off. He was grinning from ear to ear and looked in no way as if he was about to sound the death knell on our relationship.

'I really want you to come with me, Amber,' he beamed, 'and given everything you've just said it sounds like perfect timing!'

Chapter 3

Needless to say I turned down Jake's off-the-wall, but kind, suggestion straightaway. I told him that I was grateful for the offer, that I loved him with all my heart and, that if it was meant to be, our relationship would survive all the changes it was about to face, even though deep down I wasn't sure it would.

'You know I'm a city girl,' I reminded him, wrapping my arms around his neck and kissing him. 'I just don't think I could handle the country. I can't even cope with the mess you've made of my kitchen, so you can imagine how I'd be with a muddy farmyard and footprints trailing through the house.'

'I'll have you know Annie keeps a very neat and tidy kitchen,' Jake mumbled, his tone loaded with disappointment, 'and absolutely no mud is allowed in the house. It's a strictly wellies off at the door kind of place.'

'Oh, you know what I mean,' I said, shaking my head, 'and besides, what would I do?'

'What do you mean?'

'For work,' I said. 'I can't imagine there would be much call for my finely tuned corporate hospitality skills in Wynbridge, would there?'

Jake had described Wynbridge as a typical little rural market town. He told me there were a couple of churches, a market square, a museum, a few pubs and shops and a rather good café. It all sounded pretty enough, ideal in fact for a weekend away, but not exactly dripping with the kind of employment potential and lifestyle opportunities I was accustomed to.

'I thought you could help out on the farm,' Jake said hopefully, 'with the livestock and stuff.'

'Livestock and stuff!' I laughed. 'Have you completely forgotten who I am? I've never even had so much as a pet hamster!'

'Well, it was just a thought,' he shrugged, 'and as far as career opportunities are concerned, you did say you were looking to do something different.'

'Yes, well, thanks for the offer,' I smiled, kissing his cheek, 'but there's "different" and there's "way off the mark" and I think you know where you've landed with this one!'

My firm refusal, however, didn't stop me slipping the current issue of *Country Living* into my shopping basket or put me off perusing the latest range of pretty patterned wellington boots and blouses on offer from Joules. Country chic was very chic indeed, I decided, as I scrolled down the screen during a snatched minute one lunchtime.

For a giddy few seconds I could almost imagine myself baking a cake in a Shaker style kitchen and creating something decorative for the dining table with a few hedgerow blooms and some Kilner jars *à la* Kirstie Allsopp.

Sensing footsteps behind me I quickly flicked the screen back to the company homepage and stuffed the magazine in a drawer. It was Jake.

'I have a proposition for you,' he said, leaning back against the desk and looking down at me with his seductive hazel stare.

'Oh?' I smiled, running my finger lightly down his thigh. 'Another one. Do tell.'

'Next weekend,' he said. 'I want you to come to Skylark Farm with me. I'm going for a couple of days to check on Annie before I finally move there for good and I want you to see the place before you say no.'

'I have said no!' I reminded him. 'And anyway, what's in it for me?'

'Well, let's see now,' Jake smiled. 'Not much really apart from the opportunity to change your whole life, of course. The chance to really do the "something completely and utterly different" that you said you were looking for.'

I couldn't help but admire his persistence and I had to admit that I could, courtesy of the glossy magazines and online catalogues, actually feel my resolve beginning to weaken. Surely no harm could come from going and taking a quick look at the place? If nothing else it would get me away from my desk for a few hours and give me time to have a proper, uninterrupted think about everything.

'I'm not sure,' I said, biting my lip, but in reality I was feeling surer by the second.

'It's two days,' he said, 'that's all. Surely you can manage to cut the apron strings for one teeny tiny weekend?'

'Oh, all right,' I caved, an unexpected sense of excitement bubbling up. 'I'll talk to Simon and check he hasn't got anything lined up, but I'm not making any promises.'

'Amber, great timing,' Simon smiled up at me as I approached his desk, 'couldn't be better actually! I was just about to come and find you.'

'If it's about the arrangements for the polo event, everything's sorted,' I told him. 'I've even managed to book a jet to fly the happy couple out there and the paperwork will all be waiting for them when they land.'

'Great, super,' he said, offering me a seat and taking the other chair behind his wide desk. 'I never doubted you wouldn't pull it off, but I wanted to talk to you about something else actually.'

I swallowed nervously and licked my lips while mentally scanning my to-do list to reassure myself that nothing was amiss. It wasn't.

'I have a proposition for you,' he announced.

'Oh?' I smiled. Another proposition; Jake's was already being pushed to the back of my mind as my former work ethic bounced back and kicked it temporarily into touch.

'I know this goes without saying,' Simon reminded me in a hushed tone, 'but I just want to reiterate that anything said within these office walls stays within these office walls. Yes?'

'Of course,' I nodded, 'absolutely.'

I had seen one too many staff scuttling off with a cardboard box at the end of the working week to know the consequences of breaking the rules, and besides, I was far more professional than that.

'OK,' said Simon, looking at me intently, 'I'm planning to expand the business and open another office.'

I took a deep breath and tried to hide my surprise.

'Great,' I stuttered.

Another, perhaps more northerly office, would certainly help when we found ourselves most stretched.

'Liverpool or Manchester,' I asked, mulling over the most likely options, 'or perhaps Newcastle?' I was already thinking about the potentially easiest commute should I have to pay a visit.

'Dubai,' Simon said simply.

'Dubai!' I almost shouted.

Dubai was the last place I expected Simon to suggest. He'd never mentioned aspirations to expand globally, but then why should he have discussed anything with me?

'I had planned to head out there myself,' he continued, 'initially for a few months, three probably, just to make sure everything is in place and good to go, but I've had to have a rethink. Caroline's pregnant,' he proudly announced while gazing lovingly at the photograph of his stunning wife. 'There's no way I can expect her to travel and I'm certainly not leaving her.'

'Of course not,' I smiled. 'Wow. Congratulations, that's wonderful news. You must be delighted.'

Caroline was impossibly tall, elegant, sophisticated and one of the nicest women I knew. I had been terrified when I first met her and had consequently misjudged her completely. I had done her the injustice of assuming that she would be the stereotypical corporate wife – haughty, condescending and aloof; but she was nothing like that. 'I am,' beamed Simon, 'we are. However, this leaves the Dubai office without a manager so I'm looking for someone else to go in my place. '

'What about Dan?' I suggested, knowing he would snatch Simon's hand off for the opportunity to sun himself for a few months. 'He'd be perfect.'

'Actually, Amber, I was thinking of you.'

'Me?' I croaked.

'Yes,' nodded Simon, 'to manage the whole thing. You'd have a small team working under you and, although I couldn't offer you a pay rise in real terms, your flights, accommodation and expenses would all be taken care of. What do you think?'

The seconds ticked by and I couldn't think how to respond. I'd knocked on Simon's door to ask for nothing more complicated than a couple of days off to spend at Skylark Farm and before I'd so much as breathed a word I'd been offered the chance to work in Dubai for three months and have a team to delegate to.

Professionally every inch of me wanted to sign on the dotted line there and then, but personally I was thinking of the workload and Jake and the promise I'd made to consider the farm as my future home. I opened my mouth to say 'thank you, but no', but Simon cut me off.

'Don't answer now,' he said. 'Why don't you take the weekend off to think about it and let me know how you feel the week after?'

'Are you sure?'

'Absolutely,' he insisted, 'I can't remember the last time you had a break.'

I wanted to remind him that I'd never had a break, but the fact that he'd just offered me such an amazing opportunity suggested that he was well aware of how hard I'd been working since I joined the company.

I stood up to leave, feeling rather pleased with myself. Somehow I'd managed to bag it all – the weekend I wanted to spend with Jake and a dreamy job offer in Dubai to mull over.

'Just please, please remember,' Simon reminded me again, 'do not, under any circumstances, discuss this with anyone.'

Chapter 4

The rest of the week passed in a blur. By day I had Jake reminding me to pack my wet weather gear (not very encouraging) and by night I was mulling over the prospect of a secluded balcony and the opportunity to nurture a no-lines tan (seriously seductive).

I couldn't shake off the feeling that not sharing Simon's out of the blue offer with Jake was underhand and that the trip to Skylark Farm was tainted in some way as a result, but Simon had been most insistent when he said I wasn't to discuss the situation with anyone and so, with that justification in mind, I pushed my guilt to the back of my mind and carried on packing.

To justify the dubious deception even further I told myself that not even Mystic Meg could have predicted the offers that had suddenly popped up on my horizon and I owed it to myself, as well as Jake and Simon, to think very carefully before pushing ahead with either of them.

'I'll meet you at the station,' Jake reminded me for the umpteenth time before he set off on Friday morning. 'All you have to do is jump off at Peterborough and I'll be waiting.'

'I have travelled by train before,' I reminded him, 'and sometimes I've even managed to get there and back again all on my own.'

'OK, OK, don't go all Bilbo Baggins on me,' he laughed. 'I just want everything to be perfect, that's all.'

'It will be,' I said, hugging him tight, 'absolutely nothing is going to spoil this adventure.'

Less than two hours later, however, and the whole adventure was already blown out of the water. It was still only Friday morning but it was looking increasingly unlikely with every passing second that I was going to see my bed again within the next forty-eight hours let alone jump on a train to Peterborough to play Old Macdonald for the weekend.

'Please, Simon,' I said yet again, 'please don't worry. It can't be helped. Just give my love to Caroline and don't worry about anything. I've got it all under control this end, so there's no need for you to do a thing.'

Just minutes after Jake had left, Simon had phoned to say Caroline wasn't feeling well and that he was taking her to the hospital. He was in a blind panic having promised to person-ally oversee the weekend's entertainment we'd planned for the hosts of *Fast Ladies*, the nation's favourite early evening TV show. These women had a reputation for partying hard and, left to their own devices, Simon was convinced the whole weekend would go awry and we'd be left to shoulder the blame along with the bill and inevitable lawsuit.

'Are you really sure you don't mind, Amber?' Simon asked yet again. 'I'd hate to think you were abandoning anything special you'd got planned.'

'It's absolutely fine,' I told him, feeling more heartbroken by the second. 'There's nothing I can't reschedule.'

I quickly ended the call, grabbed my phone and threw myself down on the sofa. With a lump the size of a golf ball lodged in my throat I rang Jake's mobile trying not to think about how disappointed he was going to be when I broke the news. I rang at least half a dozen times but for some reason the call wouldn't connect and I couldn't phone and leave a message at the farm because I hadn't thought to ask Jake for the number. I tried his phone a few more times but with the clock ticking I had no option other than to fire off a hugely apologetic, but woefully inadequate text to his currently unavailable mobile, get down to the business in hand and keep everything crossed that at least one of the messages had got through.

I did try to make contact with Jake again that weekend, but his phone remained unanswered and there had been no response to any of my texts. I dreaded to think what he must have been thinking about the situation but the fact that he hadn't tried to contact me gave me some idea.

I was prostrate on the sofa when he arrived back at the flat early Monday morning. The floor was littered with the Sunday newspapers, many of which showed the excesses of my weekend in all its gaudy glory. You could even see me in a couple of the photos. I was the one in the background trying to hold various women upright and help them maintain an air of dignity and decorum. According to the straplines I'd failed.

Simon had telephoned and woken me, full of relief and congratulations, sometime just after seven. He was delighted by my efforts and having seen the papers said it could have been a whole lot worse. He told me not to rush into the office and that Caroline was fine. The cramps had turned out to be nothing more sinister than trapped wind, which was, literally, as much of a relief as an embarrassment. As you can imagine, I was delighted.

'So,' said Jake, dumping his bag in the hall and looking down at the usually forbidden detritus that surrounded the sofa, 'what the hell happened to you?'

I pushed myself upright and took a proper look at him. If that was what a couple of days of fresh air could do for a man I couldn't wait to see him after he'd been there a month.

'Did you forget to pack a razor?' I asked, more to ease the tension than to make a joke.

'What?'

'The stubble, it suits you.'

'Amber,' he frowned, 'where were you? I waited for an hour at the station but then had to get back to the farm. Annie hasn't been feeling all that well and I didn't like to leave her and drive off in search of a mobile signal. I've been worried sick about you. '

'I have been messaging you!' I said, jumping up and grabbing my phone. 'I sent loads of texts on Friday. Have you not seen any of them?'

'What do you think?'

'But they should have come through,' I said. 'I sent you messages explaining what had happened and why I wouldn't be coming. You should have got them as soon as your phone found some signal!'

'Well, I'm telling you, I haven't seen them.'

'But I did send them,' I insisted, my attitude dissolving the second I read the 'text failed' message. 'Oh God, I'm so sorry. Here, read them now.'

'What's the point?' he shrugged. 'I'm going for a shower.'

Considering we were now rushing headlong into what felt like an exceptionally mild spring, the atmosphere in the flat, and even at work when Jake and I were in the same room together, was decidedly frosty. Jake was busy making plans to move to Skylark Farm, which, judging by the lengthy silences, evidently now no longer included me, and Dan was spending as much time as he dared trying to convince his brother that it would probably be better all-round if Annie sold up and moved somewhere where she'd be looked after in her dotage. Needless to say Jake was doing his utmost to avoid communicating with either of us.

There were only so many times I could apologise for what had happened and I ended up using my empty, silent evenings to mull over the Dubai offer. The internet offered up endless skies, virgin beaches and a very real promise of the 'no holds barred' tan I'd been dreaming of. Even just a few months ago, the scenery itself would have been enough to have me jumping for joy, but not now.

When I flicked the monitor off and shook my mind free of the pristine beach scenes and cerulean skies, I only had to consider the weekend I'd sacrificed to know that just because I would have a team working with me, it didn't necessarily mean that I would be able to delegate to them. It wasn't that I was a control freak or anything, but Simon was and the *Fast Ladies* weekend was a prime example. There were plenty of other people he could have lined up to help out, but he'd called on me.

I suppose I should have been flattered. I'd spent years dreaming about what it would feel like to be indispensable, but now that I actually was, the feeling was nowhere near as exciting as I thought it would be.

And that, I reminded myself, was because during all those years spent dreaming and striving, I didn't have Jake Somerville in my life. For all that time I wasn't in love and I wasn't loved either. Was I really about to throw away everything I had with him for an all-over tan that would probably do me more harm than good?

Jake was offering me exactly what I told him I wanted: the chance to do something completely and utterly different with my life, and added to that there was the attraction of working far more sociable hours and with the possibility of actually taking the odd weekend off to spend some serious quality time with him.

I didn't need to look at the date highlighted in red on my calendar to know that Jake was due to leave in just a few days and neither did I need to keep looking at the shiny gold star sticker I'd used to highlight the fact that Simon was expecting an answer from me as soon as possible. It was time to make up my mind.

Chapter 5

'Well, Amber,' Simon smiled at me across his desk, 'you certainly are full of surprises!'

I smiled back. The impact and reality of what I had decided was only just beginning to sink in.

'To tell you the truth,' I admitted, swallowing hard, 'this is as much of a shock to me as it is to you.'

'I can't deny I'm devastated to lose you,' he said, shaking his head. 'I don't think I've ever had anyone leave to follow the rural idyll. Plenty of people talk about it, of course, but none have actually done it. More often than not they end up settling for an allotment at best.'

'Yes,' I said, 'I know. It is a bit of a change, isn't it?'

'Just a bit,' said Simon, nodding thoughtfully. 'But you are sure it's really what you want, aren't you? I mean, you aren't still smarting over last weekend.'

'No of course not,' I insisted, 'absolutely not. There was nothing either of us could have done about that.'

'But this is such a dramatic change from, well, everything,' Simon frowned. 'I never had you down as the outdoor type and to just pack up and move without having even seen the place or met the woman you're going to be living with—'

'I know,' I cut in, 'I know.'

I didn't want Simon to say another word about how crazy he thought my plan was. He had been kindness itself about letting me go with almost immediate effect in view of the fact I'd never taken any holiday, but I was teetering dangerously close to changing my mind. Having spent hours putting in place plans to rent out my flat and working out when and how to do an official office handover, I really didn't have the energy to undo everything and settle for what I already had.

I loved Jake and I was moving to Skylark Farm to begin a new life with him. I had ordered my new country wardrobe and wellington boots from Joules, taken out a subscription to *Country Living* and had even been thinking about the practicalities of buying myself a little 4x4.

'Well, how about,' Simon suggested, 'just in case it doesn't work out, I leave the Dubai offer open? I do have someone else in mind to send out there for the time being, but I want you to be in no doubt that if all the fresh air and interesting smells get a bit too much I'll quite happily pull them out and send you in, OK?'

I nodded, but didn't say anything. I hadn't actually factored any 'interesting smells' into my decision-making. I hoped

Skylark Farm didn't share a boundary with a pig farm or go in for muck spreading in a big way. I'd been watching old episodes of *Countryfile* online and aside from the odd complicated livestock birth I hadn't stumbled across anything I didn't think I couldn't cope with. Perhaps I would have felt differently if 'smelly vision' had been invented.

'How about we meet again in six months' time?' Simon suggested. 'Take the time off as unpaid leave and we'll have a rethink after that.'

I didn't really want to agree to the offer because it made me feel as if I was going to Skylark Farm half-heartedly, but it was such a generous compromise and it did go some way to compensating for the disappointment I felt when I realised that Simon was prepared to let me go so easily. Perhaps I wasn't quite as indispensable as I thought.

I nodded along and pencilled the date in my diary, still prepared to cling on to the coat tails of the career I was leaving behind and not really thinking about whether agreeing would have any real consequences in the future. Six months was such a long way off, after all.

'OK,' I said, 'we'll meet at the end of the summer and take things from there.'

'Well,' said Simon, pushing back his chair and standing up, 'I wish you the very best of luck, Amber. I hope the country life turns out to be exactly what you're hoping for, but if it doesn't, just remember, I'm only a phone call away.'

'Thank you,' I breathed and then quickly added, 'I know Jake has left the company already and it isn't very likely that you'll run into him again, but if you do, please don't say anything about my decision to go with him, will you?'

'Why ever not?'

'Because I haven't told him I'm going yet.'

Next on the agenda was breaking the news to Dan. My decision to tell him that I was moving to Skylark Farm before Jake was a tactical rather than a practical manoeuvre. Judging by what had been said between the pair in the build-up to my resolution I knew that Dan considered the farm to be worth quite a lot of money and I also knew that his constant nagging about the financial value of the place was taking the edge off Jake's enthusiasm for the move.

In recent days, when we had exchanged a few words, Jake had begun to sound more preoccupied and protective than excited and I didn't want anything to taint his eagerness for the move he longed for. I rather hoped that by letting Dan know that I was very firmly in his brother's corner, making him aware that Jake had another ally, would encourage him to back off and leave Jake to settle into his new life in peace.

'Are you absolutely mad?' Dan spluttered, choking on his mouthful of wine. 'Have you completely lost the plot?'

'No, I don't think so,' I said, trying to sound more sure than I felt. 'I love Jake and I want to be with him. I really want this relationship to work, Dan, and I'm prepared to make certain sacrifices to ensure that it does.'

'Yes, but there are sacrifices and there are sacrifices!' said Dan, shaking his head. 'You haven't even seen the place!'

'I know,' I said in as blasé a tone as I could muster, 'but that doesn't matter. If Jake loves the farm then I'm sure I'll love it too, and the same goes for Annie,' I quickly added before Dan threw her into the equation as well. 'And besides, this isn't *all* about him,' I explained. 'I've had enough. I really have. I want to do something completely different with my life. The timing really couldn't be better for me.'

'And what does Jake have to say about all this?' Dan asked.

He looked as if he hadn't believed a word of my rousing little speech, but I knew I meant it and that was all that mattered.

'He doesn't know,' I mumbled, suddenly more interested in the lunch menu than our conversation.

'What do you mean, he doesn't know?' Dan laughed.

'Exactly that,' I said with a shrug. 'He doesn't know yet.'

Dan shook his head and took another gulp of wine.

'Well, I can tell you now,' he warned, 'it isn't all roses round the door and *Darling Buds of May* breakfasts.'

'Well, that's good,' I said, hoping to draw a line under the conversation, 'because I don't do fried food.'

We eventually ordered and Dan poured us another glass of wine each. I sipped my water and pushed the wine further away.

'I actually have a bit of news to share myself,' he said smugly, drawing himself up and adjusting his tie.

'Oh really,' I asked, my interest piqued.

'Yes. Simon has asked if I would consider moving to Dubai to head up the opening of a new company office out there.'

'Wow!' I gasped, raising my glass and wondering if Simon had asked Dan to show the same level of discretion as he had expected from me. 'That's fantastic news. I had no idea he was looking to expand the business. Congratulations!'

'Thanks,' he grinned. 'Unfortunately it hasn't gone down so well with everyone.'

'Like who?'

'Oh, just this girl I'm seeing.'

'Anyone I know?' I wheedled.

Dan wasn't usually so coy about his private life but I knew nothing about this particular love interest. I guessed that his reluctance to reveal further details probably meant that she was married. It wouldn't have been the first time.

'Absolutely not,' he beamed, 'but never mind her. I bet you wish you'd waited to tell me about your rural aspirations now, don't you?'

'What do you mean?'

'Well, I'm sure I could have pulled a few strings and got you out there with me as my number two.'

I was saved from saying anything else as the waiter arrived at the table with our lunch. I can't deny I was tempted to tell

Dan that I'd been offered the opportunity first and ask what he thought about the fact that he was only going because I'd said I wouldn't, but I kept my mouth closed and focused on the waiter.

'Seriously though,' said Dan as we began to eat, 'if you feel that things at the farm aren't working out, just give me a call, OK?'

'And you'll do what exactly?' I asked. 'Rush back on the next available flight to help with the apple picking and egg collecting?'

'Hardly,' Dan sneered. 'Look, Amber, between you and me, Skylark Farm and the orchards are worth a pretty penny, but I just can't make Jake see the benefit of convincing Annie to part with either of them. He's more interested in keeping her happy and playing Farmer Giles. He always has been.'

I couldn't believe he was still obsessing over how much the place was worth. Perhaps he really was shallower than I'd realised.

'That's probably because he loves the place,' I said defensively, 'and Annie. It's his dream, Dan. Don't you have one?'

'Of course I do,' he replied haughtily, 'and thanks to Simon's Dubai offer, it's about to come true.'

When I arrived back at the flat that evening having cleared my desk and apologised to the rest of the team for not giving them enough time to plan a farewell party, I discovered Jake at the kitchen table comparing one way train ticket prices to Peterborough, the nearest mainline station to Wynbridge.

'How was your day?' I asked, dumping my cardboard box in the hall and pulling out the bottle of champagne I'd picked up on the way home.

'Fine,' he said, without looking up. 'Busy. What about you?'

I let out a sigh of relief as I realised he was still in a bad mood. I'd had a bit of a panic on the journey home that Dan might have called and ruined my surprise, but judging by Jake's scowl and bent head he was still thankfully none the wiser.

'Good,' I smiled, carefully setting down the bottle on the counter.

I could feel my heart suddenly picking up the pace and my palms beginning to sweat. What if I'd been presumptuous and he didn't actually want me to go with him now after all? What if Dan *had* called and this was Jake's reaction to the idea? Bit late to be thinking any of that when I'd just left my job and secretly sorted a tenant for the flat. I took a deep breath and blundered on.

'So when are you going then?' I asked, with a nod to the laptop.

'Sunday, Monday at the latest,' he muttered, still not really paying any attention to me.

'Have you bought your ticket yet?'

'I'm just about to,' he said, the cursor hovering danger-ously close to the buy button.

I took another big breath and moved closer to his side.

'Can you add an extra one to your basket?' I said quickly before I lost my nerve.

'An extra what?' he frowned, finally looking up at me.

'Ticket,' I stammered, 'if that's OK?'

'What?' he laughed, his eyes wide and his tone disbeliev-ing. 'Are you serious?'

'Of course I am!' I giggled, relief bubbling up as he pulled me on to his lap. 'Today was my last day at work. I'm coming with you! I'm moving to Skylark Farm!'

Chapter 6

Our last few days in London passed in a heady cocktail of excitement and trepidation and were punctuated by the arrival of a plethora of parcels and packages. I'd gone all out with the online ordering, and having taken full advantage of the next-day express delivery option I now had the magic outfits that would transform me from sophisticated urbanite to chic country dweller. Well, that was the theory.

'I'm not quite sure what you're imagining,' said Jake, biting his lip, 'but you're going to be sadly disappointed if you're expecting to be baking fresh bread and strolling through wildflower meadows every day of the week.'

'Not every day of the week,' I told him cheekily. 'Three or four times a week would be fine.'

I might have only been teasing, but as the packages piled up Jake began to sound more concerned, whereas I, armed with my new wardrobe, was feeling ever more confident.

'Please don't look so worried,' I insisted while sighing in admiration at the latest arrival from Boden. 'I've got some old jeans and jumpers for when you need me to help out.'

Jake raised his eyebrows and shook his head but didn't say anything. I kissed him on the cheek and dived to grab my mobile, which was ringing, yet again. I might have left the payroll of Simon Hamilton, but stupidly I'd insisted that Elena, my recently promoted replacement, could call if there was anything she needed or wasn't sure of and she was certainly making the most of my foolish offer. Up until that moment I had been selfishly flattered that Elena was struggling without me but suddenly I was beginning to wish I'd snapped rather than loosened the apron strings.

'Hi Amber,' she said in the slightly tense tone she had adopted since accepting the job, 'me again. You don't happen to have the number for Thompson's, do you?'

'Just a sec,' I said, reaching for my big black book of contacts.

So far I had kept it close to hand because every time she phoned I found myself flicking through the packed pages for some titbit of information.

'You know,' she wheedled, sounding more confident, 'it would have been so much easier if you'd left me your book. I could easily arrange for the company courier to come and pick it up if you like,' she added hopefully.

'Really,' I laughed. Evidently I had read her tone wrong and she was beginning to find her feet after all. I had to admire her nerve. 'You want me to give you my book?'

'If you don't mind,' she said, sounding relieved, 'it would make my life so much easier.'

'Look, Elena,' I said, while flicking through the pages for the section marked 'T', 'don't take this the wrong way, but creating your own contacts book is a really important part of the job. Giving you mine wouldn't benefit you at all.'

OK, so that was a blatant lie. Giving Elena my big black book would totally make her life easier, but there was no way I was going to part with it. Not even for ready cash. I'd spent three years filling the pages with every contact I had ever used, and more besides, and there was no way I was going to just pass it on, especially as I still didn't know if my life at Skylark Farm was going to be as transformative as I hoped. Some might say my reluctance to hand it over was lack of commitment, but to me it just felt like good old-fashioned common sense.

I gave Elena the number she needed and after a frosty thank you, she hung up.

'What did he want this time?' Jake asked as I filled the kettle then joined him at the table.

'It wasn't Simon,' I said. 'I've already told you, he hasn't called once. It was Elena,' I explained, failing to mention that I'd told her she could ring. 'She needed a number for Thompson's, the caterers.'

'And what's wrong with her opening the phone book or checking the details on their website?'

'Nothing,' I shrugged, rubbing my temples, 'nothing at all, but I happen to have acquired the mobile number of Paul himself and more often than not a direct line to the top makes all the difference.'

Jake nodded and reached under the table for something.

'Well,' he said, producing a neatly wrapped package and laying it on the table in front of me, 'I think it's about time you left the direct line to the top to someone else, don't you?'

'What's this?' I said, picking up the package and giving it a little shake.

'Open it,' he beamed.

I tore at the paper and looked at the box, which contained a new mobile phone.

'Thank you,' I said, feeling confused, 'but I already have a phone.'

'I know you do,' Jake laughed, picking up my trusty old lifeline and moving it to one side.

I wasn't really sure what he was getting at with his wry smile and knowing look, but I didn't want to appear ungrateful.

'So, you've bought me this because . . .?' I ventured.

'Because it's time for a change,' he said simply.

'OK,' I said, tearing ineffectually at the tape on the box. 'Is this the newer model? Do you think I'll be able to just transfer the sim?'

'Possibly,' Jake nodded, 'but you aren't going to.'

'Why not?' I asked, still not understanding the point he was trying to make.

'Because this,' he said, taking the box from me and ripping through the tape in one smooth action, 'is a new start.'

'But all my contacts, all my numbers are on my old phone,' I mumbled, feeling further confused.

'Exactly,' said Jake, beginning to sound frustrated. 'If you're really serious about making our life at Skylark Farm work, Amber, you have to leave all this behind. You can't get on the train with half your mind still on everything that's going on in that office.'

He was right, of course. Totally right, but work had been my life for so long that giving up my phone and cutting off all possible contact with what I had worked so hard for, even if it did turn out to be for just a few weeks, was a real wrench. I'd expected to feel like this when I told Simon I was leaving, but because he'd given me the six-month window to see how things panned out, I hadn't.

Of course, Jake was completely unaware of the compromise I had reached and therefore he was also blissfully unaware that I might, at some point in the future, still need both my phone and my contacts book, but for now what he was advocating made perfect sense and it was high time I parted with both. I really did need to sever all connection until after the summer and, if everything went as well as I hoped, then forever.

'OK,' I said, taking a deep breath, 'OK.'

'I'm not suggesting you should delete your friends and family,' Jake explained, 'just cut out your connections to your old job.'

I nodded but didn't say anything, surprised by just how big a step this felt and how final.

'But only if you want to, of course,' Jake added, reaching for my hand and looking concerned. 'Oh God, I've got this all wrong, haven't I? You think I'm trying to tell you what to do. That isn't how this was supposed to look, Amber.'

'I don't,' I said, squeezing his hand and feeling guiltier by the second, 'it doesn't. You're right, of course you are.'

'Really?'

'Really,' I nodded. 'I absolutely want to make this work and I can't with that damn thing going off all the live long day, can I? Turn it off,' I said, 'do it now.'

'Are you sure?'

'Definitely,' I nodded. 'It'll be a relief, to be honest.'

And it was.

I found an empty shoe box at the back of the wardrobe and inside it I put my old phone, now mercifully silent, and my contacts book and sealed it shut. I put it in the bottom of my last packing box and stacked it in the cupboard in the hall before locking the door and pocketing the key.

The cupboard was the one place in the flat that the tenant wouldn't have access to so everything personal I needed to leave behind was stowed carefully away in there like a giant time capsule.

'So this is how Harry Potter felt when he was destroying Horcruxes,' I smiled nervously as I turned my back on the door.

'Exactly,' Jake said, hugging me tight. 'Liberating, isn't it?'

I looked in wonder at the life I had reduced to a suitcase, a rucksack and my cross-body Cath Kidston bag, and yes, it did feel liberating.

The afternoon was bright, sunny and relatively warm as we boarded the train from King's Cross to Peterborough but as we travelled north the sun crept behind the ever increasing bank of grey clouds. By the time we pulled into the station the rain was pouring and the wind had an edge to it that had us rushing for the taxi rank.

'I know you said the place was flat,' I said to Jake as we left the city behind us, 'but I wasn't expecting this. I can see for miles!'

It wasn't exactly picturesque. The fields, which looked barren to my untrained eye, were stamped with never ending lines of gigantic pylons that marched across the landscape like alien invaders and the few trees I did spot were wind tortured and bent low. However, even I could tell there was something special about the place. Even through the rain and decreasing light I could appreciate the raw beauty that Jake had so passionately described.

'Almost there,' he told me.

He took my hand and kissed it as the taxi left the main road and turned up what, to my jolted spine, felt like a dirt track. I was just beginning to pity the car's suspension when we swung into a gateway and drew to a halt. My hands were shaking as I gathered my bags and Jake paid the driver.

'This is it,' Jake beamed, spreading out his arms to indicate the scruffy yard and ragtag group of dilapidated outbuildings, 'home sweet home.'

Chapter 7

The farmhouse, although clearly in need of a lick of paint and a spruce up, wouldn't have looked out of place on the cover of the *Country Living* magazine in my bag. The arched porch in the middle even had roses growing around the door (which, if nothing else, were appreciated because Dan said they didn't exist), but the mismatched jumble of boots and jackets inside were a clear indication that this was a working farm rather than a fancy weekend retreat.

'It's beautiful,' I said, smiling up at Jake and truly meaning it, 'really beautiful.'

He smiled back, raised the fox-shaped brass door knocker and hammered it against the door. The sudden din that erupted from inside had my pulse racing and my palms sweating in an instant.

'What the hell is that?' I gasped, taking a step back into the rain.

'Just the dogs,' Jake laughed, pulling me back under cover, 'they must've been asleep when the taxi arrived.'

'Dogs,' I stammered, 'you never said anything about dogs.'

'Bella and Lily,' Jake casually announced. 'The Labradors, I must have told you about them?'

'No,' I said, 'you didn't. Jake, I'm sorry, but I'm not used to dogs, or any pet for that matter. I didn't even have a gold-fish when I was a kid.'

'Oh, it'll be fine,' Jake laughed, 'these two are a doddle compared to the geese.'

I couldn't be sure if he was joking or not.

'They won't jump up, will they?' I whimpered. 'What if they don't like the look of me?'

'Oh, they won't hurt you,' Jake tutted, clearly not under-standing the gravity of the situation. 'They're pussycats really.'

'Well, they don't sound like pussycats,' I muttered, reach-ing for my suitcase and holding it protectively across my body.

Before I had a chance to find a hole to squeeze my uncer-tain self into, I heard a bolt being slid back from the inside, then the door opened, the porch was flooded with light and I was knocked off my feet backwards into the yard.

'Oh my God, Amber!' Jake shouted, rushing to rescue me. 'Are you all right?'

'No!' I shouted back, abandoning my suitcase and covering my head until he called off the hounds from hell. 'Of course I'm not all right! I knew this would happen.'

Jake dropped his bags, grabbed the dogs by their collars and pulled them away. I quickly scrabbled to my feet, my heart hammering in my chest as I brushed myself down and tried to regain my composure.

'Oh you poor dear girl,' said the woman who had answered the door as she rushed to my side, 'I'm so sorry. Are you all right?'

'Yes,' I breathed, feeling anything but, 'yes, I'm fine.'

I had been so determined to make a good first impression and already my efforts, along with the hem of my new linen shirt, were in tatters. I don't think I could have looked more of a fool if I tried.

'Auntie Annie,' Jake beamed as he wrestled with the dogs and appeared completely oblivious to my embarrassment, 'this is Amber. Amber, this is Auntie Annie.'

'I'm so pleased to meet you,' Annie beamed, swiftly pulling me into a hug and kissing my cheek.

She smelt comfortingly of pressed powder and Lily of the Valley and somehow instantly made me feel better. Whether it was the warmth of her demonstrative welcome or her obvious delight that I had decided to come I wasn't sure, but whatever it was, it helped me relax and I felt some of the tension in my shoulders disappear.

'Welcome,' she smiled, kissing me again. 'Welcome to Skylark Farm. I'm so pleased you changed your mind about coming. Jake was quite inconsolable when he thought you wouldn't.'

'Was he?' I asked.

'Oh yes,' Annie nodded conspiratorially as she scooped up my Cath Kidston bag and linked her arm through mine. 'He really was and I can see why now. She's every bit as pretty as you described, isn't she?' she said, smiling at Jake who had turned beetroot red.

'Thank you, Auntie,' he mumbled, blushing an even deeper shade of crimson. 'I'll put the dogs in the washhouse for now, shall I?'

'Yes, I think that would be a good idea, just until we're settled,' she agreed, then, turning her mischievous periwinkle eyes back to me, added, 'come on, let's go and get you a cup of tea. I'm so sorry about the dogs. I haven't been able to exercise them as much as I'd like recently and consequently they're a little hyper.'

She led me into the kitchen while Jake settled the dogs in one of the buildings attached to the side of the house. I couldn't help thinking I might have done them a disservice because they didn't look anywhere near as fearsome as they had sounded as he led them away, with their tails wagging and tongues lolling.

'Please, make yourself at home, my dear,' Annie smiled as

she slowly set about making tea and laying the table. 'You must be parched.'

'Can I do anything to help?'

'No, absolutely not,' she insisted, 'you stay where you are.'

An ancient range almost filled one wall of the kitchen and along with the scrubbed pine table there were a variety of mismatched chairs. The stone floor felt hard and cold underfoot; the only concession to comfort was a large rug that looked like it had been made from rags, in front of the range.

There was a jumble of assorted cushions on the armchairs either side of the range, evidently all handmade, and the few fitted cupboards looked like they had been in their prime decades ago. Looking around I realised the only thing the room had in common with the kitchens I'd been fantasising about in glossy magazines was the fact that this one actually was in the country.

'There we are,' said Annie, shakily placing a pretty floral patterned cup and saucer down in front of me, 'do help yourself to milk and sugar.'

Gratefully I wrapped my hands around the cup and reached for the milk jug.

'Oh Jake,' Annie scolded, when he joined us a few seconds later, 'look at the state of you, you silly boy! You shouldn't let them jump up, you know. That shirt is ruined.'

'I know, I know,' he said, shaking his head. 'Anyone

would think I'd been away months rather than days! I'm sorry, Amber, I had no idea you were scared of dogs.'

'I'm not scared exactly,' I said, trying to play down what had happened, 'I just feel a bit intimidated by them, that's all. I guess I'm just not used to them yet.'

'Bad experience as a child, no doubt,' said Annie as she eyed me astutely.

There was something in the way she said, rather than asked, that suggested that she already knew what I was going to say. The old lady might not have been as steady on her feet as she once was, but she was still clearly as sharp as a packet of pins when it came to sizing people up. Her quick glance and shrewd observations put me in mind of Miss Marple and I realised straightaway that here was a woman from whom no secrets could be hidden.

'Yes,' I admitted, 'I'm afraid so. I was at the beach with my mum and dad one day and someone's dog ran up, off its lead, and jumped up at me. I can't remember exactly how old I was, but I couldn't have been more than four or five, so it was right in my face. I haven't really had much contact with dogs ever since.'

'Oh you poor love,' Annie tutted, 'that nasty little experience should have been nipped in the bud! Didn't you ever have a dog as a child?'

'No,' I laughed. The thought of my parents coping with something as unruly as a puppy was most amusing.

'She's never had a pet,' Jake said, 'of any variety.'

'Well I'll be,' said Annie, looking shocked. 'Well, I can promise you right now, you'll be used to that pair by this time tomorrow.'

I looked at her doubtfully.

'You will,' she chuckled, 'you'll see.'

She gave Jake a swift kiss on the cheek as she passed him a cup and made her slow way back to the range.

'I hope you're hungry,' she said, 'I've got a pie in here.'

Jake looked at me wide eyed and slowly shook his head. He looked positively terrified and it was all I could do to stifle the giggle I could feel bubbling up.

'And before you say anything, you naughty boy,' Annie added without turning round, 'the pie came from town. The only thing I've done is bake a few potatoes and not even I can get that wrong!'

'I should have warned you about Annie's cooking,' Jake whispered as we climbed into bed that night. 'Be very careful about eating anything she's made herself, won't you? Her culinary skills are dubious at best, so just watch out.'

'OK,' I said, snuggling a little further under the blankets to block out the noise from downstairs. 'Do you think the dogs will be making that racket all night?'

'They usually sleep on this bed,' Jake said by way of explanation. 'They'll soon get bored and go to sleep.'

'Oh,' I said, 'I see.'

I couldn't help feeling a little guilty that they were shut out of the bedroom for my benefit. I was already less wary of them since Annie had let them back in the kitchen when we finished eating, but I still didn't really feel I knew them well enough to share a bed with them.

The pair had spent a good few minutes sniffing, licking and nudging their way under my elbows every time I stopped stroking their silky ears before settling on my feet, until it was time to go up to bed.

'So, how does Annie seem to you?' I asked. 'I didn't like to ask her about the fall, but she seemed as sharp as a tack to me.'

'Oh, there's nothing wrong with her mind,' Jake grinned, keeping his voice low, 'she's just getting a bit frail, that's all.'

'OK,' I nodded, trying to lie still and stop the bed frame from squeaking. 'From what I've seen I can't imagine she's the sort of woman who is going to slow down willingly.'

'No,' Jake said, wrapping his arms around me and pulling me to him. 'She's not, but let's not worry about that for now. Tell me, what do you really think of the place?'

'I love it,' I smiled, snuggling up to his chest. 'I really do.'

I didn't mention the surprise I'd felt when I discovered the toilet flushed with a chain or that I already knew I didn't stand a chance of catching a moment's sleep because of the steady drip from the leaking ceiling clanging into the metal bucket next to the window.

Annie had welcomed me to Skylark Farm, her home, more as if I was a long-lost family member than some stranger she was meeting for the very first time and I was determined to repay her kindness by giving my new life in the country my absolute all.

Chapter 8

I slept far later than I planned to that first morning at Skylark Farm. In fact, had it not been for the sound of laughter drifting up the stairs and seeping into the bedroom, I'd probably still be there.

Within seconds of Jake's head hitting the pillow he had fallen into a deep slumber. I, on the other hand, had not. Had I been fortunate enough to have the comfort of the pocket sprung mattress I'd left behind in London to sink into I would have doubtless quickly nodded off. What I ended up doing, however, was alternately counting splashes in the bucket rather than sheep, followed by how many times the owl hooted in an hour, then scaring myself witless trying to work out which breed of rodent was scrabbling about above my head.

Jake got up just after first light feeling refreshed and rejuvenated and went downstairs, promising to return with tea.

As I recall I muttered something about joining him, rolled over, stretched out my aching back and gratefully drifted off. It must have been, judging by the light, at least a couple of hours later when I was woken by giggling that certainly wasn't coming from Annie.

I lay for a few minutes taking in the faded floral wallpaper, heavy dark furniture and old-fashioned bedstead. Just like the kitchen and bathroom it was far from the light and airy Laura Ashley style décor I had imagined, but I surprised myself by realising I liked the place all the more because of that.

The farmhouse was a comfortable family home and judging by the little vases of fresh flowers Annie had set on the dressing table and night stand, and the pile of old paperbacks stacked next to the bed, she had gone out of her way to make me feel at home. I hoped I was capable of learning the ropes and playing a useful part in helping her and Jake run the farm as quickly as possible.

The laughter coming from downstairs was becoming more raucous by the second and I knew I couldn't put off making an appearance any longer. Taking a deep breath I pushed back the sheets and blankets and braced myself to begin the first day of my new life.

Any hopes I had of creeping down the stairs and peeping into the kitchen before entering were dashed by the creaking floorboards. Bella and Lily had obviously been listening out for me and were whining and clawing at the door before I was even halfway down.

'Oh Jake,' I heard a woman snort, 'what are you like? You don't get any better, do you?'

'Maybe not,' Jake guffawed back good-humouredly, 'but what I don't understand is why you expect me to!'

I slipped quietly into the room and having quickly looked at the not one, but two women whom Jake was entertaining, stooped to fuss the dogs. Annie was right. I might not have been completely comfortable with their enthusiastic welcome, but I was nowhere near as wary of them as I had been when we first arrived. In fact, I was grateful that they were waiting for me and that I didn't have to stand shuffling about in the corner like the new girl waiting to be introduced.

'Amber!' Jake smiled, jumping up. 'There you are!'

'Did we wake you?' asked one of the women. 'I'm so sorry. I did keep telling them to pipe down but they're just as bad as each other. I'm Jessica, by the way,' she smiled, standing up.

Jessica, resplendent in jodhpurs, Dubarry boots and matching Barbour, looked every inch the country lady. I could easily imagine myself flicking through the pages of *Country Life* and reading all about her rambling, rural family pile.

'And I'm Harriet,' said the other, knocking her knees clumsily on the underside of the table as she also jumped up.

By contrast Harriet was shorter than Jessica, her dark blonde hair was piled haphazardly on top of her head and she had holes in the cuffs of her jumper. She looked as if she would have been perfect as an extra in an episode of *The Good Life*.

'Hello,' I smiled, pushing my way through the dogs, 'please don't apologise. I'm sure I should have been up hours ago.'

'Let me get you some tea,' Jake offered. 'I never did make it back upstairs with a cup, did I?'

'Our fault again,' Jessica sighed, 'I told you we should have called this evening, Harriet.'

'I'll make the tea,' I said, grateful to be doing something.

'So, Amber, how do you like the place?' Harriet asked.

'Oh for goodness sake,' Jessica jumped in again, 'give the poor girl a chance. She only got here last night. She won't have seen anything yet!'

Jake looked at me and rolled his eyes.

'Don't worry about Tweedledum and Tweedledee here,' he whispered. 'They're always like this.'

'Hey,' said Harriet, flicking him with the tea towel.

Feeling more relaxed than I could have imagined possible when I was dithering on the stairs, I reached for the kettle and picked it up. The pain that shot through my palm was excruciating and I clumsily dropped it back on to the range, yowling in agony. Before I had time to think what to do

Jessica had grabbed me by the wrist and Harriet was turning on the cold tap at the sink.

'Bloody hell, Amber!' Jake cried, his face as red as my hand. 'I'm so sorry! I should have warned you. You can't pick the kettle up without the gloves when it's been on the range.'

'Oh,' I said, my voice trembling as I tried to play down what had happened.

I felt like a complete fool standing there while Harriet and Jessica administered first aid to me, the silly city girl, they'd met less than five minutes before.

'There,' said Harriet, gently patting my hand dry a minute or two later and blowing coolly on the burn before releasing her grip. 'You'll live.'

'Thank you,' I croaked. I felt mortified as well as in pain.

'Annie will have something you can put on that, won't she, Jake?' Jessica said. 'She's got a cure for everything.'

'How about a cure for my stupidity?' I smiled, trying to make light of the situation.

As hard as I tried to shrug it off I couldn't stop my bottom lip trembling and I knew I was ridiculously close to tears. I couldn't believe how overwhelmed I felt, and how frustrated especially when just minutes before I'd started to relax. Nothing ruffled me, ever. Yet here I was with a scalded palm and a bruised ego and I hadn't even set foot on the farm yet!

'Hey,' said Harriet, giving my arm a quick rub, 'don't say that. How were you supposed to know the damn thing was going to brand you?'

I shrugged and sniffed hard, grateful for her kindness.

'Here,' said Jake, as he set down the freshly filled teapot and clean mugs. 'I'm going to go and find Annie and ask if she has something for that burn. You girls get to know each other and I'll be back in a bit.'

'I'll be mother, shall I?' Jessica asked and reached for the pot as Jake closed the door behind him.

I began to relax again as we sat chatting around the table. Jessica told me all about her family's riding stables and how she was getting married to her fiancé, Henry, at the end of the summer. Annie had agreed to the wedding taking place in the orchards before the apple harvest and it all sounded incredibly romantic.

'I hope you'll be up for helping out, Amber,' she smiled. 'Jake has told us all about your city career and I've a feeling I might need your organisational skills before long.'

'Of course,' I nodded, surprised that there could possibly be anything that anyone as competent as Jessica couldn't organise for herself. 'I'd love to help.'

When I left London (was it really only the day before?), I had assumed there would be no call for my professional skills in the country, but apparently I was already in demand and I have to admit I was rather thrilled to think I wasn't going to be a complete waste of space.

'What about you, Harriet?' I asked, turning my attention to the other side of the table. 'What do you do for a living?'

'Well, if my father had his way,' she explained, 'I'd be following in his footsteps and taking the arable farm route.'

'But she's not,' cut in Jessica, with a wink. 'She's bucking the trend.'

'Yes, I suppose I am,' said Harriet, a slight blush blooming. 'I'm starting my own nursery,' she said proudly, then added in a rush, 'plants, not kids. I studied horticulture at the local agricultural college. That's where Jess and I met.'

'So you didn't meet at school then?' I asked, feeling surprised. 'I assumed you'd known each other forever!'

'No,' Harriet smiled wryly, 'I went to the local high school, but that wasn't grand enough for Jessica here.'

'I went away to boarding school,' Jessica patiently explained, 'a fact that my good friend here won't ever let me forget.'

'Sorry,' Harriet giggled, sounding anything but. 'She's not really as posh as I like to make out, but you can't deny she'd look good tapping a riding crop against her leg.'

Jessica scowled at her friend and I decided it was time to move the conversation on.

'So where does Jake fit in?' I asked. 'How did you meet him?'

Harriet turned a deeper shade of red and Jessica began to laugh. Neither spoke up for a few seconds and I was just beginning to wonder if there had been a romantic connection somewhere along the line, but then Harriet explained everything and set me straight.

'It was years ago now,' she cringed. 'A friend and I were collecting apples . . .'

'She means they were scrumping,' Jessica added with a wink. 'You know, *stealing*.'

'Yeah,' I laughed, 'I get the idea.'

'And Annie caught us,' Harriet continued, again ignoring her friend. 'Jake was here for a holiday and witnessed the hell we went through when Annie made us eat the apples we'd taken. He, of course, thought it was hilarious.'

'Why?' I asked. 'What was wrong with the apples?'

'It was ages before harvest time so they were nowhere near ripe,' Harriet grimaced, 'and incredibly sour.'

'Please spare us the details of the resulting stomach cramps,' begged Jessica, 'I've heard the gory details too many times before!'

'Oh,' I laughed, 'I see.'

'That hilarious debacle sealed my friendship with Jake,' Harriet shrugged. 'Jess here is a relative newcomer. She arrived with Pip the Shetland pony, but Jake can explain about her later.'

'And what about the friend you were, er . . . scrumping with?'

'Oh,' said Harriet, blushing again. 'She doesn't live round here any more.'

A quick glance passed between the two friends, but I spotted it. Clearly there was more to this missing person than either were willing to share.

'Anyway,' Harriet went on, 'getting back to your original question. Dad's given me some land and polytunnels so I can start establishing my own stock and in the meantime I'm buying in and selling from a market stall in Wynbridge.'

'Talking of which,' said Jessica, tapping her watch, 'we'd better make a move. I have a class this morning and I promised Harriet she could borrow my 4x4 to get her plants to market as her old van's off the road, again.'

She and Harriet drained their mugs and stood up to leave.

'But just before we go,' said Jessica, 'would it be all right if I said something?'

'Oh, here we go,' smirked Harriet, rolling her eyes.

'Of course,' I nodded. My stomach groaned and I couldn't shake off the feeling that I'd been summoned to the head-mistress's office. 'Say away.'

'Well,' she began, 'Jake tells us you've never lived in the countryside before. Is that true?'

'It is,' I confirmed. 'I've hardly ever even visited, let alone slept in a bedroom that isn't bathed in an orange glow.'

'Well, in that case, be patient with yourself, Amber. Don't expect to know how everything works or get everything right first time.'

'Like how to use the kettle, you mean?' I smiled, holding up my burnt hand.

'Yes,' smiled Jessica, 'even something as simple as that. Just go with the flow.'

'Oh, listen to her,' teased Harriet, 'sounding all motherly and protective!'

Jessica raised her eyebrows, but forbore to comment.

'I daresay you've already worked out that living on the farm is going to be very different to life in London,' she continued, 'so don't expect it to be perfect straightaway. Yes?'

'OK,' I smiled, rubbing my palm and thinking her words of wisdom couldn't have been kinder or better timed.

'You don't mind me saying that, do you?' she winced.

'No,' I said, 'of course not. I appreciate it and I know you're right, things here do seem very different so I will try and cut myself some slack.'

'Good. I'm so pleased you've decided to come, and I think I can speak for both of us?' she said, looking across at Harriet, who nodded in confirmation. 'To be honest, we're filled with nothing but admiration for you and what you've decided to do.'

'Really?'

'Really,' said Harriet, 'we can't even begin to imagine how transformed your life is going to be. We're used to all this,' she said, looking about her and out into the yard, 'but you aren't so if you need anything, anything at all, please ask us, won't you? Jake has our numbers and we're always about.'

'I will,' I promised, already feeling heaps better, despite the burning sensation on my palm, 'and thank you.'

'Are you coming to the pub tonight?' Harriet asked as she pulled on her boots.

'I don't know,' I said, 'I'll ask Jake.'

'Well, in that case,' smiled Jessica, 'I'm sure we'll see you later!'

Chapter 9

'Oh you poor love!' Annie tutted as she examined my hand. 'Sit yourself down. I've got just the thing to take the heat out of that. Jake, would you please get the first aid kit out of the dresser? There should be a bandage in there somewhere.'

'A first aid kit,' Jake mouthed silently at me, clearly amazed that such a thing existed under the roof of Skylark Farm.

I sat as instructed and watched as Annie disappeared into the pantry then reappeared with a potato, which she washed in the sink and then grated finely into a bowl.

'This bandage has seen better days,' Jake frowned, unravelling it on to the table, 'but frankly I'm still in shock that you have such a thing, Annie!'

'Never mind that,' Annie replied, impatiently pushing him aside and gently laying my hand palm upwards on an old towel. 'Now, my dear, this shouldn't hurt but speak up if you want me to stop.'

Very gently she covered the burn with a layer of the grated potato and secured it snugly in place with the bandage. Throughout the process, which only took a couple of minutes, I sat in stunned silence. The stinging had already begun to subside and, even though the dressing was a little cumbersome, I was grateful to be relieved of the pain. When she had finished, Annie looked at me and grinned.

'Consider that your first lesson in country lore,' she laughed. 'Raw potatoes are the best way to treat burns. Don't ask me the science behind it, but my old grandmother used to swear by them.'

'Well, it's definitely working,' I told her, 'it feels far more comfortable already.'

'We'll have a look at it again after dinner,' she winked, 'and change the potato if necessary.'

'OK,' I nodded. I wasn't really sure what to make of the whole situation, but appreciated Annie's grandmother's wisdom nonetheless. 'Thank you.'

Jake started to laugh and, I noted, pointedly used the quilted mat that hung next to the range to fill the teapot with water from the old kettle.

'Let's have another cup,' he suggested, 'then I'll take you on a tour of the farm, Amber.'

'You could even take a picnic down to the river,' Annie smiled, as she covered the bowl of grated potato and popped it in the fridge. 'It's going to be a cracking day.'

Armed with sandwiches, a couple of bottles of juice and some apples from the pantry, we ventured out into the yard. It was a warm day, clear and bright and nothing like the wet and windy evening that heralded our arrival the night before. However, not even the cloud-free skies could show the collection of ramshackle buildings in a better light. Everything carried an air of neglect and, although even to my novice eye nothing looked completely beyond repair, it was immediately obvious that there was work to do, and plenty of it.

Taking a few more steps away from the house and shielding his eyes from the glare of the warming spring sun, Jake stared long and hard at the roof of the house.

'That's going to have to be my first job,' he informed me, pointing at an ineffectual piece of tarpaulin that had obviously slipped in the gale the day before.

Where there should have been three, possibly four tiles, there was a gaping hole and exposed rafters, which no doubt accounted for the avant garde addition of the metal bucket to the décor in our bedroom.

'I need to replace some tiles up there and repair some of the others,' Jake continued. 'That hole is right up above our room. I don't know if you noticed,' he said, shaking his head, 'but the rain is actually coming through the ceiling now. Annie's put a bucket in there to catch the drips.'

'Yes,' I said with a nod, 'it had caught my eye.' I didn't mention that it had also kept me awake half the night.

'Right,' he smiled, clearly undaunted by the thought of scrambling about on the roof, 'we'll start with the hens. I'm hoping you'll be taking them on from tomorrow, assuming, of course, your hand is OK.'

'It'll be fine,' I said. 'Come on, let's get started.'

I swallowed hard and followed on as Jake made his way over to the little shed that stood closest to the house. Bella and Lily, clearly unimpressed with the tour having been on it countless times before, wandered off leaving me to explore my new office in peace.

'We've only got three hens at the moment,' Jake explained. 'We did have half a dozen just a few weeks ago, but the fox has been busy, I'm afraid.'

'You mean it's killed them?' I asked horrified.

'Yep,' Jake nodded, 'afraid so.'

'But that's awful!' I cried. 'How did it get in?'

'Well, the hens come and go as they please during the day,' Jake explained. 'They're easy targets so really, even though you might not think so, we've been lucky. More often than not a fox will keep coming back until it has had the lot. Really, I'm amazed we've still got these.'

He pointed to the edge of the yard where a couple of plump brown hens were scratching about under the hedge.

'That's Martha and Mabel,' he told me. 'All our hens are ex-battery ladies and they might look all right now, but they were in a shocking state when Annie collected them. She calls Skylark Farm the "Last Chance Saloon" for her girls and personally tends to their every whim until they find their feet and can be left to their own devices.'

I didn't ask how she prepared them for combat in case the fox came skulking.

'So,' I said, cautiously opening the henhouse door and trying not to react to the pungent smell that instantly assaulted my nostrils, 'if they're out and about in the yard, what do they use this place for?'

'They come back here to sleep and more often than not they lay their eggs in here as well, but not always, mind you. If you do find an egg in the yard, unless you're a hundred per cent sure it's fresh, it's best to discard it. Unless Annie's around, of course,' he added as an afterthought. 'As I recall she knows some old country ways of checking the freshness of an egg.'

I poked my head right in and spotted the third hen staring beadily back at me from her station in one of the nest boxes.

'That's Patricia,' said Jake with a nod. 'She is Annie's absolute favourite. She needs lifting off the eggs every morning at the moment because she's gone broody.'

'What does that mean?'

'Basically it means that she's stopped laying eggs herself, but wants to sit on any she can find and hatch them off,' Jake explained.

'Oh,' I smiled, delighted by the thought of having some cute chicks running around the place, 'why don't you just let her?'

Jake looked at me and shook his head.

'Because the eggs aren't viable,' he explained patiently. 'We haven't got a cockerel so there's no chick inside.'

'Oh,' I blushed, 'of course.'

I really did have a lot to learn.

'But if you'd like some chicks,' Jake suggested, 'I could always buy in a few fertile eggs and put them under her.'

'Would that work?'

'Yes,' Jake nodded, 'as long as she stays broody she'd hatch them off all right and you could pick which breed you like the look of. It would make a nice change to have some fancy birds about the place after years of Annie's ragtag girls. Of course we'd have to build a pen to begin with,' he added, 'just to give them a fighting chance in case the fox turns up again.'

I didn't much like the thought of losing any more birds to the horrible fox, but the lure of some newly hatched bundles of fluff and feather was very tempting.

'Right,' said Jake, leaving the picnic outside, 'I'm hoping you'll be doing this tomorrow so watch carefully. I'll lift her off and you grab what she's sitting on.'

Patricia was less than impressed as Jake gently lifted her off her makeshift nest. She squawked and flapped and took more than one peck at his hands as I looked in wonder at the bounty she had been protecting. There, nestled amongst the straw and feathers, were four large brown, slightly speckled eggs. I carefully picked them up, surprised by just how warm they were, and carried them out of the shed while Jake set Patricia down outside. She clucked off, indignantly shaking her feathers and stretching out her wings with many a disgruntled squawk thrown in for good measure.

'Wow,' I beamed, still looking at the eggs.

'Lovely, aren't they?' Jake said.

'I can't say I've ever taken all that much notice of an egg before, but yes, they are rather lovely.'

'Two of those must be the pair left from yesterday,' Jake frowned. 'Annie must have forgotten to collect them. Hens only lay one egg a day you see so—'

'Yes,' I laughed, cutting him off, 'that much I do know.'

'So,' he grinned, 'do you think you're up to taking them on then?'

'Absolutely,' I smiled back, 'you'll have to tell me what else to do with them, but yes I'm sure I could manage to look after them. Assuming there are some gloves around here somewhere that would save my hands from Patricia's vicious little beak!'

This was exactly what I needed: something completely different, something that was a world away from my old life, something simple with a very different routine. Even though I was inwardly terrified of the responsibility and strangeness of it all I was determined to say 'yes' to everything Jake suggested and not allow myself to talk my way out of anything.

'Well,' said Jake, 'let me think. You'll have to let them out every morning and shut them up at night. They find their own way back in, of course, so there's no chasing them to bed. Then you need to collect the eggs, feed and water them and clean the house and, if you could manage it,' he added, looking back inside, 'a complete sanitisation wouldn't go amiss. We don't want to be plagued with mites, especially now the weather's warming up.'

I have to admit I didn't much like the idea of scooping up chicken poo or fumigating mites, but I was determined to do my best, otherwise what was the point in coming? I might even be able to find the little basket I'd been thinking about to collect the eggs in.

'OK,' I nodded, 'consider me the new Hen Welfare Manager at Skylark Farm.'

'Very grand,' laughed Jake, 'trust you to put a spin on it! Next thing you'll be telling me you want specialist equipment.'

I raised my eyebrows, but didn't dare tell him about the basket idea.

'Anyway,' Jake continued, 'we'll see about getting some eggs for Patricia to hatch before the novelty of sitting disappears and it'll be all systems go.'

'OK,' I said, 'excellent.'

I knew one of the magazines I'd packed in my suitcase had a three page spread entitled 'Fancy Fowl' and I was already looking forward to choosing my own.

'Where shall we put these?'

We took the still warm eggs back to the house, popped them in a large earthenware bowl in the pantry and carried on with the tour. Next were the geese. There were five of them in all and they were housed in a paddock at the end of the yard. They also had their own little shed for sleeping in and, judging by the way they flapped their large wings and honked as we approached, I guessed the fox wouldn't be bothering them.

'Don't you like the geese?' I said, bending down to stroke Bella.

She had wandered up to take a look, but refused to go right up to the fence. Her thick tail thumped against my legs and the sorrowful look in her eyes suggested that the geese were no fun at all.

'No,' Jake laughed, 'she doesn't. She had one encounter too many with them when she was a puppy and she doesn't go anywhere near them these days. In fact,' he added, looking me up and down, 'I'm not even sure that you could outrun them, Amber.'

'Oh thanks,' I pouted, 'I'm pretty fit, you know!'

'I know you are, but they're nasty buggers. Come with me when I'm sorting them out by all means, but you'd best leave looking after them to me for now. Come on, let's go and meet Pip.'

Now accompanied by both Bella and Lily we made our way to the last field before the orchards began.

'So, this is Pip,' I smiled.

Jake shook a bucket filled with what I guessed was her breakfast and the little pony cantered up the field with surprising speed considering how short her legs were.

'Mmm,' said Jake, 'don't let her size and cute face fool you. She's a feisty one and not beyond giving a nip or a kick if she doesn't get her own way.'

'Harriet said you met Jessica when Pip arrived. Is that right?'

'Yes,' said Jake as the little pony thrust her head over the fence and her nose in the bucket. 'Thinking about it I haven't actually known Jess for all that long, although it already feels like forever. Her mum bought Pip for the stables. She was supposed to be an ideal starter pony for their juniors' class, but they hadn't had her five minutes before they realised she wasn't going to work out. You don't like being ridden much, do you, Pip?'

Pip shook her head and fixed me with her dark stare. Tentatively I reached out and stroked her thick black mane. She ignored me completely, which according to Jake was a good sign, and went back to her chewing.

'So basically, she's going to see out her days here at the farm?'

'Exactly,' said Jake, 'she keeps the paddock in check and Jessica pays for her feed and vet's bills and so on. Helena, Jess's mum, would have sold her on but Jess wouldn't hear of it.'

'Sell her on to where?' I asked, leaning over and roughly rubbing Pip's back.

With an indignant neigh she kicked up her heels and was off.

'I'm not entirely sure,' said Jake, shaking his head and watching her tear away.

By the time we'd completed a tour of the orchards it was almost noon and warm enough to picnic down by the river that ran through the bottom of the farm boundary.

'So, when will the blossom start to appear?' I asked, looking back towards the rows and rows of uniformly pruned apple trees.

'Probably in a couple of weeks,' said Jake as he spread out the blanket under the willow trees and glanced up at the sky, 'but if the weather stays as mild as this, it might be even sooner.'

'I can't wait to see it,' I smiled.

'And I can't begin to tell you how beautiful it is,' he sighed. 'It wouldn't matter how hard I tried to describe it, no words could do it justice. We really couldn't have moved here at a better time.'

I looked up at the blue sky and listened to the gurgling river as it wove its merry way to Wynbridge. Already I felt so at home, so relaxed. Yes, it was weird not having my phone constantly attached to my ear, but nice weird, and I knew that had I flown to Dubai, I wouldn't be feeling anywhere near as happy as I was right then sitting beneath the willows, even though the dogs were hogging the sunniest spot on the blanket.

'Harriet was telling me that you met her because of the orchards,' I said, trying to help unpack the picnic with my functioning hand.

'Yes,' Jake laughed, 'we did. Did she also tell you about the rollicking stomach ache she ended up with as well?'

'Sort of,' I nodded, 'she said she and her friend never stole anything again.'

Jake threw himself down on the blanket and I snuggled up to him. He didn't say anything else and I remembered the look that had passed between Harriet and Jessica earlier. I knew it wasn't any of my business but I couldn't resist asking.

'So who was the friend?' I said, trying to keep my tone light-hearted. 'Harriet said—'

'It was Holly,' Jake cut in. Suddenly he sounded far from light-hearted. 'Her name was Holly. She doesn't live around here now.'

'But are you all still friends?'

'No,' said Jake, turning to face me. 'Look, you might as well know, Amber: Holly and I used to be a couple. We were together for quite a while actually, but we split up and she moved away.'

'Oh no,' I joked, trying to convey that I wasn't the slightest bit fazed by his admission. 'Should I be feeling jealous of this summer teenage romance?'

'Of course not,' said Jake seriously, a deep frown appearing for the first time since we'd arrived at the farm. 'Absolutely not, but the relationship was rather more than that. I wouldn't have bothered mentioning it if Harriet hadn't first. Can we just drop it, please?'

'OK,' I shrugged, not feeling quite as unfazed as before, 'I was only teasing.'

'Life in a small community like this isn't the same as London,' Jake continued, still sounding concerned. 'You have to be prepared for a certain amount of tittle tattle here, Amber, especially in the pub.'

'Oh, that reminds me,' I said, keen to dismiss all thoughts of the girl who had occupied Jake's heart before me, 'Jessica asked if we were going out tonight.'

'What did you say?'

'I said I didn't know, but I would like to. I really liked her and Harriet. Jess even asked if I'd help out with her wedding plans.'

'Well, let's not make up our minds about the pub just yet,' said Jake as he passed me a sandwich, 'let's see how we're feeling later.'

Chapter 10

Jake and I spent our first afternoon at Skylark Farm together lazily dozing and chatting under the dappled shade of the willow trees which lined the stretch of the River Wyn that ran through the farm. For early April it was incredibly mild but, Jake was quick to remind me, that could all change in the blink of an eye if the wind swung round to the north or east.

'So,' I yawned, forcing myself to sit up and have a stretch, 'after you've fixed the farmhouse roof, what then? What else can I help with?'

'Well,' said Jake, squinting up at me, 'I know it isn't very glamorous but, as well as taking on the hens, if you wouldn't mind helping Annie out with some of the household stuff, that would be great. She'd rather die than ask, but she is struggling and I know it sounds old-fashioned but she certainly wouldn't let me do anything.'

'Of course,' I said, 'absolutely.' I understood exactly what Jake meant, but I wanted to be doing more than just household chores. 'But what about helping outside? I really want to get stuck in. That's the whole point of me being here after all.'

'Well, you could help me with the repairs to the outbuildings and learn how to look after Pip,' he suggested. 'When the harvest comes I'm going to need as much help as I can get so it makes sense to get everything as shipshape as possible now. That is, as long as you're up to it, of course,' he added, looking pointedly at my hand.

'Oh don't,' I blushed, looking at the potato packed bandage. 'I still feel such an idiot about this.'

'Could've happened to anyone,' Jake said kindly, then pulled me back down so he could kiss me. 'And of course, I was forgetting there is one other very special lesson I have to teach you about life in the country,'

'Oh,' I said, my body emitting a little tremor as he ran a trail of soft kisses along my jaw and down my neck, 'and what is that?'

'I feel it is my duty to instruct you in the art of outdoor lovemaking,' he whispered, brushing my lips with the softest kiss and slipping his arm around my waist, 'assuming of course you aren't already an expert.'

'At ease, soldier,' I laughed, pulling away slightly, 'even I know it has to be warmer than this for rolling about in the great outdoors!'

'Oh well, it was worth a try,' he smiled, releasing me and sitting up. 'Come on. We'd better go and see what Annie's been up to this afternoon. We'll walk back through the orchards.'

It was cooler walking through the trees and quiet. As strange as it might sound, I couldn't shake off the feeling that they were holding their breath, patiently waiting to give their first spectacular performance of the year.

'You know,' I said, crossing sides and reaching for Jake's hand, 'I'm surprised you haven't got any bee hives set up in here.'

'We did have,' he told me, 'a few years ago, but the chap gave them up and I'm ashamed to say we never looked for anyone to replace them.'

'Well, perhaps you could now,' I said, thrilled that the suggestion wasn't a complete non-starter. 'What with bee populations diminishing and so many people trying to keep hives at home, I bet you'd find someone local who would jump at the chance of setting up in here.'

'You know what,' he said, kissing my hand, 'I think you could be right. We'll ask Annie. I bet she'll love the idea.'

'There!' I teased. 'And you said all those magazines I was reading were a waste of money!'

We had almost made it back through the orchards when I heard, above all the other birds, one in particular. Its sweet, melodious song went on and on, the exquisite sound literally soaring up to the heavens.

'What is that bird?' I said, stopping and holding up my bandaged hand. 'Can you hear it?'

'It's a skylark,' Jake said quietly, also listening, 'they nest in the strawberry fields that lie next to the furthest edges of the orchards. I'll show you one later. They fly up and up and up and sing and sing. They're amazing little birds. There used to be a lot more about, that's why the farm's named after them.'

'That's lovely,' I smiled, 'and what's down that way?'

I pointed towards the far boundary beyond the orchards.

'A cottage,' Jake said without looking.

I had expected him to say just another field or something.

'What cottage?' I asked.

'Just a little place that belongs to the farm.'

'Who lives in it?'

'No one now,' Jake shrugged, 'it's been empty for quite a while.'

'What are you going to do with it?' I asked. 'Can we go and see it?'

'Not today,' said Jake dismissively and then looked at his watch, 'we'll go tomorrow. To be honest it's a dark, damp little place, more trouble than it's worth. If it was up to me I'd pull it down and save us the bother of keeping it.'

I was surprised by Jake's comment and sudden change of tone. I'd never heard him talk disparagingly about anything to do with the farm. I decided not to enquire further, even though my mind was already abuzz with potential ways we could make use of the place. We arrived back at the house and Jake helped me pull off my newly christened wellington boots because I couldn't manage to do it myself one handed.

'This rose around the porch,' I said, pointing at the fresh young tendrils that were winding their sinuous way through and about the front of the house, 'it's a rambler, isn't it? It looks to me rather like the one Monty was talking about on *Gardeners' World* the other week.'

'Actually,' smiled Annie who had come to the door, 'it's the very one. I thought you said Amber didn't know much about the countryside and gardening, Jake.'

'Well,' he smiled, 'she's a quick learner, isn't she?'

'Yes,' Annie smiled back, 'I think she is. Now come inside and let me have another look at that hand.'

When Jake had warned me how quickly Fenland weather could change I admit I hadn't taken all that much notice, what with the clear sky overhead and the sun smiling down through the dappled shade of the willows. That afternoon it had felt like the warmth would last well into the evening. However, as we climbed out of the taxi in Wynbridge and I leant over the bridge to get my first proper look at the River Wyn in all its glory, the icy blast that hit me square in the face offered a very clear lesson in what he'd meant.

'Come on,' he said, pulling me back and guiding me across the road, 'let's get inside.'

I took a deep breath and clung to Jake's hand as if it were my one and only lifeline.

'You aren't nervous, are you?' he asked as he lifted the latch and pushed open the heavy wooden door.

'Of course I am,' I croaked, 'can't you remember how you felt when we first started going out in London?'

Jake shrugged and turned to look at me and I realised just what a ridiculous question that was. Of course he couldn't remember being nervous or feeling socially awkward because he never was. He'd always fitted right in, wherever we went. It was that effortless, laidback style of his that had nudged me into falling in love with him in the first place. As we stepped over the threshold I couldn't help wishing that some of his confidence had rubbed off on me.

'You'll be fine,' he smiled, giving my hand a comforting little squeeze. 'Everyone's going to love you. Harriet and Jess already do.'

Knowing the pair of them were going to be there was the one thing that had stopped my nerves getting the better of me. Had I not met them earlier in the day I most probably would have refused to leave the farm for at least a few more days. Their kindness had given me some reassurance that the trip into town wouldn't be a complete car crash.

Chapter 11

The Mermaid turned out to be a low-ceilinged, traditional pub with a welcoming fire in the hearth and an equally warm welcome from the owners, Jim and Evelyn. Jim was a beast of a man, but I could tell straightaway that it was his tiny wife who really ran the show.

'Jake, my boy,' she cheered as we pushed our way through to the bar, 'you're back and, according to local gossip, for good this time!'

'I am,' Jake beamed, 'but I'm not alone, as I daresay you already know!'

Evelyn threw back her head and laughed.

'Evelyn,' said Jake, forcibly pushing me in front of him, 'this is Amber. Amber, this is Evelyn,' then added in a mock whisper that was plenty loud enough for her to hear, 'the one I warned you about.'

Evelyn laughed her rich throaty laugh again and leant

across the bar to cuff Jake who ducked out of the way. It was a manoeuvre he'd clearly exercised before.

'Hello, my love,' Evelyn smiled at me, a twinkle in her eye. 'Welcome to The Mermaid. I would shake your hand, only, as I understand it, you've had a bit of an accident.'

I held up my bandaged hand to confirm what she had heard and wondered whether it had been Harriet or Jess who'd told her.

'Why Annie can't have an electric bloody kettle like the rest of us is beyond me,' Evelyn tutted, rolling her eyes. 'But don't you worry, my love, we aren't all stuck in the dark ages.'

'Oh, it was my own fault,' I insisted, determined to defend Annie and her way of doing things at the farm, 'I've got a lot to learn.'

Evelyn looked at me then for what felt like a very long few seconds. I couldn't help thinking that she was weighing me up, just like Annie had done when I first arrived. Unable to return her gaze I fiddled distractedly with my bandage while she made up her mind. Thankfully I must have met with her approval because the next minute she was offering me a drink and Jake a pint of his usual on the house.

'Look,' he shouted above the noise once we'd got our drinks, 'there's Harriet waving at us! You lead the way and I'll follow on with the glasses.'

I squeezed my way through, past a group of musicians who were laughing and tuning up around an old piano while chatting to their expectant audience, and into an altogether quieter spot which had another fire and a couple of comfortable-looking sofas.

'I knew you'd come!' said Jessica, jumping up and rushing over. 'Come and meet Henry.' She pulled me to the sofa where she had been sitting next to a guy who complemented her in every possible way. 'Amber,' she said, 'this is Henry, my thoroughly fabulous fiancé.'

'Well, I don't know about the fabulous part,' Henry smiled, feigning embarrassment, 'but the fiancé bit is right enough!'

'Pleased to meet you,' I laughed as Jessica retook her place next to her beloved and I sat myself opposite with Harriet on one side and Jake on the other.

'So,' said Harriet, before I'd even had a chance to take a sip of my drink, 'how has your day been?'

'Brilliant,' I nodded, 'really lovely. Jake gave me a tour of the farm and, apart from the hand, I'm still in one piece, so I'd call that progress, wouldn't you?'

Before Harriet had a chance to say anything Jake leant across me to address her.

'Yes, Harriet,' he frowned, 'what did you go telling Evelyn about Amber's accident for?'

'She didn't,' Jessica quickly cut in. 'I was telling Henry when we were at the bar and she heard me, although how God only knows. She was right down the other end!'

'Because she has the hearing of,' Harriet stopped to consider exactly what she could compare Evelyn's miraculous hearing to, 'well, whatever creature has great hearing.' She frowned across at Jake, looking far more offended than I would have expected. 'You should know me better than that, Jake,' she said. 'In fact, I'm offended you even thought it was me. You know I can't abide gossip.'

'Sorry,' said Jake, looking sheepish, 'seriously, I'm sorry. I should have known better.'

'A bat!' Henry suddenly shouted.

'What?' said Jake and Harriet together.

'According to Google,' said Henry, holding up his phone and reminding me why my hands, in spite of the bandage, felt so empty, 'the bat has the best hearing in the world.'

'Now you wouldn't happen to be talking about my good lady, would you?' chuckled Jim as he walked past to the bar with an armful of empty glasses.

'No,' we chorused and burst out laughing.

Red faced and grinning we each took a swig of our drinks and settled back on the sofas.

A couple of drinks later and I was feeling much more relaxed. I'd even joined in the chorus to one of the songs the local band had treated us to.

'So,' I said, looking at a slightly flushed Henry, 'what do you do for a living? I know all about the girls' jobs, but you're still a mystery.'

'Well,' said Henry, setting down his half empty glass, 'my official title is estate manager of Wynthorpe Hall, which lies just south of the village of Wynthorpe itself, but these days with so much of the original estate sold off, it's nowhere near as grand as it sounds. I also act as a land agent for a few local farmers and land owners who are looking to buy and sell land, according to their bank balance of course.'

'Sounds interesting,' I said. 'I'm guessing there's more selling than buying going on at the moment.'

'I couldn't possibly say,' he said with a wink, 'but on that note, Jake, have you thought any more about the cottage?'

'No,' Jake shot back testily, 'I haven't.' Then he added in a slightly more affable tone, 'Give us a chance, mate. We haven't even finished unpacking yet.'

'Well, you don't want to leave it too much longer,' Henry said seriously. 'Time is ticking and the place won't look after itself, you know.'

'Yes,' said Jake, 'I do know.'

'Is this the cottage you mentioned earlier?' I asked. 'We didn't get to see it today, did we, Jake?'

Jake shook his head and took another pull at his pint. He never took his eyes off Henry.

'Well,' Henry shrugged, picking up his glass again, 'all I'm saying is, you don't want to leave it too much longer.'

Hearing Jake's sudden change in tone and seeing Henry back off so quickly ensured my interest in the cottage was well and truly piqued. Clearly there was something mysterious about the place and Jake didn't want anyone talking about it, especially, it seemed, in front of me. I made up my mind there and then to ask Annie for the keys so I could go and have a look at the place myself the next day, assuming Jake didn't offer to take me, which I couldn't now imagine for a second that he would.

'Have you heard about the fair?'

Jake, Harriet and I twisted round in our seats to look at whoever had asked the question.

'Oh hello,' said a woman, smiling down at me. Her freckled face was framed by a riot of unruly red curls and her complexion, beneath the freckles, was as pale and smooth as porcelain. 'You must be Amber.'

'Yes,' I nodded, 'I am. Hello.' I still couldn't get my head round the fact that everyone seemed to know my name and yet I knew so few of theirs. 'I'm pleased to meet you.'

'And you. I'm Lizzie. Lizzie Dixon from The Cherry Tree Café. I run the place with my best friend Jemma.'

Now that was one place I did know the name of.

'Of course,' I smiled, 'Jake has often waxed lyrical about the luscious red velvet cake and dreamy frosting you have on offer.'

'And what do you think of it?' Lizzie asked expectantly.

'Oh,' I said, my cheeks burning, 'I haven't tried it yet, but I'm sure it's delicious.'

Lizzie turned her attention to Jake, her green eyes sparkling.

'So what happened to all those pretty little cakes I boxed up for you when you were heading back to London? "This is a little something for Amber," you always told me, Jake Somerville!'

'They never made it that far,' Jake mumbled guiltily into his glass. 'Sorry, Lizzie.'

'What about "sorry, Amber"?' she teased, tapping him on the shoulder. 'Though I suppose it's a compliment really. Come and see us soon, Amber, and we'll treat you to the selection you should have sampled already!'

'Thank you,' I laughed, 'I will.'

'So,' Henry beamed, 'Jake has a sweet tooth, does he, Lizzie?'

'Oh and you can be quiet!' Jake laughed. 'You know as well as I do that you're in there every lunchtime for your caramel cupcake order!'

'Is he really?' Jessica asked, raising her eyebrows and turning her attention to her fiancé. 'You're supposed to be trying to lose a few pounds before the wedding!' she frowned. 'Can you refuse to serve him please, Lizzie? Unless he's ordering a skinny latte, kick him out.'

'I couldn't possibly do that,' Lizzie said mischievously, shaking her head and making her curls bounce all the more, 'these two are our best customers!'

'So . . . what's all this about the fair?' Harriet asked, saving the guys from further blushes.

'Apparently it isn't happening this year,' Lizzie answered, her tone completely changed as she delivered the news.

'*What?*' everyone shouted, then began bombarding each other with questions and talking over one another in a bid to discover if anyone knew exactly what was going on.

'The Harrisons have withdrawn the field,' Lizzie announced above the din. 'They said they've had enough of playing host and it's high time someone else put up with locals traipsing all over their land.'

'But the May Fair has always been on their land!' said Jessica, echoing the sentiments of the rest of the group. 'It can't just not happen!'

'Yes, but remember,' Lizzie reminded them, 'when it started up again, what was that, getting on for ten years ago now, the agreement was that various families would take it in turns to play host and that has never happened, has it? The Harrisons have been lumbered every year because no one else has ever come forward. Personally,' she added with a sigh, 'I think they deserve a break.'

'I agree with Lizzie,' said Henry. 'Everyone just assumes it will happen there every year now without question and it really isn't on. Old Mr Harrison isn't getting any younger and he's got enough on his plate what with losing his wife last year. He doesn't need to be worrying about the fair on top of everything else.'

Another woman, who I later discovered was Jemma, wandered over as Henry was talking.

'Tom told me the council are going to refuse to grant the fairground owners a licence this year if they can't find another suitable site and they won't let them back on the rugby ground car park, so my guess is it won't happen at all. And it won't be just the fair we miss out on of course, but the candyfloss and rides as well!'

'Who's Tom and what's the May Fair?' I whispered to Jake who was looking as outraged as everyone else.

'Sorry, Amber,' he said, picking up my hand and kissing it. 'I forgot you aren't familiar with the local social calendar. Tom is Jemma's husband. He works for the council,' he explained, 'and the fair is an annual country show which celebrates the area. Traditionally it has been held as close to May Day as possible and before everyone is engrossed in the rigours of harvest time.'

'Lots of craft people and community groups come together,' Jessica continued, picking up the thread, 'there's a dog show, gymkhana and lots of classes for everyone to enter. Annie usually wipes the floor with her sewing entries, doesn't she, Jake?'

'She does,' Jake laughed but then his smile faded, 'but not last year. She wasn't well enough to take part and I'd hate for her to miss out again this year.'

'Well, in that case, I'm even sorrier to be the bearer of such bad news,' sighed Lizzie, 'but unless another site becomes available, we're all going to miss out.'

'Three weeks, Tom said,' Jemma called over her shoulder as she and Lizzie rejoined the crowd around the piano. 'Three weeks to find another venue, otherwise it's all off.'

Chapter 12

I didn't get much more sleep during my second night at Skylark Farm than I had the first. Thankfully the rain had stopped and the metal bucket was, for the moment at least, redundant and consigned to the bottom of the wardrobe. I got the impression, given that there was a specific space for it amongst the boxes and bags, that it had been in regular use for far longer than Jake initially thought.

But it wasn't the rain that kept me awake that night, or the dogs. Ever since Jemma had shouted the deadline for the May Fair over her shoulder my brain had been off and running and I was wondering what my chances were of convincing Jake and Annie to offer the two meadows beyond the orchard for the event. Access to both, from what I'd seen, was more than adequate because the gates were next to the road and you couldn't have wished for a more idyllic setting for a country fair, but would Jake and Annie agree with me?

There was nothing more important to me at that moment than settling into life at Skylark Farm. Dan, Dubai and my meeting with Simon were already forgotten and my London existence felt light years away. I wanted to make a worthwhile contribution that showed everyone just how committed I was to making my new life in the country work.

Everyone I'd met so far had made me feel so welcome and I couldn't help hoping that hosting the May Fair at the farm would be the perfect way to repay their kindness. Obviously the fact that everyone seemed to already know every detail about me and my life so far was going to take some getting used to, but in a way I kind of liked it. Being part of such a close-knit community was a novelty to me and although I realised it had its pitfalls I couldn't help thinking that, from what I'd seen thus far, the benefits outweighed them.

I was the one who was up with the lark the next morning and long before either Jake or Annie. In fact, by the time Annie made it down to the kitchen I'd already fed the dogs, let them out and back in again and made a pot of tea, remembering, of course, to keep my hands well protected whenever I approached the range.

'Well, aren't you the early bird!' Annie laughed as she made her way slowly across the kitchen to her favourite chair.

'I'm going to collect the eggs and let the hens out in a minute.'

I smiled, more at the words than at Annie. I liked the sound of it. The simplicity of the morning routine was most welcome after enduring years of jostling amongst the armpits of others during the morning commute.

'Oh, I daresay you'll want this then,' said Annie as she reached down the side of her chair.

'What is it?' I asked, taking the light, haphazardly wrapped package.

'Open it,' she encouraged me. 'I found it yesterday and thought it would be just the thing for you. I put the lining in last night while you and Jake were out. I hope you like it. I have a feeling you like pretty things.'

'Oh Annie,' I gasped, discarding the paper and holding up the prettiest little willow basket imaginable.

'It's perfect,' I told her warmly as I wrapped my fingers around the handle, 'thank you so much.'

The inside was quilted and lined with what looked like a vintage floral fabric and the size and shape made it the perfect receptacle for collecting eggs.

'It was mine when I was little,' Annie told me wistfully, 'and the lining came from one of my mother's old tea towels. I'm rather pleased with how it's turned out,' she added proudly. 'I'm afraid I've been neglecting my sewing skills lately, but it was nice to have the opportunity to pick up a needle and thread again.'

'Are you really sure you want me to have it?' I felt obliged to ask as it was obviously of great sentimental value. 'If it means so much to you, Annie, shouldn't you hold on to it?'

'And do what with it?' she laughed. 'No, my love, you keep it. I'll get far more pleasure seeing it being used every day as opposed to being stuffed in the back of the cupboard!'

'Well, as long as you're sure,' I said, bending to give her a kiss, 'thank you. Thank you very much. You were right, I do like pretty things. I know Jake laughs at my wellingtons and everything but that's how I am. I like to look the part!'

'Never mind *looking* the part,' she laughed, grasping my hand, 'you *are* the part. I'm so pleased you've come to stay, Amber,' she continued, a slight crack in her voice, 'having young folk around is good for the soul. I feel heaps better already.'

'Well, I'm honoured to be here,' I said, 'and I'm thrilled you feel well enough to start sewing again. In fact, I can't wait to see what you transform next.'

Annie smiled and I remembered the plans I'd been dreaming up during the night to bring the May Fair to Skylark Farm.

'Actually, there was talk of your sewing prowess in The Mermaid last night.'

'Was there now?' Annie asked. 'How on earth did that come up?'

'Jake and some of the others were talking about the May Fair,' I explained, 'and how no one else ever gets a look in when the prizes for the sewing classes are being given out.'

'Is that a fact?' she smiled wryly and then added sadly, 'I didn't enter last year, but I think I'll have a crack at it again this year. There's still just about enough time to pull something together if I make a start straightaway. It would be good to reclaim my title from Bunty Harris.'

In my eagerness to find a way to broach the subject of putting the farm forward as this year's host I'd inadvertently got Annie all fired up again and I hoped I hadn't set her up for disappointment if the fair really did get cancelled. That hadn't been my intention at all.

'Well,' I continued, knowing I had to put her straight as kindly as possible, 'I'm not sure you're going to get the chance this year, Annie.'

'What do you mean?'

'According to the ladies from The Cherry Tree Café,' I told her, 'the fair might not be happening this year.'

'Not happening!' Annie sounded outraged and clearly viewed the potential cancellation as a personal affront. 'Whatever are you talking about? That's ridiculous, unheard of!'

'The people who usually have it on their land, the Harrisons I think it was, have withdrawn the site. They want someone else to take it on.'

'Yes, well,' Annie conceded, 'they have had quite a year so I can understand their decision, but what on earth are we going to do?'

I opened my mouth to put forward my suggestion but stopped as the dogs rushed from their baskets over to the door at the bottom of the stairs, their tails thumping in perfect unison.

'Morning all,' yawned Jake, running his hands through his hair before bending down to make a fuss of the adoring duo.

He definitely had a bad case of 'bed hair' this morning; it was sticking up in all directions and his voice was unusually gruff and gravelly.

'I know I didn't exactly hold back last night,' he confessed, 'but I feel like I've got the hangover from hell. Did you spike my drink, Amber?'

'No, of course not,' I said, shaking my head, 'don't be silly, but you do look rough. I hope you aren't coming down with something.'

'If it's a hangover I know just what you need,' announced Annie, bustling off into the pantry. 'Hair of the dog and a little something extra will sort you out.'

Jake grimaced, but didn't look as if he had the energy to argue. We waited in silence, listening to Annie uncorking bottles and, from what I could make out, cracking eggs.

'What are you two talking about so early?' Jake asked, looking warily at the glass Annie set on the table.

'Don't stand there analysing it,' she scolded, 'don't even look at it. Just knock it back in one.'

In one swift movement Jake picked up the glass and drank as instructed. I averted my gaze as the thick concoction slipped reluctantly from the glass and into his mouth. Seeing me wince wasn't going to be an incentive to keep swallowing so I turned my attention back to the basket until I heard him bang the glass back down on the table, which he did with much coughing, spluttering and swearing.

'Amber was just telling me about the May Fair being cancelled,' Annie informed him as she whipped the glass away. 'Feel any better?'

'A bit,' Jake croaked.

'Another?' Annie offered, holding up another glass.

'No!' said Jake, jumping back a little too quickly and holding on to the table until he regained his balance, 'no thanks, but maybe later if I have a relapse.'

'Such a shame about the fair,' Annie sniffed as she rinsed out the glass. 'I was looking forward to reclaiming my sewing champion title.'

'Sorry, Annie,' Jake shrugged, 'it's not going to happen and there's nothing we can do about it.'

'Well,' I cut in, with a sheepish grin, 'there might be something you can do.'

'What do you mean?' Jake asked, sitting down to pour

himself a mug of tea and refilling mine and Annie's cups. 'No field,' he said resignedly, 'no fair.'

'Well,' I said again, taking a big breath, 'what about having it here?'

'What?' Jake spluttered.

'You told me on the tour yesterday that you have a couple of meadows for grazing that are currently empty, didn't you?'

'So?'

'When you pointed them out I could see that they both had access from the road so getting everything in and out wouldn't be a problem.'

'Go on,' said Annie.

'Well, from what I can tell it would be simplicity itself. No one would have to come anywhere near the house, or even the orchards for that matter. You could keep the whole event contained at the farm's furthest boundary with the fair in one field and the fairground in the other.'

'That's a crazy idea,' Jake frowned. He looked quite ashen again. 'There simply isn't time to get it all ready and you heard last night that Tom has told Jemma the council were all set to pull the plug.'

'There can't be that much to do,' I persisted, encouraged by the glint in Annie's eye, 'not now the event has been running for so long. Surely once the fields are mown and some temporary fencing erected the rest is pretty much up to whoever is on the committee. I'm certain the fair must have one, probably more than one, and I wouldn't mind helping out with the co-ordination if needs be.'

Jake shook his head, a surprisingly 'hostile to the idea' expression fixed firmly on his handsome face.

'This isn't like one of your corporate events,' he began to explain in an infuriatingly patient tone. 'This is like nothing you've ever encountered before, Amber. There are so many potential toes for you to stamp all over you wouldn't know which way to turn! It's a crazy idea.'

'Well, it was just a thought,' I shrugged, finishing my tea and picking up my new basket. 'I guess I've got a lot to learn about country life.'

'Hang on a minute,' said Annie sternly. 'Do you mean to tell me that's it?'

'What do you mean?'

I could still see the glint in Annie's eyes but now it was accompanied by a look of shock and disbelief.

'Aren't you even going to put up a fight?' she asked.

'Um,' I mumbled, trying to ignore the air of exasperation I could feel pulsating from Jake. 'No, Annie, I'm not,' I admitted. 'Jake obviously knows what he's talking about and has far more experience in these matters than I do.'

'As do I,' said Annie, drawing herself up to her full five foot three as she walked over to me. She turned to face her nephew, the glint in her eye looking ever more mischievous. 'And I'm saying yes.'

'No,' said Jake, 'no way.'

'Yes,' said Annie. 'Jake, it would do you good.'

I didn't hang about to find out why it would do Jake good. I slipped out of the kitchen and into the yard taking the dogs with me as the two warring sides prepared to do battle. Having seen Jake's unreceptive reaction to the idea, part of me wished I hadn't said anything, but the other part, the rebellious part, was thrilled by the prospect of Skylark Farm playing host to the May Fair.

From what Jake had said about there being a plethora of 'potential toes to stamp all over' I gleaned that there were plenty of locals who were already responsible for organising, setting up and running the fair and I was more than happy to keep my head down, do as I was asked and brace myself for a timely lesson in countryside etiquette.

Chapter 13

Taking a scoopful of corn from the bag in the porch, with my basket and a pair of cotton gardening gloves safely tucked under my arm, I tentatively made my way over to the henhouse. This was my first solo outing as Hen Welfare Manager and I methodically went through the same motions as Jake had the day before.

Having opened the little hatch at the front of the house I had expected the girls to come pelting out, with the exception of Patricia of course, but nothing, not so much as a cluck. I shook some of the grain from the scoop on to the ground and in a heartbeat there was a scrabbling and scurrying and a flurry of feathers as Mabel and Martha shot out of the door and began pecking at the corn, softly clucking in appreciation.

'You're welcome,' I smiled, scattering a little more and saving the rest for the feeder.

Once I'd filled it and checked the water, I cautiously ventured round to the door at the back of the house, set down the scoop and basket, pulled on the gloves and prepared myself to face my beady eyed nemesis.

I looked at Patricia, Patricia looked at me. She ruffled her feathers and sat firm. Her stance couldn't have been more pistols at dawn! This was it. I knew that within the next few seconds the scene would be set for all future interactions.

I took a couple of calming breaths, walked quickly forward, firmly lifted her off the nest, put her on the floor and stood back up. I think she was so shocked by my actions that she forgot all about the eggs for a few seconds, and in turn, my heart racing with pride, I forgot all about her sharp little beak and lightning fast reflexes. I bent down to stroke her and in a flash she twisted round and pecked viciously at my fingers. Fortunately she only made contact with the gloves, but she didn't know that and sauntered (quite literally) out of the henhouse to join Martha and Mabel.

Somehow she had managed to manoeuvre both the girls' eggs so they were packed tightly together, snuggled on her little nest of straw. Slipping off the gloves I gently lifted the lightly speckled clutch and laid them in the basket. I wasn't sure if Round One had gone in my favour, but the hens were outside and fed and I had two eggs in my basket and that was good enough for me.

*　　★　　★　　★*

I didn't see anything of Jake for the rest of the day.

'I think he's working in the orchards,' Annie told me when I eventually ventured back to the house, 'he's certainly taken his lunch with him. What have you been up to?'

I'd thoroughly enjoyed my morning. I'd even got used to the smell of chicken poo as I swept out the henhouse and replenished the straw. After that I'd pottered about the yard, familiarising myself with the ramshackle sheds. I'd found two blackbird nests in one of them and spent a delightful few minutes watching the parents busily flitting in and out with bug-crammed beaks.

Later I'd gone down to the paddock and tempted Pip to the fence by rattling a few pony nuts in the bucket, although, as I ran my fingers through her rough mane, I couldn't help thinking she was already a little on the plump side, but perhaps the Shetland favoured a slightly more rotund figure than the ponies I remembered cajoling my parents into letting me ride up and down the beach when I was little.

Although I enjoyed relaying the details of my morning to Annie, without Jake to hear what I had been up to I have to admit some of the shine went out of the day and along with it some of the pride I felt in what I had achieved so far.

'How's the injury?' Annie asked. 'I hope you haven't got it too mucky through all your good work!'

I held up my hand and showed her the now even grubbier, grey bandage.

'I know I should have kept my gloves on,' I said, 'but you just can't get the feel of things through them, can you?'

'Spoken like a true country woman!' Annie laughed, clapping her hands together.

'I'm hardly that,' I blushed, feeling secretly pleased that under her scrutiny I had met with such approval.

'I think we'd better have that off,' she said, pointing to the bandage, 'and survey the damage.'

Where before the skin had been blistered and a violent shade of red it was now smooth and pink and virtually pain free.

'So, do you really not know how applying raw potato actually works?' I asked, while gently rubbing the scar as I washed my hands at the sink.

'Do you know,' Annie frowned, 'I really don't, but I think it must have something to do with retaining moisture, and of course the humble potato is well known for its antibacterial qualities, isn't it? I'm afraid I really don't know the exact science behind it, but my grandmother always swore by it.'

'And so do I now!' I laughed.

'Just one more day, I think, don't you?' said Annie, making up a fresh dressing.

'Is Jake still cross with me about the fair?' I finally plucked up the courage to ask as she secured a clean new bandage with a safety pin. 'I didn't mean to upset him when I suggested the idea. I just thought it might be fun and would ensure you didn't miss out on competing in the sewing classes again.'

'You're a good girl,' Annie smiled, 'and your heart's in the right place. Don't you worry about Jake, he'll come round.'

Personally I wasn't so sure and when I went to bed alone that night I was beginning to think I had made my first 'living the country life' faux pas far sooner than I had expected to.

Amazingly there was still no sign of Jake the next morning and, having slept like the proverbial log, I wasn't even sure if he'd come up to bed at all, but when I asked Annie about it she didn't sound concerned in the least.

'Oh, he'll be about here somewhere,' she told me, 'you need to stop fretting. You know what the Somerville men are like. It takes them a while to stop sulking.'

'Does it?' I said.

This was the first time Jake and I had argued. Not that you could really call what had happened between us an argument, but it was a side to him that I hadn't seen before and I wasn't sure I liked it.

'Of course!' Annie laughed. 'You only have to think about the tantrums that dope of a brother throws all the time to know that Jake must have a little of that silly stubbornness running through his veins.'

She was right about that. Dan was well known for throwing his toys out of the pram if things didn't go his way. For the first time I wondered how he was settling into life in Dubai and whether the girl he had mentioned had been left behind heartbroken and abandoned or with promises that he'd remain loyal and fly her out to visit.

'And besides,' Annie continued when I didn't say anything, 'there's a whole lot more to this moving back and sorting things out malarkey than meets the eye.'

'Is there?' I said. I wasn't sure what she meant about 'moving back'. As far as I knew Jake had only ever been a temporary resident at the farm. 'Like what?'

'Not my place to say,' she sniffed, 'he'll tell you when he's good and ready. Should have done so already in my opinion, but I've never been one to interfere.'

I couldn't get anything else out of her so, with her permission, I took the keys to the truck and headed into Wynbridge.

I parked in the market square trying not to think about what Annie meant by there being 'more to the move than met the eye', and with the intention of registering at the library and hopefully taking advantage of its Wi-Fi access. Ever since she had mentioned Dan I had been itching to check my emails and catch up with what was happening in the rest of the world. I would dearly have loved to enquire about internet options for the farm, but given the fallout over the fair I considered it best not to broach the subject for the time being.

As I locked the truck door and pocketed the key I spotted, tucked away on the other side of the square, a sign offering free Wi-Fi that didn't look like it was connected to the library at all. I hadn't taken many steps before I realised the notice belonged to The Cherry Tree Café.

As I pushed open the gate to investigate further a customer came out through the door, and the aroma of fresh coffee that followed her drew me in.

'Amber, isn't it?' smiled Jemma from behind the counter. 'How lovely to see you. What can I get you?'

'A cup of that delicious smelling coffee, please,' I said, breathing deeply. I hadn't had a coffee fix since leaving London and couldn't wait to get my first taste.

'Take a seat and I'll bring it over.'

'I'll have a croissant as well, please,' I said, looking at the pretty vintage décor and cleverly co-ordinated styling. 'This place is gorgeous,' I told Jemma as she came over with my order.

'Thank you,' she said, 'we like it. Lizzie was responsible for the cherry tree design and all the pretty finishing touches. She'll be down in a minute. She has a felting class this morning. That's her space at the back,' she said, pointing to the back of the café. 'She runs her crafting courses from there.'

'Oh wow,' I said. 'Jake never mentioned those. What a fabulous set up.'

'It's working well,' Jemma said proudly, 'but it's hard work what with juggling the kids and everything, but we wouldn't change a thing. Now, is there anything else I can get you?'

'No, I don't think so, thanks. I came in with the intention of taking advantage of your free Wi-Fi, but as I'd originally planned to go to the library I didn't bother bringing my laptop.'

'You can borrow mine if you like,' Jemma offered. 'I don't mind.'

Jemma fetched her laptop from the kitchen and I spent a few minutes chatting to Lizzie who then introduced me to Angela, the other lady who helped in the café and was, according to Jemma, 'the glue that held everything together'. I relished every mouthful of the coffee and Lizzie had refilled my cup before I had a chance to ask.

Needless to say, having not checked my email account for a couple of days, my spam folder was fit to burst and my inbox was crammed with requests from Elena who, having discovered my old mobile was no longer switched on, had changed tactics. I scrolled down the screen methodically ticking everything that had her name on it and pressed delete. I did feel a brief pang of guilt but the emails were already tailing off and it was about time she launched her solo voyage.

There was just the one email from Dan, titled 'Wish you were here'. Flicking through the dozen or so photos he'd sent and watching the clouds begin to gather outside I have to admit I did rather wonder at the wisdom of the choice I had made, if only with regards to the contrasting weather. The plush apartment looked as appealing as the scenery, as did the restaurants, balcony and beach view. However, the one thing Dan didn't mention was work and there were no pictures of the office or the team he had working for him. Clearly he was taking his time to settle in. I imagined Simon would be thrilled about that.

'Can I offer you another?' asked Angela, who was hovering at my elbow with the coffee pot again.

'No,' I said, 'thank you.'

Her eyes flicked momentarily to the screen then she looked at me again and smiled.

'Looks nice, doesn't it?' I said.

Angela bent down and took a longer look.

'It looks nice enough,' she said, 'reminds me of where my daughter lives in Australia. All right for a holiday, I daresay,' she smiled, 'but home is where the heart is, don't you think?'

I nodded, but didn't say anything. Just for the moment I was experiencing a tiny pang of doubt about my new home. It was obvious, after my conversation with Annie, and Jake's reaction to Henry mentioning the cottage in the pub, that there was something he wasn't telling me, and as much as I hated to admit it, it was shaking my faith in my hasty decision to pack up my life and move to the country.

'Thanks for that,' I said, passing the laptop back over the counter to Jemma, 'I'm all caught up now.'

'How did Jake get on yesterday?' Lizzie called through from the crafting area where she was still setting up.

'What do you mean?' I asked as I wandered over.

'He was at the council offices, wasn't he, Jemma?' she called through to her friend.

'I really couldn't say,' shrugged Jemma. 'It wouldn't be appropriate for the wife of a council employee to discuss council business.'

'It isn't like the doctors,' laughed Lizzie, 'you aren't breaking any oath!'

'Well,' I said, 'I shouldn't worry. I'm sure I'll find out whatever it's all about soon enough.'

Chapter 14

I reversed out of the parking space and headed back to the farm with mixed feelings. The day had turned the same shade as my spirits, dull and grey, and by the time I pulled back into the yard a steady light rain had begun to fall. I parked the truck in its allotted spot and went back to the house.

'Where have you been?' Jake said, jumping up. 'I've been looking all over for you.'

'I could ask you the same question,' I retaliated.

Jake nodded, but didn't say anything.

'I drove in to Wynbridge,' I told him, then added with a touch of defiance, 'I wanted to check my emails. See if there was anything that needed my attention.'

'And was there?'

'No,' I admitted, knowing I had lost the point I was trying to score.

'Well, never mind that now,' he said. 'Come and sit down. I have something to tell you.'

'What?' I said, filling the kettle and ignoring the chair he had pulled out for me.

He reached for my wrist as soon as I'd set the kettle to boil and pulled me into his arms.

'I'm sorry,' he said, kissing me lightly on the lips and making my stomach flip, even though my brain was telling it not to.

'I was worried about you,' I said quietly, 'it wasn't nice being left all on my own.'

'You had Annie,' he smiled, kissing me again.

'Yes, but I could hardly ask her to come and protect me from the rodent in the rafters, could I? Talking of which, it's raining again and you still haven't fixed the roof.'

'I did come up to bed,' he whispered in my ear, while softly caressing my neck, 'so technically I was there to protect you, and as for the roof, I'm going to have a look at it in a minute.'

'Good,' I said, resisting his less than subtle seduction technique and not really caring that he was going to get wet through. 'Because I'm not sleeping another night in that room with that wretched bucket at the foot of the bed.'

'Amber.'

'What?'

'Please sit down and listen.'

Reluctantly I gave in and sat and waited to hear what he'd been up to for the last twenty-four hours.

'As you know,' he said, taking the seat opposite, 'when you suggested having the May Fair here, I wasn't very keen on the idea.'

'Yes,' I said frostily, 'that much I had worked out.'

'But Annie was.'

'Yes,' I smiled, 'Annie was.'

'And as you've probably already worked out,' he continued with a wry smile, 'what Annie says, goes, as far as this place is concerned anyway.'

'Yes,' I said. 'I had rather worked that one out.'

I could feel the beginnings of the hope that I had felt when I first made the suggestion surging back up again.

'So, to cut a long and very tedious story short—'

'I'm rather beginning to wish you would.'

'We're having the May Fair here!' he said in a rush.

'Really?'

'Yes.'

'Skylark Farm is hosting the May Fair this year?' I squealed.

'Yes.'

'And you're happy with that?'

'Yes.'

I jumped up, threw my arms around his neck and kissed him passionately on the lips. I wasn't sure why hosting the fair was so important to me, but it was. Perhaps because it offered me the opportunity to contribute to the farm and the area in a way I felt comfortable with, or perhaps it was more to do with making sure Annie got the opportunity to fight for her sewing crown. Regardless of what it was, I was thrilled that it was going to happen and I couldn't wait to get started.

Chapter 15

Much as I had expected, organising a traditional rural fair was very similar to overseeing the corporate events I had become used to project managing in the city. A great deal of patience, persistence and dogged determination was needed, along with the all too familiar commitment to be on hand at the drop of a hat to iron out the wrinkles that had a habit of popping up when you least expected them.

However, unlike the business dealings I was used to, the May Fair had the added complication of a million and one unwritten, but firmly established rules that I found myself having to grapple with, and make allowances for. A problem made all the more difficult by the simple fact that I didn't know what any of the rules were.

Take the mowing of the meadows, for example. To me it was perfectly logical that Mr Smith, our closest neighbour, should be granted permission to do it as he was on hand;

however, that did not take into account Mr Richards further along the Drove who had always prepared the old site and was mortally offended when he heard that his services would not be required. It took me an hour of sweet talking and several halves of bitter in The Mermaid to rectify the situation, but rectify it I did, although I would imagine that Mr Richards's recollection of my heartfelt apology was somewhat hazy.

And this was just one tiny detail. Throw in other such tiresome delights as who would be supplying the tea urns and tables, the chairs and tablecloths (paper versus fabric), along with who would be judging the 'waggiest tail' in the dog show and the most striking floral arrangement on a tea tray and I soon realised, that in my haste to settle into rural life and play a valuable role, what I'd actually done was set myself up for a potential breakdown.

All this tedious time wasting, as I considered it, did of course pass my beloved by. When Jake had told me the farm would be playing host to the fair he had, in the very next breath, made it clear in no uncertain terms that even though he would attend the fair with me he would not, under any circumstances, have time to help with the organising and preparations, as there were other far more pressing things to attend to, such as fixing the roof of the house.

'Have you thought any more about the fancy dress theme for the under nines?' Harriet asked, one particularly fraught Thursday a couple of weeks before the main event.

'I've thought of little else,' I told her seriously, as I flicked through the file that had all the paperwork relating to the children's competitions crammed inside it.

'And whether or not there'll be a fourth ice cream van?'

'Not yet,' I said in a clipped tone. 'I've scheduled that in for around three tomorrow morning.'

She stopped flicking through her own pile of papers and looked up at me.

'I thought you were being serious,' she frowned.

'Sorry,' I said, throwing the file down on the table and rubbing my eyes. 'Sorry.'

'How are you bearing up?' she asked, wrinkling her nose and bracing herself for the answer.

'Really?'

'Yes,' she winced, 'really.'

'Well now,' I began, 'let me see. When I first suggested this idea I did so kind of on the assumption that there were already various established committees who would make all these ridiculous decisions and take responsibility for the vast majority of components that make up this damn fair!'

'Oh,' smiled Harriet, '*damn* fair now, is it?'

'I had thought,' I raged on, 'that all Jake and I, sorry,' I corrected myself, '*I* would have to do is sign a few bits of paper and point various lorries and vans in the right direction when the time came, but oh no! Now I'm even being asked to give an opinion as to whether there should be a tray bake *and* a tear and share category in the home bake competition or if we should just stick to one or the other!'

'Talking of baking,' said Jessica, who poked her head round the kitchen door, 'how's the cake making coming along?'

'Oh bollocks!' I shouted, rushing over to the range and rescuing an ever so slightly burnt pair of sponges from the oven. 'I'll never get the hang of this when I've got so much else to do,' I said resignedly. 'I give up.'

I threw the tins on the table and even the dogs turned away in disgust. Clearly they had eaten one too many failed offerings in the last few weeks.

'How is it,' I said to Jessica and Harriet, 'that I've ended up with all this work when the fair has run for years, according to Annie, without a hitch?'

Jessica flicked through the piles of clipboards, making a note of all the red squiggles which indicated the things that I had been asked to help with.

'Looks to me like you've been lumbered with the tricky bits,' she said.

'What do you mean?' I sighed. 'What are the tricky bits?'

'All the things that cause problems every year,' Harriet chipped in. 'All the decisions that put people's backs up. All the things that require a shed load of tact and diplomacy, along with an intimate knowledge of everyone's family history going back at least three generations. All the—'

'Yeah, OK,' I said, putting up a hand to stop her, 'thanks. I get the idea. Do you think they're trying to catch me out on purpose?' I'd been wondering that ever since I'd made the mistake with the mowing. 'Do you think they're out to prove that I can't do it and that as an incomer, I don't even have the right to try?'

'Absolutely not,' said Jessica firmly. 'Everyone in The Mermaid was singing your praises last night, weren't they, Harriet?'

'Yep,' she agreed, 'they all know that without you and the farm the fair wouldn't be happening at all this year and of course they also know what you did for a living in London. And don't forget, you did say from the outset that you were willing to help out. It's the same old situation, I'm afraid.'

'Which is?'

'If you say you'll help out,' said Harriet.

'Then you'll be helping out forever,' finished Jessica.

The only time I got any real respite from organising and checking and telephoning was late in the evenings, and as I ticked off the days on the kitchen calendar my baking skills were improving at about the same rate as my sewing . . . with painful slowness.

Annie had convinced me to enter one of the sewing classes as well as the baking. She said it would take the pressure off the cake making, and during the time the tins were in the oven, completing a few stitches would stop me opening the door to check the cakes' progress and consequently ruining all possibility of them rising. I agreed, feeling most grateful that the weather was warm and that Mabel and Martha were able to supply me with an egg every day and that the farm next door always had a half a dozen for sale at the gate.

'How are you getting on?' I asked, looking at the quilt Annie was sewing.

She had decided to focus all her attention on just one entry this year and was throwing every spare second into perfecting the quilted design of Skylark Farm she had come up with. The farmhouse took centre stage, complete with embroidered roses around the porch and hens clucking at the door. The edge was embellished with apple trees in every season to represent the orchards and the River Wyn appeared as a sinuous blue thread just as it did around the farm boundary. There was even a pair of patterned wellington boots propped up against the wall next to the porch.

Lizzie Dixon from The Cherry Tree wasn't allowed to take part in any of the competitions as she made her living from sewing and crafting, but she had been a regular visitor since Annie began the quilt, questioning her about who taught her to sew and how she'd learnt this and that stitch.

'She's doing amazingly well,' Lizzie answered for Annie. 'And this is really something,' she added for the umpteenth time, as we all sat together at the kitchen table. 'I've learnt almost as much from Annie as I did from my grandmother.'

It turned out that Lizzie's gran and Annie had been firm friends. Their love of sewing had held them together when other childhood friendships had wavered and gradually faded into memory.

'And what do you think of my bookmark?' I said, holding aloft my simple cross-stitch effort.

Annie scrutinised my stitches for a few seconds and then looked at me over the top of her half-moon glasses. 'I would do that whole left side again if I was you and,' she added with a nod to the range, 'I hate to say it but I think you've burnt your cakes.'

OK, so I was rubbish at sewing and I was certainly taking my time to get into my stride as far as the baking was concerned, but life on the farm was a dream. You only had to look at the state of my pretty patterned wellington boots to see that I had really got stuck in with running things. I loved the hens; especially Martha who would quite happily sit tucked under my arm, placid, docile and clucking softly as I went about my chores.

Patricia and I had never really hit it off, however; she was still sitting tight and now had four eggs under her that Jake had sourced and I had high hopes that they would hatch any day now.

'Have you made up your mind what you want yet?' he had asked me one morning over breakfast. 'Only Bob Richards up the road has a few Pekin Bantam eggs ready to go. He only wants pennies for them.'

'What do they look like?' I asked, trying to pick them out of the 'hen fancier's line up' featured in one of my magazines.

Jake grabbed the poultry keeper's guide from the dresser and flicked through the pages.

'He can't guarantee what colours they are,' he explained, spinning the book round to show me, 'but this will give you an idea.'

I looked at the tiny, fluffy feet and array of colours. They all looked lovely to me, but the lavenders were particularly pretty.

'Oh yes,' I said, 'these are adorable.'

'They'll only lay small eggs but what with the other three girls that'll mean we aren't inundated. Oh and by the way, I meant to tell you yesterday, I've found someone interested in putting some hives in the orchard. He's bringing them at the weekend.'

With the May Fair on the horizon, bees in the orchard and the prospect of fluffy chicks scratching about the yard it really did feel as if life at Skylark Farm was shaping up to be perhaps more hectic than I first expected, but perfect nonetheless.

Chapter 16

A couple of days before the May Fair the weather dawned sunny, warm and bright and I was woken by Annie shouting up the stairs and Jake pulling the covers off the bed.

'Come on!' he shouted excitedly, pulling on his jeans and T-shirt. 'The fair's here!'

To say it was a tight squeeze manoeuvring the lorries, caravans and trailers down the Drove and into the field was the understatement of the millennium and by the end of the morning it felt as though my heart had spent far more time in my mouth than it had in my chest. Jake, however, was in his element and for the first time he actually looked and sounded genuinely excited about the prospect of his beloved farm playing such an integral role on the community calendar.

By teatime everything was calm and in place, although far from quiet. The massive generators whirred away and the fairground children ran from ride to ride each with their own set of jobs and responsibilities, while their parents tweaked light bulbs and checked cables were secure and safe.

'Jake tells me this was all your idea,' said Luca, the fairground owner, smiling down at me as he surveyed his family flitting about the field.

Luca was a mountain of a man. Thick set and strong with a head full of dark curls and a penetrating gaze that I discovered I couldn't quite bring myself to return.

'Sort of,' I told him, my cheeks glowing. 'I just hated the idea of the May Fair not happening at all, especially as it was going to be the first time I would have seen it. This,' I said, indicating the freshly cut meadow, 'just seemed like the ideal solution to me.'

'Oh, absolutely,' he said. 'To tell you the truth, I'm extremely grateful you came up with the idea. I was beginning to wonder where we were going to end up.'

I hadn't really given the fairground's schedule any thought when I made the suggestion of us hosting the fair, but I could see what Luca meant. They could hardly keep riding the roads until their next scheduled stop, could they?

'Of course, as an incomer,' I added, shaking my head, 'I didn't realise just how much hard work it was going to be when I suggested it.'

'Nothing wrong with a bit of hard work,' Luca grinned.

Having watched him complete the work of three men throughout the day I guessed that sitting idle and watching the world go by was an alien concept to him, and indeed all his family.

'And sometimes,' he smiled, his dark gypsy eyes sparkling, 'an incomer is just what a place needs to come along and shake things up a bit.'

I didn't say anything, but scuffed at the turf with the toe of my boot.

'So what do you think?' Luca shouted to Tom and another council official who were striding towards us with a file full of paperwork. 'Is everything looking shipshape?'

'Of course it is!' grinned the official. 'I wish everyone took as much pride as you lot, Luca, it would make my life far easier!' He handed over what I guessed was the licence to operate to Luca and another couple of sheets to me. 'Please pass these on to Annie, could you, Amber?'

'Of course,' I said, taking the papers. 'How do you think the other field is looking?' I asked, hoping he was going to be as happy with the actual May Fair site as the fairground.

During the day, as the fairground rides were being built, the large marquee had been erected along with three or four smaller ones. Workmen had also put in place the fencing, blocking access to the river, and the posts and ropes that made up the boundary of the show ring where the gymkhana, dog show and displays would happen.

'It all looks just as it should,' said Tom. 'I know there are plenty who don't like change, but when they come I think they'll see the benefit of having the fair somewhere else for a change. I for one think the site looks great.'

'Yep,' agreed his boss, shuffling his papers together again, 'so do I, and I'll be back tomorrow night with the kids for opening night.'

The fairground was going to run on Saturday night ahead of the fair itself, which was happening on the Sunday and then again from mid-afternoon on Sunday until around midnight. The council was happy to grant a slightly later than usual operating licence because, unlike at the Harrisons, there were no other houses close by.

When Tom and his boss had left and Luca had retired to his caravan for tea, Jake and I stood and surveyed the two fields and tried to imagine what it would be like when the event was in full swing.

'Are you still cross about it all?' I asked, wrapping my arms around his waist, safe in the knowledge that I already knew what he was going to say.

'No,' he said, kissing my hair, 'not at all. In fact, I love it.'

'Really,' I asked, twisting round to face him just to be sure, 'you really mean that?'

'Yes,' he said, 'I really do. I couldn't see it at the time, but Annie was right, and you of course, this is just what I need, what Skylark Farm needs. It's high time we shook the place up a bit and had some fun!'

Chapter 17

Leaning as far as I dared out of the bedroom window early Saturday morning I could just about make out the fairground rides and caravans and the sun bouncing off them as the wind twisted the endless lines of washing that had been strung up between them. I quickly dressed and rushed my breakfast, eager for the day to start.

'When I've done my chores, Annie,' I said as I swallowed my last mouthful of toast, 'I'll walk you down.'

I grabbed my basket, pulled on my wellington boots and rushed for the door.

'I've got a feeling the chicks are going to have finished hatching this morning,' I said excitedly. 'And before I come back I'm going to run down and check on Pip. She seemed a bit . . . I don't quite know how to put it really. Well, she was sort of placid yesterday.'

'In that case,' said Annie, 'check her by all means and

twice if necessary. Placid isn't a word I've ever heard associated with that little rascal!'

My instincts about the chicks were spot on, not that it would have taken a genius to work it out. Jake had told me as he climbed into bed the night before that he had taken one last look under Patricia and could see some definite chips in two of the eggs. Of course, I had wanted to go rushing down to see for myself, but he said it was best not to disturb her again and that hatching generally took a while.

Isolated from Mabel and Martha in a broody box, Patricia had been sitting tight for what felt like forever to me. For the last few days her every whim had been catered for and she had even been fed and watered on the nest. She was far easier to deal with once she realised we weren't going to keep trying to throw her out every day and stuck fast to her post. I don't think a bomb could have moved her.

I let Mabel and Martha out of the little door at the front and quietly slipped in the back, which we'd purposefully been keeping slightly darker and quiet.

'Good morning,' I whispered, 'any news?'

I changed the water and replenished the little bowl of feed. I was desperate to move her to one side and see what she was hiding, if anything, but I knew better than to interfere. I smiled to myself as I made everything shipshape for the prospective new mum.

A memory from my former life flashed through my mind as I remembered how breathless, stressed and tight-chested I'd been while waiting for my ruby red Jimmy Choos to arrive from the US. The tension and expectation had been palpable, but it was nothing compared to this. Given the way my stomach was gurgling and my heart racing you'd have thought I'd laid the eggs myself!

I was just about to call it a day and leave Patricia in peace when she slowly stood up and ruffled her feathers. Nestled together in the warmth of her soft and fluffy underside were four slightly bedraggled, wobbly necked little chicks. Suppressing the squeal of delight bubbling up in my chest, I stared in wonder, and although they weren't in any way pretty, they nonetheless melted my heart. I quickly removed the fragments of shell, told Patricia what a very clever girl she was, and raced back to the house to tell Annie the good news.

I'd never thought about the possibility of having a baby of my own, but a sudden image of Jake with a small child in his arms popped into my head and I could see it all as plainly as if it were really playing out in front of me. I watched him taking the toddler over to the henhouse to see the chicks and I imagined how idyllic a setting Skylark Farm would be in which to raise a family. Where better to spend long summer days and cosy winter nights?

'They've hatched!' I told Annie, plonking the broken shells next to the sink and quickly shaking off my own unexpected maternal feelings. 'I saw all four of them.'

'Oh, that's wonderful news,' she smiled. 'Hens or cockerels?'

'What?' I frowned, momentarily forgetting my manners.

'Hens or cockerels,' she said again, 'are they boys or girls?'

'Oh,' I said, trying to think what they all looked like, 'crikey, I didn't look. Sorry. I don't know.'

Not that I had a clue how or what to look for, of course. Annie started to laugh.

'I'm just teasing, you silly girl,' she said, wiping her eyes with her handkerchief, 'you won't be able to tell that for a good while yet!'

'Oh Annie,' I blushed, 'you know how rubbish I am about that sort of thing.'

'You are far from rubbish,' she said, the laughter suddenly disappearing from her lips, 'far from it.'

'Well anyway,' I puffed, 'they're all here safe and sound. Jake said they'll be fine left to their own devices for a day or so and I've filled Patricia's water bowl with pebbles so if they do have a wander and fall in, they'll only get damp.'

'Like I said,' nodded Annie, her eyes shining, 'far from rubbish. Now, go and check on Pip and see what surprises she has in store this morning!'

Many a true word is spoken in jest and when I opened the top half of the stable door I got the shock of my life. Chicks I could cope with, but I was in no way prepared for the sight that met my urban eyes. I ran back up to the house and burst into the kitchen just as Annie was running a bowl of hot water to wash the breakfast dishes.

'Whatever's the matter?'

'It's Pip,' I said, bending over to cradle the stitch in my side, 'she's lying down and it looks—'

'It looks what?' Annie said, grabbing the towel and drying her hands. 'It looks what, Amber?'

'It looks,' I said, hardly believing the words that were coming out of my mouth, 'like there's a pair of feet sticking out of her back end.'

'Oh good grief!' said Annie, throwing down the towel and reaching for the phone. 'I thought she was getting fat and I did mention it to Jessica but in the end we just put it down to the fact that the chubby little thing wasn't getting as much exercise as she used to. I'll call Kate. She's our vet, but I don't know when she'll be able to get here. You'll have to go back down there and help her, Amber.'

'Me?' I cried. 'Where's Jake?'

'Down checking the fair,' she said, quickly tapping in numbers, 'and you know he won't have a signal. Now get back down there, girl, and do what you can.'

By the time I got back to the stable the situation had moved on and along with a pair of feet I could clearly make out a pair of nostrils and a tiny mouth. Pip was straining hard but I could see nothing was happening. Without thinking, without giving my fear a second to take hold, I rolled up my sleeves, sat on the straw behind her and prepared myself for her next contraction.

It didn't take long and this time as the little mare strained I took hold of the pair of slippery hooves and gently but firmly pulled. Unsure of just how hard to tug I was only able to help move the foal the tiniest bit and as the contraction passed it slipped back a little and Pip began to whinny and tremble. I crawled towards her head and stroked her rough, shaggy mane.

'Come on,' I whispered, 'next time we'll do it.'

Pip seemed to go calm for a moment and then began to strain again, her eyes wide in distress. I rushed back and grabbed the tiny feet once more, pulling more forcefully this time and not letting go.

The next few seconds were a blur and before I could move out of the way I found myself surrounded by a pool of liquid with the tiniest foal practically on my lap. I wiped the sticky residue away from its nostrils and watched as it shook its head a little and its chest began to heave. Checking the umbilical cord was no longer attached I gently nudged the foal up to Pip's nose, just as I'd seen vets do on television programmes, and she began to lick and whinny again, but softly now and not in fear.

There was no point trying to wipe down my jeans or shirt, so I sat with my back against the wall, my breath sharp in my chest, trying to get a handle on what had just happened. I had always expected life on the farm to throw up new sights and experiences but this was beyond anything I had imagined. I closed my eyes for a second and let out a long, slow breath.

'Oh well done you,' a brisk voice cut through the quiet as a tall, dark haired woman wearing overalls strode into the stable. 'Very well done indeed. Now, how do you fancy giving me a hand with the placenta?'

Chapter 18

'So, tell me again,' whispered Jessica as we peeped over the bottom half of the stable door at the cosy scene within, 'how did you know what to do?'

'I've already told you,' I shrugged, 'I didn't. I just thought back to all the things I've seen on TV and hoped for the best. It was all pot luck, and Pip of course. She knew what she was doing really.'

'But if you hadn't got in there and helped her do it,' said Jake, kissing my hand, 'neither she nor that little fella would probably even be here. I'm so proud of you, Amber,' he whispered so quietly that only I could hear.

I still couldn't really believe what had happened. Not only had I helped deliver the little black velvety colt, I'd also assisted Kate and cleaned and tidied the stable after she left. Mother and son were now beautifully bonded and settled and fortunately, we all agreed, far enough away from the bustle and noise of the funfair for it not to disturb them.

'I still can't believe she was pregnant,' Jessica tutted with a shake of her head. 'Mother is absolutely furious. We would never have passed her on to you, Jake, if we'd known.'

'How long are ponies pregnant for?' Harriet asked, squeezing us all closer together so she could get another look.

'Eleven months,' Jessica and I said in unison.

I had been doing a bit of research during the afternoon, just to prepare myself for any other little surprises the diminutive mare might have tucked up her sleeve, or anywhere else for that matter.

'So to be fair, Jess,' said Harriet equably, 'when you first had her she was only just pregnant. There's no way you could have known, is there?'

'But even so,' said Jessica frowning. 'We'll help out with Kate's fees and so on,' she said to Jake.

'Jess,' Jake laughed, 'please stop worrying. It's fine. We're delighted. It's just one of those things. Now come on. Let's go and have some dinner and get ready for the fair. I don't know about you lot, but I'm in the mood to celebrate!'

'Here she is!' Annie smiled, clapping her hands together when we arrived back at the house. 'My clever girl.'

'Oh Annie, please don't,' I blushed, 'I've told you it was all down to Pip really.'

But Annie was having none of it.

'This is a sign,' she insisted as she plated up the fish and chips that Henry, Jess and Harriet had brought with them, 'first the chicks and now this little colt. It's been a long time since anything was born on this farm and now all this happens in one day. This is down to you, Amber. You've helped Skylark Farm turn a corner. I see good things on our horizon.'

I was immensely proud of what I'd done, even though I still couldn't believe it was really me who had played such a crucial part in it all. I thought of the wobbly legged little black foal with the white flash down his muzzle and smiled.

'Have you got a name for him yet?' Henry asked through a mouthful of mushy peas.

'Me?' I said.

'Oh yes, Amber,' said Jessica, 'you have to name him, doesn't she, Jake?'

'Absolutely,' grinned Jake, toasting me with his mug of tea.

'I'm not sure,' I said, shaking my head. 'What about Star or Flash, because of that white splash on his face?'

Annie wrinkled her nose, clearly not sure about either suggestion.

'Well, all right,' I said thoughtfully, 'how about Blaze then?'

'Perfect!' everyone agreed.

'Absolutely,' said Annie, passing around more chips, 'makes him sound like a proper little rock star!'

Whether it was because I hadn't been to a funfair for such a long time or whether it was down to all the other excitement of the day I couldn't be sure, but the evening at the fairground was the best night out I'd had in years.

The entire experience was a full-on, fabulous assault on the senses and we were bombarded with music, madly flickering bulbs of every colour and the smell of hot dogs and candy floss, toffee apples and fried onions. I watched on, enraptured, as local children ran madly between the rides screeching and carelessly throwing toxic filled neon glowsticks high in the air, oblivious to the warning cries of their parents.

'What shall we go on first?' Harriet shouted above the din, rubbing her hands together.

'Whatever's loudest and fastest!' I yelled back. 'I could do with a good scare!'

We lurched dizzily from ride to ride, meeting up with some of Jake's other friends from the town and a few of Jessica's colleagues from the riding stables. As the evening wore on we became increasingly breathless and raucous, our aching bellies filled with every sickly and unsavoury treat we could lay our hands on.

'I can't eat anything else,' I pouted as Harriet handed me a red sticky dummy the size of my hand. 'If I eat one more thing I swear I'm going to throw up!'

By half past ten the fair was winding down; ever mindful of the licence the council inspector had issued the day before, Luca wasn't prepared to push his luck and stuck rigidly to the hours he was allowed to run the rides and sell his wares. Everything would be in full swing until midnight after the May Fair, but the way I was feeling after all the excitement the day had thrown up, I was grateful that the fun on Saturday was capped to a more reasonable hour.

The families had long gone and only the gangs of local teens, usually bored witless by life in a small town, remained along with Jessica, Harriet and me as we searched in vain to find Jake and Henry. I knew they'd been watching us when we strapped ourselves on to the Eliminator, but I'd been so dizzy when we spilled off it that I hadn't noticed they had slipped away.

'I bet they've gone to check on Pip again,' said Jessica sensibly. 'Don't worry, Amber, we'll walk you back to the house. Our car is in the yard anyway.'

We were just about to set off when we noticed, tucked away in the furthermost corner of the field, close to the caravans, a small tent standing alone with practically no illumination or hint of ostentation, unlike everything else.

'What's that?' I said, nodding my head in the direction of the tent as I tried in vain to painfully pull the last bite of candy floss out of my hair.

'Aha!' Harriet grinned. 'This'll be a laugh! Don't you agree, Jess?'

'Oh yes!' Jessica squealed, dumping her sticky dummy in the nearest bin and linking arms with me.

Frogmarched would be the best way to describe my brisk walk towards the tent, which was, I discovered, the domain of the much revered fortune teller, Rose.

'Have you got any silver?' Harriet whispered.

'What?'

'To cross her palm with!' she urged.

'I don't think it works like that in real life!' I giggled, conscious of violating the subdued aura that seemed to pulsate from and around the little tent.

'Please, come, sit.'

The three of us, shamed into silence, entered the incense scented, dimly lit confines. Suddenly the noises of the fair winding down were barely audible and the lights and music from earlier quickly forgotten.

'Just you,' said the woman, pointing at me with a bony clawlike finger, 'you two wait outside.'

Before I could make a grab for them Harriet and Jessica slipped back outside.

'Sit.'

I sat.

'Let me see your face.'

I looked up at the covered head of the woman. Her face was almost impossible to make out and her body was draped in layers of sequin-edged shawls in spite of the oppressive heat. The smoke from the incense was thick and heady. It stung my eyes and throat.

'What is it you want?' she asked me.

Part of me wanted to run straight out of the tent, but the other part kept my bottom firmly attached to the chair. After all, what harm could possibly come from playing along? I thought carefully for a few seconds before giving her the most honest answer I could think of.

'To live here,' I said eventually, 'at Skylark Farm. And to be happy.'

'But you aren't from here. You have only just moved here.'

'That's true,' I said. I wasn't at all suspicious that she already knew this. Doubtless Luca had told her who I was. 'But I already love it and I love Jake and Annie and I want to make a new life for myself here.'

I'd expected her to tell me that all would be well, that my wish was granted, but her demeanour, or what I could make of it, appeared decidedly doubtful.

'I see problems ahead,' she said slowly, 'and arguments. Things are not going to go smoothly for you but you don't know why yet. Someone is keeping secrets from you.'

I swallowed hard and tried to dismiss her pronouncement, but her words struck an answering chord in my heart. I did feel there were things I didn't know about Jake and the life he had lived at the farm before I arrived, but that was only to be expected. He'd spent the best part of his life associated with this place whereas I had only been here a few weeks. There were bound to be things I would probably never know.

The woman stared at me intently and I quickly looked back down at the table.

'I see the prospect of sunshine on your horizon,' she said languorously with her eyes half closed, as if she herself was dreaming of far off places, 'and intense heat, but only if you choose it.'

I pushed back my chair and pulled the last of my change out of my jeans pocket. I didn't want to hear any more.

'But don't forget,' she said triumphantly as I turned to walk out and she scooped up the change, 'you yourself are both the deceiver and the deceived.'

Chapter 19

I was surprised to find Jake was already in bed when I got back to the house. I'd somehow managed to fob Jessica and Harriet off with some nonsense about living a 'happy ever after' from fortune teller Rose and was mulling over exactly what she might have meant about people keeping secrets from me and whether or not I was suspicious enough to believe that there was anything of value in her prediction.

'Are you all right?' I whispered as I slipped into bed, determinedly claiming the tiny space next to Jake left for me by the dogs. 'I was worried about you,' I said, nuzzling up behind him.

'I'm fine,' he said.

I couldn't work out if he sounded genuinely sleepy or more like he was coming down with a cold.

'I just wanted to check on Pip and Blaze,' he eventually added.

'But why didn't you come back?' I asked. 'I missed you.'

'Sorry,' he mumbled, 'I thought you were having fun with Jess and Harriet and decided to leave you to it. I hope that was all right?'

'Fair enough,' I yawned, moving even closer and slipping my hand around his waist, 'and were they OK?'

'Who?'

'Pip and Blaze of course, they weren't upset by all the noise and commotion, were they?'

'No,' he whispered, finally turning over and pulling me into his arms, 'they were fine, absolutely fine. I can't begin to tell you how proud I am of you, Amber.'

I felt myself blush in the darkness.

'I never thought I'd see you doing anything like you've done today,' Jake continued.

'Me neither,' I admitted.

I wasn't altogether sure if I was offended by his remark or quite certain of what he meant by it. However, assisting a mare in labour was hardly in the same league as waiting for a few eggs to hatch so I guessed I could let him off. If anyone had told me, even just a few weeks ago, what I was going to find myself doing that morning I never would have believed them either.

'By the way,' I said, having decided not to look for any deeper and probably unintentional meaning behind his words, 'you were right about the eggs. When I went to check them this morning all four had hatched. I meant to tell you before, but with Pip stealing the limelight I forgot all about the dear little things!'

'I think that's allowed,' Jake chuckled, kissing my hair.

'I expect they'll be up and about tomorrow,' I said, yawning again. 'I'll go and have a look at them first thing. I've had enough for today. I'm dead beat.'

'I know,' Jake agreed, 'it has been something of an "in at the deep end" kind of day, hasn't it?'

'Just a bit,' I muttered, while mentally ticking off the hundred or so things from my to-do list. 'Oh God!' I shouted, suddenly sitting bolt upright and making the dogs jump. 'I forgot the bloody cake!'

'What cake?' said Jake, trying to pull me back down beside him.

'My cake for the show tomorrow,' I sobbed, 'I'm supposed to be entering a Victoria sponge!'

'Oh, don't worry about that,' Jake said, trying to placate me, but actually making the situation even worse. 'That's one of the fiercest classes there is. Believe me, you're better off out of it.'

'Don't you think I can do it?' I frowned, pulling further away from him and feeling wide awake again. 'Are you afraid I'm going to show you up?'

'Of course I'm not. For goodness' sake, Amber, that isn't what I meant at all!'

'What did you mean then?'

'Look,' he sighed, 'you're going to be under enough scrutiny tomorrow as it is and I just thought you could do without any extra pressure. Given all the trouble you've gone to I want you to enjoy tomorrow, not be worrying about what people think of your baking skills.'

'What pressure?' I laughed. 'What people? No one's going to be the slightest bit interested in me . . .'

My words trailed off as I began to imagine the car park filling up and hundreds of people descending on the meadow and all wondering who exactly was responsible for the fiasco that all of a sudden I was convinced the entire day was going to be.

'Everyone will be interested,' said Jake significantly and consequently cranking my paranoia up another notch. 'Everyone knows the suggestion to have the May Fair here was initially your idea and naturally they'll all want to see what sort of job you've made of it.'

Inwardly I felt my insides squirm and I groaned at the thought. In the city I knew what I was doing. I knew the right things to say and the right clothes to wear, but I hadn't been here long enough to have fathomed any of that out. What if I gave off the wrong kind of image, teamed the wrong shirt with the wrong shoes? I knew my new friends wouldn't be bothered about all that, but what about all the locals who were looking forward to their annual get-together? What if I failed them, and not just in my choice of outfit? What if my efforts simply weren't good enough? I'd never live it down.

'Believe me,' Jake continued, clearly oblivious to the fact that he'd already said more than enough, 'there'll be dozens of people to meet. Everyone is going to want to catch a glimpse of the girl who's been stirring things up on the farm.'

His tone was light, but I knew that in truth I was most likely going to be the talk of the town, or the show anyway.

'Where are you going?' Jake hissed as I swung my legs out of bed and made a beeline for the door.

'To make this damn cake,' I whispered back. 'It won't bake itself, will it?'

In the end, May Fair day didn't begin quite as I had expected it to. In my rose tinted, unrealistically idyllic vision, I had fantasised that I would wake from an uninterrupted night's sleep, throw on a vintage floral print frock and skip down to the field in the sunshine. I'd charm everyone with my easy manner and kind words and then drift away leaving a rose scented haze in my wake.

Unfortunately the reality couldn't have been any further from what I'd spent the last month dreaming about. The first thing I was aware of was a crippling pain in my neck, a damp patch on my cheek and freezing cold ankles.

'Have you heard?' I heard someone shouting.

I thought it sounded like Harriet, but what would she be doing in the bedroom and at such a godforsaken hour?

'Have you heard who's back?' came the voice again, which this time I could definitely identify as belonging to Harriet and sounding much closer than before. 'What the hell are you doing?'

Suddenly it all came flooding back to me and self-consciously I wiped the dribble on my dressing gown sleeve and tentatively levered myself into a sitting position.

'Have you been there all night?'

'Not quite,' I croaked, quickly scanning a note Jake had left at my side explaining that he'd had to go out early and that he didn't like to disturb me. 'When I got to bed last night,' I elaborated for Harriet's benefit, 'I remembered I hadn't made my cake.'

'Don't tell me it's taken you all night to bake a Victoria bloody sponge?' she smirked, filling the kettle and placing it on the range.

'No,' I said testily, 'it has not taken me all night to bake a "Victoria bloody sponge" as you so elegantly put it. It's taken me all night to bake seven.'

'Seven!'

'They kept going wrong,' I said defensively, shooting her a glance to warn her off taking the mickey, 'and by the time I'd managed one I was happy with I simply didn't have the energy to crawl back up the stairs to bed so I sat down here for a few seconds and, well, you can guess the rest.'

I stretched my aching back and tried to rub some feeling back into the sorest spot on my neck.

'So where is this masterpiece?' asked Harriet as she looked around.

'They're all in the pantry,' I told her. 'You can help me assemble it in a bit. I still haven't completely made up my mind which is the best, to be honest. Anyway, never mind my cake, and not that you aren't welcome, Harriet, but why exactly are you here?' I yawned. 'And more importantly who is back from where?'

'What?'

'You were yelling about someone being back,' I reminded her as I caught sight of Jake pulling into the yard in the truck.

'Never mind,' said Harriet, rushing for the door, 'I'll help you in a bit.'

In the end I got on with making a pot of tea myself and, in the absence of any help, I selected the two sponges I considered most capable of showing off my baking skills at their best and holding their own amongst the Wynbridge WI et al. According to Annie the ladies from the WI alone had over seven hundred years' combined experience and therefore centuries more expertise than me. As I slipped the cake inside Annie's prettiest tin I tried not to think about what I was letting myself in for or remind myself that the whole fair debacle had been all my idea.

With practically no time left I drained my cup, retied my dressing gown and pulled on my wellies to go and check on Patricia and the chicks. I could see Jake and Harriet down at Pip's stable and although I couldn't hear what they were saying, judging by the head shaking, gesticulating and arm waving, I could tell it was none too friendly. The scene came as something of a shock. Jake and Harriet's relationship had always seemed perfectly amicable to me. My mind drifted back to Rose the fortune teller and her timely mention of secrets and deceit.

I shook off my creeping suspicions and got on with my chores. I let Mabel and Martha out at the front of their house before slipping in the door at the back to see how things were progressing in the nursery wing. To my surprise Patricia was up and about and she looked much like any other new mum to me – worn out and a little unkempt – but when I peeped inside the box I could understand why she had been sitting tight. The four little chicks were no longer loose necked and bedraggled; now they looked like they had had a sharp blast under a hairdryer.

I smiled to myself as I watched three of them exploring the straw and cheeping to one another. The fourth was sitting quietly but I guessed that the effort of hatching was more than gargantuan for such a tiny little thing and therefore it deserved a rest. It was hard to believe that just a couple of days before they were all still firmly ensconced in their eggs.

'Amber?'

'I'm in here,' I said, poking my head back out of the door so Jake could see me and I didn't have to shout. 'Come and see.'

Jake joined me in the henhouse and quietly re-closed the door behind him.

'Oh wow,' he grinned, giving me a hug. 'Well done you!'

'Nothing to do with me,' I laughed. 'It's Patricia you should be congratulating.'

'You know what I mean,' said Jake, looking around him. 'I've never seen this place so spic and span, inside and out.'

I shrugged my shoulders to indicate that it was nothing, but actually it was and I was delighted that Jake had noticed all the trouble I'd gone to. It had taken me more hours than I cared to add up to transform the place to its current smart state and it was now finally beginning to look something like the henhouses I'd coveted in the magazines I had poured over in the run up to our move.

'I'll go and get some chick crumbs ready in a minute,' said Jake, carefully picking up the quietest ball of fluff and examining it. 'What with the fair and everything we might not get to check on these little guys again today, but they'll be OK. Can you do the water?'

'Of course,' I nodded, as he returned the tiny bundle to its warm, straw bed.

'Um,' he said, giving it a final stroke as it snuggled back down and made no attempt to join the other three.

'What is it?' I asked. 'What's wrong?'

'I think we might need to keep an eye on this one,' he said seriously, 'probably nothing to worry about. Could just be a slow starter, but I'd like to see it up and about a bit more by now.'

'I thought it was just tired out from the effort of hatching,' I whispered, staring at it intently and willing it to jump up and start cheeping.

'You're probably right,' Jake shrugged, 'don't worry about it today.'

'Should I come back and check later?' I said, reluctant to leave.

'There won't be time,' Jake reminded me. 'Best just let nature take its course.'

I didn't like the sound of that but knew we had to get ready for the fair.

'How's Pip this morning?' I asked, finally tearing my eyes away from the chicks.

'She's fine,' smiled Jake, 'and so is Blaze. I still can't believe it really. Kate's going to be at the fair to help out with the gymkhana so she's going to have another look at them when she gets a chance.'

He stopped for a second, his hand on the latch of the door and a faraway look in his eye.

'Are you all right?'

Looking at him properly I could see dark circles under his eyes and his smile didn't quite make it all the way from his mouth to his eyes. I'd expected him to be excited about the fair, especially now the day was here, the sun was shining and everything was good to go, but he looked more careworn than carefree.

'I'm fine,' he said unconvincingly, 'really.'

'Did you see Harriet?'

'No,' he said, turning to go, 'not since last night. Come on, we'd better get ready.'

Chapter 20

Engulfed by fear, trepidation and excitement I soon forgot about the chicks and braced myself for whatever the day planned to throw at me. I'd never seen Annie so animated and excited and although I knew there was something not quite right with Jake, a definite something he wasn't telling me, I was still delighted that Annie had the opportunity to enjoy the fair so close to home.

'What's up with you?' she asked, watching me rub my neck and trying to stretch it back into a slightly less painful position.

I decided not to fill her in on the details of where I'd spent most of the night.

'I think I must have slept funny,' I said instead. 'I've just got a bit of a stiff neck, that's all. I'll be fine.'

She abandoned folding her precious quilt so it was ready to take down to the marquee and began noisily rifling through the packed drawers of the old dresser.

'I've just the thing,' she said, scattering balls of twine and elastic bands far and wide. 'This'll sort you out.'

'Oh no really,' I said lightly in a vain attempt to shrug off the problem, 'honestly, it isn't all that bad.'

I couldn't bear the thought of attending the fair with a wasp-attracting pineapple poultice or blueberry neck brace, or any of Annie's concoctions strapped to me for that matter.

'Aha!' she announced triumphantly, tossing me a box that was agony to catch.

She went back to her folding and I examined what she had been looking for.

'Ibuprofen,' I laughed. 'Really, Annie?'

She looked up and winked.

'And there was you thinking I was going to send you to the fair with a fresh pig's bladder draped around your shoulders!'

I popped two of the tablets out of the packet and gratefully swallowed them with a mouthful of water.

'Mmm,' I admitted, 'I was thinking something along those lines.'

'Give me some credit,' she muttered, 'we won't try that until tonight.'

To see the meadows so miraculously transformed was, in my humble opinion, simply breathtaking and totally worth the endless phone calls and late nights that had accompanied taking the event on. The early mist that had played around the furthest reaches of the river, clinging to the banks and slipping under the hedges, had soon burnt off and the prospect of a gloriously sunny day stretched thankfully ahead.

Whereas the evening before everything had looked perfectly prepared but tranquil and still, the marquees poised for action and the white spray paint marking the spots for the various ice cream and crepe vendors to park, everything was now abuzz with frenetic activity. A small army of locals and members from various committees bustled about with tea urns and floral displays, raffle tickets and boxes of crockery and it was hard to imagine the transformed fields could ever have been earmarked for a quiet, empty summer.

Protectively I wrapped my hands around Annie's old cake tin and in turn Annie clung fast to her treasured quilt as we searched for our respective areas in the big marquee. The bunting barely stirred under the immense canvas roof and the air inside was already bristling with more than the heat of just the sun.

'Is that a cake?' asked Jeannie Russell, one of the top ranking WI members who appeared as if from nowhere at my elbow and steered me quickly towards the baked goods table. 'You'll need to see Mrs Summers if you can find her,' she said briskly, 'she's the one in charge.'

Inwardly I groaned at the sight of the white cloth covered trestle table already packed with cakes and biscuits of every description. It was immediately obvious that the Victoria sponge class was the most popular and, so obviously out of my depth, I wished with all my heart that I'd left my effort back in the kitchen. For the moment, Mrs Summers was nowhere to be seen.

'Let's find you a spot, dear,' smiled Jeannie Russell, indicating a minuscule gap at the front.

'No, no,' I said, retreating, 'I'll just pop it at the back.'

I could feel at least a dozen pairs of eyes turn their attention from their own plates to mine as I popped the lid off the cake tin. Carefully and with shaking hands, I lifted out my cake and placed it amongst the others and, to be honest, in the cold light of day I didn't think it looked too shabby.

'Is that jam homemade?' pounced one of the group.

'Yes,' I said, relieved that it was, 'it's Annie's from last year.'

Every member of the group took a half a step back and there was even a sharp intake of breath from some. Immediately I recognised my mistake, but it was too late to retract my admission. Knowing who had made the jam I couldn't imagine there would be any judge in the land brave enough to sample it and I was bitterly disappointed to have scuppered my chances with such a rash comment.

'Doesn't look too bad,' said another of the group to her neighbour.

Her comment was met with a dismissive sniff and raised eyebrows and I felt some of the tension in my shoulders ease a little. Perhaps my humble cake wasn't such a disaster after all.

'And the jam looks all right,' said another. 'Surely not even Annie can get fruit and sugar wrong.'

A few minutes later we were all herded together and ushered back towards the meadow in preparation for the marquee doors to be closed so judging could commence. Considering I had absolutely no expectations of seeing a card anywhere near my plate I was certainly feeling the tension, and poor Annie, despite being an old hand at competing, looked on the point of collapse.

'Come on,' I told her as we linked arms, 'let's have a wander, get a breath of air and a bite to eat.'

We lingered as long as we dare at the other end of the marquee admiring the skilful array of crafts and seasonal produce on show. Beautifully smooth tablets of beeswax, any number of extravagant floral displays and, my particular favourite, comic knitted tea cosies made me rather pleased to find myself in the role of competitor as opposed to judge.

When I'd decided to abandon my cross-stitch entry I had felt a pang of guilt, but seeing the quality of everyone else's stitches I was relieved. My jumbled little contribution would have been laughed off the table.

'However will they decide?' I said to Annie, torn between favouring a cupcake cosy over one in the shape of a gigantic striped bee.

'Thank you, ladies,' said a stern voice from the doorway of the marquee, 'I'm afraid I'm going to have to hurry you.'

Poker straight and infuriatingly slowly Annie, clinging to my arm a little tighter than was absolutely necessary I felt sure, slackened her pace. I could hear many a tut and sigh as we reached the canvas door, which was pulled tightly closed the second we were through it.

'So,' said Jake and Harriet as they rushed up to us together, 'how did you get on? How did it look compared to the others?'

'Fine,' said Annie, quickly recovering her airy, confident attitude. 'I wouldn't usually be so bold, but just between us I've got rather high hopes this year.'

Harriet rolled her eyes and Jake shook his head.

'We were talking to Amber,' Jake frowned, 'as well you know!'

'Oh, her cake fitted in a treat,' she smiled, 'didn't it, dear?'

'I hope so,' I said nervously, fiddling with the waistband of my dress, 'time will tell, I guess. Nothing I can do about it now.'

Having found Annie a seat in the shade where she could see both the show ring and the door to the marquee and plied her with yet more tea, Jake and I made our slow way round the field, welcoming the visitors to Skylark Farm and checking all was well amongst the vendors and groups who were adding the finishing touches to their stalls and displays.

'Where's Harriet disappeared to?' I said, noticing that she'd slipped away.

'Back to the plant stand I shouldn't wonder,' Jake confided.

'I'm surprised she didn't have a stand herself,' I said, craning my now slightly less painful neck in the direction of the trade stands.

'I think she's rather sweet on the competition,' Jake added with a wink, 'so she's decided to sit this one out.'

'Oh really,' I smiled, 'you'll have to point him out to me. She's never mentioned she's on the prowl for anyone in particular.'

'Well,' said Jake, discreetly nodding his head towards a pretty dark haired girl in the ice cream queue wearing a floral cotton frock similar to my own. 'That's Rachel. She's the one Harriet's on the prowl for.'

'Oh,' I said, 'I see. Well, in that case she's got very good taste then, hasn't she? Rachel looks a bit of a stunner to me.'

'Hmm,' said Jake dreamily, 'I've always thought so.'

'Hey you!' I laughed, digging him in the ribs.

We turned to see Jemma and Lizzie heading towards us. Lizzie was holding the hand of a very pretty little blonde girl and Jemma was pushing a pram from the depths of which I could see a pair of tiny hands and feet appearing and disappearing as the occupant kicked and punched the air.

'Congratulations!' beamed Jemma. 'This all looks amazing. How lucky have you been with the weather?'

'I know,' said Jake with a grateful glance at the clear blue sky overhead. 'To be honest that was my biggest concern, but this won't change.'

'Mummy,' said the little girl tugging at Jemma's skirt, 'can I have an ice cream, please?'

'Come with me,' said Lizzie, 'I'll get you one. See you later, guys.'

'Are you going to have a dance around the Maypole?' Jemma called mischievously over her shoulder as she followed on behind her daughter and her best friend.

'No,' said Jake, 'I think I'll give it a miss this year, but Amber's going to give it a go.'

'No Amber is not,' I gasped, cuffing him lightly. 'No way.'

Before we knew it preparations for the first class of the dog show were well under way and a stealthy, but nonetheless vicious fight between two rival terriers had just broken out when Jake nudged me and pointed towards the marquee.

'Time to discover your fate,' he said with a wry smile as we watched the judges streaming out. 'Do you want to hang back or get it over quickly?'

'Look at Annie,' I said pointing. 'By the looks of it I'll be taking the "getting it over quickly" option.'

Annie had already abandoned her chair and was gesturing wildly for me to join her. I took a deep breath and smoothed down the front of my dress. Considering I had convinced myself that taking part was just for fun and that it didn't matter if my cake was placed or not, my heart was doing a miraculous job of suggesting otherwise.

'Are you coming?' I asked Jake, who didn't budge when I started to move.

'They let competitors in first,' he explained. 'I'll wander over in a bit. Good luck,' he added, planting a swift kiss on my cheek.

I still couldn't put my finger on what was wrong with him, but there was definitely something. It was as if a thin mist had descended between us and no matter how hard I tried I just couldn't push my way through it to reach the real Jake, the guy I had fallen in love with. He had held my hand, spoken to the visitors and sorted out the few inevitable niggles happily enough and if you'd asked anyone else what was wrong with him they would have all said 'nothing', but I knew. I knew something was bothering him.

'All right,' I smiled, conscious that I was keeping an impatient Annie waiting. 'See you in a bit.'

The atmosphere inside the marquee had obviously been merely warming up before, because when we walked back in it was positively buzzing with high velocity electrical emotional charge.

'That,' said a woman as she stalked back outside, 'is a total bloody travesty.'

She made no attempt to move aside as we passed one another and consequently she ended up practically shoulder barging me out of the way. Both momentarily halted we made eye contact for a split second and for some reason I was the one who said a hasty 'sorry', before she continued on her way towards the exit.

'Who was that?' I hissed at Annie.

'I didn't see. Come on,' she said, plucking at my sleeve, her eyes focused on the table where she'd set up her quilt.

A small crowd had gathered there and they shuffled apart as we approached giving us a clear view.

'Congratulations, Annie!' called one of the group. 'Lovely to have you back, my dear.'

A general murmur of appreciation and consent rippled through the assembled ladies and Annie proudly caressed the corner of her first place card.

'Wouldn't surprise me if you get the best in show rosette with that,' chirped up another voice.

Annie turned, her face flushed with pride. She looked at me for less than a second and gave the merest trace of a wink.

'Thank you, Bunty,' she said graciously, 'very kind of you to say so.'

Next it was my turn.

There was an even bigger crowd around the baked goods table and, if possible, the atmosphere surrounding cakes and fancies was even more highly charged than over at the crafts. Peering over the top of everyone I realised my cake was nowhere in sight and I hoped the mention of Annie's jam hadn't consigned it to the bin already.

'Well done,' said one of the women, 'congratulations. We didn't have you down as a baker.'

'Oh yes,' laughed another, 'well done you! You've certainly stirred things up round here. It's almost worth not being placed at all just to see the look on certain folks' faces!'

Finally securing a full view of the table I spotted Annie's pretty chintz plate nestled between first and third with my cake still on it.

'You've come second!' Annie cheered, clapping her hands together. 'Oh Amber, well done!'

I stood and looked at her open mouthed and rooted to the spot. Not only was I stunned that I'd somehow managed to teach myself how to produce a prize winning cake, but also that it actually meant so much to win. I couldn't help wondering what the old me would have thought of my domestic accomplishments. My London kitchen hadn't seen any action beyond heating a bagel and providing my first caffeine hit of the working day.

'Have you always baked, my dear?'

'No,' I choked, my throat tight and dry, 'no. I only started about six weeks ago when I moved here with Jake.'

'Even better,' laughed the woman who first congratulated me. 'Cat and pigeons springs to mind,' she winked to her neighbour and together they went off giggling.

'Come on,' said Annie, 'let's go and find Jake and tell him the good news.'

The rest of the day passed in a blur. As predicted Annie was awarded best in show and we celebrated with a bottle of cordial and some sandwiches under the still cool shade of the willow trees next to the river.

'Good idea putting these fences up,' I said to Jake with a nod towards a group of young boys looking for a way down the bank.

'Don't even think about it!' Jake called to them and they skulked off back towards the show ring looking downcast and disappointed. 'I was rather hoping for a slice of prize winning cake,' he smiled at me.

'Entries have to stay put until the end of the day,' Annie said drowsily from under the brim of her battered straw hat.

'But won't they dry out in the heat?' Jake frowned, looking disappointed. 'I want to sample second place at its absolute peak.'

'Oh, I shouldn't worry about that,' I told him, 'there's loads back at the farm and I reckon they're all pretty much as good.'

'Oh, get her,' said Harriet as she flopped down next to me on the blanket and planted a perfunctory kiss on my cheek. 'There'll be no living with her now!'

'I didn't mean it like that,' I blushed, embarrassed that she thought I was showing off.

'I know you didn't,' she laughed, 'I'm only teasing.'

'You're in a fine mood, aren't you?' I said, sitting up properly and looking at her sun-kissed face. 'Anything to do with a certain Rachel by any chance?'

Harriet looked absolutely stricken and shot an accusing glance at Jake.

'Wasn't he supposed to say anything?' I whispered, grabbing her hand. 'God, Harriet, I'm sorry. I didn't think. I haven't upset you, have I?'

'Don't you care then?' she said, looking right back at me. 'Doesn't it matter to you that I . . . that I . . .'

'That you what?'

Harriet didn't say anything, but began furiously tearing at the grass around the edges of the blanket.

'Like girls,' I said in a low voice.

'Yes,' she said.

Her tone was almost challenging and she looked me in the eye for the merest second before snatching another handful of grass.

'Of course it doesn't,' I said, reaching for her hand again. 'Harriet, I haven't known you for long but I love you to bits. You've made settling in here so easy and been such a good friend. Whether you like girls, boys, both or neither is of no consequence to me. You've been a good friend to me right from day one, that's all that matters.'

'Really?'

'Of course really,' I insisted. 'Honestly, who do you take me for?'

'Sorry,' she said, sighing heavily, 'it's just that, well, let's just say my coming out hasn't exactly been welcomed by everyone around here.'

'Narrow minded hypocrites,' Annie chipped in, 'you send them to me, Harriet, and I'll soon set them straight!'

Any further discussion was halted by the show announcer.

'Would Annie, Jake and Amber please make their way to the show ring? Annie, Amber and Jake to the show ring as soon as you can, please.'

Jake jumped up, trying to pull me along with him in the process. Out of the corner of my eye I had been watching a small crowd of adults and children, resplendently decorated in ribbons and flowers, gathering around the Maypole, which was similarly bedecked.

'If this has anything to do with dancing,' I said, stubbornly refusing to budge, 'then you can forget it.'

'It'll be the judging,' said Annie from beneath her hat.

'The what?' said Harriet, who had hastily forgiven my mention of Rachel in the face of such a potentially amusing and, for me, humiliating situation.

177

'You won't have to dance, skip or anything else, Amber,' Annie tried to reassure me, 'but as hosts of the May Fair we three are expected to judge the best dressed child.'

'Well, come on then,' said Jake impatiently. 'Look lively, Annie! If we don't get a move on we'll throw the whole schedule out and no one will be happy.'

'I'm not coming,' Annie announced.

She clearly thought the whole idea was preposterous.

'Why not?' I asked. 'Please, Annie,' I pleaded. 'I could really do with your moral support.'

'Absolutely not,' said Annie, refusing even to open her eyes. 'You pair are on your own. You have to remember, Amber, that I know practically all those rogues waiting over there, and most of their children. One misplaced rosette and friendships of decades will be in tatters.'

'What about *my* friendships?' I pouted.

'You haven't been here long enough to establish any with that lot,' she said mischievously, 'so no one's going to blame you if you make a pig's ear of it, not for long anyway.'

'Oh thanks,' I muttered, as Jake dragged me from under the trees and back towards the show ring.

'Who shall I pick?' I hissed as we approached.

'I don't know,' he said distractedly, 'but I daresay in line with the fair's tradition you'll be selecting a girl and I'll be choosing the boy.'

'You've got to be kidding!' I laughed.

'Actually,' he smiled, 'I'm not.'

All the children looked lovely to me, boys and girls, but there was one little lady who was slightly smaller than the rest and she caught my eye straightaway.

Dressed in a simple embroidered white cotton dress, with bouncing blonde curls, a white hair band and green shoes and socks she was the perfect image of spring and the cheerful little daisy she was representing. She even had a small hoop decorated with delicate silk flowers.

I breathed a sigh of relief as even the rest of the competitors, along with their parents and eagle eyed grandparents, clapped and cheered when the winners were announced. Clearly I had made the right choice. With hands that weren't quite steady I knelt down in front of her and carefully attached her flowery rosette.

'Thank you,' she said shyly, giving me a little smile, 'my name's Eliza.'

'Well, congratulations, Eliza,' I told her, 'you look very pretty.'

It wasn't until she reached up to offer me a daisy crown of my own that I realised there was something amiss with her arm. Her mum rushed forward to help and Eliza abandoned us to take her place for dancing around the pole.

'She lost most of her lower arm to meningitis last year,' said the woman, pulling a handkerchief out from her sleeve.

Her husband stepped forward and slipped his arm around her waist.

'This time last year we didn't even know if she'd be here,' he said, his eyes filling with tears and fierce pride, 'but she's a little fighter, our Eliza, she's had to be.'

'Thank you for choosing her,' said Eliza's mum as she ran a hand over her swollen belly, 'it means a lot to her to be told she's pretty.'

'Well,' I sighed, 'she's beautiful.'

'Be careful what you wish for when it's your turn,' the woman smiled as she positioned herself in the best spot to watch her daughter.

'My turn for what?'

'To dance,' she said. 'A couple of years ago I asked for another child.'

'She didn't get one that year,' grinned her husband, 'but now she's carrying two!'

'Oh, don't worry about me,' I smiled, eyeing the Maypole warily, 'I'm not going anywhere near it!'

They both laughed and I made my excuses to join Jake who was still standing near the boys as they self-consciously prepared to join in.

'Now don't you look a picture,' he smiled warmly, pointing at my crown, 'you look like the May Queen herself. You should go round,' he said, pointing at the dancers, 'just once.'

'No fear!' I said, taking a step back. 'Not after what I just heard!'

I'd never been prone to superstition but what Eliza's parents had told me stuck fast in my mind. Life in the countryside had made quite enough of an impact on me during the last few weeks. I was already living a totally transformed life and doing things I hadn't even dreamt of six months ago. However, the one thing I certainly didn't need to change or enhance was upping my chances in the fertility stakes.

'Not even for me?' Jake wheedled.

'Absolutely not,' I laughed, 'do you know what will happen if I do?'

'I've got a pretty good idea,' he smiled, wriggling his eyebrows suggestively. 'And I don't think it would be the worst thing that could happen, do you?'

Suddenly the music and the shouting and the dancing seemed a very long way off. I wasn't even sure if the ground beneath my feet was solid enough to carry my weight. Jake caught a free ribbon for himself and passed me another, and for the next few minutes we circled around and around, ducking, dodging and weaving but without once breaking eye contact and not for one second without unbridled laughter on our lips.

'Oh, you've done it now,' I giggled, finally falling into his arms as the music came to a stop.

'I certainly hope so,' he said.

He brushed my tangled hair away from my face and kissed me deeply. Finally it felt like my Jake was back.

Chapter 21

'Just who the hell does she think she is?'

'Lady of the Manor probably.'

Squeezed into the stiflingly hot Portakabin loos I listened intently to what was doubtless the latest round of local gossip being chewed over and spat out in front of the mirrors. The way the two women, just inches from where I was standing, were going at it made me feel grateful that I wasn't the object of their sharp tongues.

'Swanning around the place like she owns it,' said the first sneering voice again, 'and picking the Patterson kid. She must have known.'

My heart sank as I quietly closed the loo seat and perched on the edge.

'Of course she did, someone would have told her.'

'But I don't really care about that. What's pissed me off is that they let her enter the baking class. Mum should have been second, not her, and that scheming old bag Annie shouldn't have entered anything either. Best in bloody show. I ask you!'

'But I don't think there's any rule saying they couldn't enter.'

'I'm well aware of that,' snapped voice number one. 'But it's simple show etiquette, isn't it? Anyone even half familiar with the system knows that. The host never enters. Old Mrs Harrison supplied dozens of scones and cakes to sell over the years, but she never expected to win a sodding rosette for them, did she?'

'Do you think the judges felt obliged to place her then?'

'Of course they did.'

'But that's terrible. I'm not sure that can be right. Everyone seems to really like her. They say she's fitted in really well.'

'Well, of course, they would say that, wouldn't they? Little Miss "Butter Wouldn't Melt" with her Boden blouses and patterned wellies is utter perfection, isn't she? But I'll tell you something.'

'What?'

'I'll bet you anything you like she knows nothing about me and Jake or why he went scurrying off to London trailing after that clever brother of his with his tail between his legs.'

Stifling my sobs I waited until their cruel laughter had died away, then, having splashed my face with cold water, I made my way stealthily back to the marquee. I snatched my cake from the table, dumped it in the first available bin and went back up to the house with Annie's chintz plate and tin and a cracking headache courtesy of the dozens of questions now whirring about in my brain.

It didn't take a genius to work out that the person slagging me off in the loos and the person Harriet had been shouting about 'being back' were actually one and the same, and once that connection had been made, it was a short leap to the name of Jake's ex-girlfriend: Holly.

I guessed she was also the one responsible for the shoulder-barge manoeuvre in the marquee and I mentally retraced my steps trying to remember what she looked like. However, it had all happened so quickly and so many other things had happened since, that the only thing I could recall about her with any real clarity was that she was tall, blonde and rather angular.

Chapter 22

The following morning, as I sat under one of the towering oak trees that bordered the fields, I watched on as the fairground was dismantled and packed away, along with the marquee which, collapsed on the damp grass, now looked as impressive as a deflated balloon. My heart felt like that marquee: squashed flat and trodden all over; and although in reality I knew it was only the end of the May Fair it felt like it was the end of so much more.

Unable and unwilling to put it off any longer I strode off down the track towards the cottage, which Annie had told me was called Meadowview Cottage, in search of some answers. I had been mulling things over and was now convinced that must have been where Jake and Holly had lived together. Once I'd finished there, I determined to find Jake and insist on being told exactly what all the furtive whispering and hushed conversations were about. If there really was a battle looming on the horizon I couldn't possibly take part if my alleged allies were holding back the ammunition that could help me win it.

The single-storey cottage came into view as I turned the final corner on the dusty track. It looked innocuous enough, somewhat run-down but nonetheless potentially picturesque, nestled in a small dip and in the middle of its own patch of garden. I remembered Jake's suggestion that tearing it down was an option he had been considering and felt rather sorry for the little place as I struggled to open the gate.

A closer look revealed that the garden was very neglected and overgrown and when I finally reached the window to the left of the door and peered through the grime, I stepped back in surprise. The bed in the room was dishevelled and unmade as if someone had only just pushed back the covers and climbed out and I half expected to find a face staring back at me and yelling about trespassing.

I waited for a few seconds, my heart hammering in my chest and then, as no one had appeared, took a deep breath and slipped along the weed covered path that ran down the side of the property. The back garden was in much the same state as the front and the rooms at the back looked similarly abandoned. There were dishes around the sink in the kitchen and a newspaper lay open on the table. Even the big clock above the door was still keeping time.

For a moment I wondered if maybe someone had broken in and was living there undetected, but the grass I had walked over hadn't been disturbed for a long time and there was no sign of forced entry anywhere. Surely if someone was squatting there would be some tell-tale sign around the place; they couldn't have just flown in.

I was certain that this mysterious cottage held the answers to unlocking the secrets everyone was keeping from me and I marched back to the farm intent on finding the keys and having a proper look inside.

It was still quiet in the kitchen, not even the dogs were up and about. Tired out from the exertions and excitement of the May Fair, Jake and Annie were doubtless making the most of a rare lie in. A fact I took no time in taking advantage of as I began my search for the keys to Meadowview Cottage, but what I found was much more worrying.

'Jake,' I hissed, sending the bedroom curtains flying back along the poles and letting the sun stream in, 'Jake!'

He groaned and turned over, pulling one of my pillows over his head.

'Come on,' I said, pulling it off again, 'I need to talk to you. This is important.'

'What now?' he groaned, his voice sounding muffled from under the bedclothes.

'I need you to come down to the kitchen. I've got something to show you.'

'If it's plans to hold the May Fair here next year, you're on your own. I've got work to do.'

'But you might not have for much longer!' I warned him. 'Come on, this could be important.'

A few minutes later Jake stood with me in the kitchen, his arms firmly crossed as he surveyed the pile of unopened letters I'd discovered in my quest to find the cottage keys.

'Where did you find these?' he frowned, running a hand through his dishevelled hair and rubbing his tired eyes.

'They were in the back of the dresser.'

Neither of us were sitting at the table. Instead we were keeping a safe distance in case the contents of the envelopes spontaneously combusted.

'What were you doing in the back of the dresser?'

'Looking for envelopes,' I lied, 'but that doesn't really matter now, does it? The fact is that no one receives this many letters from their bank when it's got good news to share, do they?'

Jake shrugged his shoulders.

'Look at the postmarks,' I said, reaching for the envelope on top of the pile. 'You need to open them!'

'No way!' he shouted, then lowered his voice. 'They're addressed to Annie. I can't go rifling through what isn't mine. And you shouldn't either,' he added crossly.

'Well, I'm sorry,' I said, throwing the letter back on the table, 'but I've kind of reached the point where I feel like I have to start trying to find things out for myself.'

'What do you mean by that?'

'Nothing.'

'No, come on. If you've got something to say, let's hear it.'

Creaking floorboards overhead warned us that Annie was on her way and Jake grabbed the pile of letters and quickly stuffed them back in the dresser.

'I think that's called denial,' I muttered, picking up my basket and heading back out of the door.

I was relieved to find chick number four was decidedly brighter and continued with my chores feeling relieved that at least everything on the hen front was in order. However, on entering the kitchen after checking on Pip and Blaze, I discovered the atmosphere was its usual sunny self and knew instantly that nothing had been said about my worrying discovery.

'Can I take the truck?' I asked, setting down the basket and washing my hands at the sink.

'Of course,' said Jake equably, 'I'm working in the orchards this morning and catching up with the bee man so I won't be needing it.'

'Doesn't he have a name?'

I know I sounded peevish but Jake's obviously jolly effort to make out that everything was fine and dandy was infuriating.

'Charlie, I think,' he said, scratching his head, 'but everyone round here just calls him "the bee man".'

'I'm glad you're feeling better, Amber,' said Annie. 'We missed you at the fairground last night but given all the work you'd been putting in I can't say I'm surprised it caught up with you. Shame it couldn't have held off until today, though.'

'Or not arrived at all,' smiled Jake.

'Oh no,' said Annie, 'there's always a price to pay.'

'What do you mean?' I asked, hanging the hand towel over the range rail.

'In my experience,' Annie explained, 'everything pleasurable in life, everything you love, comes with a price. It's getting the balance right and making sure the positives outweigh the negatives, that's the tricky part.'

'You know,' I said, 'I think you could be right. Listening to a certain girl slagging me off yesterday was probably the negative sent to balance out all the fun I'd been having. I'm guessing that the thought of her presence must have been the issue you were skirting around, Jake, when you were deciding whether or not you wanted to play the host.'

Jake dropped the paper he had been reading and Annie fixed him with a steely stare.

'I said to you, you should have told her!' she shouted, banging down her fist on the arm of the chair. 'Didn't I warn you no good would come from keeping secrets?'

'You don't even know it was her,' Jake said wearily.

Annie, tight lipped, her face contorted with anger I would never have thought her capable of, said nothing. I'd had enough of the pair of them and their silly game playing.

'Annie,' I said, ignoring Jake's comment, which was actually more of an admission than he had probably intended it to be, 'people in glasshouses really shouldn't throw stones.' With that I grabbed the keys and stormed out of the house.

I pulled out of the yard and headed towards Wynbridge wondering what was being said in the kitchen and feeling increasingly guilty that I had taken my frustration out on Annie. I tried to focus all my attention on the road ahead and not think about Jake single-handedly struggling to squash all the worms back into the can that I had just ripped open.

How was it really possible that so much could change in just twenty-four hours? I had been so happy, so content, but all that had been taken from me in the course of two minutes trapped inside a portable toilet. I found myself wondering whether it was too soon to plead with my letting agent and ask them to find a legal loophole to clear the tenant out of my flat so I could move back to London. Not that I really wanted to go back, but nor did I want to live this new life if it was destined to be filled with deceit.

I parked the truck in the market square and bagged myself a tucked away table in The Cherry Tree Café.

'What can I get you, my love?' smiled Angela.

'Whichever slice of cake is most calorific,' I nodded, 'oh, and a coffee, please, a vat full.'

'Oh dear,' she said sympathetically, 'that bad, eh?'

I nodded and watched her bustle back to the kitchen, then waved to Jemma who popped her head through the beaded curtain and mouthed 'hello'.

'Mind if I join you?' said a voice behind me.

It was Jessica.

'Of course not,' I said, patting the seat next to me. 'No work today?'

She hung her bag over the back of the chair and eyed the coffee and towering plate of pretty cakes Angela was setting down in front of me.

'No,' she frowned, 'I'm running errands. What is all that?' she asked, looking up at Angela wide eyed.

'A little bit of everything Amber should have already sampled, according to Jemma,' Angela chuckled. 'As I understand it, all the cakes Jake took were devoured en route back to London.'

'Oh yes,' said Jessica, greedily eyeing the treats, 'I remember now. I'll have the same, please, Angela, and a pot of tea.'

'You'll never fit into your dress,' I warned her.

'Then they'll jolly well have to let it out a bit then, won't they?'

I'm not so naïve to think that the entire world's problems can be cured with tea, coffee and cake, but having devoured roughly two thirds of what had been put in front of me I was feeling much happier and far more willing to share my concerns with Jessica than I had been when she first arrived.

'So,' she said, laying down her fork and wiping her lips with her cupcake patterned napkin, 'what's up?'

Not an easy question to answer as no one had told me anything much, but I owed it to myself to try to figure it out before the situation escalated to irretrievable.

'Are you on a bit of a show comedown or is there more to it than that?'

Given her tone and the concern knitting her brow I guessed she already knew some of what I was going to say.

'Ever since I moved here,' I began with a sigh, 'everyone, Annie included, has gone out of their way to make me feel welcome and part of the community.'

'And that's a problem because?' she asked, selecting herself another iced fancy.

'Because there's something else going on, something they aren't telling me. I know that Jake practically grew up on the farm and I also know that he had a relationship with Holly whatshername, but I get the distinct impression that there was more to their parting than just a simple relationship break-up and I can't shrug off the feeling that everyone's still thinking and talking about it behind my back.'

The words came out in a rush, spilling over themselves and almost tripping me up in the process, but at least they'd been said. If I did end up scurrying back to London with my tail between my legs at least there was one person who knew the real reason why.

'Oh, I don't think that's true,' Jessica said, shaking her head, 'no one's talking about anything. Why would they be?'

'Because she's back,' I said simply. 'This Holly whatsher-name is in Wynbridge and don't even pretend you didn't know. Harriet obviously knows so you must too.'

'I haven't clapped eyes on her,' said Jessica sheepishly, 'but I admit that Harriet had mentioned she'd been seen.'

'And heard,' I muttered.

'What do you mean?'

Blushing furiously I then went on to explain what I'd heard Holly and her friend saying about me.

'It's obvious she's out to change people's opinions of me,' I sniffed, 'or maybe just wants to put me in my place. I really was a fool to think I could fit in here so quickly, wasn't I?'

'Absolutely not,' said Jessica, sounding cross. 'You've never put a foot wrong, you've made sure the May Fair happened this year and you've been nothing but kindness and generosity itself, Amber. Don't you think for one second that *her* opinion is the same as anyone else's! Everyone loves *you* to bits.'

'So why is she going round telling everyone I've got ideas above my station and that I'm a fake?'

'Because she's jealous maybe,' Jessica suggested, 'and who can blame her? She's doubtless heard how happy you and Jake are and seen for herself at the fair how much of a go you're making of things, and decided to stick her nose in.'

That kind of made sense but it still didn't explain *why* she would want to stick her nose in.

'Look, you need to talk to Jake and Harriet,' said Jessica sensibly. 'If you explain exactly how you're feeling about all this they'll soon think better of keeping quiet and tell you what went on before she left.'

I gave her my most pleading look but it was obvious she wasn't going to spill any more beans; however, at least my hunch had been proved right. I knew there was more to this unsavoury situation than just post-relationship break-up sour grapes.

'My guess,' Jessica continued, reaching for her purse so she could settle the bill, 'is that she's come back here because she's bored or she's run out of money or fallen out with her latest man. I daresay she'll be gone again as soon as mummy and daddy have replenished her bank account, but that doesn't mean that you shouldn't know what she did. I for one think that you should be told and I'm frankly surprised that Jake hasn't explained already. It might even help you understand why he still hasn't got around to clearing out the cottage.'

I nodded but didn't say anything, my mind abuzz with this freshly gleaned information.

'Talk to Jake and Harriet,' Jessica said again, patting my hand. 'They're the only ones who know the full story. Really, I'm almost as clueless as you are and have probably got the wrong end of the stick anyway.'

The drive back to Skylark Farm was slow, purposefully slow, and when I pulled back into the yard and spotted Harriet's little truck parked outside the back door I guessed she and Jake had already had their heads together. To be honest, as the miles had slipped by, I had fast reached the point where I was beyond worrying about myself and whether or not I was going to have a meltdown when I heard what they had to tell me. I was more concerned about the parting shot I'd left with Annie. Had she worked out that I'd found the unopened letters from the bank, and if so could she forgive me for mentioning them?

Jake and Harriet were walking back up from Pip's paddock and I waited for them to reach the yard before walking over.

Jake was the first to speak.

'Amber,' he said, 'we need to talk.'

'Yes,' I said, 'I was rather hoping you were going to say that.'

We walked over to Annie's swinging seat and the little table and chairs that were haphazardly arranged in what she called 'her garden', at the back of the house. The lawn was in need of a cut and the borders definitely needed tidying. The garden had been on my list of jobs for the following week, a sort of cathartic form of post-fair withdrawal symptom therapy, assuming of course that I was still here.

'Is Annie inside?' I asked, nodding towards the house.

'No,' said Jake, 'she's gone for a walk in the orchards.'

'And is she,' I croaked, 'is she all right?'

'She's fine,' said Jake, 'we'll talk about her later. Right now I'm more interested in sorting out the mess that even just the thought of a certain someone has managed to stir up again.'

'I take it you mean Holly,' I said, looking squarely up at him. 'If that is who you mean then please just say her name. I think there's been more than enough confusion, don't you? And by the way, I know you don't really want to believe me, but I'm certain it was her I heard at the show.'

'Having thought about it,' Jake agreed, 'I think you are probably right. That's exactly the sort of thing she would say.'

I was relieved that Jake agreed with me now, but I just wanted to get on with clarifying the situation.

'OK,' I said, quickly continuing before either of them could stop me again. 'Let's just get this over with. I know that Holly is back in Wynbridge, I know she hates my guts and I also know that she's going around slagging me off. What I don't know is why.'

'Because she's poison,' Harriet muttered darkly.

'But is that really what you think of her, Harriet?' I frowned. 'I kind of got the impression that the two of you were friends. I thought she'd just moved away and that you'd drifted apart.'

'Actually, that isn't the half of it,' she sighed.

'Then you'd better fill me in, hadn't you?'

I sat, poised for her to continue, but it was Jake who finally spoke up.

'As you know, Holly and I used to date,' he said, his words rushed, 'and I'm guessing that you've worked out that we lived for a while down at the cottage.'

'Yes,' I confirmed, 'it had crossed my mind. But why,' I added, the thought only just occurring to me, 'didn't you live in the house? Like you and I do now?'

'Because Annie couldn't stand Holly,' Jake said plainly, 'she never could. Ever since that day she caught her scrumping in the orchards with Harriet, she maintained that Holly was the one responsible for the trouble the girls found themselves in. She tried to warn me off, she was always telling me that the girl was devious and sly, which was exactly what she turned out to be.'

'So why did you fall in love with her then?'

'Do you know,' he said, 'looking back, I have absolutely no idea.'

I wasn't sure if that was a comforting thought or not.

'Everything down at the cottage was fine to begin with,' he carried on. 'I worked on the farm and Holly kept herself out of Annie's way. Then, gradually, she began talking about how much the place was worth and what we could do with the money if Annie decided to sell. Annie had never mentioned leaving the farm and I had no idea where Holly had got these grand ideas from.'

I stole a glance at Harriet who was staring pointedly at the grass.

'In the end it became unbearable. She said she wasn't going to spend the rest of her life chained to this place, that she wanted me to make something of myself like Dan had. She was obsessed with leading the sort of lifestyle I had no interest in at all and spent every waking minute trying to convince me to supply it for her.'

'Sounds to me like she should have been dating your brother if she didn't want to earn it for herself,' I remarked as Harriet shifted uncomfortably in her seat. 'But how did she even know him? I thought Dan never came here.'

'Sometimes he would come up for the day,' Jake explained, 'he'd roll up in his fancy car with gifts from London that no one, except Holly of course, actually wanted. I think she fell in love with the idea of urban penthouse living because of him, and as a result, run-down, ramshackle Skylark Farm fell well and truly out of favour.'

'And where do you come into all this?' I asked Harriet who had so far had little to contribute beyond calling her former friend 'poison'.

'I came to see Jake at the farm one day,' she said, clearing her throat, 'and found Holly in the house going through a pile of Annie's papers. She didn't know I was watching her to begin with but when she started to put some of the documents in a separate file I let her know I was there.'

'And what did she say? What was her defence?'

'She didn't bother to come up with one,' Harriet shrugged. 'She was convinced I wouldn't tell Jake what she was up to.'

'Why?' I frowned. 'Why would she think you'd keep her dirty little secret?'

'Because,' Harriet sighed, 'because she . . .'

Jake reached across the table and grasped Harriet's hand.

'Because,' he explained, 'she was the only person at the time who knew that Harriet was gay and she said that if she said anything to me about the letters, then she'd "out her" in the pub in front of everyone.'

'But that's preposterous!' I gasped.

'Well, that's what she did,' Jake sighed.

'You mean she actually did it?'

Jake nodded.

'I'd gone straight to Jake, of course,' said Harriet. 'What else could I do? I knew Holly had the wherewithal to manipulate her way into getting what she wanted and I was terrified Jake and Annie were in danger of losing the farm. I wasn't ready for everyone to know the details of my private life, but what choice did I have?'

'And what did you do,' I said, turning back to Jake, 'when you discovered what she was up to?'

'I locked her out of the cottage,' he explained, 'locked myself out too and in my temper threw the only set of keys for the place I had in the river.'

'The place is exactly as they left it,' Harriet smiled, 'and no one's seen her since, until now that is . . .' she faltered.

'You mean you didn't even let her back in to pack?' I asked.

'Not a thing,' Jake said smugly. 'All she had was her phone and the clothes she stood up in.'

'And she never put up a fight?' I questioned.

'She didn't dare. Harriet had discovered she had been secretly meeting someone behind my back, hadn't you?' he said turning to Harriet.

'Who?' I asked the pair of them.

'I never found out,' Harriet shrugged. 'She'd left before I got to the bottom of it all.'

'So that was the end of it,' Jake said, shaking his head. 'I told her I'd go straight to the police if she gave me cause and the next thing I heard she'd left for good. I don't know how she managed to fund her move or where she went, but she was out of my life and that was all I cared about.'

'And was that when you came to London?'

'Yes,' said Jake. 'I needed to get away from here for a while. She'd tainted everything I loved with her spiteful behaviour and when I first left, and Dan set me up with the job with Hamilton, I wondered if I'd ever come back. It didn't take long, though. Well, you know that, Amber,' he smiled, 'you soon brought me back to life and before long I was going on about the place again.'

I couldn't help feeling a little cheated. When we started dating I had no idea I was 'bringing him back to life', but we'd never delved into each other's former relationships before, not even serious ones. Was I being a fool, letting the circumstances surrounding his move to the city get to me, or was I right to suddenly feel fearful that I was a rebound relationship and one that he might be prepared to move on from if someone else came along? Was that a natural reaction to what I'd just discovered, or an overreaction?

Suddenly I couldn't resist asking:

'Why didn't you tell me about any of this before?'

'I guess, because it didn't matter. Holly was history, she wasn't important any more. I'm in love with you, Amber, and bringing you here has been all about the future. I didn't want you coming here and comparing what you were doing with what she did.'

'I would never have done that,' I said, 'and besides, there is nothing to compare. She never wanted to work on the farm and that's all I wanted to do from the day I arrived at Skylark. All you've done is made me feel a fool and vulnerable to boot. If I'd known that there was an ex lurking who would object to my being here I could have prepared myself. This is just all so unexpected.'

'But we never thought for one second that she'd come back,' Jake insisted. 'I really believed she had gone for good.'

'Jake never meant to hurt you, Amber,' pleaded Harriet. 'His keeping quiet was more about me than him. I'd been so humiliated that I just wanted to let the whole thing drop, so if you want to blame anyone for not speaking up, then blame me.'

I didn't want to blame anyone but I couldn't help wishing I'd known what I was letting myself in for when I came here. Clearly I was nothing like Holly. She was a manipulative, selfish bully who was out to use Annie, the farm, and even the man she claimed to love, all to suit her own needs; whereas I was looking for a fresh start and a new life with the man I loved just for who he was, not because of what he and his auntie had. No motive, no strings, no hidden intentions.

We didn't analyse the situation any longer, and as the dust began to settle that afternoon, I realised what a relief it was to finally know that everything was out in the open, well, everything other than the contents of those letters from the bank, of course. Obviously they still had to be dealt with, but in the spirit of renewed solidarity I hoped we could tackle those together.

As far as Holly was concerned, if Jake wasn't bothered by her being back in Wynbridge, then I was going to have to accept the situation and let it drift off down the River Wyn and out to the North Sea. It sounded simple enough, but with their former life still preserved in Meadowview Cottage like some macabre mausoleum, I hoped I was going to be able to live up to my seemingly accommodating attitude towards it all.

I waved Harriet off and went to check on the chicks again, sternly telling myself that my current priority was to stand side by side with Jake and Annie and put on a united front. What with a harvest to prepare for and Jessica and Henry's wedding to finalise, there were more exciting times on the horizon for Skylark Farm and I wasn't prepared to let anything take the shine off, or stop me from enjoying my first summer here. 'I'm sorry I didn't tell you about Holly before,' Jake said as we snuggled up in bed that night. 'If I'd thought for even a second that she'd have the cheek to turn up again I would have explained sooner.'

'It doesn't really matter,' I said, stroking his chest. 'To be honest I'm feeling rather smug.'

'Smug?' said Jake. 'What do you mean?' He sounded thoroughly bewildered.

'Well, Annie has never had any qualms about having *me* in the house, has she?'

As soon as I said it my mind flitted back to the unopened letters and I wondered if Jake was thinking the same. Perhaps if she knew what I'd discovered hidden in the dresser she'd think differently.

'No,' he said, 'she hasn't.'

'Jake,' I said, 'about those letters. I wasn't snooping through her stuff.'

I didn't want him thinking I was in any way the same as Holly and therefore I didn't mention that I had been searching for the cottage keys either.

'I know you weren't snooping,' he said, kissing the top of my head, 'and besides you came straight to me. It wasn't like you opened them or sneaked one away.'

'Of course not,' I told him, 'I was just worried. I am still worried. Jake?'

'Mmm?'

'You know we're going to have to deal with them at some point.'

'I know,' he yawned, 'I know, but not now, eh? Let's give it a couple of weeks and see if Annie mentions them.'

I wasn't altogether happy with the idea of letting more time pass, but I had no choice but to agree.

'OK, we won't worry about them for now. Are you very tired?' I asked, running my hand down his chest and under the covers.

'You know the bed squeaks,' he warned.

'I do,' I grinned, 'but the floorboards don't, do they?'

Chapter 23

The next couple of weeks were busy on the farm. Three of the chicks had grown beyond all recognition and, for a while, the smallest, which I had named Tiny T, seemed to be finally catching them up, until one morning I discovered the little bundle lifeless in the corner of one of the nest boxes. The once bright eyes were forever closed and the tiny beak firmly shut.

The blow had been hard to take and although I tried outwardly to tough it out, inside I was devastated. Not even Annie's sensible 'survival of the fittest' speech could rouse me. Privately I buried the little soul beneath the hedge in Annie's garden and marked the spot with a smooth flat stone.

While all this was playing out, at the other end of the yard Blaze was enjoying the new found freedom of the paddock. Kicking up his heels in the warm sunshine he was already

Heidi Swain

testing his mother's patience and everyone agreed it was doing Pip no harm at all to have a taste of her own medicine.

According to Jessica and Harriet, Holly was still in Wynbridge but after the unmitigated success of the May Fair and the fabulous write-ups in the local press I was on cloud nine and, to begin with, barely gave her continued presence a second thought.

'How do you fancy a trip to the pub tonight?' I suggested to Jake a couple of days after I had buried Tiny T. 'It seems like ages since we met up with everyone.'

I was still madly in love with life on the farm, but given what had happened, I didn't think a change of scene would do either of us any harm. Also, as it had been a while since we'd ventured into town I didn't want people thinking that we were hiding away or avoiding Wynbridge just because Holly was still in the area.

I was more than capable of handling myself, and her, for that matter. No, it was actually Jake who seemed reluctant to leave the confines of the farm and face his demons. So far he had managed to head me off every time I mentioned clearing the cottage, asking Annie about the letters from the bank or suggesting a trip out, but he couldn't hold out much longer, could he?

'Oh, I don't know,' he shrugged, rubbing his eyes. 'I'm actually pretty whacked.'

To be fair he did look tired but I wasn't prepared to let him off again. It was time to change tack.

'Fair enough,' I smiled, purposefully checking my purse was in my bag and reaching for the truck keys, 'I'll just have a quick shower, then head off.'

'You're still going then?' he questioned, sounding surprised.

'Yes,' I said, 'you don't mind, do you? I've hardly seen Jess and Harriet since the fair and Henry's going to be there as well,' I wheedled.

'Oh, all right,' he reluctantly gave in, 'I'll come, but not for too long, OK?'

As always on a Friday night the crowd in The Mermaid was filled with an unbridled sense of excitement and optimistic expectation for the weekend to come. Everyone was determined to get their two days of heady freedom off to a flying start.

The second I closed the pub door I spotted Jessica and Harriet pointing wildly towards the end of the bar and, coupled with watching the colour drain from Jake's face, it didn't take me many seconds to scan along the row of bar stools and spot the skinny ex-girlfriend from hell.

I took advantage of the fact that she hadn't yet spotted us and had a long look at her. Physically we were polar opposites: I was dark, she was blonde; I was slim (but only just.

How I had managed to put on weight doing a far more physical job was beyond me), whereas she was thin. And last, but not least, I was beginning to feel increasingly tense whereas, if her shoulders were anything to go by, she looked infuriatingly at ease. I needed to nip this feeling in the bud.

'You go and grab a seat,' I said to Jake, pointing him towards Jessica and Harriet, 'and I'll get the drinks in.'

'Are you sure?' he said, worriedly.

'Absolutely,' I smiled, giving him a little shove.

I squeezed my way through and finally, after some careful manoeuvring, ended up exactly where I'd planned, between Holly and Charlie the bee man.

'Hello, Charlie,' I smiled brightly, 'can I fill that up again for you?'

'Oh hello, Amber,' he smiled back, his round face already ruddy, 'thanks. That would be most appreciated.'

I ordered the drinks from Jim, but it was Evelyn who I was really hoping was going to give me the opportunity to have a bit of fun. I could feel Holly's feline green eyes appraising me but I was determined not to give her the satisfaction of returning her steely gaze. I was just about to head off with my tray when Evelyn came to my aid.

'Hello, stranger!' she laughed. 'Long time, no see. Where have you been hiding yourself?'

'Oh, you know me, Evelyn,' I quipped, 'I like to be with Jake on the farm doing my bit and getting stuck in. This is such a busy time of year and he likes to have me close to hand.'

The twinkle in Evelyn's eye told me she knew exactly what I was up to and that she was more than willing to play along.

'I know,' she nodded, 'and I also know that you're just what that place needs, someone who is prepared to muck in and get their hands dirty.'

'Well,' I sighed, 'I love it there just as much as he does and of course Annie has made me feel so welcome. I'm a lucky girl,' I smiled, 'and I'm looking forward to helping the place go from strength to strength.'

'Good for you,' said Evelyn firmly, 'that's the attitude. I know there's some folk round here, folk that were actually born and bred here, who would rather see the orchards ripped up.' She shook her head at the thought. 'Funny that an incomer such as yourself can see the value of the place, when others can't.'

'Well, you know me, Evelyn,' I said, carefully lifting up the tray, 'stick me in my Boden blouse and patterned wellies and I'm good to go!'

Round One to me, I smiled as I headed over to the others and relayed the conversation. Everyone except Jake was roaring in their seat by the time I'd finished retelling my tale, which needed no fabrication or embellishment to hold them enraptured.

'You shouldn't wind her up,' he mumbled, 'you don't know what she's like.'

'Sly, vindictive, manipulative,' I reeled off, 'shall I go on?'

'I just don't want any aggro,' said Jake, quickly draining his glass. 'I don't want her to have any reason to retaliate, for Harriet's sake as much as ours.'

When I had looked at Harriet she had been laughing along with everyone else but having Jake put me in my place did make me feel rather foolish. I'd had my moment; perhaps it was time to put my claws away. After all, no real good could come from lowering my behaviour to Holly's level, could it?

'So, barbecue at ours next weekend then?' Jessica confirmed as we were beginning to think about making a move later in the evening.

'Yes,' the rest of us chorused.

'I'll do some puddings,' I offered.

'And I'll bring salad and drinks,' Harriet chipped in, 'and how about . . .'

She stopped mid-sentence and we all twisted round in our seats to see what or who had stopped her.

'I saw you were getting ready to go and I just wanted to come and say, well, I don't know what I wanted to say really.'

I had to hand it to her, Little Miss High and Mighty had sheepish and vulnerable down to a tee. Holly stood behind the sofa, wringing her hands together and looking as if she was about to burst into tears.

'Come on,' said Jessica, pulling Henry to his feet, 'time to go.'

'Please don't,' said Holly, 'just give me a minute? Please, there's something I want to say, need to say really,' then added with a look of intense regret, 'should have said ages ago actually.'

Jessica sat back down with a thud and pulled Henry back down along with her.

'I know I have absolutely no right to come over here,' Holly began, her eyes darting around the group, 'and even less to talk to you, Jake, and you, Harriet,' she added softly, 'but I just wanted to say that I'm sorry.'

Harriet harrumphed in disgust and began pulling on her jacket.

'Harriet,' said Holly, 'I really, really mean it. I've been doing a lot of thinking since I've been away and what I did to you, the way I treated you, my oldest friend of all people, was utterly despicable.'

Harriet looked at her, but didn't say anything.

'And you, Jake,' Holly continued, looking down at him, her eyes brimming with tears at precisely the right moment, 'I'm sorry for what I did to you and the farm. I had no right to expect you to change or leave the place. You've always loved being there but I thought that I could make you love me more. I was selfish and deluded and I'm sorry I betrayed you, and Annie.'

I began to wish I could disappear into the sofa as I felt Holly's eyes finally alight on me.

'I know you've moved on now,' she said to Jake while looking at me, 'and Amber, I know you love the farming life and I wish you all the happiness in the world at Skylark Farm. Don't make the same mistakes that I did, will you?'

'I have no intention of making any mistakes,' I told her.

'I don't expect any of you to forgive me,' she smiled, addressing the group again, 'and if I was in your shoes I would have told me to bugger off by now, but I wanted to say that I really am sorry for what I've done and I want you all to know that. And for the record, Amber,' she added, 'I don't know what people have been telling you about what I've been saying, but I think you look very pretty in your Boden blouses and wellies.'

A stunned silence fell as she left us and went back to the bar. I knew without any shadow of a doubt that the voice I'd heard in the loos at the May Fair was Holly's and I was just about to say as much when Harriet spoke up.

'Did that really just happen?'

Her tone was incredulous but there was a smile on her lips that I hadn't expected to see.

'Did she really just come over here and apologise?'

'I think that's the gist of it,' said Henry, equally as shocked.

'Well, I shouldn't get too carried away,' said Jessica briskly, 'I can't imagine for one second that she meant a single word.'

I was relieved to finally hear one voice of reason.

'But you don't know her like we do,' Harriet said, shaking her head, 'does she, Jake?'

Jake said nothing.

'Holly doesn't do apologies, Jessica, not ever and she certainly wouldn't lower herself to come over here and say all that without good reason.'

'Oh, I bet she had good reason all right,' retaliated Jessica defensively.

'I don't know,' said Harriet thoughtfully.

'Oh come on,' said Jessica, again pulling poor Henry to his feet. 'Have you forgotten what she did to you, Harriet? Have you forgotten the way she treated Jake? I know I don't know all the gory details, but surely you can't think that she meant any of that little sob story?'

Harriet shrugged and stood up.

'All I'm saying is that I've never heard her apologise before and of course I haven't forgotten what she did, but what just happened was a bit of a shocker to say the least, wasn't it, Jake?'

'Just a bit,' he said, 'just a bit.'

I couldn't help feeling somewhat panicked by both Jake and Harriet's reaction to this unexpected turn of events and began to wonder if Holly had just played the ultimate master stroke.

'So you do believe her then?' Jessica demanded, the tension cranking up a notch.

'I don't know,' Harriet shrugged. 'Time will tell. I guess.'

Chapter 24

The way Holly managed to worm her way back into the group's affections was pure genius. In fact, there were moments in the weeks that followed where even I was tempted to lower my guard and play into her pristinely manicured hands. However, still convinced deep down that she was as clever and cunning as the fox Annie feared, I privately stood my ground and clung fast to the belief that she had an ulterior motive. However, with everyone else seemingly bewitched, I didn't dare mention my reservations for fear of turning myself into the villain.

The week following the night of her out of character apology was relatively prickle-free but after that I noticed there was an increasingly steady drip, drip of Holly into our lives. She started, predictably enough, with Harriet.

'Hello, Harriet!' I called from my vantage point in Annie's little garden.

'What are you doing up there?' Harriet laughed, her hand flying up to her heart when she spotted me precariously balanced near the top of the ladder.

'Come and see,' I told her as I climbed carefully down. 'I'd appreciate an expert opinion.'

'Not bad,' she nodded as she surveyed my most recent handiwork. 'Actually,' she said, taking a closer look, 'not bad at all.'

'I know it's probably the wrong time of year to be cutting back and tying in roses, but this brute of a thing was completely out of hand and I was sick of catching my sleeves on it every time I came in here. What do you think of the rest?'

'I think you've done a beautiful job,' she said as she looked about her. 'I can't remember the last time it actually looked as good as this. Crikey,' she laughed, pointing at the lawn, 'I'd forgotten there was a path through here.'

The winding brick path through the lawn was just one of the many gems I'd discovered when I'd decided to rescue Annie's little garden from the rampant and unruly clutches of Mother Nature. I'd found the borders enclosing the lawn were crammed full of cottage garden plants. There were hardy geraniums and irises, Alchemilla mollis and old-fashioned highly scented pinks. Amid the general chaos of the crowded yard and outbuildings, it felt like a most welcome oasis of calm.

'What does Annie make of all your hard work?' Harriet asked as I poured us both a glass of refreshing elderflower cordial.

'She loves it!' I admitted. 'She hasn't spent an evening with us in the house since I rearranged the table and chairs and cut the grass and she's been making Jake take photographs of everything! But I have to say, I've enjoyed it just as much as she has. It's been fascinating learning all the names of everything.'

'You've really turned things around here, Amber,' Harriet said generously, 'and I don't just mean in this little garden. I admire you, you know. It can't have been easy.'

'Easier than you think,' I confessed. 'I was more than ready for a change when I moved here.'

My body emitted a little tremor as I remembered the noise and bustle of the city and the seemingly endless commute. Once upon a time it had suited me well, but Skylark Farm was where I felt I genuinely belonged. My heart was well and truly sold on life in the country.

'You all set for tonight?' I asked, keen to forget all about my former existence.

Harriet didn't say anything, but drained her glass and put it on the table.

'Do you want another?' I offered, holding up the bottle.

She nodded and I poured her a refill.

'Actually,' she said, picking up her glass again, 'that's what I wanted to talk to you about.'

'You are still coming, aren't you?' I demanded. 'Don't tell me you're working late again! We've already changed the date once.'

'No,' said Harriet shyly, looking more vulnerable than I'd ever seen her, 'I'm not working. I've got a date.'

'I'm not sure blowing out arrangements with friends for the sake of a date is allowed,' I pouted.

'It's with Rachel,' she said, her expression suddenly as soft as her romantic heart.

'Oh,' I said, 'well, that's completely different.'

'I thought you might say that,' she grinned sheepishly.

'Are you nervous?' I asked, suddenly remembering the anguish that outweighed the optimistic excitement that wove its way around and through the potentially life-changing first date.

'Terrified,' she admitted, turning deathly pale. 'I haven't managed to eat a thing all day.'

'Oh you silly sod,' I laughed, trying to make light of the situation and allay her concerns, 'you'll be fine. It's about time you two got together.'

'I know,' she smiled, looking a little surer, 'you're right, it is, but I still can't quite believe it's going to happen tonight.'

'What did Jessica say?' I asked, keen to hear the whole story. 'I mean, does she want me to take anything extra?'

The second question was an afterthought but quickly added when I realised just how far I was sticking my nose in.

'Actually, I've got the stuff I was supposed to be taking to dinner in the back of my car,' she admitted. 'I was wondering if you wouldn't mind taking it with you.'

'You mean you haven't told her?'

Harriet shook her head.

'Wimp,' I teased. 'You do know she'll be thrilled when you explain why? She knows how much you like Rachel, and besides, she's the one you always talk to about her, isn't she?'

'I know,' said Harriet, running her hands through her hair. 'She is and actually that's just what makes the whole situation even more awkward.'

'What do you mean awkward?' I frowned. 'I was only teasing about breaking off arrangements with friends. You know that, right?'

'Yes,' she said, 'of course.' She was looking more flustered by the second. 'Oh God,' she groaned, 'I wasn't going to say anything.'

'About what?'

'Right,' she said, taking a deep breath, 'don't go mad.'

'OK,' I said, beginning to feel both concerned and suspicious.

'It was Holly who set the whole thing up.'

'*What?*'

'I ran into her in The Cherry Tree and we got chatting. She asked me if I was seeing anyone and I mentioned Rachel.

Next thing I knew, she'd pulled out her phone and was arranging the whole thing. They're distant cousins or something . . .'

Her words trailed off as she took in my stricken expression.

'I see,' I said.

'Do you?'

'Of course.'

'I wasn't going to tell you, but I knew someone would go gossiping that they'd seen us in the café and I didn't want you getting the wrong idea.'

'Harriet,' I said as I gathered up the bottle and glasses, 'it's absolutely nothing to do with me.'

And it wasn't, but that didn't stop me hating the situation. An image of Harriet and Holly sitting in the café with their heads together flashed through my mind and I admit I felt jealous, even though I had absolutely no right to.

'I really think she just wants to make amends,' Harriet continued, 'Holly I mean, but it doesn't make any difference to me, not at all. I still haven't forgotten what she did. Although—'

'Although what?' I snapped, my tone sounding harsher than I meant it to.

'It doesn't matter,' said Harriet, clearly picking up on how I felt about it all.

'No, come on,' I said more gently, 'what were you going to say?'

'Just that sometimes,' Harriet said tentatively, looking everywhere but at me, 'sometimes I can't help wondering if she actually did me a favour when she told everyone about me.'

I felt my mouth fall open in shock.

'You can't possibly be serious.'

'Well, you see,' she shrugged, 'I was really struggling to find a way to tell everyone.'

'Oh please,' I said, making for the garden gate. 'Please don't try to justify what she did to you. I don't think I could stand it.'

Harriet followed me back to the yard.

'I hope you have a good time tonight,' I smiled, trying to squash down my anger and frustration. 'I really do.'

I wasn't going to let Holly come between us. Harriet had been such a supportive friend since I arrived at the farm and there was no way I was going to lose her.

'Thanks,' she said, 'and I hope you guys have a good evening too.'

I leant forward and kissed her on the cheek.

'Call me tomorrow,' I said, juggling the bags of salad and drinks along with our glasses and the cordial. 'I want to hear all the details. Well, almost all the details.'

I watched her back out of the yard, a smile fixed on my face. Holly had given Harriet exactly what she wanted and by my reckoning that meant Round Two had gone to the skinny blonde lurking on the side lines. And, if Harriet was such a pushover, I couldn't help wondering what she'd got up her sleeve to try to win Jake around.

I didn't mention the real reason for Harriet pulling out of the barbecue to either Jake or Annie. I couldn't trust myself not to rant and, to be honest, ever since Jake, wide eyed and with a trace of a smile on his lips, had relayed Holly's whole apology-in-the-pub act to Annie, she herself had kept incredibly quiet. She had sat and listened as Jake retold events and threw in the odd 'well I'll be', and 'you don't say', but beyond that she had remained frustratingly silent. I still couldn't weigh up her feelings about the situation and consequently thought it best to keep my own opinions to myself.

I was canny enough to have worked out that bitching about Holly to either Jake or Harriet, or even displaying the slightest contempt for her, was enough to make *me* look like the bitch. For some reason, the soppy pair seemed hell-bent on giving her a second chance.

Fortunately for my sanity, however, Jessica had firmly, and without a care for how her attitude came across, very definitely plonked herself in my corner.

'You have got to be kidding me!' she burst forth the second I finished telling her the real reason behind why Harriet hadn't come to the barbecue.

It wasn't the fact that she was seeing Rachel that she objected to, rather the way the whole set up had been established.

'Sshh,' I hissed, closing the back door of her and Henry's recently renovated cottage. 'Keep your voice down.'

'But don't you see?'

'Of course I see,' I said soothingly, 'but no one else does, so just keep it down, will you?'

'What have you told Jake?' she demanded.

I didn't get the chance to explain that I hadn't told him anything.

'Come on, Jess!' Henry bellowed through the window. 'Do you want these steaks cooked or cremated? A few plates wouldn't go amiss!'

We sat down to eat in their sunny back garden and eventually talk turned to the absence of the third 'musketeer', as Henry had annoyingly taken to calling us.

'So she's finally bagged herself a date with Rachel,' he smiled, piling coleslaw and salad on to his plate. 'You might actually get some peace now, Jess!'

'Oh I doubt it,' I jumped in before Jessica had a chance to open her mouth.

'Why not?' Henry frowned.

'Well, she's going to want to share all the details with her best friend and confidante, isn't she?'

'I'm not sure I fill that particular role any more,' Jessica muttered darkly.

Henry looked at me across the table and let out a long, slow breath.

'I wonder if Holly had anything to do with it,' Jake suddenly chirped up.

He asked the question and said her name as if it was the most natural word in the world to trip untroubled off his tongue. I laid down my knife and fork and felt my stomach clench and twist in protest.

'What makes you say that?' Henry asked, clearly confused by the mention of her name and blissfully unaware of the potential storm he was about to unleash.

Jake looked up from his plate and realised we were all staring at him. I was appalled to notice that he was blushing slightly.

'Oh, I ran into her a couple of days ago in town,' he said dismissively, 'and she happened to mention that she was back in touch with a few old friends and something about how she was a distant cousin of Rachel's or something to that effect . . .'

'So, when exactly,' I said, choosing my words with as much care and as little contempt as I could muster, 'did you have this little chat?'

I knew I sounded jealous and peevish and completely over the top and, had it been anyone else in Wynbridge, anyone else in the world for that matter, it wouldn't have mattered one jot. But this was Holly we were talking about and it did matter. The fact that Jake hadn't mentioned that he'd run into her hurt like hell.

'Look,' he smiled, trying to placate me, 'it was two seconds. We literally passed one another in the car park. She asked after you actually, Amber.'

'Oh did she?' I spat, before taking a huge mouthful of wine.

'Yes,' he sighed.

I couldn't help thinking how tired he sounded and I guessed he hadn't said anything because he knew exactly how I was going to react to the mere mention of her name.

'She offered to come and help clear out the cottage.'

'What?'

'Well, considering half the stuff in there belongs to her, she said it was the least she could do. I thought you'd be pleased.'

'So why didn't you tell me sooner then?'

'Because it slipped my mind,' Jake smiled. 'Honestly, Amber, don't turn this into something it isn't. How about you come along to help us clear the place as well? At least that way we'll all be doing it together.'

'Oh thank you,' I said, pushing away my barely touched plate of food, 'that'll be a real treat.'

'Well, don't then,' snapped Jake, throwing down his napkin, 'whatever.'

'Oh, I'll be there,' I said vehemently. 'I might not like it, but I'll be there, don't you worry about that.'

Out of the corner of my eye I spotted Jessica and Henry looking uncomfortable. What a fine way to repay their hospitality and what a time to have such a silly row. Suddenly I realised just how ridiculous it all was. Of course I wanted to see the cottage cleared and yes, it probably would be easier with Holly on hand to take her stuff there and then, but the thought of her standing in the loos at the May Fair, bitching about me behind my back, was not something I was going to forget in a hurry.

Chapter 25

Listening to Harriet rave on about the fun she and Rachel were enjoying in the first flush of romance was almost enough to soften my hardened heart against Holly . . . almost.

'I just can't believe how much we have in common,' Harriet said yet again, shaking her head in wonder at the magic of it all, 'and did I tell you that she wants to set up her own nursery as well?'

'Plants, not kids,' I jumped in.

'What?'

'Plants, not kids,' I said again, 'it's what you said the day we met and you were telling me what you wanted to do with your life.'

'Oh I see,' Harriet laughed, regarding me for the briefest second before looking dreamily across the garden and down towards the orchards again. I wasn't sure what she was actually seeing in her befuddled state, but I was pretty sure it wasn't the flowers and trees. 'Can you imagine,' she said with a sigh, 'if we could do something together, if Rachel and I could set up a nursery together?'

'Come on, Miss Daydream,' I said, waving my hand in front of her face and drawing her back to reality, 'let's get the rest of these out of the car. It looks like the heavens are about to open.'

'Right,' said Harriet, sounding marginally more alert, 'of course. Let's put them under cover and I'll explain how to plant them up.'

When I had finally finished renovating and repairing Annie's garden there was little to do beyond cutting the grass and keeping on top of the weeds. Not only did I miss the exercise, but also the sense of achievement that came with the transformation. Consequently, having admired the beautiful seasonal containers created by Monty Don every Friday evening, I asked Harriet to supply me with some summer bedding of my own so I could attempt to put together something similar myself.

She had turned up early that morning, her smile as sunny and bright as the cheerful trays of plants crammed into the back of her van, and furnished me with a quick but competent 'how-to' masterclass.

'What are you going to plant them in?' she asked as we finished unloading.

'I've found a couple of old troughs in the shed,' I told her, 'and a few galvanised buckets, but beyond that I'm not sure.

To be honest I wasn't expecting quite so many plants,' I laughed.

'Well, you want to make an impact, don't you?'

'Definitely,' I nodded.

Yes, putting my stamp on the place felt like even more of a priority now that I knew Holly was going to help clear the cottage. She would be coming to the farm at some point and I wanted to leave her in no doubt that the place was very definitely my turf.

'I tell you what,' Harriet said, biting her lip, 'you want to get up to Wynbridge. There's an auction today. You're bound to find something suitable there and it won't cost the earth.'

'What sort of things do they sell?'

'Anything and everything,' Harriet expanded, 'stuff for the house and garden, small farm machinery and a couple of times a year there's even a livestock sale. I know you're a fan of all that battered vintage stuff in those magazines of yours and the auction is always rammed with bits like that. I don't know why I didn't mention it sooner actually.'

'Oh wow,' I squealed, my excitement mounting, 'that sounds like a perfect idea. I had no idea the town had its own auction, and no,' I chastised, 'I can't believe you didn't mention it sooner either!'

'Well, you'd better get cracking,' she said, tapping her watch, 'it'll be starting in an hour or so.'

'Right,' I said, 'I'll go and get changed and head up there now.'

Harriet slammed shut the back door of the van and climbed into the driver's seat. She was about to turn the key in the ignition and, even though I hated myself for doing it, I couldn't help asking.

'So,' I said, as if it was the most natural question I could possibly ask, 'what does Holly make of your burgeoning relationship with Rachel? As official match-maker I would guess she's feeling pretty pleased with herself.'

Harriet looked at me for a second and I wasn't sure if she was going to answer. Given my previous reaction when the 'H' word came up, I could hardly blame her if she decided to keep quiet.

'To tell you the truth,' she said eventually, 'I've hardly seen her. I had thought she'd be full of herself and pestering me for details and some thanks or recognition. The old Holly certainly would have been, believe me, but I've only seen her for five minutes and that was just as I was leaving to come here.'

'She came to see you?'

'No,' said Harriet, 'she spotted me locking the gate as she drove by and pulled up for a quick chat. She was pleased that Rachel and I had hit it off but she didn't put it down to her match-making skills, as you put it.'

'Oh well,' I said a little begrudgingly, 'maybe she has changed after all.'

'Maybe,' Harriet shrugged. 'Anyway you get yourself to Wynbridge and see what you can find at the auction.' She turned the ignition over and began to pull away. 'And ring me if you want a hand planting up!'

'I will,' I called after her. 'Thanks, Harriet.'

By the time I'd finished my farm chores and driven myself to town I had a job to find a parking space that I felt confident enough to squeeze the farm truck into. Thankfully the threatened rain had held off and the market square was abuzz with more people than I'd ever seen in the whole town. I had hoped to grab a quick coffee and a slice of something delectable from The Cherry Tree Café, but there wasn't a seat to be had, inside or out.

'It's always like this on auction days,' Angela told me as she bustled around me with her order pad and pen. 'If you'd have come an hour ago we could have squeezed you in!'

'No matter,' I shrugged, 'I'll pop back later.'

'Good luck at the auction,' Angela called after me. 'I take it that's where you're heading?'

'Yes,' I called back, as I dodged through the crowd. 'I'll let you know how I get on.'

It didn't take many seconds to work out where the auction was taking place. I simply followed the steady stream of locals heading towards the old town hall, which I had always assumed was locked up and redundant.

Having registered at the desk and collected my numbered bidding card, I had just a few minutes to rush around and look at everything before the viewing ended and the auction began. The time limit turned out to be a definite blessing because I could have spent a small fortune on vintage kitchen paraphernalia for the house, and that was before I'd even considered the garden!

'Seen anything that takes your fancy?' said a voice behind me.

'Hello, Jim,' I smiled, 'you made me jump. How is it possible with your bulk to creep up on someone?'

'I'll have you know I'm very light on my feet,' he chuckled, 'always have been.'

Looking him up and down I decided not to comment further.

'I'm looking for planters for the farm,' I said instead, 'thought it might be nice to spruce the place up a bit for the summer. Harriet has sorted me out with some lovely plants and now I need some pots and hanging baskets to show them off, you know the sort of thing.'

Jim nodded along, looking very pleased with himself.

'Follow me,' he said, 'I've seen just the things. I was thinking about bidding for them myself but Evelyn would go mad, and besides,' he added, rubbing his stubbly chin, 'I don't think we've got the space.'

In the months since my move to the farm every visit to The Mermaid had been a revelation. As the time passed, less and less brickwork and footpath had been visible, and now, heading towards mid-June, the whole front looked to be entirely covered with an explosion of colourful summer bedding. It was Jim's pride and joy, and I knew, from Evelyn telling anyone who stood still long enough to listen, that he spent hours dead-heading and watering.

'Here,' he said in a whisper as he nudged aside a couple of other lots with his size elevens, 'what do you reckon?'

'Oh Jim,' I grinned, 'they're perfect, but I don't think I'll be able to afford them.'

Jim looked at me as if I was talking another language.

'Seriously,' I said, 'these things are highly sought after.'

'Never,' said Jim, looking from me to the two large galvanised and cobweb encrusted dolly tubs that he had discovered and back again. 'I just thought they'd be ideal because of the size of them. Are you sure they're worth something? I remember my great-grandmother did the weekly wash in one of these.'

'You mark my words,' I told him, rifling through the various other pots and baskets, 'I'll try for them, but prepare to be amazed!'

My prediction (courtesy of the hours spent perusing the pages of various rural lifestyle magazines) turned out to be spot on. The higher the price went, the further Jim's jaw dropped and the harder I found it to focus on how much I was bidding and stifle my giggles.

The pair of old wash tubs were indeed the perfect containers to flank the little porch at Skylark Farm and I could easily imagine them in situ, overflowing with colour in the summer, fairy lights at Christmas and tulips and daffodils in the spring.

Locked in a fierce bidding war with another buyer, who was conveniently tucked out of sight behind a pillar, I quickly exceeded my good sense and the price soared higher and higher. Had it not been for Jim plucking at my sleeve and eventually snatching away my bidding card I would probably have ended up having to re-mortgage my flat to pay for them.

'That'll do,' he hissed, hanging on to my card until the sound of the gavel had rung out and the crowd let out a collective and incredulous sigh, clearly disappointed that the fun was over.

'Bugger,' I muttered, when he finally thought it was safe to relinquish my card. 'They were *exactly* what I wanted.'

'Well, I for one am relieved you didn't get them,' said Jim, fanning his flushed face.

'What?' I whispered fiercely. 'You were the one who pointed them out to me in the first place!'

'Exactly,' smiled Jim, 'and if Annie had found out how much you spent on them she would have skinned me alive!'

He was right, of course, but I was still disappointed. I looked around the packed crowd for any sign of who had managed to outbid me. Who, I wondered, looking amongst the faces, had also known that they were on to a good thing? Unable to pick anyone out of the throng I paid for my other few bits and pieces, decided to skip squeezing in at The Cherry Tree and accepted Jim's offer to help me carry my spoils back to the truck.

'You've got a nice little haul there,' he said with a nod towards my motley collection, 'considering what you paid,' he added cheekily.

'Could've been nicer,' I tutted. 'Never mind.'

'Better luck next time, love,' he laughed as he waved me off.

Chapter 26

Back at the farm I'd just finished unloading the truck and was about to make a quick sandwich when a 4x4 I didn't recognise pulled into the yard. I walked over to greet our visitor, wondering where Jake and Annie had got to.

'Can I help you?' I asked as the window slid slowly down. 'Or did you want to see Jake?'

'No, it's all right,' said a familiar voice, 'I was looking for you actually.'

Totally taken aback I automatically smoothed down my shirt and hoped my hair wasn't the usual top-knot tangle it tended to turn into after a morning spent outdoors. Furious with my traitorous response to the appearance of the designer sunglasses and sleek curtain of blonde hair that was Holly's crowning glory, my subsequent question sounded begrudging and probably harsher than she deserved.

'What do you want?' I demanded, quickly lunging for the dogs to stop them jumping up and scratching the paintwork. 'I'm busy.'

'I don't want to keep you,' she said, opening the door a little so I had to take a step back. 'This is just a flying visit.'

Bella and Lily took one look at the slender frame of the farm's former resident, pulled free from my grasp and skulked back towards the house.

'Look,' she said, seeming slightly less sure of herself now her feet were on my turf, 'I know we haven't seen one another since that night in the pub but I meant every word I said. I really am ashamed of the way I treated Jake and Harriet and I'm truly sorry for all the hurt I caused.'

I looked at the ground, not knowing what to say. This wasn't my argument to settle.

'I know I can't undo any of what I did,' she continued, 'but I don't want to carry on living in Wynbridge knowing that this is all everyone is still talking about. I just want to clear the air once and for all. I'll do anything to make amends.'

'I'm sorry, Holly,' I said, finally finding my voice, 'but you really are talking to the wrong person.'

Not that I wanted her talking to Jake, of course, but this whole situation had nothing to do with me. She and Jake and Harriet would have to settle this one for themselves.

'But I'm not though, am I?' she said, her voice beseeching me to understand.

'What do you mean?'

Holly rolled her eyes and allowed herself a small smile.

'Everyone round here knows that Jake is head over heels in love with you, Amber.'

I was relieved to know that she was aware of that and felt a slight blush beginning to bloom.

'And that Annie loves having you here, especially now you're so cleverly returning the old place back to what it once was.'

'So?' I said, determined not to let her well timed praise go to my head.

Holly sighed.

'Look,' she said, 'Jake will never give me so much as the time of day if he thinks you and I don't get on, on top of everything else. Your opinion really counts around here, Amber, and if you and I can be friends then I know he'll be able to see that I've changed.' She shook her head. 'I don't mean to sound so selfish but I miss Harriet and I miss Jake. Not,' she added quickly, 'that I'm interested in interfering in your relationship. I just want everyone to know that I really am sorry and not have to feel on tenterhooks every time I leave the house.'

Given what Jake had said about clearing the cottage with her and the fact that he had acknowledged that she had helped Harriet and Rachel along the path to true love, I guessed he was already feeling pretty forgiving, but I wasn't going to tell Holly that.

'I'll talk to him,' I said eventually.

'Will you?' Holly gasped, grabbing my arm.

'Yes,' I said, annoyed to find myself amused by her reaction.

'Really?'

'Yes,' I said again.

If I hadn't been privy to the horrid ins and outs of the whole debacle I probably would have laughed at the child-like excitement that suddenly transformed Holly's ordinarily composed features.

'I've got a little something for you,' she said in a rush, 'I hope you don't mind.'

'You don't have to give me anything, Holly,' I frowned.

'It's sort of a peace offering,' she said, ignoring my protestations and walking round to the back of her elegant 4x4.

My stomach rolled as I thought how Jessica would react when I relayed this whole scene to her. She'd be furious that I hadn't thrown Holly out of the yard as soon as she set foot on it and I told myself that no matter what she had tucked away in her boot I couldn't possibly accept it.

'When I saw Harriet earlier,' Holly rushed on as she fumbled ineffectually with the door catch, 'she mentioned that you were doing some gardening and I happened to be passing the auction in town earlier,' she struggled on, 'and spotted these.'

With a sudden ping the door sprang open.

'Apparently they're all the rage at the moment. I thought they'd look nice either side of the porch.'

I burst out laughing. I could hardly believe that Holly was the rival bidder tucked around the corner of the pillar in the auction room, but the evidence, stowed carefully away in the boot of her expensive off-roader, was proof enough.

'What's so funny?' she frowned, looking from me to the dolly tubs and back again. 'Aren't these the right things? I thought they were the ones in all the magazines.'

'They are,' I said, trying to compose myself. 'Holly—'

'What?' she pouted, looking crestfallen.

'I was the other bidder!'

'You mean to say I paid all that money because it was you who was bidding against me?'

'Yep,' I nodded.

This was the kind of karma I liked: quick and precise. I couldn't prove to anyone else that Holly had been the one bad mouthing me in the loos at the May Fair, but I knew it, she knew it and apparently so did karma, and knowing how much she'd had to part with to pay her dues almost made it worth binning that Victoria sponge!

'What's the joke?' called Jake as he pulled into the yard looking bewildered.

'I'll let Amber explain,' said Holly, giving me a little nudge as she rolled her eyes.

'Can you help us unload these?' I asked, shaking my head and pointing to the tubs.

'Whatever are they?' asked Jake as he tried to work out how to manhandle them without compromising the flawless paintwork of the 4x4.

'I'll tell you what they are,' said Holly, looking at me and grinning, 'bloody expensive!'

Chapter 27

As predicted by Jim, Holly and myself, the pair of dolly tubs, once cleaned and planted with a tall fuchsia in the centre and a variety of vibrant summer bedding spilling over the edges beneath, did indeed look very pretty flanking the porch of the farmhouse. However, as much as I had coveted them and as much as I loved them, I couldn't shake off the feeling that they were tainted and had come my way with an even higher price tag than the cash one I had been prepared to pay for them.

Since explaining the somewhat dubious details of their arrival to Jessica she had remained sullen and distant and I was pinning all my hopes on the impending wedding plans to pull us back together. It wasn't as if I wanted her lumbered with some major gown crisis or anything, just a little niggle that she would need me to help sort out would do, something that would put me back on her radar and pull me further up her friendship list again.

'Post!' I shouted into the kitchen as I finished emptying the last few drops from the watering can on to the eclectic collection of pots outside the back door.

I flicked through the pile of letters, my eyes lingering longest on yet another addressed to Annie and marked urgent from the bank.

'Jake,' I called up the stairs, 'can you come down?'

Annie was another one who had become increasingly distant during the last couple of weeks and although, like Jessica, she wasn't happy about Holly being back on the scene, I got the distinct impression that there was more behind her brooding than the persistent reappearance of Jake's ex.

'There's another letter from the bank for Annie,' I said, dropping the pile of mail on the table with hers on the top. 'This can't go on, Jake.'

'I know,' he said resignedly, running his hands through his hair and grimacing, 'I know.'

'Would you like me to leave you to it?' I asked, turning back towards the door. 'I've still got Pip and the hens to sort out.'

'Actually,' said Jake, biting his lip, 'I was rather hoping you would be the one to talk to her.'

'Me?'

'If you wouldn't mind, I'm sure she'd open up to you. You've developed such a close bond.'

'But what about you?' I said, my heart already resigned to the fact that I was going to be the one who would have to broach the tricky subject. 'She's your auntie.'

'Please,' said Jake again. 'I'll go and sort out Pip and the hens.'

He looked thoroughly miserable and I knew I had no choice. As daunting as the deed was, I was the one who was going to have to see it through.

'All right,' I sighed, 'but don't blame me if she ends up resenting me for it.'

'She won't,' he said kindly, 'I'm sure of that.'

'You can take this for the eggs,' I said, passing him my beloved basket, 'but please be careful with it.'

I had already finished pouring the tea and slicing Annie her bread and butter to go with her boiled eggs when the creaking floorboards overhead announced her imminent arrival. I gently lifted the two smooth, slightly speckled eggs into the cup she had used since childhood and placed the mail next to her plate where it couldn't be missed.

'Morning, Annie,' I said brightly, determinedly masking my nerves by immersing myself in the comfort of our early morning ritual and chit chat.

'Morning, pet,' she replied, taking her familiar seat at the table. 'No Jake this morning?'

'He'll be along in a minute,' I smiled, 'he wanted to check up on Blaze himself today.'

'And how are you?' said Annie, fixing me with her beady stare. 'You look a bit peaky to me.'

'Oh, I'm all right,' I shrugged, 'a bit tired, but that's no wonder, is it? We've been so busy here these last few weeks, haven't we?'

'Hmm,' she said, clearly not convinced.

'There's some post for you,' I said, nodding at the pile as I spooned sugar into my tea. 'That top one looks important.'

'Is this today's post?' Annie countered. 'I reckon Bob must be on holiday. I'm sure this other fella's skimping on deliveries. I bet he's only calling every other day and that's how we've ended up with all this lot. You know,' she continued, 'I've never known the post to come so early.'

'This one looks like it's from the bank,' I batted back, prodding the pile and feeling ever more resolute that I wouldn't be side-tracked by the intricacies of rural mail delivery rounds. 'Are you going to open it?' I added impatiently. 'It might be important.'

Annie slowly cracked the top off her first egg and eyed me astutely. I fiddled with my toast and honey, suddenly remembering the night I arrived at Skylark Farm and how she had made a mental appraisal of me then too.

'It looks to me,' I buckled, cracking under the pressure of her all-seeing gaze, 'it looks to me,' I said again, 'exactly like the dozen or so I found in the dresser. They hadn't been opened either.'

There, I'd said it and there was no going back.

'Where?' said Annie, banging down her spoon.

She sounded absolutely outraged and I hoped Jake hadn't made a mistake asking me to be the one to broach the thorny subject.

'Here,' I said, ducking into the dresser and pulling out the pile Jake had stuffed back inside weeks before. 'This lot,' I said, adding them to the one that had just arrived.

'Oh those,' said Annie airily. 'They're just circulars, aren't they? I've been saving them up to light the fire with when the weather changes in the autumn.'

'Here,' Annie said, pushing the pile towards Jake, who had finished the early morning chores in record time, 'you do it.'

'I can't imagine it's anything too bad,' he said reassuringly as he slit the first envelope with Annie's father's ancient paper knife. 'If there was anything really wrong Mr Walker, the manager, would have called, surely.'

Annie sniffed but didn't say anything and Jake and I exchanged worried looks.

'I can't believe you know the name of your bank manager,' I said. 'I couldn't tell you who mine is.'

'Mr Walker has looked after us for decades,' said Annie fondly, 'for almost as long as I can remember.'

'From what I know of him,' explained Jake, 'he does

things the old-fashioned way. Personal service counts for a lot as far as he's concerned.'

I nodded but didn't say anything else, just watched as the pile of opened letters steadily grew and his expression became more and more furrowed.

'Well,' I demanded, the second he finished reading the last one, 'what do they say?'

'It isn't that bad, is it, lad?' Annie whispered. She was deathly pale and there was a waver in her voice that I hadn't heard before. 'It can't be. We're keeping our heads above water, aren't we?'

'No,' said Jake uncertainly, 'not quite. According to this, Annie, we're dangerously close to reaching the farm's overdraft limit. I didn't even realise we had an overdraft limit. Why didn't you tell me things were this tight?'

Annie shrugged, looking shame-faced.

'But we manage, don't we?' she said, her bottom lip trembling. 'There's always food on the table.'

'Yes,' said Jake, 'and fuel for the range but very little else. From what I can make out, we're sinking a little deeper every month. It's been a long time since any real income was paid in to balance things up a bit.'

Annie sighed resignedly and wiped the corners of her mouth with her starched napkin.

I couldn't help thinking that had she opened the first letter when it landed on the doormat and shared the contents with

Jake then the whole situation could have been nipped in the bud. She had wasted so much time and the situation was obviously now far worse. However, taking in her forlorn expression I didn't have the heart to say anything and, really, what would have been the point?

'This isn't good,' said Jake, taking hold of her hand. 'The bank is advising us to be aware of the spiralling situation and redress the balance before it becomes irretrievable.'

'What exactly are you saying?' said Annie, narrowing her eyes and paying far more attention now she realised her beloved farm might not have the rosy future she thought.

'What I'm saying,' said Jake with a sigh, 'is that if you really want us to carry on living here, Annie, and keep the orchards going, then we need to find a way to increase our income. Find a way to make this place pay beyond the harvest. The money the apples raise nowadays simply isn't enough to make the future here sustainable. We might not be in desperate trouble just yet but give it even just a couple of months and all that could change.'

'But in my father's day—' Annie began.

'In your father's day, Annie, things were very different. We're going to have to diversify,' Jake said, turning to me. 'Keep the orchards, of course, but find more ways of making money from the farm, and I don't just mean selling a few bunches of flowers and some jars of honey at the farm gate either.'

'No,' said Annie stubbornly, 'I'll not have this place turned into some sort of playground for out of town folk. There are enough farm cafés and kids' play areas springing up on farm-land as it is. What we have here is history, Jake. Orchard farming as it was originally intended. Skylark Farm is an integral part of Fenland farming history and I won't have it lost.'

'All right then,' said Jake, beginning to sound angry, 'we'll just bury our heads in the sand for a bit longer and when the bank comes knocking, which they will, grub out the orchards and sell the land for development. The history you care so much about will be buried under bricks and concrete with no chance of being rescued. The three of us will carry on living in the house, of course, but don't expect to see much of us, Annie, because Amber will have to commute some-where to work and I'll have to find work on another farm. How does that sound? Perhaps we could play farms at the weekend out there in the yard with new houses and roads springing up around us.'

'Jake!' It wasn't my place to interrupt, but I couldn't abide the stricken look on Annie's face a second longer. 'Have a heart.'

'Sorry,' he said, running his hands through his hair, 'sorry.'

'What are we going to do?' whispered Annie. There was a definite wobble in her voice now and it tugged at my heart as I watched her shakily reach up her sleeve for her hankie. 'I thought,' she sobbed, 'I was leaving you a healthy legacy, not a noose. Perhaps we should sell up. Perhaps you should stick me in a home.'

'Now stop that,' I said firmly, 'there'll be no talk of nooses or giving up. Skylark Farm has a lot to offer and potentially a very bright future. I didn't give up everything to move here and see the place fail. We just need to stop panicking, put our heads together and come up with a plan. I bet there's a whole heap of as yet untapped potential that will pull this place into the future without,' I said, looking squarely at Annie, 'compromising its integrity.'

'I really am sorry,' Jake said again, gripping Annie's hand a little tighter. 'Amber's right. We'll come up with something. We'll find a way.'

I was relieved my rousing little speech had pulled my beloved out of his despair but for the moment I couldn't even begin to imagine what we could do to turn around the fortunes of the farm. It was all very well that I'd encouraged Jake to increase the poultry numbers and made the place look pretty with a few plants and pots, but this was serious. There wasn't time to play at being a farmer any more, it was time to step up and really prove my worth.

Chapter 28

I spent the next few days in a perpetual fug. Just when I thought I'd come up with something it slipped away again, and Annie following me about, her eyes filled with hope that she would be there the moment I pulled the rabbit out of the hat, was not helping my creative juices in the slightest.

Jake had asked me not to tell either Harriet or Jessica about the potential problems we were facing, which was a real shame because it would have been the perfect excuse to talk to Jessica, who I still hadn't had the opportunity to talk to since Holly had given me the dolly tubs. And also I was convinced that my friends' wealth of local knowledge would have provided just the inspiration I was lacking, but I could understand his reluctance.

The day he'd opened the letters he'd called his parents and was left with a thumping head and a foul mood because, as always when the farm was discussed, they had trotted out the same 'sell the place' mantra that Dan adhered to. From the sanctuary of their villa in the Algarve I imagined Skylark Farm was as distant a memory to them as the country they had left behind upon retirement to a sunnier clime. The ailing fortune of the farm was simply not their problem.

'We'll find a way,' Jake whispered to me at some ungodly hour of the night, 'won't we?'

'Of course,' I said, giving his back an obligatory but hopefully reassuring rub. 'Of course we will.'

'You said yourself there's bound to be something we can do, didn't you? Some undiscovered potential we can tap into.'

'Absolutely,' I whispered into the darkness, knowing another sleepless night loomed ahead.

Tired of chewing the top of my pencil and staring at a blank sheet of A4, early the next morning I called the dogs and took the three of us off for a walk around the farm to have a proper look at what the place had to offer.

The fields at the furthermost boundary, where the May Fair had been held, hadn't been touched since everything had been packed away, and they wouldn't be until Jessica and Henry's wedding in a few weeks' time. I admit I didn't know much about farming – grazing and the like – but to leave such an expanse of land empty and unused seemed like a waste to me. I made a note to ask Jake to reconsider how the land that was currently sitting idle could be utilised. Pip had a more than adequate paddock for her and Blaze to canter about in, and even the geese (who still terrified me) had a plot which could be reduced if necessary.

Walking around the perimeter of the orchards I admired the apples, which had begun to swell. Even my untrained eye could see the branches were packed, some almost weighed down under the burgeoning weight. Annie's family had always picked, packed and sent the apple harvest away to auction and I knew that selling at the farm gate wasn't really an option, but what if there was some way we could make use of some of the apples on site or even find something to sell alongside them?

My mind flicked back over the pages of one of the magazines I'd been so fond of in the run up to the move and I raced back to the house, desperate to share my idea and the thunderbolt of inspiration which had finally, thankfully, struck.

'What have you got there?' laughed Jake when he came back to the house for lunch.

The table was littered with notes, scraps of paper and magazines open on various pages.

'Sit down,' said Annie, ushering him towards the table. 'She's a clever girl this one,' she chuckled, 'this'll keep you out of mischief, my boy.'

Jake looked at me and grinned and began moving the magazines around.

'Don't move a thing,' I told him, 'and don't start reading anything either. We'll look at all this when I've explained what I'm thinking, but only if you decide it's a good idea, of course.'

'OK,' said Jake, slowly pulling his gaze away from the table and back up to me. 'What exactly have you come up with then, oh wise one?'

'Well,' I said, determined not to rush too far ahead and ruin the whole explanation, 'I went for a walk around the farm with the dogs earlier and a couple of diversification ideas sprang to mind.'

'Just stick to the big one,' said Annie impatiently, 'see if he can guess.'

'I was looking at the hives,' I carried on, ignoring Annie, who was plucking at my sleeve like a child beseeching its mother for ice cream at the end of the school day, 'and I remembered how pleased you were to have them back again. Do you remember?'

'Of course,' said Jake, his confused expression suggesting that I wasn't making a very good job of explaining myself at all. 'But we can't make a significant amount from selling honey, Amber,' he said patiently, 'and besides, the bee man takes most of it.'

'She isn't talking about selling honey, you infuriating boy!' Annie scolded. 'Let her finish.'

'But she said—'

'Never mind,' I said, cutting in before the confusion escalated further.

Secretly I was thrilled with the idea I'd come up with and had no desire to have the revelatory moment ruined because of crossed wires and my inability to explain myself succinctly.

'The point I'm trying to make about the honey,' I said, taking a big breath, 'is that I think you love the project all the more because it is so in tune with the farm and the rural landscape. That little venture, the whole apple trees and bees set up, well, they complement one another, don't they?'

'Definitely,' Jake nodded, 'but I don't see—'

'What else would you say complements apples?' Annie interrupted, narrowing her eyes at her nephew.

I knew she was about to shout out the idea from the rooftops and I willed Jake to reach the logical answer before she had a chance.

'Especially when served up with apple sauce,' she couldn't resist adding.

I watched as a slow smile spread across Jake's face.

'You're talking about rearing pigs here, aren't you?' he smiled at me.

'Hallelujah!' Annie shouted, then collapsed into her chair and picked up one of the magazines as if her work was done for the day.

'Yes,' I grinned, 'but not on a huge scale. According to a couple of magazine features I've read, letting pigs clear up the windfalls in orchards is a traditional farming method which is currently enjoying a bit of a revival.'

Having worked out what had got me so excited Jake began flicking through the pages and picked up the notepad and lists I'd started to make.

'If you choose the right breed and can guarantee the welfare, slaughter and butchery standards are top notch then the pork fetches quite a premium. From what I can work out there's the potential to make a considerable profit,' I went on, 'and if you like the idea and fancy going to have a look at how the system works, I've found a couple of farmers not a million miles from here doing something similar who would be willing to show us around.'

Jake didn't say anything, but carried on scanning through the notes I'd made.

'I've only had time to make some preliminary notes about set up costs and so on,' I said, 'but to be honest, I don't think it would be as much to get off the ground as you might think.'

I stopped then, feeling slightly out of breath and a little worried that I might have jumped the gun. Perhaps I should have mentioned the idea in passing before I got so carried away making phone calls and so on.

'And what about the apples?' Jake asked, his eyes never leaving the page he was reading.

'What about them?'

'Well, haven't you come up with any ideas about how to make them earn their keep while you've been planning all this?'

He threw down my notes and spun round the magazine on the table that was closest to him.

'Organic apple juice and cider!' he laughed.

'And pigs,' I joined in, 'raising pigs and making cider at Skylark Farm. How does that sound to you, Annie?'

'It sounds good to me!' she smiled, raising her teacup in a toast to us both.

'See,' I laughed as Jake came round the table to give me a hug, 'I told you all these magazines would come in handy!'

Never one to rest on his laurels, Jake grasped the two ideas with both hands and between us we had the wheels in motion by the end of the week. The cider venture was definitely happening but only on a very amateur level to begin with. Jake had cobbled together some bits and pieces, including an old garden shredder, in readiness for the harvest and planned to make a few batches for friends and neighbouring farmers to see if it was worth pursuing the idea any further before we invested too much money in production.

The pig keeping idea, however, was to my delight the main focus of securing the farm's future and Jake and I had wasted no time in arranging a visit to one of the farmers featured in my favourite magazine. The farm was in Suffolk and although not all that far we decided to set off early so we could make the most of the day and enjoy some rare time away from the farm.

'Are you sure the chicks are in the run?' Annie said for what felt to my ears like the hundredth time. 'Only I heard that old fox again last night and I'd hate us to lose any more of our girls.'

'Or boys,' said Jake. 'I'm sure one of those chicks is a cockerel.'

'Well, whatever,' said Annie, 'that fox won't be choosy when he comes calling and I don't want to lose a single one of them.'

'Don't worry, Annie,' I reassured her, 'I checked the gate myself and if it makes you feel any better I'll do it again before we go. I've got them all confined to the run today and no fox can get at them in there, no matter how wily!'

'Thank you, my love,' she nodded, 'you're a good girl.'

I checked the gate as promised and Jake packed the truck.

'I wish she wouldn't worry so much,' he said as he nestled our picnic lunch amongst the blankets in the back. 'Sometimes I think our being here doesn't make her feel any safer or give her any comfort at all. I know I can't turn back time but I'd rather hoped our presence here would somehow stop her feeling her age. I want her to feel that she's still safe here, no matter how old she gets.'

'She does feel that way,' I said, climbing in next to him. 'I'm sure she does, but I guess she's got used to at least one of us always being around now. I daresay she isn't used to being on her own any more, and besides, you know how much she fusses over her girls, how much she loves them, especially dear old Patricia. They're like her babies, Jake. It's only natural she's worried if she's heard a fox. Only last week I saw one myself with three cubs scampering about in the far end of Pip's paddock. They're so brazen. Beautiful,' I admitted, 'but brazen.'

'I suppose so,' relented Jake, looking back towards the house. 'Do you think she'll be all right on her own all day?'

'Of course she will,' I laughed. 'Now *you're* worrying! She's just getting old, Jake, there's nothing physically wrong with her.' Seeing the frown on his face I stopped myself and added, 'How about I text Harriet when I can get a signal and ask her to look in on her later so we don't have to worry about rushing back? You know Annie won't thank you for it but would that make you feel better?'

'Yes,' he smiled, turning the key. 'You know, Annie's right about you.'

'What do you mean?' I asked, waving my phone about in the cab in a fruitless search for even just a single bar of signal.

'You are a good girl.'

Chapter 29

As business names go, Jake and I reckoned 'Posh Pigs' was about the worst we could imagine; however, the warm welcome and fabulous set up was second to none. Nestled just inside the gently undulating Suffolk border, the Palmers' farm was a far cry from Skylark, but the land and orchards were a similar size and I could easily imagine emulating what had been created here at the place I now considered home.

'So,' said Billy, the burly Suffolk farmer with hands the size of hams, 'what do you think?'

He leant on the wooden gate he had just closed and surveyed the idyllic world he had made for his friendly Oxford Sandy and Black pigs.

'I love it,' said Jake, also taking in the view. 'I really think we could make this work at our place, don't you agree, Amber?'

'Absolutely,' I nodded, revelling in the thought of the farm as 'our place'. 'I don't see why we can't secure the two empty meadows so the weaners can have the run of them during the spring and summer, then clear up in the orchards in autumn before they go to slaughter. They could even roam in the little woodland area at the far end, assuming, of course, they aren't too destructive.'

'A couple of arks in the field for them to bed down in,' said Jake, a faraway look in his eye, 'and the freedom to potter about filling their bellies with apples.'

'Not all of them, though,' I reminded him, with a nudge. 'You'll want some for the cider, remember?'

'Oh, I like the sound of this,' chuckled Billy, 'I think I might be paying you two a visit before long.'

'Well, you'd be most welcome,' smiled Jake. 'I'd appreciate any advice or ideas you might have.'

'Supply me with cider, lad, and a bit of supper and I'll gladly come along.'

After a final lingering glance at the high speed antics of the latest litter as they pelted around the tree trunks and between their patient mother's legs, Jake and I said our goodbyes, stowed away the pack of plump sausages Billy's wife Sally had insisted we take to sample and set off to find a spot to eat our picnic.

'So, what did you make of it all then?' said Jake as we drove off. 'Do you really think we can make a go of it?'

'Of course we can,' I told him. 'We don't need a breeding system like Billy's, though. We'll keep it simple. Buy the piglets in the spring, fatten them up during the summer ready for slaughter in the autumn and let the land recover over winter before the next ones arrive. We've more than enough room to rotate every year. It's perfect!'

Jake laughed and reached for my hand.

'Bit of a difference to securing tickets for polo matches and the Wimbledon final, isn't it?'

'Just a bit,' I laughed along with him, 'but I wouldn't change it for the world. Not one thing. Although . . .'

'Although what?'

'Well, we might not be able to get too ahead of ourselves just yet.'

'Why not?'

'Jess and Henry's wedding,' I reminded him. 'I can't imagine Jessica would be very happy to have pig arks in the background of her photos!'

'Oh crikey,' smiled Jake, obviously picturing her mutinous expression, 'can you imagine?'

'Unfortunately, yes,' I sniggered.

'Well, not to worry,' said Jake, 'I'm seeing the bank manager with Annie tomorrow. At least now we've got some definite ideas to share with him, and in the weeks leading up to the wedding we can get sourcing and planning ready to welcome the first porkers next spring.'

We found a space and Jake parked alongside the river, which was awash with little tourist boats making their slow and steady way through the meandering Broads.

'That sounds like a good idea to me,' I said, reaching into my bag for my phone to text Harriet, 'and if all goes according to plan, I've got a little something else up my sleeve to keep me occupied as well, assuming you can spare me, that is.'

'Well, we'll have to see about that, won't we?' Jake joked. 'Does this particular venture have the potential to swell the farm coffers?'

'It does.'

'And will it entail you leaving the farm and working elsewhere?'

'It will not,' I giggled.

'OK,' said Jake, rubbing his imaginary beard and thinking hard, 'will Annie approve of what it is you have hidden up your sleeve?'

He inched a little closer and began lightly caressing the inside of my wrist with a view to peeking up aforementioned sleeve for a clue as to what I was suggesting.

'I hope so,' I said, trying to shrug off his caress, 'although I have to warn you there may be the need to speculate before much accumulation can be seen.'

'Right,' he said, edging even closer and kissing my neck with soft and gentle butterfly kisses. 'That's normal procedure in business, I think. I'll see if the bank will bear with us a bit longer. So, are you going to tell me?'

'No,' I said, trying to push him away, 'I am not, and if you don't stop, we're going to have to find somewhere else to eat our lunch.'

'Why?' he said dreamily and continued to blaze a trail towards my cleavage.

'Because there's a woman walking her dog over there,' I murmured, 'and she's beginning to look seriously shocked!'

Without a word Jake drew back, jumped out of the cab and retrieved the picnic basket and blanket from the back seat.

'Afternoon. Lovely day for a picnic, don't you think?' he called to the woman, who tutted and turned tail.

I mulled over my plan as we wove our slow way home through the late afternoon sunshine. It was true that I had come up with a project that I felt was better suited to my skills than helping Jake with the piggy idea, but that didn't mean that I wasn't going to be involved. If anything I was rather looking forward to wandering through the orchards with a bucket of pignuts, leaving a trail like the Pied Piper for the piglets to follow wherever I led them. Well, that was the theory.

No, this particular idea was a little different to the getting-down-and-dirty one I had suggested to Jake, but I also knew it probably wouldn't be as easy to get under way. For a start I needed Annie's blessing and, having seen her initial quick and feisty reaction to the idea of any sort of diversification at the farm, I found myself holding my breath as I decided how best to broach the idea. I decided I would ask her that evening. She was bound to be enthralled by all we had learnt from Mr Palmer and it would be far easier to convince her if she was already buoyed up by the prospect of the Skylark Farm Piggy Plan.

We pulled up at the farm, next to Harriet's work van. I was surprised to see Jessica's car also parked in the yard, but it wasn't until the sound of an approaching ambulance reached our ears that we realised something was wrong. Jake tore out of his seat and raced towards the house, stopping only when he made it to the door and turning as voices reached him from the opposite direction. As if on autopilot I undid my seat belt and followed.

Slumped with her back against the henhouse door was Annie, surrounded by blood and what looked like a clump of chicken feathers.

'It was the fox,' she said breathlessly as Jake and I reached her, 'he came back.'

'Don't try and talk,' said Jessica, pressing what looked like a red towel on the back of Annie's head, 'don't get yourself all worked up again.'

Harriet was looking decidedly queasy.

'Harriet,' said Jessica, her tone firm and commanding, 'go back over to the house and see if you can find some more towels, would you?'

'I'll go with her,' I said, grateful to leave the first aid administration in Jessica's competent hands.

'Has she banged her head?' I asked Harriet as soon as we were out of earshot.

'Scalped it more like,' said Harriet with a shudder. 'When I got here she was just lying there. I tell you, Amber, I thought she was dead.'

'What happened?'

'Search me,' she said, piling towels from the dresser drawer into my arms. 'My guess is she heard the fox in the yard, went out after him and fell.'

'But I locked the gate,' I insisted, a cold dread settling over me at the thought that I was the one responsible for what had happened. 'I locked the henhouse as well. There was no need for her to go out. I even double checked before we left because she said she was worried.'

'Well, he must have got in somehow,' shrugged Harriet. 'Come on. Jess is going to need these.'

The ambulance had arrived and we rushed back over. Jessica, after explaining what had happened, handed Annie over to the paramedics. I noticed her hands were shaking as she stepped back, covered in blood.

'Come over to the house,' said Harriet to her friend, 'and we'll wash your hands. These guys know what they're doing.'

Within minutes the paramedics had assessed the situation, applied a dressing, put a very ashen faced Annie on to a chair and moved her to the ambulance.

'I'll follow on behind,' said Jake as he jumped back into the truck.

'I'll come with you,' I said and pulled open the passenger side door.

'No,' said Jake, turning the engine over, 'you stay here and sort things out. You'll need to check the others and see where the damn fox got in. I'm sure Annie would feel better knowing you were here looking after things. Is that all right, Amber?'

'Of course,' I croaked, my eyes filling with tears. 'I did lock that door, Jake,' I sobbed, horrified to think that he blamed me for what had happened. 'I know I did.'

'I know,' he said, kindly. 'I'll ring you in a while. Jessica and Harriet will stay with you. I'll call you later.'

The three of us searched and searched, we went around and around the perimeter of the hen run looking for signs of forced entry, but there was nothing. With every step I took I knew it was looking more and more likely that the only way in and out was through the door and therefore I had to be the one to blame, but I also knew, without a shadow of a doubt, that I had locked that damn gate.

'At least he only got one,' said Harriet, rubbing my arm sympathetically.

'But why did it have to be Patricia?' I sobbed, noisily blowing my nose on the kitchen roll Jessica passed me. 'Out of all of them, why her? You know how Annie feels about her.'

'I guess she was trying to defend the chicks,' said Jessica, which did nothing to make me feel better.

'I just can't understand how this happened,' I said, shaking my head and pulling on the latch, 'it just doesn't make any sense.'

Chapter 30

Even though I knew I hadn't done anything wrong I was still riddled with guilt and misplaced remorse and dreaded the thought of Jake coming home that night, especially if he brought Annie back with him. How could I possibly face her knowing that, even though she wouldn't say it, she must be blaming me for what had happened? There was no logical explanation for the unthinkable chain of events other than that I hadn't locked the hens up properly.

I waved Jessica and Harriet off having promised to let them know the second I heard anything, grabbed the house keys and called for the dogs to come with me for a walk. I needed to do something, and sitting at the kitchen table, waiting for the phone to ring, wasn't going to help settle my sanity.

It was a perfect summer evening. A gentle breeze lifted the slender branches of the willows on the riverbank and the young rabbits ran wild and unchecked around the periphery of the empty fields. I had set off towards the furthest reaches of the farm with the intention of considering how we could tie the land in with the orchards when the pigs arrived, but my eyes kept being drawn back to those gambolling rabbits. No wonder the fox had come back to the yard for the hens. They must have been far easier pickings than the ballistic bunnies I could see tearing about.

I called to the dogs and walked through the orchard, passed Pip and Blaze who were at the far end of the paddock, and back up to the yard still feeling no calmer.

'Come on then,' I said to Lily, who hadn't left my side, 'let's go and see if Jake's left a message, shall we?'

I looked around, but Bella was nowhere to be seen.

'Bella!' I shouted sharply, my heart picking up the pace.

I'd already lost Annie her prize hen. If anything happened to Bella I might as well go and pack my bags and head straight to Peterborough train station because I couldn't cope with the thought of disappointing her again.

'Bella!' I called, even louder this time.

A distant bark met my eager ears and together Lily and I set off to see what the silly dog was up to. Bella had recently developed a fascination for hedgehogs. She would stand guard over them, barking furiously and prancing about on all fours like a lamb, but I didn't think this was such a prickly scenario because she was too quiet and, when I finally spotted her, too still.

Standing square on with her tail swaying from side to side and her ears pricked forward, she stared pointedly at something under the hedge that she obviously wanted me to investigate. I hoped it wasn't the fox. Rural novice as I still was I had no idea how one would react when cornered and had no intention of finding out first hand.

'What have you found?' I said, gingerly bending down next to Bella, her tail thumping all the harder because I was showing some proper interest in her quarry.

I looked a little closer and spotted what had got her so excited. It was Patricia. Annie's beautiful, clever dog had found her precious, darling hen.

Patricia looked at me and I looked at Patricia. Her ever present suspicious beady stare reminded me of our former battles and it was a tentative hand that reached under the hedge to gently draw her out. I held my breath and waited for the inevitable stabbing peck, but it didn't come. As carefully as I could I manoeuvred her out from her hiding place and drew her close, trying not to look at the blood soaked feathers on her back or think about the possibility of losing her now she had, thanks to Bella, been found more or less in one piece. My heart was brimming with relief and I could have quite easily plonked myself under the hedge and sobbed, but I put my emotions on hold and dealt with the situation, quite literally, in hand.

Lily rushed ahead, leading the way back to the house and Bella trotted along by my side, keen to claim the credit for the treasure she had recovered. In the porch I grabbed the empty cardboard box we kept for parcel deliveries and, having quickly lined it with one of the towels Harriet had found earlier, I gently laid Patricia inside and carried her into the house.

'Kate!' I shouted into the phone, then, remembering the delicate state Patricia was in, I lowered my voice. 'It's Amber, from Skylark Farm. Oh thank goodness you've answered!'

'Whatever's wrong?' asked Kate, sounding worried. 'It isn't Pip, is it, or Blaze?'

'No,' I said shakily, 'it's Patricia, Annie's favourite hen.'

I explained that the fox had almost made a meal of her and about the wound on her back.

'Well,' sighed Kate, 'I don't reckon much for her chances. It'll be the shock that has the potential to do for her rather than the injury from what you've described. You've done the right thing isolating her and putting her in the box. Just keep her somewhere warm and quiet for now, like the pantry, and try not to disturb her if you can help it.'

'OK,' I said, taking a big breath. 'Is there really nothing I can do beyond that?'

'Afraid not,' said Kate, 'but she's a tough old bird. She might pull through yet, although I wouldn't get your hopes up. Give me a call tomorrow if she's still with us and I'll come and have a look at her then.'

She'd hung up before I had a chance to thank her and I was grateful she'd offered to come out. Kate was brisk and a consummate professional and I knew that she was probably thinking it really was a lot of fuss over an old ex-battery hen, but she was also kind hearted and knew how much Patricia meant to Annie. Carefully and as gently as I could I lifted the box, with Patricia nestled calm and sedate inside it, into the pantry and quietly closed the door.

Annie was a tough old bird as well and I was certain that she was going to pull through, but I had no intention of telling her that her pet had been found until I was absolutely sure her feathered friend was going to make it. In my experience false hope was about as helpful as no hope.

Jake came home alone that night. It was almost eight by the time I heard him pull into the yard. I took his dinner out of the warming drawer, assuming he had enough of an appetite to eat it. I know I certainly didn't. My mind alternated between worrying about Annie ensconced in the hospital and Patricia paralysed in the pantry. I couldn't even swallow away the lump in my throat, so there was no hope for cottage pie.

'Well,' I pounced the second Jake opened the back door, 'is she going to be all right?'

'She'll be fine,' he said, wrapping his arms tight around me and kissing the top of my head. 'Or at least she will be, if she stops moaning and lets her consultant and the nurses do their job.'

'As bad as that?'

'As bad as that,' Jake sighed.

Limp with relief I buried my head in his chest and clung to his warm embrace as my tears fell unchecked.

'I did lock that gate,' I said eventually, sniffing inelegantly.

'I know you did,' he said, 'and I know you checked it again when I was packing the truck. I saw you and I told Annie that.'

'And did she believe you?'

'Of course she did.'

Well, that was something but it didn't alter the fact that the crisis had happened.

'So how did the fox get in then?' I said, looking up at him. 'It just doesn't make any sense. Jessica, Harriet and I have checked every inch of that hen run and we've found nothing. Not so much as a nick in the fence anywhere.'

'And the gate was still bolted shut, wasn't it?'

'Yes, yes, it was.'

In all the panic I don't think I'd really taken that fact on board.

'Do you know what?' said Jake, looking down at me and shaking his head. 'If I didn't know any better, I'd say someone deliberately let that hen out.'

'But that's absurd,' I frowned, untangling myself from his arms. 'There was no one here, and besides, who would do that?'

Jake shrugged and went to wash his hands at the sink before sitting down to eat.

'Anyway,' I said, 'talking of *that* hen, you'll never guess who Bella found.'

Chapter 31

Despite my worst nightmares, and believe me, there were a few that night, Patricia was still with us the following morning and if anything I thought she was looking decidedly brighter. She even took a few pecks at the handful of corn I offered her, although whether she was feeling hungry for food or my fingers, I couldn't be sure. Either way I was encouraged by her apparent improvement.

'If it's all right with you,' I told Jake as I quietly closed the pantry door and went to wash my hands, 'I won't come with you to the hospital today, but I've packed a few bits and pieces ready for you to take.'

'But Annie will be expecting you,' Jake frowned. He sounded bemused as he helped himself to more toast. 'She doesn't blame you, Amber. You do know that?' he added, eyeing me astutely.

'I do,' I said, still feeling a little unsure, 'but there's so much to get on with here and remember you've got to go to the bank afterwards so there's no telling how long you might be. I would hate to be away from Patricia for too long, especially now it's beginning to look like there might actually be some hope for her.'

'That,' said Jake, glancing at his watch, 'is actually a very good point. OK,' he finally relented, 'you keep things ticking over here and I'll check up on Annie and go straight on to the bank. But Amber,' he said sternly, 'you are going to have to face her at some point. The nurses won't tolerate her nonsense for long.'

'I know,' I said again, 'and I do want to see her. I just think it's more important to focus on making sure Patricia is really on the mend for when Annie comes home.'

Jake had only been gone a few minutes when the house phone rang.

'So,' said Jessica, 'how's the patient, any more news?'

'Not since last night,' I told her with a sigh, 'so I'm guessing she must be behaving herself.'

Jessica laughed.

'The day Annie starts behaving herself will be the day that we really need to start worrying!'

The line went quiet for a second and I geared myself up to say what I should have done yesterday.

'Jess,' I began, 'I didn't get a chance to say anything yesterday, what with the ambulance and everything.'

'What did you want to say?'

'Thank you, for starters,' I told her. 'Thank you for everything you did for Annie. I dread to think what would have happened if you hadn't turned up when you did.'

I remembered how calm she had been the first time we met, when I had burnt my hand on the kettle handle, but Annie's scalping incident was in a totally different league. I wasn't sure how I would have reacted if I'd arrived at the farm and found her crashed out in the yard.

'It was nothing,' said Jessica dismissively, but I could tell she was smiling. 'You'd have done exactly the same if you'd got there before me.'

I wasn't sure I could have.

'Well, thank you anyway,' I said again. 'It was good to see you, even under such horrid circumstances. I haven't seen anywhere near enough of you lately,' I told her. 'I miss you.'

'Do you?' she asked, sounding surprised. 'I thought you and Harriet had a new best friend to play with now.'

'If you're talking about Holly,' I told her honestly, 'I haven't seen her for ages, and I can't vouch for Harriet, of course, but I haven't heard talk of her at all.'

I couldn't help thinking what a relief it was that things on the Holly front had quietened down. I wasn't sure I could have coped with my paranoia about her being back in Wynbridge on top of everything else that had happened. I suddenly realised that the gift of the dolly tubs along with Holly's adamant confirmation that she no longer had designs on Jake really couldn't have been more fortuitously timed.

'Although,' I added, thinking it was best to be completely open with Jessica, 'that could all change in a few days if Annie agrees to my new plan.'

'Oh!' squealed Jess, ignoring my admission that this idea of mine would mean crossing swords with Holly again. 'What new plan is this then? I'm intrigued. First the May Fair and now this! Come on, spill the beans!'

I could have bitten my tongue off for letting my guard down. Both Jake and Annie had been most insistent that they wanted to keep the farm's current ailing fortunes strictly private and, for the sake of wanting to get back into Jess's good books and tell her the truth, I'd got carried away. Of all the people too! Jess was as sensitive as a springer spaniel's nose in an airport when it came to winkling out secrets.

'Jess,' I said apologetically, 'I'm sorry but I really can't say anything else. However,' I added, hoping that offering her a consolation bone would throw her off the scent for a while, 'I promise that as soon as I can talk about it, you'll be the first to know.'

'Oh, all right,' she said sulkily, 'you promise?'

'I promise.'

'Well, just be warned,' she said, sounding somewhat mollified, 'if it really has got something to do with Holly, then watch your back, front and everything in between because I still don't trust her as far as I can throw her.'

'OK,' I said, 'if what I'm planning ends up throwing us together,' knowing full well that it would, 'then I'll be on my guard.'

I wanted to add that if Jake and Harriet had moved on and that if I could tolerate knowing Holly was around, dolly tubs or no dolly tubs, then perhaps it was time Jessica moved on too, but I didn't. I was so relieved to have my friend back finally that I didn't want to upset the apple cart again.

'So,' I said instead, 'how are the plans for the wedding coming along?'

By the time we had finished discussing the merits of roses versus lilies and Henry's dubious musical entertainment suggestions for the reception, half the morning had gone and I was seriously behind with my chores.

I had just finished obsessively checking on the hens and was heading down to the stable when Holly herself, as sleek as the 4x4 she drove, pulled into the yard. I thanked my lucky stars that she'd turned up after my conversation with Jessica.

'Hello, Holly,' I said politely, ignoring the urge to check my watch, 'have you come to admire your dolly tubs?'

'My what?' she said, with a frown.

'The tubs,' I said again, this time pointing towards the porch. 'Don't they look stunning?'

'Oh, yes,' she said, throwing them a fleeting glance, 'yes, great.'

She had barely noticed the beautiful display and on closer inspection I could see her hands were shaking slightly and she looked tired and pale, nothing at all like her usually cool and composed self.

'Are you all right?' I asked, concerned that she was going to keel over and that, unlike Jessica, I didn't have the first aid skills to aid her recovery. 'Holly?'

'Yes,' she said, 'yes?'

'I asked if you were feeling all right. You look a bit peaky.'

She nodded distractedly and I encouraged her to get to the point.

'So, what can I do for you?'

'I was just wondering how Annie is,' she said, a definite wobble in her voice.

'Oh good grief,' I groaned, 'news really does travel fast around here, doesn't it?'

I hoped the residents of Wynbridge weren't all thinking that the 'wet behind the ears incomer' was responsible for what had happened.

'Did you hear about it in the pub?'

'Something like that,' she said impatiently. 'So, how is she?'

I really couldn't understand Holly's concern. According to what I'd been told, she and Annie barely tolerated one another. However, I told her as much as I knew and she seemed somewhat reassured.

'I was worried,' she said by way of explanation when she realised I was confused by her questioning. 'I might not get on with her, but I did live here after all and I wouldn't want to think she had been badly hurt, or hurt at all for that matter.'

That was fair enough, I guessed, and decided to put her apparently genuine sincerity down to her recently transformed personality. Secretly I had everything crossed that now she had all the details she would head back to town and defend me to the regulars in The Mermaid at least.

'Look, Holly,' I said, when she made no attempt to say anything else or climb back in the driver's seat, but instead stood rooted to the spot looking blank. 'I hope you don't think I'm being rude, but I really need to get on. You're more than welcome to come with me,' I added so she wouldn't think I was trying to get rid of her, 'but I do need to see to Pip and feed the geese.'

I said the last chore with a little shudder, but Holly didn't even flinch at the mention of the geese. Then I remembered that Jake had told me how little she had to do with the actual nuts and bolts of running Skylark Farm and I realised she was probably completely unaware of what a menace they were.

'No, it's OK,' she said, finally retracing her steps to the safety of her plush leather interior. 'I didn't mean to hold you up. I just wanted to check that everything was OK. Bye.'

Leaving a cloud of dust behind her, and me feeling more confused than ever, she blazed a trail back towards the gate and was gone.

'So,' I said when Jake arrived back later that day, 'how's Annie? When's the hospital going to let her home and what did the bank say?'

'What have you done to your hand?' Jake frowned, ignoring my barrage of questions and honing in on my heavily plastered fingers.

'*I* haven't done anything,' I told him sheepishly, 'it was the geese.'

'They pecked you when you fed them?'

'No,' I said, stuffing my hand in my trouser pocket to try to divert his attention.

'What then?' he asked, biting his lip.

I was annoyed to see the trace of amusement dancing in his eyes and felt even more determined not to tell him what had happened. Why should I be the one to furnish him with his daily dose of a good belly laugh? However, if I wanted my questions answered, which of course I did, then I didn't see that I had much choice.

'I filled the feeder first,' I told him, keen to let him know that I had done everything as he had instructed. 'Just like you do,' I added for good measure, 'then, when I had a clear view of the gate, I let them out.'

'Go on,' smiled Jake.

'Oh, all right,' I snapped. 'To cut a rather long, but I daresay hilarious, story short they out-flapped me to the gate and I caught my hand on a sharp piece of wire as I tried to vault over without opening it.'

'Ouch,' said Jake, trying to smother his grin with concern.

'Yes,' I scowled in warning, 'Ouch is one way of putting it.'

I didn't add that as I had touched down on the other side of the gate I'd caught my feet (for once not in their wellies) in the bucket of cold water I'd run for Pip and ended up slipping over and soaking both my feet and my legs.

'Did you clean the cut properly?' Jake asked, now sounding serious.

'Of course,' I nodded, crossing the fingers on my injury-free hand and hoping that the cursory wipe with the kitchen roll was enough to stave off anything nasty.

'Come on then,' he said, 'let's get a drink and I'll fill you in on everything.'

The upshot of Jake's trip to Wynbridge was that Annie was coming home the following day with strict instructions to sit still and behave. The bank thought the Piggy Plan was an excellent idea and had, in theory, even agreed to wait it out for us to make a dent in the overdraft, and approved a small loan to help with the initial set up costs.

I drained my glass of elderflower cordial, feeling relieved that life at the farm was getting back on track. It had been a traumatic and tempestuous couple of days, well, twenty-four hours really, and even though in reality it wasn't as long as it felt, I was pleased we had turned such a positive corner.

Even Patricia seemed almost back to her old self. The wound on her back, now bathed and scrutinised, was more of a graze than a gaping gash and I was pleased I could return her to Annie almost as good as new.

'And what about your idea?' wheedled Jake. 'You still haven't told me what you've got planned.'

'All in good time,' I told him as I refilled our glasses. 'I'll talk to Annie as soon as she's settled and we'll take it from there.'

'You,' said Jake, sliding off his chair and heading towards me on his knees, 'are a tease.'

'No I'm not,' I giggled, squirming in my seat before he'd even reached me. 'I just don't want to get your hopes up in case Annie says it's a no-go.'

'Do you think she might?'

'I don't know,' I said, 'and you can stop fishing for details because I'm not going to tell you anything.'

'Really?' he said as he lightly placed his hands on my knees.

'Really!' I laughed and tried to brush him off.

'Fair enough,' he shrugged, moving closer and pulling me off my chair and into his arms. 'Now,' he said, 'let's see if

287

you'll be more willing to talk about what you want to do tonight, shall we?'

'Tonight?'

'Well, think about it,' he said, wrapping his arms tighter around me, 'Annie is safe and sound in hospital and we have the whole place to ourselves.'

'You didn't mention that last night,' I reminded him.

'Well, I was worried then, wasn't I?' he said, lowering his head to kiss my neck and ears.

'What, about Annie, you mean?' I asked, closing my eyes and savouring every sensation his tender touch aroused.

'Yes,' he said, then added with a wicked grin, 'but tonight I'm feeling deliciously carefree.'

Chapter 32

The old farm truck wasn't designed with passenger comfort in mind and squeezing three into the cab was really out of the question. So, early the next morning, Jake set off alone again, only this time with the promise of returning with Annie. Although I was nervous about seeing her I was pleased she was coming back so soon. The place just didn't seem right without her. I missed her, and although a part of me did feel incredibly guilty about not visiting her, I simply didn't think I could cope with the sight of her in a hospital bed being told what to do (irrespective of whether or not she chose to do it).

I spent much of the morning flitting about the house and Annie's little garden checking everything was shipshape for her return. The bedrooms all had clean linen and vases of fresh flowers and the fridge and pantry were stuffed with enough supplies to see us through a zombie apocalypse. As the time wore on even the dogs seemed to pick up on the atmosphere and it became increasingly difficult to keep Patricia confined to her barracks.

'Not much longer,' I told her soothingly, 'I promise.' She eyed me beadily and I swear I heard her huff.

Finally, just as the clock in the kitchen struck eleven I heard the truck pull up close to the porch.

'Can you give us a hand?' Jake called through the open door.

He sounded flustered and impatient and I braced myself for what was to follow.

'I can manage!' was Annie's testy response. To my ears her voice sounded reedy and thin. 'You stay where you are, Amber.'

I hopped from foot to foot, unsure of what to do. I didn't want to leave Jake to struggle, but I didn't want to upset Annie either. I couldn't imagine she thought there was anything worse in the entire world than being beholden to or needing help from anyone.

After what felt like hours rather than a couple of minutes I heard the truck doors slam shut and a shuffling of feet in the porch.

'Here you are, you stubborn old bugger,' said Jake, his tone softer than his words suggested, 'back where you belong.'

I rushed forward and had my first glimpse of the woman who had changed my life in the space of just a couple of months and tried not to gasp in shock. She had looked ashen when I last saw her, being transferred to the back of the ambulance, but now, despite the fact that her demeanour was the same, she certainly didn't look anything like her old self. I was appalled to discover that she appeared tiny, frail and not at all sure that she could trust her feet to take her where she wanted to go. Her complexion was pale, waxy almost, her eyes dull and the skin on the back of her hands, as I took them in my own, felt paper thin and dry.

'Welcome home,' I croaked, my voice barely making it out of my throat and betraying my vain attempt to sound as if nothing had changed when one further glance at Annie reminded me that so much had. 'We've really missed you.'

Annie nodded but didn't say anything and I felt a wave of heat course through my body and land in my face flushing my neck and cheeks until they burnt. Jake, Jessica and even Harriet had gone out of their way to reassure me that Annie didn't blame me for what had happened, but her silence seemed to be suggesting that was not the case at all.

Slowly and carefully I walked her across the kitchen to her favourite chair next to the range and gradually lowered her into it. I took a step back and only then realised why she hadn't answered. Thick, heavy tears rolled silently down her cheeks and I rushed forward with my handkerchief, desperate to stem the flow.

'Thank you, dear girl,' she said kindly, taking my hand and this time gripping it with the little strength she had. 'I shouldn't be crying. It makes my head thump, but it's such a relief to be home.'

'How is your head?' Jake asked, dumping Annie's few things from the hospital on the table. 'Apart from the throbbing, I mean. The consultant did say it might feel a bit uncomfortable after the journey home, didn't he?'

'It's all right,' said Annie. 'Not really any worse than before. Do you know,' she said, turning her eyes back to me, 'they glued it back together?'

I felt my squeamish stomach roll at the thought.

'Who would have thought it,' she smiled, a twinkle of the old mischief lighting up her periwinkle eyes, 'who would have thought that I'd end up like old Humpty Dumpty?'

'Not quite,' laughed Jake. 'If you remember, all the King's horses and all the King's men couldn't put him back together again, whereas you,' he smiled and kissed Annie's hand, 'are almost as good as new. And talking of eggs, don't you have something for Annie, Amber?'

'Of course!' I said, suddenly remembering. 'Close your eyes and hold out your hands.'

'I hope it's a cup of tea,' said Annie, 'I'm absolutely parched.'

Jake threw me a glance, a concerned frown knitting his brows.

'You only had a cup of tea before we left the hospital,' he said, 'not that I begrudge you another one, of course,' he added.

'Oh, I didn't drink that,' said Annie, 'I haven't had a cup since I left here.'

'What?' said Jake. 'Why ever not?'

'Two reasons,' said Annie in a sing-song voice. 'Firstly it tastes like muck, and secondly, according to the man in the bed next to me they put drugs in it.'

'Drugs?'

'Yes,' she said conspiratorially, 'to keep everyone quiet.'

Jake didn't bother arguing but looked at me, rolled his eyes and reached for the teapot.

'That explains a lot,' he said in a hushed tone.

'What do you mean?' I whispered back.

'The state of her skin and the tears,' he hissed.

I shook my head still not understanding.

'She's dehydrated,' he said. 'You wait, by this time tomorrow, with her system swimming in her body weight of tea, she'll be back to her old self.'

'Well, I hope so,' I said, throwing her a quick glance, 'it will be nice to have the old Annie back.'

'What are you two whispering about?' Annie's voice suddenly boomed out making us both jump.

'There you are,' Jake grinned as if that proved it, 'just the thought of a cup of tea and she's coming back to us! Are you going to fill us in on where you stashed all the cups you didn't drink?'

'Never you mind,' said Annie mysteriously.

'Have you still got your eyes closed?' I asked her, already feeling far better than I had ten minutes ago.

'Yes,' she snapped, 'I'll be asleep at this rate.'

Jake laid an old towel on Annie's lap and I collected Patricia from the pantry whispering sweet nothings into where I guessed her ears were and begging her to be quiet. Seemingly aware of the importance of the occasion she played her part admirably and allowed herself to be transported with the minimum amount of fuss from her box to her mistress's lap.

'There,' I said with a relieved sigh as Annie's hands wrapped around the old bird, who immediately settled contentedly on the towel and readied herself for the fuss and attention that would follow.

Slowly Annie opened her eyes and Patricia closed hers, each revelling in the moment of joyful reunion.

'She was under the hedge,' I explained, a lump the size of a golf ball lodging itself in my throat. 'Bella found her,' I added with a nod to the dogs who, unusually subdued, had settled at Annie's feet awaiting their share of her attention. 'I never left that gate open,' I blurted out before I could check myself. 'When Jake and I left here it was bolted shut. I know it was.'

All morning I'd been telling myself that I wouldn't mention it, that it didn't matter because Jake had told me that Annie already knew, but seeing her so fragile and frail as a result of what had happened had sent my plan out of the window and it was impossible not to say anything.

'I know,' she said, looking right at me. 'I know it wasn't you and I don't want you for one second thinking that I think any different because I don't. But I'll tell you both something,' she said sternly, looking between me and Jake, 'I'm convinced someone opened that gate. They let my girl out and then closed it again and when I remember who it was, there'll be hell to pay.'

'Whatever do you mean?' I gasped. 'Are you saying someone was here?'

'I'm fairly certain of it,' she said, gently shaking her head, 'even though it is all still such a muddle, but it'll come back to me at some point. You mark my words.'

I was terrified by the implication of what Annie was suggesting, but my conviction that the gate had been shut tight when Jake and I left meant that her idea could very well be the only logical explanation.

Chapter 33

Jake's hunch about Annie's hydration was spot on and, as predicted, it wasn't long before she was back to her old self in spirit if not quite in body. We had been taking things slowly, too slowly according to Annie, but her head was healing beautifully so it was worth putting up with her impatience and moaning. Just getting up and down the stairs and in and out of the garden took it out of her physically, but her mind and quick wit were both as sharp as ever, and although I was sorry that she still couldn't get about as quickly or as independently as she liked, I was grateful for the ample opportunity it gave us to sit together and chat.

'You know,' she said to me one evening as I helped her into the bath, 'I could get used to all this pampering.'

'Yes,' I said, arranging the bath pillow for her to rest her head on, 'it has come to my attention that you are rather coming round to the idea.'

We looked at one another and smiled.

'You're a good girl,' she said, 'I don't know what I would have done without you these last few days,'

'And Jake,' I added, not wanting to hog all the limelight.

'Of course,' she said, 'but I can't imagine he'd be so keen to wash my back. No, I mean it, Amber, if it wasn't for your willingness to help out then I'd have been trundled off to a home somewhere by now.' She shuddered at the thought. 'And once they get you in one of those places there's only one way out.'

'Well,' I said, keen to change the subject to something more cheerful, 'we need you here, don't we? There's so much going on what with the Piggy Plan to organise and Jess and Henry's wedding to prepare for that we need the whole Skylark team fighting fit. Everyone here has to pull their weight,' I smiled, mimicking Annie's own mantra.

'Cheek!' she laughed. 'Are you warming my towel?'

'Yes,' I said, 'of course. I haven't forgotten yet, have I?'

'No,' said Annie, looking serious again, 'as busy as you are, you don't forget a thing whereas I'm struggling to remember lots of things right now.'

'Be patient with yourself,' I told her. 'The consultant said it will all come back, but pushing yourself to remember won't actually make any difference, will it?'

'Well, there is one thing I remember,' she said.

'Oh,' I said, wondering if the potential mystery visitor was about to be unmasked. 'What's that?'

'Jake told me,' she began, 'when he was explaining how the Piggy Plan was coming along, that you had had an idea. He said that you told him you'd thought of another way to make the farm pay, but I haven't heard mention of it since. I am right, aren't I?'

'Yes, you are,' I said, feeling a little disappointed but wondering if now was the moment to broach the subject nonetheless. 'I have thought of something but what with everything else that's been going on I've kind of put it on the back burner.'

'Well, come on,' said Annie impatiently, 'out with it. Only top this water up first, would you? It's getting cool.'

Once the bath water was back up to a more comfortable temperature Annie again fixed me with a stare, not dissimilar, I realised, to the one favoured by her prized hen. Patricia, having decided she ruled the kitchen, the dogs and, if she could get away with it, both Jake and me, had been hastily reunited with the chicks and Mabel and Martha in the henhouse. She was still sulky about the demotion in her living quarters but slowly settling back to life as an ex-battery hen rather than a token human.

'So,' said Annie, 'what have you been thinking about?'

I took a deep breath and braced myself for the potential rejection.

'I've been thinking about Meadowview Cottage.'

'Huh,' huffed Annie.

'And what a waste it is, just sitting there locked up going to wrack and ruin.'

'You and me both,' she said bitterly.

Well, that wasn't the response I was expecting but then I hadn't delivered the main part of my plan yet, had I?

'I told Jake months ago that the place needed sorting,' tutted Annie. 'It isn't right to have it sitting there like some sort of macabre time capsule. It hangs over us all like a shrine to a time that should be forgotten. I can't bear to go anywhere near it.'

I hadn't thought of it like that. I hadn't thought about the possibility that Jake actually wanted it all kept as it was. It suddenly dawned on me that it might be a precious reminder of his relationship with Holly, before everything went wrong. I'd always assumed it had been left because he'd thrown the key in the river and then moved to London, but was that the real reason behind his reluctance to deal with it? It was madness that he had started a relationship with me and not cleared it out before he asked me to move here, and whatever sort of fool was I just to accept the situation and not demand that he got it sorted?

'So you want it emptied as well then?' Annie said. 'I'm not surprised. It can't be nice having his life with someone else set up down there.'

'No,' I said, a definite wobble in my voice, 'now you mention it, it isn't.'

'You weren't thinking of moving in there with Jake yourself, were you? I can't see how that would make us any money. If anything it would cost us to be running two homes, but,' she added with a sigh, 'I understand if you want your privacy. It can't be easy being stuck here with me.'

'No,' I said quickly, trying to dismiss all thoughts of the life Jake and Holly had led down at the cottage, 'no, that's not what I had in mind at all.'

I couldn't possibly think of living there myself knowing that the place was already riddled with memories of another relationship, no matter how sour it had turned.

'What then?'

'I was thinking about redecorating it, if it needed it, giving it a bit of a makeover and setting it up as a holiday let.'

Annie opened her mouth to say something but I carried on talking, pretending I hadn't noticed.

'I know you don't like the idea of people using the countryside like some gigantic playground, but the cottage and the setting are so pretty that I think you could easily earn more from it than if you were to put a tenant in it. Also, tourists are just coming round to the idea of what the Fens have to offer, so I think the timing would be perfect. It isn't fair to the beautiful Fenland landscape to keep it under wraps and not spread the joy. We could at least give it a try for a year and see what it brings in.'

I reached for Annie's towel. The water must have cooled again and I didn't want her catching a chill on top of every-thing else. She let me help her out of the bath and sat on the toilet seat while I dried her feet and legs. We went through the whole routine without talking and I smiled to myself thinking how well we worked together. We could have been doing this for years rather than just a few days.

'I think it sounds like a very good idea,' she said at last as I carefully slipped her nightdress over her head.

'Do you?' I gasped, tangling her arms in the sleeves. 'Do you really? I thought you'd hate it.'

'In some ways I do,' she admitted, pulling herself free, 'but I know it's time for a change and the cottage is private enough not to impact on the farm. I think I've reached the point where I would do anything to save this place and be able to pass it on to you and Jake. But I want you to be in charge of this idea, Amber. You came up with it and I know you're more than capable of making it work. You leave the pigs to Jake and focus on bringing Meadowview Cottage back to life.'

Had Annie really said she wanted to pass Skylark Farm on to me as well as Jake? I flushed at the thought of living my life here forever and taking the place on as Jake's partner in both business and life, rather than the role I had now as someone who was just trying it on to see how it fitted. Personally I already knew how it fitted – like a handmade glove, and the prospect of wearing it forever thrilled me deeply.

'I suppose you'll have to have *her* here when you empty the place,' Annie said with a disgusted sniff, 'what with so much of it belonging to her, but as you're all friends now I suppose it won't be quite so bad.'

'I wouldn't go quite that far,' I said, tying Annie's dressing gown and hanging her towel over the heated rail, 'but yes, Holly will help clear the place. She's already offered actually.'

I couldn't help thinking of Jake and his apparent reluctance to sort the cottage out whereas Holly had already offered to get it done. Well, Annie had assigned me project manager of the cottage's transformation, so he was just going to have get on with it whether he liked it or not.

Chapter 34

When we finally got down to it, Jake didn't seem upset by the thought of emptying Meadowview Cottage at all. In fact, I was relieved to realise, he seemed rather keen on the idea. I gave myself a stern talking to as I watched him scroll through his phone for Holly's mobile number and tried not to dwell on why he might have it.

'Here it is,' he said eventually, 'and in case you were wondering, it's a new number she asked Harriet to pass on so I could get in touch when we got round to emptying the cottage.'

I felt my face flush, embarrassed that my suspicious train of thought was so transparent.

'I still can't believe Annie's agreed to the holiday let idea,' he went on, shaking his head and pulling me into his arms. 'You've got everyone wrapped around your little finger, haven't you?'

'I wouldn't say that,' I told him, deftly relieving him of his phone so I could transfer Holly's number into my own, 'but you've got yourself some serious competition now.'

'What do you mean?' he frowned.

'Piggies versus mini-breaks,' I smiled up at him. 'Who do you reckon will make the most profit by the end of next year?'

'That will probably depend on how much money you spend doing the place up, won't it?' he laughed, nodding at the piles of magazines I had spread across the table.

I didn't tell him the magazines were purely for inspiration and that I was planning to make full use of the Wynbridge auction and various online bargain sites when it came to furnishing the place and making it look the part. If he thought he'd won the financial challenge before we'd even started then that was fine by me. I was already looking forward to presenting him with a healthy bottom line in a few months' time.

'Right,' I said, kissing him quickly and pulling myself free, 'let's get this project up and running, shall we? I suggest a trip to The Mermaid to see Holly, and then we can meet up with Harriet, Jess and Henry afterwards. How does that sound?'

'Do we really have to see her?' he groaned, sounding more like a temper throwing toddler than a fully grown man.

'Yes,' I said, waving my phone in front of his face, 'you might have a number for her but that doesn't mean we can get a message to her, does it? You know as well as I do that the signal here is rubbish.'

'So use the landline.'

'Look,' I said, sounding increasingly like the mother of the aforementioned toddler rather than the life partner, 'we're going to the pub, she'll be there, we'll set a date, end of.'

'But what about Annie?'

'Annie will be fine,' said the lady herself as she made her slow way from the porch to her chair. 'I've been telling Amber all week to arrange a night out for the pair of you. You haven't left the farm since I came home from hospital and it's high time you did.'

'What do you think?' I said to Jake, batting my lashes. 'It's been ages since we've seen everyone.'

'Oh, go on then,' he relented, 'but only if you promise to behave yourself, Annie.'

'That'll be the day, dear boy,' she laughed mischievously, 'that'll be the day!'

I couldn't wait to see everyone again and have a good catch up. I was even looking forward to seeing Holly, much to Jake's bemusement.

'You must be crazy,' he laughed when I told him as we set off to town, 'not only are you the most understanding girl-friend in the world, you're also the maddest!'

Maddest I could appreciate, but I wasn't so sure what he meant about the understanding part.

'What do you mean?' I quizzed.

'Well, this whole Holly scenario,' he said, his eyes focused on the wet road ahead, 'it wasn't until Annie and I were talking about your plans for the cottage that it really sunk in about how it must all look to you, me keeping everything exactly as we left it, I mean.'

I shrugged, but didn't say anything.

'Annie said I'm lucky you've put up with it for all this time, but to be honest I hadn't even thought about it like that. I'm sorry if it's been upsetting you, Amber. The only reason it's still all there is because I'm too lazy to break in and sort it out. It's not as if I've been sneaking off and sitting amongst it all crying over the past, is it?'

I know it was silly, but it was a relief to hear him say it.

'So,' I sighed theatrically, making light of the situation now I knew the truth behind it, 'you aren't secretly hoping that you and Holly are going to get back together and pick up where you left off then? You aren't planning to send me back to London and carry on living there again?'

'No! Christ no!' Jake shouted, swerving a little as he twisted round to look at me. 'Oh bloody hell, Amber! Is that what you've been thinking?'

'No,' I said, laughing at his reaction, 'of course not, but it was worth saying it just to see your face. Now, keep your eyes on the road, will you?'

'Oh you sod,' he breathed, clutching his chest and puffing out his cheeks until his face returned to its normal healthy colour. 'So tell me, why exactly are you looking forward to seeing Holly?'

'Well, for a couple of reasons, I guess,' I told him. 'Firstly, like I already explained, so we can set a date to get the cottage cleared. I'm hoping to have it emptied, decorated and furnished by the time the apples are ready to harvest.'

'And I'm sure you will,' Jake smiled. 'I know how quickly things happen when you set your heart on them. Come October we'll be toasting your success with a flagon of Skylark cider!'

'Oh,' I said cheerfully, 'I like the sound of that.'

'And what's the other reason?'

'I want to check she's OK,' I explained. 'She turned up the morning after Annie's accident looking decidedly peaky and sounding, well, a little odd actually.'

'You never mentioned it before,' said Jake. 'What do you mean "odd"?'

'I don't know,' I shrugged, 'she just wasn't her usual composed self.'

Holly's appearance that morning had been playing on my mind but I hadn't mentioned it to either Jake or Annie. There was just something about the entire visit that didn't sit right with me but I couldn't put my finger on exactly what it was.

'And,' I said, picking up my phone and scrolling through the photo album, 'I want to show her how good the dolly tubs look. I suppose it's my way of saying no hard feelings and moving on from the May Fair fiasco and I couldn't just send them to her mobile because until a minute ago I didn't know we had her number, and anyway the damn signal is too inconsistent! You know what, I'm seriously thinking of joining one of those militant "Wi-Fi for rural communities" action groups!'

As it was raining so hard Jake dropped me at the door of The Mermaid and went off to find a parking space in the market square. The pub was fairly quiet for once and I spotted Holly, poker straight on a bar stool, right away. She waved when she caught sight of me and I made my way over thinking she actually looked far more composed than the last time I saw her.

'What a night!' I laughed, addressing both her and Jim as I peeled off my coat and sprayed the pair of them with droplets of ice cold rain water. 'Sorry,' I said, 'I was only in it for a few seconds and look at the state of me. Poor Jake's gone to find a space. He'll be soaked right through by the time he gets here.'

'In that case,' said Holly, 'why don't we get the drinks in and bag the sofa by the fire? I had thought it was ridiculous seeing you'd lit it in June, Jim, but now,' she said, giving a little shudder, 'I'm rather grateful for it.'

We ordered and paid for our drinks and I followed her to the sofa, taking in her skinny frame from behind. If she gained a few pounds she probably wouldn't feel the cold was the first thought that sprang to mind, but in honour of good-will and getting our relationship off to an amicable start I let it drift away without giving it a voice, and gratefully threw myself on the sofa in the cosiest nook the pub had to offer.

We had just finished admiring the photos of the dolly tubs when Jake came bursting through the door. His hair was plastered to his head and his shirt clung to him in all the right places. I couldn't hold back the little sigh that escaped my lips. He looked so hot that I didn't really want to dry him off next to the fire, but a quick glance at Holly who, given her glazed expression, was obviously thinking exactly the same thing, hastily changed my mind. I tucked my phone back in my pocket and reminded myself that perhaps I shouldn't let my guard down too soon.

'Here, lad,' shouted Evelyn from behind the bar as she tossed him a towel, 'dry yourself off with this, we don't want all the female customers overheating, do we?'

'Thanks, Evelyn,' he smiled sheepishly, rubbing his hair until it stuck up in all directions.

'Jake,' called Holly, waving her beautifully manicured hand, 'over here!'

He walked towards us, self-consciously peeling his shirt away from his tantalisingly toned torso.

'Here,' said Holly as she patted the seat next to her, 'come and dry off next to the fire.'

'Budge up,' he said, flicking me lightly with the towel, 'I want to get warm.'

I couldn't be sure whether he hadn't heard Holly or whether he'd chosen to ignore her, but either way she looked rather glum and I began to wonder if she really was trying to win him back as Jessica had suggested to me on more than one occasion.

'So,' she said, pushing Jake's pint across the table and recovering in less than a second, 'what can I do for you two lovely folk?'

As the conversation continued I gave myself a little shake and again dismissed Jessica's suspicions. Holly was paying me just as much attention as she was Jake, more in fact, judging by the eye contact and I really couldn't imagine she'd be so brazen as to try to flirt with him in front of me. As far as this situation was concerned I needed to get some perspective. My mind flitted back to the dolly tubs again and the heart-rending apology she had made to everyone in the pub before that.

'We need to ask a favour,' Jake explained. 'Amber has come up with the most amazing plan but we need your help to get it off the ground.'

In an instant I zoned back in to what was being said. Strictly speaking we didn't really need her help at all. If we wanted to we could just dump her stuff in the cottage garden and let her sort it out from there, but we weren't the type of people who would do that, I reminded myself, hoping that Jake wasn't going to reveal any more details about what I'd come up with for the place.

'Do you remember,' he continued after taking a long pull of his pint, 'that when we chatted before you said you'd come and help clear the cottage?'

'Yes,' said Holly, 'of course.'

I couldn't be sure, because I didn't know her well enough, but to me she looked a little crestfallen by the recollection.

'Well,' Jake carried on oblivious, 'if you're still up for it we want to get it done, don't we, Amber?'

'Yes,' I said, 'and the sooner the better if that's OK with you?'

'Absolutely,' smiled Holly, the disappointment or whatever it was now banished, 'just say the day and I'll be there. To be honest I was hoping you were going to ask soon. I'm moving into a flat in town and I could do with some more stuff to make it look homely. I didn't want to buy anything until I'd checked out what I still had in "the cottage that time forgot".'

Jake didn't say anything and I felt surprisingly awkward hearing her talk about her possessions still being at Skylark Farm, especially now the place was my turf.

'So you're definitely staying in Wynbridge then?' I asked after taking a sip of wine. 'I kind of got the impression that you didn't like it much round here. I had you down as an urbanite.'

'Well, you know what they say,' shrugged Holly, 'a change is as good as a rest and actually my change of heart is mostly down to you, Amber.'

'It is?'

'Yes,' she laughed, 'you coming here and loving it all has kind of made me see the place with fresh eyes.'

'Oh great,' I smiled, thinking it was anything but, 'that's brilliant. What are you planning to do for work?'

'Well, Dad has his own estate agency and he's been talking about setting up some sort of holiday let business to run alongside it. I'm hopefully going to be spearheading that eventually, when I've learnt the ropes a bit, that is.'

I could feel Jake all aquiver next to me.

'Well, that's wonderful, isn't it, Amber?'

'Yes,' I said, raising my eyebrows so high they almost disappeared into my hairline and hoping he'd take the hint.

'Excellent in fact,' he ploughed on, 'as Amber's plan is to get Meadowview Cottage up and running as a holiday home. It could be your first month's commission, Holly!'

He sounded so pleased with himself, and Holly, her eyes darting between the two of us, looked equally ecstatic.

Neither of them noticed the thunderous look which crossed my face.

'That's a fantastic idea,' said Holly, clapping her hands together. 'Let me grab my diary and we'll set a date to clear the cottage right now!'

I bit my lip and kept my mouth shut. I had no intention of earning any commission for her, or anyone else for that matter. Jake didn't know it but I'd already made tentative plans to set up a website and Twitter account and was arranging to do all the sales, marketing, promotion and bookings myself. This was one ship I was more than happy to sail alone!

Chapter 35

With the following Monday pencilled in as 'clear out cottage day' and our glasses drained I was kind of hoping that Holly would take the hint and leave us to it. I really wanted a few minutes before the rest of the gang arrived in which to bend Jake's ear about 'operation blabbermouth' in private. Unfortunately, however, she looked installed for the duration and I had to resort to dragging him to the quietest end of the bar on the pretence of ordering another round.

'What a bit of luck!' he beamed, his chest puffed out and his eyes shining.

Clearly he was delighted with the unexpected course the plan had lurched off on. I waited, drumming my fingers on the bar, while he ordered drinks for everyone.

'What if they don't all turn up?' I hissed, pointing at Evelyn's busy back as she bustled about filling glasses.

'What?'

'You're going to be lumbered with all these drinks if they don't show. What a ridiculous waste of money!' I pouted.

'What's with the face?' Jake frowned, finally realising something was amiss with my usually sunny outlook. 'Look,' he said, pointing to the door, 'everyone's here now. Stop worrying.'

I spun round to see Harriet and the pretty girl I remembered from the May Fair as Rachel exchanging hugs with Holly, while Jessica dumped herself down on the opposite sofa and Henry loitered between them all clearly not knowing what to do.

'Oh great,' I said, throwing up my hands in resignation, 'that's all we need, pistols at dawn between Holly and Jess. This wasn't quite what I had in mind when I suggested we spent the evening with friends.'

Jake paid for the loaded tray of drinks and gingerly picked it up.

'I thought this was what you wanted,' he said as he began to weave his wobbly way back to the sofas. 'As I recall, Amber, this was all your idea in the first place.'

'Yes, well,' I hissed behind him, 'even the simplest ideas have a way of getting out of hand, don't they?'

'What?'

'Nothing.'

Jake slowly turned to look at me, the glasses slipping a little on the tray as he did so.

'Have I done something wrong?' he frowned. 'I thought you'd be over the moon about Holly sorting out the bookings for the cottage.'

'*I* was going to sort out the bookings,' I snapped, unable to keep it to myself a second longer. 'I'm already making plans to set up a website and everything. I've no intention of paying someone else to do a job I'm more than qualified for. This project is supposed to be about increasing revenue from the farm and clearing the overdraft, remember?'

'But surely it'll be better to pay a professional and get the job done well,' said Jake in a low voice, 'someone who knows a bit about the business.'

'Knows a bit about the business?' I seethed. 'Tell me you aren't serious. I don't believe Holly's ever done a day's work in her life let alone specialised in anything!'

Other than making trouble, I thought, but I kept that particularly mean-spirited observation to myself.

'And anyway,' I added, in defiance of Jake's crackpot idea, 'Annie put me in charge of Meadowview Cottage, so I'll be the one doing the hiring and firing and I'm more than capable of doing a professional job myself, thank you very much.'

'But I've already said she can do it now,' he said. 'She'll be upset.'

'And that's my problem why exactly?'

Perhaps it was my problem if my boyfriend was so worried about upsetting his ex-girlfriend.

'Because I want us all to get along,' he said, looking even more confused than before.

He didn't really look as if he knew what had hit him and I walked straight over to the table before he could put both feet even further in his mouth. Unfortunately the atmosphere around the fire felt more highly charged than that between me and Jake.

Apparently unaware of the combustible tension, however, Jake handed round the drinks and Harriet was just about to introduce me properly to Rachel when Jessica piped up.

'I understand congratulations are in order,' she said, raising her glass as her eyes flashed around the group.

Henry, brave man, put a steadying hand on her thigh, but she quickly brushed him aside.

'As I understand it,' she continued, addressing me, 'you and Holly are going into the holiday home business, Amber.'

I looked between her and Holly who shrugged her shoulders and mouthed 'sorry', her expression a picture of innocence, but really it wasn't her fault, was it? It was Jake who had let the cat out of the bag. Oh how I would have liked to give him a flogging, and not in the kinky way I'd been imagining earlier when he walked in looking all Mr Darcy in his wet shirt.

'I take it,' Jess went on excruciatingly, 'that this is the big idea, the grand plan that you were promising to share the details of?'

I was devastated that she sounded so upset. When I'd promised her that she'd be the first to know I'd really meant it.

'Yes,' I nodded, my voice barely more than a strangled croak.

'Sorry?'

'Yes,' I said again, a little louder this time.

'Well, I wish you the very best of luck,' she smiled, raising her glass to her lips and downing the entire contents in one, 'you're certainly going to need it!'

No, this was definitely not how I imagined the evening would turn out. I perched myself uncomfortably on a stool dragged over from the bar and we all sat in silence alternately fiddling with our glasses and staring between the carpet and the fire. Eventually, when I couldn't bear it any longer, I struck up a conversation with Harriet and Rachel who, despite the chilly atmosphere, seemed to have plenty of heat between them.

Risking a quick glance at Jessica, now wedged between Jake and Henry, I could see she still had a face that could curdle milk and Holly, dainty and demure next to Rachel, seemed to be taking forever to finish her glass of sparkling water.

'Well,' she said after a while, 'as much as I'd love to stay and chat I've got a date, and besides,' she smiled, looking round our dejected little gathering and adding, I hoped, to try to ease the tension rather than to get a rise, 'I don't think I can keep pace with you lot.'

She stood up and I quickly followed her to the door, keen to make sure she was really leaving.

'So, we'll see you next week then,' I said. 'Monday we decided, didn't we?'

'Yes,' she said, 'around ten. Oh, and Jessica!' she called over her shoulder.

'What?' came the gruff response from the sofa.

'It wasn't Amber who told me about the plans for the cottage, it was Jake. If you want to be cross with anyone it should be him really. Sorry, Jake,' she added, 'but you did rather put your foot in it, didn't you?'

I could have kissed her for saying that. Just when I was beginning to suspect that she was playing devil's advocate she went and totally redeemed herself. She'd got me off the hook with Jessica and put Jake in his place in one well aimed sentence. However, when I re-joined the group, sitting in the space Holly had just left (the irony of which was not lost on me), the look on Jessica's face told me that Holly might as well have not bothered to explain anything at all.

'I suppose you think she's even more bloody perfect now,' she scowled at me, 'trying to make us all friends again before she drifted off on her Miss Dior scented cloud.'

'Miss Dior?' chirped up Henry twisting round to look at his betrothed. 'That was Chanel Number Five, surely?'

We all stared at him open mouthed but it was Rachel who got the giggles first.

'What?' said Henry, turning bright red. 'Well, it was, wasn't it?'

Rachel's laughter was infectious and within seconds we were all laughing along with her, even Jessica.

'Darling, I wish you wouldn't come out with things like that,' she said, leaning across and kissing his cheek. 'I don't want people thinking I'm marrying the only gay in the village.'

'Oh bugger off,' said Henry, standing up and tossing his hair in the most camp way he could manage. 'Who wants another drink?'

'I do,' said Harriet as she jumped up to accompany him to the bar, 'and I'll have you know,' she winked at Jessica, 'as far as I'm aware, Rachel and I are the only gays in the village.'

Jessica's face was an absolute picture. She looked totally mortified.

'I'm joking,' said Harriet, 'Jess, I'm only messing.'

'Oh God,' said Jessica, 'me and my big mouth. I'm so sorry. I didn't mean anything by it.'

'That's all right,' said Harriet, 'we'll forgive you, won't we, Rachel?'

'I suppose so,' Rachel muttered, 'you have to expect a small town attitude in a place like this.'

Jessica looked as if she wanted the floor to open up and swallow her and then Rachel started laughing again.

'Oh you sods!' breathed Jessica. 'I thought I'd really offended you.'

'Take a lot more than that,' laughed Harriet, linking arms with Henry. 'Come on, you promised us drinks.'

The atmosphere lightened considerably after that and we spent a happy evening together talking about the wedding and my supposedly secret ideas for Meadowview Cottage. Jake didn't mention the Piggy Plan and neither did I. It was a bit late in the day for him to remember that all the changes we were making were supposed to be a secret, but there was no point dwelling on what was done.

'So, will that be OK?' said Jessica as Jim rang the bell for last orders. 'I know you've got Miss "Holier than Thou" visiting, but it would be great if I could just grab you for five minutes on Monday, Amber.'

'Of course,' I nodded enthusiastically, 'absolutely.'

I was so thrilled to be back in her good books that I would have agreed to anything she suggested and to be honest it was quite nice that she and the others knew about the cottage. At least I could share my progress with them, and any potential failures of course, although I was hopeful there wouldn't be nearly as many of those.

'And you won't mention the cottage idea to anyone, will you, guys?' Jake reminded them as we headed for the door. 'Annie doesn't want anyone knowing about what's happening at the farm just yet.'

'Do I take it from that that there are more changes afoot?' asked Henry astutely as he waggled his eyebrows.

Jake blushed crimson and I rolled my eyes. It was a miracle he hadn't told me about the abandoned cottage as soon as I told him I was moving to the farm because he was proving himself to be an absolutely rubbish secret keeper.

'We won't say a word,' said Harriet, tapping the side of her nose, 'but I can't vouch for Holly, of course.'

'Oh well,' I said, not wanting to dive back into that particular can of worms just yet, 'we'll just have to keep our fingers crossed that she knows the meaning of discretion, won't we?'

Jessica threw me a withering glance and Henry shoved her out into the night before she could say another word. We all said a hasty goodbye as the rain continued to lash down and Jake and I set off back to the farm and the exciting prospect of our new ventures.

Chapter 36

All that weekend Annie nagged at Jake to go down to the cottage and break in so he and I could make a start on clearing the place, but he wouldn't.

'I don't see why you need *her* there to get going,' said Annie scathingly. 'If it was up to me I'd just hire a skip, dump her stuff in it and tell her to pay the bill.'

I was delighted Annie was back to her old self, even if she wasn't quite as steady on her feet as before, but I could have lived without her constant reminders that Jake wouldn't tackle the cottage without Holly by his side. It was going to be tough enough seeing the evidence of the life they lived there without thinking about why Jake wouldn't just get on with it as Annie kept suggesting.

By Sunday afternoon the situation had reached boiling point and Annie, her expression militant, was all prepared to set off with a hammer and knock the door down. I took yet another deep breath and tried to immerse myself in the cross-stitch sampler she had set me up with in an attempt to pass on her sewing legacy.

Unfortunately I was pretty rubbish at it. Baking seemed to be more my forte, but I didn't want to let her down so I toiled away while the rain lashed down and the distant sound of thunder sent Bella and Lily scurrying back under the table. I held the fabric at arm's length and squinted in the half light. Annie had always made it look so easy as she sat in her chair with her needle rhythmically flashing in and out, but mine just looked a mess. I was supposed to be practising the alphabet but it looked more like alphabet spaghetti than regimented lettering.

'Would it be all right,' I said as I threw the fabric, needle and all, down on the table, 'if we just stopped going on about this? Tomorrow can't come soon enough for me but keeping on about it won't make the time pass any quicker.'

'Are you all right, my lovely?' frowned Annie. 'I didn't mean to upset you.'

'Of course she isn't all right,' snapped Jake.

'I just want to get it over and done with,' I said to Annie. 'I can't wait to get started on the transformation and in my head I can picture exactly how I want it to look, even though I haven't been inside yet. I'm just not looking forward to what we've got to do before I can get on with it, that's all.'

'You do know why I want Holly there, don't you?' said Jake.

'No,' said Annie.

'I was asking Amber,' Jake shot back testily.

'No,' I said, in much the same tone as Annie, 'not really.'

Jake ran his hands through his hair and came to sit with me at the table.

'Don't get me wrong,' he began, 'I do believe that she meant it when she said she was sorry about what happened, but that hasn't erased the memory of what actually happened.'

'Of course not,' I said.

'I've seen Holly at her very worst,' he said bitterly, 'we all have, and although I can't deny she does seem to have changed, I'm not going to give her any opportunity to go around saying that any of her stuff was broken or missing. When I open that door tomorrow I want her to be there and I want her to acknowledge that no one has been in since I locked the place up all those months ago.'

'I see,' I said, some of the pieces of my life slipping back into focus.

That did make sense. If Holly thought we'd broken in without her and that I'd had the opportunity to have a snoop through everything she might well take offence and I could understand that Jake didn't want to give the old Holly any excuse to resurface. His reasoning for not wanting to go inside the cottage without her left me in no doubt that he still didn't trust her, even though she had displayed incredible patience in waiting for her possessions. Yes, it was far better to wait and do it all together.

'Do you really see?' said Jake, looking relieved. 'Because what I said about the place before was all true. I just wanted to forget about it, even though Annie wouldn't let me. To tell you the truth, if you hadn't come up with your brilliant holiday let idea and I could have got away with it, it would probably have been rotting away forever.'

'Rotting! Oh God, don't tell me there was stuff in the fridge?' I asked, wrinkling my nose at the prospect of seeing for myself the transformation of cheese and milk that had been left for the best part of a couple of years.

'Probably,' Jake shrugged, 'although Holly was a real one for diets. With any luck she was on a dairy-free fad at the time so we'll be spared anything too gross.'

'But Annie does have a point,' I said, 'we will probably need a skip. The fridge will need replacing for a start, unless of course you fancy tackling the cleaning?'

He looked less than impressed with the idea.

'Personally,' I added, 'I'd be much happier knowing the appliances were brand new, as we're letting the place out.'

'And the bed,' Annie chirped up.

Why did she have to mention the bed? That was the one piece of furniture I was really dreading seeing. Jake shot Annie a withering look and reached for my hand.

'If you'd rather not come down,' he said, 'I would understand.'

'No,' I smiled; there was no way I was going to leave them to it. 'No, it'll be fine. Many hands make light work and all that.'

I glanced over at Annie and she gave me the merest wink. It wasn't that I didn't trust Jake, but obviously, judging by what he and everyone else said, there was clearly more to Holly than I had seen and even though I always tried to look for the good in everyone I wasn't quite ready to leave her alone with my boyfriend just yet.

'Don't forget Jess is dropping by at some point this morning,' Jake reminded me as I fed the hens on Monday morning and set about helping him choose the best set of tools for breaking and entering. 'You know, I've got a feeling,' he said, thinking back to the job in hand as he looked at what we had gathered together, 'that there might actually be a key in the back door.'

'Really? Crikey, that would make life a lot easier, wouldn't it?' I said, thinking of the cost of having to replace just one lock rather than two.

'Yes,' said Jake thoughtfully, 'the kitchen door was always locked in the mornings as I recall and I shut us out of the front. It was definitely the front door keys I launched into the river.'

'Why didn't you have the back door key on the key ring as well?'

'We barely used that door,' he shrugged, 'actually Holly never did. She wasn't one for gardening. As I recall she never even sat outside. Definitely the front door key,' he said again.

'Remind me never to fall out with you,' I laughed, shaking my head.

'Not likely,' said Jake, dropping the tools in a bucket and pulling me into his arms.

'Oh,' I giggled, 'and why's that?'

'Because we want the same things, you and me,' he said, kissing me softly. 'We haven't got anything to argue about.'

'That,' I told him, thinking of how much I loved Skylark Farm, 'is very true.'

We were already waiting outside Meadowview Cottage when Holly pulled up in her 4x4.

'God,' she groaned, as she jumped out, 'look at this place. However did you convince me to move in here, Jake? It's so dark and dingy.'

Jake looked at me and raised his eyebrows.

'No offence,' she quickly added, patting my arm.

'None taken,' I smiled.

'As I recall,' said Jake, 'you had your sights set far higher than this place, Holly, didn't you? I don't think your plans involved us living here for very long.'

Touché! Round One to Jake. I didn't have him down as the bitchy type but Holly seemed to have a god given gift for bringing out the worst in people. First Jessica had displayed her fiery side and now Jake had bitten back too. I couldn't help wondering if I would be adding my own name to that list by the end of the day.

'It won't be dark and dingy much longer anyway,' I quickly jumped in before the sniping got out of hand. 'I'm planning to have all these straggly conifers taken out, then there'll be loads more light and room for a proper little garden.'

'Well, thank God!' laughed Holly.

Jake looked at me and rolled his eyes, picked up the bucket of tools and followed Holly through the gate up the weedy, overgrown path to the front door.

'I remember you carried me across this threshold,' she smiled dreamily up at Jake and then looked apologetically at me. 'Sorry, Amber,' she said again.

I had an increasingly sneaking suspicion that she was going to try to make this experience just the wrong side of comfortable for me. I could understand that there would be memories flooding out of every corner but I hoped she wasn't going to draw them all to my attention. My tolerance would only carry me so far and Jake, who was having none of her simpering, seemed to have reached the end of his already.

'No chance of that today,' he said, brushing roughly past her and making her step back on to the sodden grass. 'Come on. I'm breaking in round the back.'

'I do hope this won't be too awkward for you,' Holly smiled as she trotted along in Jake's wake. 'Quite frankly I thought you wouldn't be here.'

'Oh no,' I said as the sound of breaking glass met my ears, 'I wouldn't miss this for the world. I can't wait to get a look inside and see what potential the place has to offer.'

'Well, I hope you won't be disappointed,' she said, her voice full of concern, 'and actually that isn't quite what I meant.'

'Hurry up, will you?' called Jake. 'I'm in!'

I knew exactly what she meant and that was exactly why I was there.

Chapter 37

My first job was to send the dusty curtains flying back along their poles and to throw open the windows. The air wasn't exactly unpleasant, more unmoved rather than musty and damp, which was a pleasant surprise.

While Holly rushed around cooing over this and sighing over that and Jake fixed some plywood over the hole where he'd smashed the glass, I moved from room to room trying to ignore the cosy set up, instead picturing the space transformed courtesy of my cheap and cheerful renovation ideas. Holly did have a point about it being dark and dingy but I knew that I was right about that being down to the overbearing conifers. Once they were down the place would be halfway to transformed and able to breathe.

The kitchen and dining space at the back of the cottage faced east and overlooked what was currently a tiny overgrown garden. The few kitchen units, Jake informed me, had only just been fitted before he and Holly moved in and the simple Shaker style suited my plans perfectly. Apart from a thorough scrub, a fresh lick of paint, some pretty curtains and decorative touches, the room needed little else, and it was the same in the bathroom.

The sitting room was small but cosy with a tiny wood burner and front facing windows. The space would easily accommodate four and I could imagine how snug it would be with the fire lit and the wind raging outside. I tried not to think about Holly and Jake sitting together on the sofa feeding one another marshmallows and wearing matching sweaters.

'Isn't it a hole?' said Holly, shaking her head. 'I did try and warn you. There's no way I'm going to secure many bookings if it stays looking like this.'

'Actually I think it's wonderful,' I said, looking at Jake who grinned back. 'In fact,' I told her, 'if I wasn't so happy up at the farm I'd even consider moving in here myself. And while we're on the subject, Holly, you won't need to worry about the bookings because once I've got the place ready I'll be sorting them out myself.'

Holly choked on her insulated coffee mug that she'd brought with her.

'Oh. Well,' she called over her shoulder as she left the room, 'the commission on somewhere like this would have hardly made it worth the effort anyway. I won't be long,' she added. 'An hour, two tops, and I'll be out of your hair.'

'Do you really like it,' Jake asked when he was sure she was out of earshot, 'or did you just say that to wind her up?'

'No,' I said, 'I really mean it, it's lovely. Not as homely as I'd imagined, but you know, each to their own.'

Truth be told I had expected the place to be as chic as Holly, but it wasn't. If anything it was even more barren than the flat I'd left behind in London. I'd been bracing myself to face paintings she and Jake had picked out together and photo frames crammed on every surface, capturing the wonderful life they'd shared. That is, before Holly showed her true colours and revealed her grand plans to move them up and out, but beyond the odd Ikea lampshade and vase, there was nothing. The cosiness that I'd first shied away from when I crossed the threshold came more from the cottage itself and the snug dimensions of the rooms rather than anything of sentimental value.

A sharp rap on the front door made us both jump.

'That'll be Jess,' said Jake. 'Shall I run round and head her off so their paths don't cross?'

'No,' I said, laughing at his panicked expression, 'you stay here and I'll go and meet her.'

'Sure?'

'Of course I'm sure,' I said, planting a kiss on his stubbly cheek. 'I think I can trust you not to run off with Holly while I'm gone.'

Jake looked at me and shook his head.

'Only if you do decide to elope,' I said, 'would you leave the key on the front step because I can't help thinking this little place has had enough of being shut up.'

'She's in there then,' said Jessica in a loud sing-song voice the moment she saw me.

'Yes,' I hissed in a hushed tone, 'she's in there.'

I had no idea which room Holly was in but I wasn't taking any chances. I didn't want her hearing Jessica running her down. The day was going to be tricky enough without having to smooth out any arguments or problems that could be avoided.

'Come on,' I said, 'let's head up to the house and check on Annie and you can tell me what it is you want to talk about.'

Annie was as amazed as Jessica that I'd left Holly and Jake alone at the cottage.

'You can't trust her,' she said for the hundredth time, and Jessica joined in where she left off.

'You don't know what she's like,' Jessica chimed in, shaking her head defiantly.

'Yes, but what you both seem to be forgetting,' I said sternly as I poured us all tea, 'is that I *can* trust Jake and I *do* know what he's like.'

'That's true,' said Jessica.

'It is,' said Annie, 'but I still wouldn't put it past her to try something.'

'Annie!' I scolded, beginning to feel cross and increasingly paranoid. 'Please stop.'

'Sorry,' said Annie, dunking her shortbread.

'Yes,' said Jessica, 'me too.'

As Jessica requested we walked back through the orchards having stopped on the way so she could have a look at Pip and admire Blaze.

'What a start this pair gave you to your time at the farm!' she laughed. 'I can't believe you've only been here, what is it now?'

She tried to count up on her fingers and I did the same.

'Must be around three months,' I said eventually. 'Is that right? It can't be, four maybe. It seems so much longer to me, but I don't think it is.'

I couldn't shake off the feeling that I'd been living at Skylark Farm and immersed in country life for years. So much had happened in such a short space of time that it didn't feel possible that I had ever had time to live any other kind of life. It was true that I had settled in quickly; just the thought of moving back to London and picking up the threads of my old life made my stomach churn.

For the moment my promise to have a meeting with Simon about the Dubai job seemed like something that was looming on someone else's horizon. It certainly didn't feel as though it had anything to do with me. Perhaps I could resolve the matter by email, but I wasn't going to worry about it just yet. I had ages left before my time was up and he was expecting me to make a decision.

'Well,' said Jessica, laying her hand on my arm as I closed the orchard gate behind us, 'however long it's been it feels like forever to me.'

'Really?' I smiled, thrilled that she felt the same way.

'Really,' she said.

I remembered that she had asked to come out and see me with something specific in mind and, suddenly aware of how long Jake had been with Holly down at the cottage, I tried to push the conversation along.

'So,' I said, 'was there something specific you wanted to talk about?'

'Yes,' said Jessica smiling.

'Well,' I told her, 'you know, if there's anything I can do to help with the wedding I will. My corporate skills might be a bit rusty but I'm sure I'll soon get the hang of them again.'

Jessica laughed and we linked arms.

'So am I kicking arse?' I asked. 'Is the caterer dragging her heels or the photographer not pulling his weight?'

'No, nothing like that,' said Jessica, 'but there is something I want to ask you.'

'Go on,' I said, 'it isn't like you to be lost for words!'

Jessica stopped and turned to face me. Her face was flushed and her usual confidence and self-assuredness seemed to have slipped a little.

'OK,' she said, licking her lips. 'I know we haven't known each other very long even though it feels like we have, and I was wondering,' she smiled shyly, 'if you would consider being my bridesmaid.'

'Really?' I squealed.

'Really,' she laughed. 'Harriet is the old-maid of honour and I have a curly haired little niece lined up for cute and I was hoping you'd consider filling the role in between?'

'Jessica,' I told her proudly as I wiped away a tear, 'I would be honoured to be your bridesmaid and fill whatever role necessary.'

'Excellent,' she grinned, squeezing me tight, 'I knew you would.'

'There's only one stipulation,' I told her, pulling myself free, 'no taffeta, oh and no meringues.'

'OK,' said Jessica, sounding disappointed, 'how do you feel about bows and layers of shocking pink lace?'

Arm in arm we made our way back down to the cottage. It was all quiet as we entered the kitchen. I'd told Jessica she could come in to tell Jake the news but only if she promised to play nice with Holly.

'Where are they?' she mouthed to me, heading towards the hall.

I shrugged my shoulders and followed on behind. I didn't find the fact that she was whispering particularly encouraging and I felt my heart somersault when I heard hushed voices in the bedroom. Jessica put up her hand to stop me and we held our breaths as we listened through the closed door.

'Oh my God, it's huge,' Holly gasped, 'even bigger than I remember.'

'I bet you never thought you'd see it again, did you?' Jake laughed. 'I'm surprised it's come out to be honest. Do you dare grab it?'

'I can't,' said Holly, 'what if it tries to bite me?'

I'd heard enough. I burst through the door to find Jake and Holly standing on the bed staring up at the ceiling looking terrified.

'What the hell is going on?' I gasped.

'Oh thank God,' said Jake, his shoulders dropping as he caught sight of me, 'thank goodness you're back.'

He shot off the bed and out of the door leaving Holly rooted to the spot.

'What are you doing?' I asked him as he cowered behind me holding out a plastic jug he'd snatched from the bathroom.

'The ceiling,' he said with a shiver, 'look.'

In the corner of the ceiling above the window was potentially the biggest spider in the known free world. I knew Jake absolutely hated them and apparently so did Holly. I smirked to myself at the thought of leaving her there for the rest of the afternoon, but my humane side won the tussle and I knew I couldn't do it.

'That's the same spider that lived here when we did,' said Holly, finally daring to make a dash for the door as I approached the offender with the jug. 'I'm sure of it, but it was nowhere near as big back then!'

In one smooth movement I knocked the spider into the jug and tossed it out of the window. Doubtless it would make its way back in at some point, but the terrified pair wouldn't be bothered by it for the next few hours at least.

'Thank you, Amber,' said Holly. She was shaking all over and Jessica was laughing behind her.

'Yes,' said Jake with a shudder, 'thank you, darling.'

'You really are the perfect pair, aren't you?' Jessica laughed.

Jake, not at all fazed that his phobia had been on display in all its glory for her to see, grabbed me round the middle and squeezed me tight.

'Absolutely,' he said, kissing me full on the lips. 'She's the yin to my yang, the left to my right, the black to my white—'

'Yeah, yeah,' said Jessica, walking away, 'we get the idea. Don't we, Holly?' she added pointedly.

'I'll grab some boxes from the car,' said Holly, following Jessica back outside.

I decided not to dwell on how Holly and Jake had ended up on the bed together. I simply wrapped my arms tight around him, feeling content to be the other half of whatever pairing he came up with.

Chapter 38

The blessed absence of personal knick-knacks meant that Holly was packed by the end of the day. Jake was more than happy for her to take the few decorative items, along with most of the crockery and kitchen utensils. The fact that her father had arranged for a van to collect the larger pieces of furniture (including the bed, hurrah) ensured that the place had been purged of all things Holly by teatime. Less than eight hours from start to finish and at last I had the blank canvas I had been dreaming of.

'So,' said Jake after we waved Holly off, 'what do you think now it's empty? Do you still think it has potential?'

'Absolutely,' I told him enthusiastically as I went from room to room closing the windows and curtains. 'I meant what I said earlier, I really love it and I know people will pay good money to come and stay here.'

'But you're forgetting one thing,' he reminded me, looking around the empty kitchen, 'we, or should I say you, are on an extremely tight budget.'

'Oh believe me,' I said, biting my lip, 'I haven't forgotten about that at all. I think the biggest expense is going to be getting those wretched conifers taken down.'

'That won't be a problem,' said Jake, 'I know someone who can do that, and in fact,' he added, looking particularly pleased with himself, 'he owes me a favour.'

'Well, in that case,' I smiled, 'let's go and have some dinner and you can telephone your chainsaw wielding friend and set a date.'

Back at the farmhouse all was calm and quiet. Jake and I exchanged glances as we saw the table already set, with a large bowl of salad picked from the garden at its centre.

Jake washed his hands and threw me the 'watch yourself' warning, reminding me to be on guard when Annie revealed what she had cooked. I knew that whatever it was, I was going to have to eat some of it. This was the first meal she'd cooked since her stint in hospital and I was determined not to let her efforts end up in the bin.

'Don't panic,' Annie laughed, when she came in and spotted us loitering nervously next to the table. 'Ham and pork pie from the butcher and some new potatoes. Nothing exotic! I love the pair of you too much to risk poisoning you.'

We sat together around the table and piled our plates high. Evidently it was hungry work this house clearing malarkey.

'So,' said Annie, 'how did you get on?'

'All finished,' said Jake, helping himself to more salad.

'What, already?' asked Annie, wide eyed.

'There wasn't actually all that much,' I told her. 'Quite a lot of clothes, which according to Holly were only fit for the charity bag now as they were so out of style, and a few bits of furniture. That was pretty much it.'

'We didn't live there long enough to transform it into a home,' Jake shrugged, 'and besides, Holly was hardly ever there. Neither of us made much effort to turn the place into somewhere we wanted to spend time together.'

'She never struck me as a particularly home loving girl,' Annie sniffed, then smiled warmly at me, 'not like some. Anyway, that's enough about her. Tell me, Amber, what's next for Meadowview Cottage?'

I told her about my plans to have the surrounding conifers felled to let in more light and take advantage of the striking Fenland sunrise and sunsets, and showed her the list I had started, detailing all the bits and pieces that I felt would suit the style of the place. Once she had finished reading it she passed it over to Jake.

'This is all old-fashioned stuff,' he said, looking up at me when he'd finished scanning the page. 'Or should I say vintage?'

'Yes,' I nodded, 'it is. I'm guessing the cottage was built in the fifties, early sixties perhaps, and I thought it would be great to fill it with bits and pieces from around that time, assuming I can find them. Vintage is very popular right now and the setting and style of the cottage will lend itself perfectly to the bespoke holiday experience.'

I could easily imagine the boisterous and beloved Larkin family from *The Darling Buds of May* bustling about down there, eating gargantuan dinners and enjoying cocktails.

'Sounds great,' said Jake, 'but it's all pricey. Are you sure you can pull it off?'

'Absolutely,' I said, thinking of the auction and all the things I had seen there that would be ideal. 'And I know just the place to go to start buying,' I added mysteriously.

'Well,' said Annie, looking particularly pleased with herself, 'before you part with any money, you might want to have a look in the loft.'

'Really?' I said, looking from her to Jake and back again.

'Don't ask me,' Jake shrugged, shaking his head, 'I don't think I've ever even been in the loft. In fact, I don't even know where the hatch is!'

I couldn't wait to have a look through what Annie had squirrelled away over the years. I hoped it turned out to be more exciting than the Christmas decoration box and TV aerial my parents kept in theirs.

'I've been putting stuff in that loft,' Annie carried on wistfully, 'for more years than I care to remember and my mother before me and her mother before that. It's most likely all junk, but you're welcome to make use of anything that might be suitable. The loft space here runs under the eaves and it goes on forever. There are even some old pieces of furniture up there, although it's all a bit cramped now. To be honest it's probably high time someone had a good sort through it all.'

'So where is the hatch exactly?' I said, my fingers itching to get started and the backache I'd incurred after helping Jake and the van driver lift the sofas earlier now quickly shrugged off.

'I'll show you tomorrow,' said Annie as she began to gather the dishes together. 'You look tired out to me and there's no rush.'

She was right, of course, there was no rush and I knew that once I'd started I wouldn't be able to stop. It was probably best to spend the evening refining my list and to start with fresh eyes tomorrow.

'What did Jessica want?' Jake asked as he carried the dishes that Annie had piled together over to the sink. 'You never said.'

I couldn't believe I'd forgotten! After the furore with that blasted spider my exciting piece of news had been completely side lined.

344

'You'll never guess,' I giggled, my face flushed with pride and excitement.

'What?'

I took a deep breath and bit my lip.

'Oh come on,' said Annie impatiently, drumming her fingers on the table, 'out with it!'

'She's asked me to be one of her bridesmaids!' I said in a rush, jumping up and down on the spot.

'Well now,' smiled Annie, 'there's a turn up for the books!'

'I know,' I beamed. 'Harriet's going to be old-maid of honour, as Jess put it, and she's got a niece as her flower girl and now me! I've never been a bridesmaid before!'

'There,' said Annie, clapping her hands together, 'how lovely is that? Perfect actually. You'll both be all dressed up in formal wedding party outfits for the occasion.'

'Both?' I said, turning to look at her. 'What do you mean?'

'While you were off with Jess,' Jake explained, 'Henry popped down to the cottage after looking in on Annie. I'm surprised you and Jess didn't bump into him actually. Anyway he's asked me to be one of his ushers.'

'Oh wow,' I laughed, 'that is perfect then!'

As I drifted off to sleep that night I couldn't help thinking about how different everything had felt just twenty-four hours ago. The previous evening I'd struggled to nod off, filled with trepidation and dreading the thought of having to watch Holly and Jake pick through the remains of their life together. Whereas tonight, I couldn't nod off because I was bubbling with excitement. Not only did I have Jessica and Henry's wedding to look forward to, but also the prospect of filling the cottage with treasures that already belonged to Skylark Farm.

Every time I thought the place had given me everything it could, I made another little discovery and living here became even more magical. Was this finally it, I wondered, or was there something else? Had I reached my limit or were there more surprises to come?

Chapter 39

Early the next morning I could hear Jake bustling about in the bedroom but I refused to acknowledge his fidgety presence for as long as I could.

'So, are you coming then or what?' he eventually asked when it became obvious that I wasn't going to spring out of bed fresh faced and ready to go without a bit of coaxing.

'Where?' I yawned, refusing to open my eyes. 'Where am I supposed to be coming to?'

'Down to Meadowview Cottage, of course. Tony's coming with his chainsaw to take the conifers down.'

'Today,' I said while opening one eye, 'what, now? What time is it?'

'Just gone seven,' said Jake as he tried to pull off the covers.

It was a move he'd practised before and I clung on tight.

'It isn't as if we have to worry about disturbing the neighbours, is it? Come on, lazybones!' he laughed, reaching under the duvet and tickling my legs. 'I've already done your chores as well as my own.'

'All right,' I gave in, 'all right. Give me ten minutes and I'll be there.'

'Five,' he grinned, 'tops.'

By the time I got dressed, piled my hair loosely on top of my head and bumbled down to the kitchen, I realised there was more to the way I was feeling than a restless night. However, as Jake was already revving the engine, there was no time to feel sorry for myself.

'You all right?' frowned Annie as she thrust a steaming mug into my hands after I'd pulled on my wellies.

'Didn't sleep,' I told her, 'too excited.'

'Are you sure that's all?'

'Yes,' I nodded. 'Yes, I'll be fine in a minute or two.'

'Well, when you come back I'll show you where the loft is,' she winked, accepting my explanation. 'And don't forget to grab some gloves from the porch if you're planning on helping the boys.'

'Gloves,' I laughed, 'I thought we'd agreed we don't do gloves.'

'That was before you were asked to be a bridesmaid,' she said sagely. 'Wouldn't look good on the photos if you had hands like an old farmer, would it?'

'No,' I said, reaching for the smallest pair I could find, 'I guess not. Will you be all right?'

'I'll be fine,' she nodded, 'I've told Jake I'll keep the dogs here with me. They'll only get in your way and chainsaws can be tricky things.'

Jake gave a blast on the horn and I rushed outside, mug and gloves in hand, ready to begin the day.

If I didn't know any better I would have said that Jake's mate Tony, Treetop Tony to his pals, was probably a tree himself in a former life, a willow most likely. Tall, thin, with colossal feet in reinforced safety boots, but with a voice that barely rose above a whisper, he made short work of felling the first conifer and it soon became obvious when we stood back to admire the view that this was going to be the making of Meadowview Cottage.

'I'm not a fan of taking down healthy trees,' he told me when we stopped for a breather, 'but these things are a menace. I bet they've never been checked or cut back since they were planted.'

I didn't know much about trees, practically nothing in fact, but I could see where he was coming from. The ground around the stumps was dry and dusty and there was nothing growing there. As far as I could see all these brutish things did was provide a windbreak and a wall of darkness.

By lunchtime all that remained of the row out the front were a few uneven stumps, which Tony said he would level off when he'd finished out the back.

'Will they grow again?' I asked, no doubt showing my ignorance, but curious nonetheless.

'No,' he said, 'that's it for them. Done and dusted. Personally I wouldn't plant anything where they've been. If you want to create a garden then bring the boundary further in, otherwise you'll spend a fortune trying to enrich the soil and forever digging out the roots.'

I felt a bit sad that I had been the one to instigate the conifers' demise but stepping over the threshold into the cottage soon soothed my guilty conscience. The moment I entered the kitchen at the back I could see just how dramatic the change in light was.

The front of the cottage faced west so the sitting room and one of the bedrooms would benefit from the sun later in the day while the kitchen, bathroom and second bedroom would enjoy the sunrise. I thought about Tony's suggestion of creating a garden. Which plants would work well with the vintage theme, I wondered? Perhaps I could ask Harriet and Rachel to help me out with some ideas.

I walked from room to room revelling in the transformation and as I stood quietly, before the sound of the chainsaw ripped through the air again, I swear I heard the cottage sigh. For the first time, literally in decades, it could breathe again.

'Would you mind if I went back up to the house?' I asked Jake later that afternoon. 'Annie has promised to show me the loft and to be honest I'm shattered.'

Jake looked at me for a long few seconds then pulled off one of his gloves and felt my forehead with the back of his hand.

'You do look tired,' he said, 'I'll run you back up in the truck.'

'No,' I said, 'don't worry. I can walk easily enough. I just don't think I can drag any more of this stuff about.'

'All right,' he nodded. 'You are pleased, though, aren't you? I mean, personally I think it's a minor miracle, but is it how you imagined it would look?'

'Even better,' I told him. 'I guess this is how it all would have looked when the place was first built, and I know you'll probably think I'm being silly but I'm sure the cottage is pleased as well.'

'What do you mean?'

'Well, when I went inside it felt to me as if the place let out a huge sigh of relief. Does that make sense?'

'Not really,' he laughed, 'but it does sound like the sort of thing you and Annie would say, so you're probably right!'

Annie was asleep in her chair next to the range when I got back to the house. The dogs, docile at her feet, barely moved as I lifted the latch and slipped quietly in.

'Some guard dogs you are,' I smiled at the pair of them, remembering how just a few months ago I'd been totally resistant to the idea of sharing a house with them, never mind a bed.

Unwilling to disturb her, I settled myself in the chair opposite Annie and had just begun to doze off myself when she stirred.

'How's it going down there?' she asked, gingerly stretching her back and stifling a yawn. 'I've been listening to the chainsaw going, surely he must be almost done by now.'

'Yes, almost,' I explained, sitting up straighter to stave off my own sleepiness, 'just a couple at the back left now.'

'They were tiny when we planted them,' Annie told me, her eyes shining at the memory. 'My father got them from the market in Wynbridge for pennies. They were only ever supposed to reach six foot but what with everything else that needed doing on the farm and with no one living down there they soon got forgotten. The poor little place has never been much of a priority around here. I'm pleased that's going to change. It deserves a chance to shine.'

'Well, I hope I can do both you and the cottage proud,' I smiled.

'Cottage,' she said pensively, 'I never really understood why it was called a cottage. Delusions of grandeur on my mother's part most likely.'

'I have to say I've been mulling over the name myself,' I admitted, remembering how when I first saw it I couldn't help thinking that the word cottage had never been less appropriately applied to a dwelling, but now I had explored the inside and got a feel for the place I felt differently.

'Well, it's hardly a cottage, is it?' said Annie, echoing my first impressions perfectly. 'It's just a little bungalow really, nothing more.'

'I suppose it is,' I nodded, 'but Meadowview Bungalow just doesn't have the same appeal, does it? I think your mother was right to award it such a pretty name, delusions of grandeur or not.'

'Yes,' she conceded, 'I suppose you're right. Now, let's go and have a look in this loft.'

Annie called the space a loft but actually 'veritable treasure trove' would have been a more accurate description. Stooping through the tiny door, hidden behind the chest of drawers in Annie's bedroom, was like stepping back in time, and if it wasn't so crowded, I would have run up and down all day sifting through the treasures.

At the furthest end of the space were the oldest bits and pieces while closer to the door were the most recent additions. Surveying the gems Annie and her family had stashed away it looked as though nothing had been parted with for generations and I knew I could quite easily equip the entire cottage with what had been hoarded away for as long as Skylark Farm had existed.

'Are you sure I can use all this?' I asked Annie for the umpteenth time. 'What if any of it gets damaged or broken?'

'Amber, it is sitting up here stagnating just like that little cottage has been. It's high time it was sold or put to good use.'

'There are things in here we should have downstairs in our kitchen!' I laughed as I unwrapped a beautiful glass jug and six matching glasses with daisies printed on them. 'Can you imagine serving Pimm's in these after a long day picking apples? And these flour and sugar dredgers,' I gasped. 'I can't believe all the baking I've been doing downstairs and all the while these have been sitting up here crying out to be used!'

I knew I was getting carried away, but I couldn't help it. Immersing myself in all those magazines, I had fallen in love with every piece of retro kitchen paraphernalia I saw and here it all was; a delightful smorgasbord spread out before me.

'Those,' said Annie from her seat on an upturned tea chest, 'belonged to my grandmother.'

'Wow,' I said, handling them with even more reverence, 'so why have you packed them away up here?'

As soon as the question left my lips I knew the answer. Along with the few pieces of furniture and various boxes of bedlinen there was a plethora of kitchenware but nothing to do with sewing.

'Am I a cook,' asked Annie, looking amused, 'or a master baker?'

'No,' I giggled, biting my lip.

'Well, there you are then. I was never likely to use any of these things so up they came. However,' she said kindly, 'if *you* want to make use of them we'll get Jake to give us a hand carrying them back down.'

'No,' I said, putting them back where I had found them, 'I couldn't. It's enough that you're letting me use everything for the cottage. These are your family heirlooms and treasures, Annie. I've no right to them. They should stay safe up here.'

'Are you not family then?' said Annie, raising her eyebrows and fixing me with her all-seeing stare. 'Don't you consider yourself one of us?'

I didn't know what to say. Jake and I were a couple, of course, and I was living in his family home but I didn't think I'd lived at the farm long enough to be considered family, even though Annie had already told me that the place was going to be as much my future as Jake's.

'Like I said,' Annie smiled, her eyes never leaving my face, 'I'll get Jake to help us carry everything down.'

Chapter 40

'So,' said Jessica, 'what do you think? Mum keeps telling me they're too revealing but I've told her this style is perfect. It isn't as if you're teenagers, is it? My niece, Mia, has something in the same fabric, but a totally different style obviously.'

This was the first glimpse Harriet and I had had of the dresses Jessica had lined up for us to wear at the wedding and, judging by her expression, Harriet was obviously of the same opinion as me. We both absolutely loved them.

'They're gorgeous,' said Harriet, lightly fingering the soft green fabric. 'I know I'm no girly girl but these are stunning.'

'And what do you think, Amber?'

The matching dresses were halter neck, backless, calf length and very fifties in style. They were elegant and extremely sophisticated. I guessed that a clear theme for the wedding had been revealed in Jessica's choice and I wondered if she and Henry would consider spending their honeymoon in vintage splendour at Meadowview Cottage.

'Adorable,' I told her, 'absolutely adorable. If these are what you've picked out for us I can't wait to see what you're wearing!'

We didn't get so much as a hint as to what Jessica's dress was like, but Harriet and I didn't really mind. We were too busy enjoying ourselves ducking in and out of the fitting rooms of the boutique in Norwich, sipping fizz and being thoroughly pampered as we looked at the array of shoes and accessories before getting down to the business of choosing the right sized dress. I was rather taken aback when the zip on the size of dress I would normally pick out refused to meet anywhere near the middle.

'Have you been eating everything you bake?' teased Harriet. 'You're supposed to share the cake, Amber, share. Can you remember that?'

'Leave her alone,' said Jessica protectively. 'Country living requires a little padding and besides we don't want her looking like Holly, do we? I'm sure Jake prefers a little meat on the bone.'

Padding! A little meat on the bone! Just how much weight had I gained exactly? I turned to look at myself side on in the mirror. Given the amount of exercise I got at the farm I was surprised I had gained as much as an ounce but then I didn't use the gym any more so a certain amount of 'padding' or 'meat' was inevitable I guessed.

'Does Wynbridge have a gym?' I asked, sucking in my stomach and cheeks.

Both Jessica and Harriet began to laugh.

'I'm actually being serious,' I frowned, flouncing back to the fitting room to ask the assistant if she could help me find the next size up.

Having suffered the humiliation of upping my dress size, a stopoff at The Cherry Tree Café back in Wynbridge was the last temptation I wanted, but as Jessica had chauffeured both Harriet and me all day I felt I had little right to object.

'I'll have a slice of coffee and walnut and a pot of tea, please,' said Harriet, grinning at me as she gave Angela her order, 'and could you make sure it's a big slice? I've worked up quite an appetite today.'

I stuck out my tongue and carried on wistfully perusing the cakes lined up on the counter while Jessica made her rather more calorie conscious mind up.

'And Amber,' said Angela, turning to me with her pencil and order pad poised, 'what can I get you?'

'I'll have,' I said, trying to ignore Harriet's scrutiny, 'a pot of tea and a red velvet cupcake, please.'

'Good for you!' cheered Harriet, making the people at the table closest jump. 'For a second there I thought you were going to crumble,' she laughed out loud, nudging my elbow completely off the table. 'You had a little breathing space in that larger dress, didn't you? Plenty of time to fill it yet, isn't there, Jess?'

'Remind me,' I said, rubbing my arm and scowling at her, 'why exactly are we friends?'

This time it was Harriet who stuck out her tongue while Jessica tutted and rolled her eyes.

'It's all right for you two,' she said, 'all eyes are on the bride on the big day so I can't keep wolfing down all these sweet treats.'

'So why have you brought us here,' frowned Harriet, 'when stuffing yourself silly on all these creamy and frosted delights is out of the question?'

'I've asked Jemma to make the cake,' Jessica whispered excitedly, 'and I just wanted to check everything was in hand.'

Watching Jemma bustling about the kitchen I couldn't imagine there would be any problems but it was Jessica's big day and I knew better than to argue. I watched as she rifled through her bag for her notebook and pen and went off to the kitchen to check Jemma's progress with her beloved cake.

Minutes later she was back and all three of us were just tucking into our order when the café door opened and in breezed Holly. She swept up to the counter looking, I thought, skinnier than ever but that could have just been because she was bare legged. Her knees, I saw with a jolt, were actually the widest part of her beanpole legs.

I felt a twinge of guilt as I thought of my own knees and calves, and wondered if Jake minded that I'd piled on a few pounds. Had he even noticed? He hadn't said anything if he had. I didn't like this sudden awareness of my weight and body shape. I'd never really given my figure much headspace before and I had no intention of starting now. After all, if I hadn't just had to try on a bigger bridesmaid's dress I probably would have never even noticed in the first place. It was true I had liked to squeeze in a couple of gym sessions a week when I lived in London but that was more about working off the frustrations of a week in the office than working on my figure.

'Ten quid says she can't walk out of that door without passing comment,' hissed Jessica, earning herself a stern look from Harriet.

'Are you still on her case?' she whispered, sounding cross. 'If Amber and I can be civil to her then I don't see why you can't.'

I kept my head down and didn't say anything. This whole Holly, Harriet, Jake scenario was nothing to do with me really and I refused to get drawn into taking sides, especially on what had been such a special day.

Holly gathered together her bottle of water and what looked like some sort of seed bar in a bag, not dissimilar to the wedge Jessica was about to sink her teeth into, and turned around to leave.

'Oh hello, ladies,' she smiled when she spotted us, 'I didn't see you all there.'

'Hello, Holly,' said Harriet through a very crumbly mouthful. 'How are you?'

'Hi,' I said, waving my fork vaguely in her direction.

Jessica didn't say anything.

'Nearly the big day,' said Holly, looking pointedly at the silent member of the group, 'and if you don't mind me saying, Jessica, you are looking stunning. You're positively glowing with that healthy bride vibe. Don't you think, Amber?'

'Mmm,' I nodded, giving Jessica a cursory once over. 'Yes. I guess.'

'Are you doing the fasting thing?' she said to Jessica. 'Not that you need to, of course. All that horse riding has always kept you in trim.'

'I have been thinking about giving it a go,' said Jessica, looking up for the first time, 'just until the wedding.'

I couldn't believe it. What had happened to the ice maiden? One piece of perfectly placed flattery and Jessica was beginning to melt. You certainly had to hand it to Holly. She was the queen when it came to playing the game. Harriet prodded my leg under the table and grinned at her plate.

'And what about these things,' said Holly, waving the seed laden slice she'd just paid for and daintily sitting herself on an empty seat, 'any good?'

'Definitely,' said Jessica, 'although personally I like the one with cranberries in best.'

The conversation between the two continued as Harriet and I devoured our sugary treats and drank our equally sweet tea. I couldn't be sure about Harriet but personally I'd tuned out when they started on about living life without pulses. Quite frankly if I listened to another word I don't think I would have had a pulse myself for much longer. I'd never been one for fad dieting and I wasn't about to change just because the waistband on my jeans was a bit snug.

'Well,' said Holly, just when I was thinking of ordering something else, 'I'd better get going. I told Dad I'd only be gone for five minutes.'

'One of the perks of working with family,' agreed Jessica, 'not that much gets past my mother, of course,' she added darkly.

'See you later then,' said Holly, briefly kissing Jessica's cheek as she stood up.

Actually kissing Jessica's cheek!

'But if I don't see you before, have a wonderful day. Oh and girls, you should take a leaf out of Jess's book, go easy on all that sugar.'

She was gone before I had a chance to retaliate, not that I would have known what to say.

'Well,' said Jessica, her cheeks flushed and eyes shining from all the ego boosting, 'you know, I really think she might have changed.'

'Oh thank God!' said Harriet, punching the air and again attracting the attention of the other customers. 'Does that actually mean we might all be able to meet in The Mermaid without fear of a beating if you catch us talking to her?'

'Don't be so melodramatic,' tutted Jessica as she picked up her bag from under the table. 'I haven't been that bad.'

Harriet raised her eyebrows and placed her hands on her hips.

'I just wanted to be sure she really meant it when she said she was sorry,' Jessica conceded, 'that's all. I didn't want to see anyone get hurt again, especially you.'

'Well, I appreciate your concern,' said Harriet, 'but does this really mean this whole feud is finally over?'

'Absolutely,' nodded Jessica, as she went to have a final word with Jemma. 'I can't see the point in holding a grudge. All that scowling can't be good for the complexion, can it?'

Chapter 41

Heading into high summer at Skylark Farm was quite literally the stuff of dreams, but not the sort of dreams that I'd ever had, of course. The previous summer I'd been sweltering in the city along with everyone else and dreading the sweat soaked commute and air conditioned nights, but this year, July and August were simply blissful. The halcyon days were truly upon us and I couldn't imagine that life could possibly get any better.

I split my time between either working on the cottage, helping Jessica with the wedding, undertaking my farm chores or assisting Annie around the house. Everything happened, everything got done, but the pace was relaxed and easy-going and even Jessica had turned from potential Bridezilla to chilled out bride. In fact, she'd chilled out so much that, having first checked that I wouldn't mind, she'd invited Holly to the wedding reception!

The dogs spent their days asleep either under the trees in the orchard or spreadeagled on the cool flagged kitchen floor and even the geese had knocked their assault tactics down a notch. The chicks, now militant, straggly teens rather than balls of soft fluff, strutted about the hen run (one more purposefully than the others, to my eye), while Mabel, Martha and Patricia, who had thankfully made a complete recovery, basked in dust baths with their beaks open and their eyes trained on the skies praying for rain. Even Pip was calmer in the heat, but the same couldn't be said for Blaze who still favoured a canter around the paddock whenever the sun was shining in the clear, blue sky.

Annie was finally fighting fit again and enjoying pottering around her little garden. Relieved that the fox seemed to have disappeared for good she was relaxed and spent much of her time sewing in the shade. Jake was equally busy but also relaxed, keen to get everything in place for the Piggy Plan to launch the following spring and preparing for what seemed set to be a bumper apple harvest. He was looking forward to a more than bright future at the farm, as was I.

'How do you fancy taking a picnic down to the river this afternoon?' he asked one sunny August morning before heading off to meet Henry to discuss the positioning of the wedding marquee. 'We could even go for a swim,' he suggested temptingly. 'If this morning is another scorcher like yesterday it might not be a bad way to cool off.'

'I would,' I said, 'but I haven't got a bathing costume or a bikini. I didn't think of packing anything like that.'

'So,' said Jake, shrugging his shoulders, 'who said anything about bathing costumes or bikinis?'

'Oh,' I smiled, 'I see. That's how things happen around here, is it?'

I didn't welcome it but an image of him and Holly skinny (in her case literally) dipping in the river sprang to mind.

'No,' grinned Jake, 'but there's always a first time!'

'Oh, so not something you and Holly used to indulge in then?'

I hated myself for asking, but the words simply refused to stay in my head.

'God no,' said Jake, 'I wouldn't have even bothered asking! She was a bit too uptight for that sort of thing.'

Well, I guess that was something.

'OK,' I told him, 'it's a date. I'll get everything together and meet you down there later.'

It was, as Jake predicted, another scorcher and the soft breeze under the willow trees was most welcome. I'd just finished painting the final room in the cottage and, feeling exhausted, I was grateful for the excuse to take a break. I was no interior design expert but even I knew it was fast work when the paint dried on the walls the second it left the roller.

Thankfully the ceilings, doors, skirting boards and windows hadn't needed any attention and I had only really painted the walls to give the place a more homely touch. Now it was finished I could finally get stuck into the fun part. Jake thought my mood boards and scrapbooks full of magazine clippings were all highly amusing so I was looking forward to putting everything in place and watching him eat his words.

I slipped off my shoes and buried my feet in the relative cool of the long grass. It was already gone twelve and I hoped Jake wasn't going to be too much longer. Painting was hungry work and the picnic basket was calling. I tied some twine around the necks of the elderflower cordial bottles and carefully lowered them into the river. The water was silky soft as it caressed my hands and I couldn't resist it any longer.

I hitched my dress up, tucked it in my knickers and sat with my feet and calves dangling over the bank in the water.

'Sorry I'm late!'

I jumped up and turned round smiling only to discover that he had brought Henry and Jessica with him.

'Oh!' said Henry, turning his back, like a true gentleman.

'Sorry,' said Jake, 'I tried to text but, you know, no signal.'

'Just be thankful I wasn't skinny dipping,' I told him, 'and anyway, Jake, I haven't even got my phone. You can turn round now, Henry!'

Poor Henry was beetroot red, but I couldn't fathom the expression on Jessica's face. She eyed me quizzically for a second or two then plonked herself down on the blanket.

'Are you two staying for lunch?' I asked as I opened up the picnic basket.

'No,' she said, 'you're all right. We'll leave you to it.'

'I've packed plenty,' I told her. 'Stay and tell me how things are going with the wedding.'

'Shall we?' she said to Henry.

'Well, I am a bit peckish,' said Henry, running an appraising eye over the containers I was setting out.

'As long as you're sure,' said Jessica, 'this one eats like a horse.'

'I'm sure,' I told her, passing Henry a plate. 'How did the marquee meeting go?'

'All sorted,' announced Jake. 'The guys have suggested setting up at the orchard end of the field so if the weather is good—'

'Which of course it will be,' I cut in for Jessica's benefit.

'Which of course it will be,' added Jake, 'then the guests will be able to walk through the orchards in the evening without having to negotiate the rest of the field.'

'And also,' said Henry, helping himself to a spoonful of avocado salad, 'that will mean that the cars can all be parked nearer the field entrance, although we're not expecting too many vehicles as most people are planning to walk down from the church, assuming—'

'Don't say it,' said Jessica. 'I'm beginning to get paranoid about the weather. Everything else is going so well at the moment that the only potential disaster I can see is if this glorious weather breaks.'

'It won't,' said Jake, reaching for a cup, 'not for weeks yet. Where's the cordial?'

'In the river,' I told him, 'the string's under the stone.'

'Oh clever you,' he said, kissing the top of my head as he went to retrieve it. 'Anyone would think she's always lived here, wouldn't they?'

'I would,' said Jessica.

'And me,' joined in Henry, 'I can't imagine Skylark Farm without Amber here to keep it on the straight and narrow!'

'Thanks,' said Jake, 'so what have I been doing all these years?'

'Jogging along,' said Jessica, 'nothing more, nothing less. Amber here is the one who has stirred things up.'

'Thanks, guys,' I said, feeling my face glowing as red as Henry's.

'And with that thought in mind,' Henry said, 'might I have a word with you before we go, Amber, in private?'

'If it's about flashing my undies,' I told him, 'then I absolutely promise not to do it at the wedding.'

'No,' he said, turning red again, 'nothing like that.'

'So how is the guest list shaping up?' I asked Jessica, leaving Henry to regain his composure. 'Everyone present and correct, I hope.'

'Yes,' she said, rolling her eyes, 'finally. Some people have really taken some chasing, I can tell you.'

'And what about Holly,' I asked tentatively, 'has she confirmed yet?'

'What?' Jake choked.

'Oh, I forgot to tell you,' I said, 'Holly and Jess are best buds now! Having bonded over diet recommendations, she was granted an invitation to the reception.'

Jessica threw me a filthy look before answering, while Henry sniggered behind his napkin.

'No, I didn't have to chase her,' she said haughtily. 'And yes, she is coming. She RSVP'd straightaway actually. Apparently she's out of the country until a couple of days before the big day and, unlike some, didn't want to forget about replying.'

'So much for learning the ropes from Daddy,' I said to Jake, 'so much for her professional attitude.'

'Oh, all right,' said Jake, 'can we please not have this discussion again?'

I looked at him and laughed. I liked the way that when it was mentioned in front of friends it was a discussion, but when I was bending his ear in private about offering Holly the right to make the cottage bookings it was an argument!

'Fair enough,' I said, slipping my shoes back on. 'Come with me a minute, Jess. I've got an idea for the wedding I want to share with you.'

'Don't be long,' Henry called after us, 'I've got to get back to work.'

'So,' I said, 'what do you think?'

'Perfect,' smiled Jessica, clapping her hands together, 'absolutely perfect.'

'I didn't want to say anything in front of Jake because he always laughs when he knows I've found an idea in a magazine.'

Jessica held out her hands and held up the glass jar I handed to her, admiring its simplicity.

'So if we start collecting jars now—'

'Any size,' I reminded her.

'And I get some lengths of ribbon and lace to tie around the necks—'

'And tea lights to go inside.'

'Then these can be dotted around the tables in the orchards and light up the path to the marquee.'

'Exactly,' I said, 'you can pass them all on to me if you like. I don't mind making them and if I start now it won't be one of those rushed last minute jobs that turn into a nightmare.'

'Oh, we won't be having any of those,' Jessica said sternly, 'rushed last minute nightmares are simply not allowed.'

'Of course,' I smiled, 'message understood. Now, why don't you go and get Henry so we can have our little chat before he has to go back to work?'

Henry's 'little chat' turned out to be quite a big ask in the end and more akin to the work I had done in London than feeding hens and painting walls at Meadowview Cottage; for the first time since moving I wished I had my contacts book and old phone with me. I was going to have to call in some favours to pull this one off, but Henry was desperate.

Right up until the last minute he'd thought the honeymoon was sorted. He'd even forked out a massive deposit which now seemed to have gone AWOL along with the company he had booked through. He knew where he wanted to take his bride and what they were going to do when he got there but beyond that, having already had his fingers burnt, he was feeling pretty clueless.

'You're my last hope,' he had said, wringing his hands together. 'Well, I don't mean that exactly.'

'I know,' I told him, 'don't worry. Just leave it with me.'

'I knew you'd be able to sort it,' he said, already sounding relieved and more than happy to pass the dilemma on.

Personally I wished I shared his confidence but I was determined not to let him and Jessica down, whatever the cost.

Chapter 42

Henry's little favour ended up taking far longer to arrange than even I could have imagined when I offered to take it on, but of course with no internet at the farm and access limited to The Cherry Tree Café and library opening times it was inevitable that my progress was going to be hindered. With the phone signal at the farm being so intermittent more often than not I ended up driving to a layby up the road just to check my emails, and only then if the wind was in the right direction and the truck was parked in precisely the same spot.

A few days after our clandestine chat, with the wedding looming ever closer and Henry's blood pressure and stress levels rising so rapidly that it was looking increasingly doubtful that he would have the stamina to attend the ceremony, I was almost there. I just needed one final push and some peace and quiet to check everything over and make sure every little detail was in place.

'I'm just going to town!' I called up the stairs to Jake. 'I should be back around lunchtime.'

Annie was sitting at the kitchen table eagerly seeking out titbits of gossip from the local paper.

'You don't mind, do you?' I frowned as I gathered my things together and looked guiltily at the dozen or so boxes crammed into the kitchen. 'I promise I'll take all these down to the cottage tonight.'

'Don't worry, dear girl,' Annie told me with a dismissive wave of her hand, 'it can't be helped. There's no rush. I'm sure whatever you're helping Henry with is important otherwise you wouldn't be running yourself ragged trying to sort it, would you?'

'It *is* important,' I told her, grateful that she was being so understanding. 'Thanks, Annie.'

'But what about this lot?' moaned Jake, stumbling into the kitchen with a frown firmly etched on his face. 'You can't just leave it all here now you've got something more exciting to do, Amber. What if Annie trips over one of these boxes?'

'Excuse me,' said Annie, twisting round in her chair and staring sternly at Jake over the top of her glasses, 'if anyone around here is likely to trip, it's you. Flying about the place with your size tens and snapping people's heads off before you've even said good morning! Whatever's the matter with you?'

'I just want to see the cottage finished,' he said sullenly. 'I thought it was supposed to be done by now.'

'So did I,' I said, glancing up at the clock, 'but Henry—'

'Henry nothing,' Jake cut in. 'I asked him what's going on when I saw him yesterday and he said he didn't know what I was talking about.'

'Well, he would, wouldn't he?' I snapped back, annoyed that Henry couldn't drop his guard just enough to keep me out of Jake's bad books. 'You know it's all supposed to be a secret.'

'Well, whatever's going on,' he continued, his tone loaded with sarcasm, 'I can't see why it's taking this long. I know you like keeping busy but you can't just flit from one thing to another without finishing anything.'

'Helping Henry is taking this long,' I reminded him, 'because we have no internet here and precious little phone signal. You know that. And I don't flit from one thing to another, thank you very much. This is just bad timing, that's all. What's with the attitude and loaded questions?'

'Nothing,' he said and moodily nudged one of the boxes with his foot, 'nothing.'

'Fine,' I said, throwing up my hands and heading for the door. 'I'll see you later.'

Aside from the blip when I'd suggested hosting the May Fair, this was a side of Jake I'd rarely seen and I can't say I liked it much. If I'd known that helping Henry was going to be such a problem then I never would have agreed to it, but I couldn't back out. Everything was signed, sealed and practically delivered and if I abandoned Henry now it would all be lost and he'd be heartbroken.

'I just don't want you to get sucked back in,' Jake blurted out the second my fingers touched the latch on the door.

'What do you mean?'

'This whatever you're doing for Henry is related to your old job, isn't it?'

'Go on,' I said, unwilling to either confirm or deny his suspicions.

'And I can see what a buzz you're getting from it.'

I didn't have a clue where he'd got that idea from. Most of the time I was feeling dizzy, nauseous or increasingly panic stricken that I wouldn't be able to make it all happen in time.

'I'm not getting any kind of buzz,' I told him. 'Believe me.'

'Look,' said Jake, 'I loved you when we lived in London, I really did, but I love you so much more here.'

'I don't understand,' I frowned. 'What exactly is it that you're trying to say?'

'Just that you've changed so much since you've been here and I know how much you love the farm and the truth is,' he sighed, looking utterly miserable, 'I'm just scared that something's come along that has the potential to take you away. I don't want to see you pulled back into the life you had before. The life you said you were ready to leave behind, remember?'

'I'm not getting pulled back in to anything,' I told him and crossed the kitchen to give him a hug. 'And I'm not going anywhere either. My heart belongs to the farm,' I said, looking right into his eyes, 'and I promise you it always will. Please don't be in any doubt of that. OK?'

'OK,' sniffed Annie, noisily blowing her nose, 'I won't.'

Jake and I pulled apart. For a minute I'd forgotten she was sitting there. Well, at least now they both knew just how deep my allegiance to the farm ran.

'Look,' I said, 'I have to go. I'm hoping this will be the end of it today but if it isn't please don't question my commitment to this place, or to you for that matter. You're stuck with me now,' I said with a smile, 'you both are.'

I drove to Wynbridge with a very heavy heart, disappointed that Jake had even thought about questioning my dedication to Skylark Farm and the exciting new projects we were beginning to see come to fruition. I loved him and Annie and the farm and everything associated with it. I had from the very second I arrived and not just because of all the glossy magazines I had been reading. I wished he would just take a second to remember that I loved it all even though he had kept his relationship with Holly, and the fact that they'd lived in the cottage, to himself for so long. I loved life at the farm so much that I'd made the gargantuan effort to get over and see beyond all of those things.

By the time I found a parking space both the library and The Cherry Tree were open, but choosing which one to go to was a complete no-brainer. The library might have been the quieter choice but it was definitely lacking in calorific comfort food.

'Morning,' smiled Lizzie brightly as she bustled about setting up for one of her crafting classes, 'you all right? You look a bit down in the dumps.'

'I'm fine,' I said, trying to return her cheery welcome with a smile to match. 'Just rather a lot on my plate at the moment and it's a complete pain not having internet access at the farm. Although,' I added, eyeing the counter display of freshly baked cakes, 'this place does have its compensations.'

Lizzie, obviously used to the presence of so much creamy frosting, didn't follow my gaze.

'I don't know how you manage without internet at home,' she said, shaking her red curls in dismay. 'I'd go mad if I couldn't check Twitter and my emails every day.'

'I guess I've just got used to it,' I told her, 'and I don't have a Twitter account at the moment.'

'Oh well,' she sighed, 'each to their own. Just give me two secs and I'll get Jemma to come and take your order.'

'Thanks, Lizzie.'

I set up my laptop and kept my head down, determined to get the loose ends tied up as quickly as possible.

'Morning, Amber,' smiled Jemma. She sounded as cheery as her best friend. 'What can I get you?'

'Morning,' I smiled back, scanning the breakfast menu.

My stomach groaned loudly in response and I felt myself blush, knowing there was no way that Jemma wouldn't have heard. Fortunately she was too polite to comment.

'I know it's really early,' I said as I pushed the menu back between the cruets, 'but do you think I could just have a mug of hot chocolate and a double chocolate muffin?'

Hardly the healthiest of breakfasts but it was just what I fancied and, as Harriet had joked, I did have a little space to fill in my bigger bridesmaid's dress.

'Of course,' smiled Jemma, making a note on her order pad.

'It's all I've got the taste for,' I said by way of explanation, not that she was expecting one. A new email pinged into my inbox and I eagerly scanned to see if it was the news I had been waiting for. 'My appetite is all over the place at the moment,' I added distractedly.

'You aren't pregnant, are you?' whispered Jemma.

'What?' Instantly my eyes snapped from the screen back to her.

I couldn't tell from her expression if she was joking or not. Her next comment suggested not.

'When I was pregnant with my two I turned meal times on their heads,' she said, as if it was the most natural thing in the world to be talking about. She tapped her pencil on her order pad and carried on wistfully. 'Just for the first few months, it was pizza for breakfast and porridge for lunch and—'

'No,' I cut in, with a nervous little laugh, 'no, definitely not pregnant.'

'Oh well,' she shrugged, 'it was just a thought. Besides,' she added in a whisper, 'you and Jake did take a turn around the Maypole, didn't you?'

I didn't answer and she bustled off to prepare my order.

With Jemma's off the wall suggestion ringing ever louder in my ears I quickly fired off the confirmations Henry had failed to secure, typed up an itinerary along with all the details and links listing what he had to do next and sent the whole lot off to his inbox. It was done, finally, and I should have been relieved but I wasn't. In fact the completion of the project barely registered.

I closed my laptop with a snap, left some cash on the plate, abandoned my half-eaten muffin, called the cheeriest 'cheerio' I could muster and headed for the chemist. Ordinarily so organised with little gold stars on my kitchen calendar and with my office desk diary acting as a reliable back-up, the arrival and demise of my period was monitored with military precision. Any more than half a day behind

schedule and I would be drumming my fingers on my desk
and willing it along, but at the farm I had none of those
visual reminders and if I was being completely honest my
awareness of my monthly cycle had flown out the window
since the move.

I wracked my brains as I scanned the shelves trying to
remember the last time I'd taken a trip down the 'feminine
aisle', as my mother called it, but my thoughts were so addled
I couldn't even hazard a guess. Panic had well and truly
gripped me by the time I rushed back to the car park with
not one, but three pregnancy tests (just to be on the safe side)
and feeling grateful that I hadn't recognised anyone in the
queue.

'Oh great,' said Jake, opening the truck door before I'd
even turned off the engine, 'you're back.'

I quickly stuffed the transparent cheap and cheerful chemist's carrier bag behind my laptop and jumped out, clasping it
all protectively to my chest.

'I'm really sorry about before,' he said, his feet scuffing up
stones on the dusty ground like a guilty child.

He looked about twelve and I knew he was genuinely
sorry. To a certain extent I could even see his point.

'It's OK,' I said, eager to make quick use of the bathroom.
'Really, I understand.'

'Promise?' he asked sheepishly.

'Promise.'

'OK,' he grinned, 'here, let me give you a hand.'

'No,' I said sharply, gripping everything even tighter, 'it's fine, I can manage.'

The smile disappeared and was instantly replaced by that increasingly familiar frown again.

'I really am sorry, you know,' he said, clearly no longer convinced that I really had forgiven him for being so suspicious.

'I said I know,' I nodded, brushing past him and into the house. 'Sorry, I'm just desperate for the loo.'

'Fair enough,' he shrugged, beginning to look sulky again. 'Well, get a move on then and we'll move those boxes down to the cottage.'

Chapter 43

'Amber!'

I heard Jake calling up the stairs, but his voice sounded like it was a million miles away. For all I knew he could have been hollering from an entirely different galaxy.

'Have you fallen down the damn loo?' his voice called again. 'Are you coming or what?'

'Yes!' I called shakily, my voice cracking. I cleared my throat and tried again. 'Just give me a sec.'

I stared at the three plastic wands fanned out on the windowsill, my hands gripping the sides of the basin so hard my knuckles had turned white. I took a deep breath and forced myself to herd together my scattered thoughts.

Having finally stopped retching I had read and re-read each and every piece of information that had been supplied with the tests and shook as a steady numbness crept in and over me. It had started somewhere just below my knees but seemed hell-bent on enslaving my brain as well as my body.

Not just fat then. Not just gaining a few pounds in the boob department because I'd been eating cakes and tray bakes almost faster than I could stick them in the range.

No, not fat. Pregnant.

I closed my eyes to block out the sight of the regimented blue lines but they were still there when I opened my eyes again. The first one had appeared with alarming speed, as had the third. It was the second that had taken its time, but it was there nonetheless, conclusive evidence that I was going to have a baby. Jake's baby.

Beyond dancing around the Maypole we'd never so much as even talked about our thoughts on children. Our relationship so far had been solely focused on us and the farm and Annie, but we were going to have to talk about them now. And although I wasn't at all sure about how I was feeling (I hadn't even begun to allow myself to think about the tiny life I had growing inside me right there and then), one thing I did know was that this wasn't how it was supposed to happen.

Surely Jake and I should have been 'in on it' together? We should have, by mutual consent, been trying for a baby after a period of cooing over everyone else's. We should have chosen the tests together. He should be sitting holding his breath waiting for me to wave the blue lines in his direction and then enfolding me in his arms, one hand protectively stroking my still flat stomach—

'Amber!'

He certainly shouldn't have been bawling at me from the bottom of the stairs.

'I'm on my way!'

I clumsily swept everything back into the carrier bag from the chemist's, rushed along the hall to the bedroom and shoved it all in the top drawer of my nightstand.

'Sorry,' I said breathlessly, when I finally made it down to the kitchen. 'Sorry.'

'God, are you all right?' he frowned, the heat instantly disappearing from his voice. 'You look awful.'

'I'm fine,' I said, 'probably too much rushing around.'

This was certainly not the time to blurt out the truth. I wanted to get my own head around the unplanned pregnancy situation before I filled his. I might have made a hash of the whole 'dream / test / discovery' scenario but the scene setting for sharing the news with the father-to-be needed to be utter perfection.

'Oh, you've loaded up already,' I said, noticing the sudden absence of all the cardboard boxes that had been cluttering up the kitchen. 'I really am sorry they were left in here for so long. I know the situation has been less than ideal.'

Jake shook his head.

'No,' he said, 'I'm sorry. I should have been more help with the whole project, you've done practically everything on your own, and,' he added, 'I really am sorry for what I said earlier.'

'I know you are,' I told him reaching for his hand. 'And don't worry about the cottage. You've got enough on your plate, what with the Piggy Plan and the harvest coming up, and besides, I did say I'd sort it all out on my own. I just wasn't expecting Henry's project to take so long. One thing's for sure, though, no matter how it looked, I hated every minute of it. Although,' I added with a wry smile, 'when you know the details you'll understand why I couldn't turn him down.'

'Amber,' Jake sighed, pulling me into his arms, 'you really are a good girl, aren't you?'

I couldn't help but giggle as I listened to him paraphrasing Annie again.

'You always put everyone else before yourself and make everything better.'

'Well, I try my best,' I smiled, wondering if this whole unexpected pregnancy scenario was going to make everything better or complicate things too soon.

'I'm sorry I lost sight of that,' Jake continued. 'I should have known better than to question you. You've put up with a lot since you gave up your career to come here and I love you for that, I really do. If I start acting like a jerk again, just do us both a favour and tell me, will you?'

'Oh yes,' I said with relish, 'you can count on me.'

★   ★   ★

Unpacking the boxes of Annie's vintage hoarding and putting the finishing touches on everything was without doubt the very best part of the whole cottage project. Annie had even managed to make curtains and cushions from the piles of fabric I'd discovered. Every room was so incredibly authentic that I fully expected Ma Larkin herself to come bustling through from the kitchen, complete with a tray of sausage rolls or Bullseye cocktails.

'So,' I said, twitching the final curtain into place, 'what do you think?'

The vast majority of this final phase of unpacking had happened on autopilot because my mind had been thinking back over the last few weeks and exactly when this unexpected arrival might have landed in my life. You wouldn't know it, though, and even in my befuddled state, I could see how good it all looked.

The fact that I was feeling so calm came as something of a shock. For someone who had just discovered that her entire life was about to change beyond all recognition I was almost serene, but really, what would have been the point of panicking? Stressing out wouldn't have changed any of what had happened, and thinking back to Jake's expression as we took our turn around the Maypole, I couldn't really imagine that he was going to be anything other than ecstatic when he got over the shock of this unexpected addition.

If this had happened to me a year ago I would have felt as if my life was over, but living at the farm, happy with Jake, Annie and all our hopes and plans I felt that the gift of a baby could well be the final piece of the puzzle that made our picture complete.

Jake came and stood next to me. He looked around him and shook his head as he took in the light, airy room and pretty vintage furnishings.

'You know when we first talked about this place and I said I was considering tearing it down?'

'Yes,' I said tentatively, fingers firmly crossed that he wasn't going to tell me that he wished he had.

'Well, it kind of feels as if it's happened,' he beamed.

'What do you mean?' I frowned. 'What are you talking about?'

'All this,' he said, throwing his arms open wide, 'it all feels brand new. Everything about the place is so different, so light and fresh.'

'Well, everything is different,' I laughed, 'and the light is down to the conifers being culled.'

'No,' he said seriously, 'it's more than that. The whole place has an entirely different aura. It feels as if it's been cleansed or something.'

'Cleansed?' I laughed again, wondering what the hell he was talking about.

'Exorcised then,' he said. 'No, don't laugh. I know what I mean. The whole atmosphere has changed. I never thought

I'd be comfortable in here,' he reached for my hand, 'but you've made it happen. When you first told me about your plan to do the whole vintage thing I thought you were bonkers, but you've stuck to it and done it and it's utter perfection.'

'Thank you,' I grinned.

I could feel my cheeks burning and wondered if this was perhaps the right time to tell him about the baby after all.

'You really do make everything better, Amber, don't you? You just have this knack of bringing out the best in everything whether it's for the good of everyone like at the fair or more personal things like this for the farm. You make me incredibly happy and I think,' he said, lifting me off my feet and carrying me to the bedroom, 'I think we should be the first to christen this room with a little afternoon love-in. Don't you?'

He set me down again and I was grateful that he didn't comment on the extra tonnage he'd just had to manoeuvre.

'Bugger,' he muttered, frantically searching through his wallet, 'oh well, maybe not.'

My head was screaming at me to tell him that lack of contraception at that precise moment really wasn't an issue but my heart was pretty adamant that this wasn't the moment, and besides, the announcement wouldn't have made for the best foreplay in the world! Telling my beloved that I was carrying his baby required some careful scene setting and a very special occasion. Perhaps I should consider making the most of a few snatched moments with him at Jessica and Henry's wedding when the farm would be looking its absolute best.

Chapter 44

Manic. That would be the best way to describe the final few days before the wedding.

Friends of the happy couple had been dropping off various glass jars and bottles for us to transform into candle holders to light up the orchards for the evening. And, unbeknown to Jessica, I had hired lengths of pretty floral fabric bunting from Lizzie at The Cherry Tree to help complete the look, along with some pastel painted tins filled with fresh flowers for the few outdoor tables.

Secretly I was also planning to use a few of the tea lights to illuminate the way down to Jake's favourite spot by the river, which was where I had decided I would finally tell him about the baby. I had played out the scene at least a thousand times in my head, I even had a little speech prepared, and I was becoming as impatient as Jess for her wedding day to dawn so that Jake and I could share the excitement together.

Fortunately, the glorious weather was still with us and the marquee went up on the Thursday without a hitch. Unfortunately, the same couldn't be said for Jessica's spiralling stress levels, which were in danger of escalating completely out of control.

'You see,' she said, bursting into the farmhouse kitchen and dumping a box of jam jars on the table so that they rattled fearfully together, 'it's all these little things that are going to tip me over the edge!'

'I've told you a hundred times,' said Harriet, rushing in after her and depositing half a dozen carrier bags next to the box, 'that we can do all this. You're getting yourself worked up over things that aren't even an issue. You need to get a grip, Jess, and let someone else take some of the strain.'

Annie and I exchanged a quick glance as Jessica shot Harriet a killer stare capable of curdling fresh milk.

'You know you can leave all the orchard stuff to us, Jess,' I said, quickly standing between the two friends and thus preventing further friction. 'We've told you a dozen times we'll make all the bits and pieces and set everything up; you just concentrate on the marquee and caterers.'

'Henry's dealing with those,' she said, noisily blowing her nose.

'Well, the cars and flowers then,' I suggested.

'Mum's on top of those and the church and entertainment, and before you say it, the cake is almost done and it is utter perfection.'

'So,' said Harriet, her hands now firmly placed on her hips, 'what is it exactly that's got your nuptial knickers in such a knot?'

'Yes,' I cut in again, 'what have you got left to do, Jess?'

'I'm going to Norwich to collect the dresses,' she said, checking her watch, 'and pick my cousin up from the airport.'

'Well, I can see why you're panicking,' joined in Annie, a wry smile etched across her face, 'all that within forty-eight hours, you'll never make it up the aisle, Jessica!'

'I know, I know,' puffed Jess, a tiny smile finally appearing as she sucked her bottom lip, 'I'm a bit out of control, aren't I?'

'A bit!' snorted Harriet.

'Well, you didn't think I'd make it to the big day without having at least a few Bridezilla moments, did you?'

'No!' we all chorused and Jessica laughed.

'Are you going to come with me just to be on the safe side,' she asked, looking squarely at me, 'just for one last fitting?'

'No,' I said, swooping down on the carrier bags to hide my blushes, 'I'm going to get on making these, and besides, it fitted last week and I'm sure I haven't eaten that many cakes since!'

★   ★   ★

It turned out to be a blessing that I hadn't gone with Jessica to Norwich because Harriet, it turned out, was certainly not blessed in the craft department. When I looked up to see how she was getting on I had just completed my eleventh tea light holder whereas she was still struggling with her third.

'How is it,' I frowned at her across the kitchen table, 'that you can sow such tiny seeds, and handle those fragile little cuttings, but you can't tie a length of sodding ribbon around a glass jar?'

'I don't know,' Harriet grinned sheepishly.

'Here,' I said, passing her the ribbon and scissors, 'you cut the lengths of ribbon and drop in the tea lights, otherwise we'll be here all night!'

'How are things going down at the cottage?' she asked, pulling a length of ribbon from the reel and instantly getting it in a tangle.

'All done,' I told her proudly, 'and it looks amazing even if I do say so myself! I can't wait to welcome the first guests now.'

'And is Holly still lined up to organise the bookings?' she said, her eyebrows raised.

'Absolutely not,' I scowled. 'How did you know about that?'

'She mentioned it in the pub the night Jake put his foot in it. I think the pair of you were at the bar. I got the impression she was quite keen actually.'

'Well, thankfully,' I said, relieving her of the scissors before there was no ribbon left to work with, 'I had the opportunity to set her straight the day we cleared the cottage and we haven't heard a word from her since she took off on holiday. Between you and me I'm rather hoping she's so busy working on her tan that she won't give any thought to persuading me to change my mind. Do you know where she's gone?'

'No idea,' said Harriet. 'Actually she was a bit cagey when I asked her and she never did end up giving me a proper answer. Ordinarily she would have been bragging about it for weeks, but this time I'm as clueless as you are. It wouldn't surprise me if there was a new man involved somewhere along the line.'

'Here,' I said, ignoring her gossip and throwing a pack of lavender scented tea lights across the table. 'See if you can manage to pop one of these in each of the jars without anything coming to harm.'

Harriet laughed and set about her new, simple task with gusto. We worked in companionable silence for the next few minutes and I imagined Holly turning up at the wedding reception, bronzed and beautiful. Had I decided to take up my boss's offer to work in Dubai a few months ago my own glow would have rivalled hers, but I was glad I hadn't. The thought of Dubai, however, reminded me that my time was almost up.

I had known within minutes of setting foot on Skylark Farm land that this was where my heart belonged. I didn't want to go flying halfway round the world for the sake of a no-lines tan and a more stressful job than the one I'd just left behind in London. I knew it was wrong that I hadn't let Simon know sooner, but to be honest I had been so busy settling in to my new life that I hadn't given the old one a thought . . . until now. I promised myself there and then that straight after the wedding I would telephone and explain. I would even share my news about the baby if Jake was as happy about it all as I hoped he would be.

I put down the jar I was dressing and absentmindedly ran a hand across my belly.

'You all right?' said Harriet.

'Never better,' I smiled.

Chapter 45

Much to Jessica's relief, and mine, my bridesmaid's dress still fitted beautifully. It showed off my new round curves, thankfully, just on the right side of modest and demure, and although Jess's mother had declared the style a 'racy' choice for a wedding, the few other people who had seen the dresses agreed that they were stunning.

Having shocked her mother further by refusing the offer of a rehearsal dinner, and telling Henry in no uncertain terms that he and his rugby mates would definitely not be flying to Dublin to indulge in the 'stag do to end all others', no one dared decline when she requested their presence in The Mermaid the evening before the big day.

'So,' said Annie as I walked her back to the house from the marquee that evening, 'is everything all set for tomorrow?'

'Yes,' I said, 'finally. It took a while to hang the bunting, but it was definitely worth it, not that I'm sure Jake would agree, though.'

Jake was less than impressed that he had lost almost an entire afternoon to help, not when he had his own list of jobs from Jessica to get on with, but I didn't think wobbling about on top of a ladder to string fairy lights and bunting in my condition was the best of ideas. Not that Jake was privy to my condition, of course, which I hoped accounted for all the grumbling. Had he known I was pregnant I felt sure he would have been far more chivalrous.

'I don't see why Harriet can't help you do all this,' he had moaned as I passed him the seemingly endless lengths of fabric and lights.

'Because she's overseeing proceedings in the marquee,' I reminded him.

That, I admit, was only half the story. Having seen the hash she'd made of the lanterns I couldn't even begin to imagine what she was capable of doing with a few metres of loose bunting and a light breeze and had decided not to mention that I needed any help.

'We'll get finished a lot sooner,' I goaded Jake, 'if you stop complaining.'

'Oh, don't worry about Jake,' Annie smiled, 'when he sees you in that dress tomorrow he'll forget all about bunting and twinkly lights!'

'Well, I hope so,' I blushed.

'In fact,' Annie continued, 'it wouldn't surprise me if the two of you aren't making an announcement of your own before long. A country wedding, in my experience, always brings out the romantic spirit in everyone.'

My heart skipped a beat at the idea, but then I began to worry if Annie was perhaps a staunch traditionalist, and that she'd be disappointed that our own announcement was, in the traditional sense of the word, going to be the wrong way around.

'Well, I don't know about that,' I said, trying to pull her off the bridal path, 'but tell me, Annie. What do you really think of the changes we've made to the cottage? You do think it looks all right, don't you?'

I had been shocked by Annie's initial reaction as I walked her through the rooms for the very first time since the make-over had been completed. She had been quiet for much of the tour and when I finally dared to steal a glance at her, mortified that I had got it all wrong, I discovered to my surprise that her face was wet and there were tears coursing unchecked down her cheeks.

'I adore it,' she said, nodding enthusiastically, 'absolutely adore it, although I admit it was a shock seeing so many of the things my mother had known and used all back together again. It almost felt as if she could walk into the room at any moment.'

'But how do you feel now about keeping all of those precious things in there?' I frowned. 'Please say if you'd rather I put everything back in the loft and sourced the bits and pieces from somewhere else. The auction proved invaluable when it came to furniture so I'm sure I'd have as much luck there with finding everything else.'

'Absolutely not,' she said, patting my hand, 'everything is perfect. Don't for one minute think about changing a single thing,' she added with a wink.

'OK,' I said, kissing her cheek and feeling relieved, 'I won't.'

I dropped her back at the house and while waiting for Jake to finish up in the orchards and take us to The Mermaid, I made a quick inspection of the small box I had hidden under the shelf in the porch. I planned to put the blanket and extra lanterns on the riverbank early the next morning before I drove over to Jess's to get ready. I felt my heart flutter wildly as I pictured Jake and me sitting under the willows as I told him about the baby, our baby. I still couldn't believe it. Physically I didn't really feel any different, but my brain was struggling to think of anything other than the fragile new life I was carrying inside me.

'You ready then?'

I spun round, my heart very definitely hammering in my chest now rather than fluttering.

'God, you scared me,' I said, clutching my chest. 'Yes, yes, I'm ready.'

'I'll just wash my hands and change my shirt and we'll get off then. We'd better not keep Jess waiting.'

'Quite,' I smiled. 'To tell you the truth I'm not sure whether I'm looking forward to this evening or not.'

'Me neither,' Jake grinned conspiratorially. 'We'll give it an hour and if she's too much, duck out early.'

'If we dare,' I giggled.

By the time we got to the pub everyone else was already there and thanks to a celebratory bottle of champagne from Jim and Evelyn, Jessica was considerably more relaxed than she had been when I saw her earlier.

'I've only had half a glass,' Henry whispered with a naughty grin, 'and giving Jess the rest seems to have done the trick. She's more relaxed than I've seen her in weeks.'

'But she's been too nervous to eat anything since breakfast,' I whispered back. 'You don't want to get her completely squiffy.'

'Oh, I didn't think of that,' said Henry, looking rather disconcerted and definitely less pleased with his crafty plan.

'If she has a hangover tomorrow,' Jake joined in with a throaty chuckle, 'your life won't be worth living, mate!'

'Hello, you two,' said Jessica, rushing over and enveloping us both in a rib crushing hug. 'I was beginning to think you weren't coming.'

'We wouldn't have missed this for the world,' grinned Jake, passing me a glass of wine, 'would we, Amber?'

'Absolutely not,' I agreed, wondering what on earth I was going to do with the glass, 'but if you don't mind,' I said, pushing it back towards him as inspiration struck, 'I'm going to stick to juice tonight. I think at least one of us should have a clear head.'

'I don't mind,' said Jake, 'I'll drive us home if you like.'

'No,' I insisted, 'it's fine. Pass this on to Harriet.'

'Well, if you're sure?'

'Definitely,' I nodded, 'you have a pint with Henry. He's missing out on Dublin after all.'

'Well, that's very generous of you,' smiled Henry, giving me a swift kiss.

'Hey,' slurred Jessica, 'there'll be no canoodling with my bridesmaid, thank you very much.'

'Have you seen who just walked in?' said Harriet, suddenly appearing at my elbow. 'Would you look at the colour of her. She didn't get that sitting on the beach at Cromer!'

'Hello!' beamed Holly, immediately heading in our direction. 'And how are the bride and groom feeling? Any last minute nerves kicking in yet?'

'Not yet,' said Jessica, kissing the air about a metre either side of Holly's flawless face, 'but there's still time. Where on earth,' she said, holding her at arm's length and looking her up and down, 'have you been to get a tan like that?'

'Secret,' said Holly smugly, 'all will be revealed tomorrow.'

'Oh,' said Jessica, 'I'm intrigued.'

'Good,' laughed Holly, 'that's the idea. You are sure it's still OK if I bring someone, aren't you?'

'Absolutely!' said Jessica, sloshing champagne over the side of her flute. 'The more the merrier.'

Harriet and I exchanged stunned glances. That wasn't what she'd been saying when she'd asked us to help her out with the intricacies of the marquee seating plan for the evening sit down supper! Just how, I wondered, did Holly do it? I was going to have to study her technique a little more closely because her ability to wrap people around her little finger was astounding.

'Excellent,' she smiled, dazzling us all with her pearly whites, which of course looked all the whiter next to her gorgeous, golden skin, 'can't wait. Anyway, I mustn't stand here any longer, paling you all into insignificance!'

She said it with a smile on her lips, but I wasn't entirely convinced that she wasn't laughing at us, rather than with us.

'What did you make of that?' I said to Harriet as we watched her sashay away.

'Classic Holly,' said Harriet, rolling her eyes.

'Oh really?' I said and turned my gaze back to her.

'God yeah,' laughed Harriet, 'you might think you've got away with it, but then it sinks in and it's too late for a comeback.'

'A proper jellyfish,' I said.

'Exactly,' nodded Harriet, 'you don't feel the sting until she's gone. She might have apologised to everyone, but she'll never change.'

I was surprised by Harriet's admission.

'Hmm,' I said, watching Holly slide elegantly on to a stool and engage Jim in conversation. 'What do you think she meant by "all will be revealed tomorrow"?'

'God knows,' sighed Harriet, 'dread to think.'

'You don't think she's planning to upstage the bride and groom, do you?' I asked, wide eyed.

'I doubt it,' said Harriet, 'not now she's gone out of her way to make friends with everyone again.'

'So what is she up to then?'

'No idea,' Harriet shrugged, 'but, don't worry about it. If she starts getting out of hand we'll just ask her to leave.'

'Are you sure?'

Before she had time to answer Henry stepped forward and we all quietened down and looked at him politely, expecting some kind of pre-wedding speech.

'Right,' he announced, 'I'm going to take Jess home.'

'What?' chorused Harriet and I.

'You aren't serious?' frowned Jake. 'We've only just got here!'

'I know,' he said, 'but I think I've rather buggered up on the champagne front.'

'I'm fine,' said Jessica with an accompanying hiccup that ripped through the air and made us all laugh, 'absolutely fine.'

'Yes,' I said, looking at Henry, 'I think perhaps you have.'

'Oh God,' he groaned, 'her mother's going to go mad.'

'Take her for a brisk walk,' Jake suggested, 'that'll sort her out.'

'What, my prospective mother-in-law?' said Henry, looking confused.

'No, you twit,' laughed Jake, 'Jess, take Jess for a walk to help her sober up.'

'I think I'd better come with you,' said Harriet, 'just in case she needs someone to hold her hair back on the journey home. God, I get all the best jobs.'

'What a disaster,' moaned Henry. 'I'm really sorry, everyone.'

'Don't worry about it,' I told him, patting his arm and stifling a yawn. 'Probably just as well if we all get an early night. See you at the church tomorrow.'

'Oh no,' said Jess, giving me another hug, 'are you going already? You've only just got here.'

'Oh for pity's sake,' tutted Harriet, 'let's get her out of here, Henry; the sooner we put her to bed the better!'

Chapter 46

Jessica and Henry's wedding day dawned exactly as everyone had been praying it would, sunny and bright but with a light breeze that had just enough strength to stave off the intense heat. My first job was to meet Harriet at the marquee and await the arrival of Jemma and Lizzie from The Cherry Tree. It was our responsibility to ensure the cake was displayed on the right table and that everything else was shipshape, the finishing touches perfected and up to meeting Jessica's exacting standards.

I set off through the orchards and down to the marquee, determined to ensure I played my part in making Jessica and Henry's special day as seamless as possible, before quickly rushing down to the river to set up the blanket and lanterns for later. I was sure the butterfly feelings in my stomach last night were more to do with the baby than nerves and I was even more excited to share the news with Jake now.

'I hope you don't mind but we've made a start already!' called Jemma, as I approached.

I walked around the back of the marquee and discovered a pristinely restored Morris van loaded with rigid cake boxes parked next to the caterers' entrance. Taking in the pretty cherry tree and cupcake livery it was immediately obvious that the cake was in safe hands and that Jemma and Lizzie had the same lofty standards both within and beyond the café walls.

'Morning, Amber,' smiled Jemma as she appeared slightly out of breath in the doorway, 'I've almost finished with the cake.'

'Hello, hello,' laughed Lizzie, 'nice day for a white wedding, don't you think?'

I laughed along as Jemma rolled her eyes and the pair carried on bustling about in their spotless matching aprons each stylishly embellished with the same cherry tree design as the van. The pair worked together in a well practised fashion, and not for the first time I thought what a splendid set up they'd created.

'So,' I said, checking my watch and feeling appalled to discover that the time was already ticking away far faster than I realised, 'how is it all shaping up?'

'Come and see,' said Jemma, standing aside to let me into the marquee.

The pastel cupcake tower, floral bridal favours, kids' craft goodie bags and endless other clever touches completed the simple but stylish vintage country theme that I had already worked out Jessica was going for, as did the hand painted banner that was now artistically hung behind the top table.

'That's just a little extra gift from us,' Jemma smiled, 'Lizzie's idea. What do you think?'

'Oh wow!' Harriet, who had finally arrived, beamed. 'That is stunning!'

Lizzie blushed an even deeper shade of red than her hair and waved her hand dismissively.

'Well,' she said, 'I hope they like it. It's the first one I've made. I can soon take it down if you think it's not their sort of thing.'

'No,' I told her, 'absolutely not. You leave it right there. I know they'll love it, it's really beautiful.'

'Right,' Jemma announced, once she and Lizzie had again checked everything was in place, 'we'd better get back to the café. Lizzie has a felting session this afternoon and I've about a thousand cakes left to frost, but before I go,' she said, turning so only I could hear her, 'Amber, can I have a quick word?'

'Of course,' I nodded and followed her out to the back of the van.

'About what I said at the café the other day,' she said awkwardly, her eyes never leaving her feet, 'about whether there might be a chance that you were pregnant.'

'What about it?' I said, as I tried to focus on my breathing and stop my face flooding a tell-tale shade of puce.

'I hope I didn't offend you,' she said, looking at me quickly, 'only you'd gone a few minutes later and I can't help thinking it's because of what I said.'

'No,' I told her, trying to keep my tone light, 'absolutely not.'

'Are you sure?' she said, her eyes now searching my face. 'Because I would hate to think it was.'

'No,' I said again, 'honestly. I was just in a rush, that's all. You'll find out why at the reception later,' I blagged.

'Oh well, that's all right then,' she sighed. 'I've been so worried that I'd upset you!'

'Not at all,' I smiled, giving her a swift hug.

'Come on, Jem,' called Lizzie from the driver's seat as she revved up the engine, 'we're late!'

'Coming!' she called back, rushing round to the passenger door and jumping in. 'OK, leave the cake covered until the last minute and have a fabulous day!'

'But you are coming back later, aren't you?' Harriet called after them. 'The more the merrier!'

'Yes, we promised Jessica! As soon as the café's closed we'll be back for the reception.'

We watched the van bounce across the field and went back inside for one final look at everything.

'Stunning, isn't it?' Harriet sighed dreamily.

'Yes,' I said, nodding in agreement, 'if I was getting married this is exactly what I'd want.'

My former Caribbean poolside wedding fantasy had been kicked firmly into touch since I'd arrived at Skylark Farm and happily found myself ensnared by the raw splendour of the Fenland horizon and the romantic beauty of the orchards.

'There'll be plenty of time to think about that,' winked Harriet, pulling me out of my reverie as she impatiently tapped her watch. 'Are you ready to go? Time's pushing on.'

'Can I just have ten minutes?' I begged. 'There's one final thing I have to do.'

'I'll go and wait in the car,' she said, 'but if you aren't there in five minutes I'm leaving without you and you can incur Jessica's hangover wrath all on your own.'

'Crikey,' I giggled as we closed the marquee doors, 'she was in a state, wasn't she?'

'I don't know what Henry was thinking,' she laughed back. 'God help him if his bride-to-be is feeling anything less than radiant!'

Just a few minutes later, with the tea lights, lanterns and blanket arranged at Jake's favourite stretch next to the river, Harriet and I set off to enjoy Jessica and Henry's big day.

I'd never been much of a gusher when it came to showing emotion and neither, from what I'd seen, had down to earth

Harriet, but the sight of our friend in her bridal gown sent us both rushing for the tissues.

'I know it isn't a meringue or anything,' Jessica smiled as she span around in front of the floor length mirror in her bedroom, 'but it is right, isn't it? It is me.'

'It's perfect,' I told her, smoothing down my own similarly styled dress, 'in every way.'

Jessica had opted for a cream strapless, calf length, fifties number with a green waistband and silk pink roses in her hair and bouquet. The bridesmaids' dresses, with their halter necks, were the same soft green as Jessica's waistband and our clever silk posies and hair accessories matched the pink of hers perfectly.

'Aren't the roses fabulous?' Jessica beamed.

She appeared to have absolutely no lingering hangover from the champagne Henry had so foolishly pressed on her and Harriet and I had already exchanged relieved glances when we found her so happy and excited.

'Lizzie made them. Which reminds me,' Jessica said suddenly, 'how are things at the marquee? Everything is all right, isn't it?'

'It all looks beautiful, Jess,' Harriet sniffed. 'I don't think I've ever seen such a pretty wedding venue. It's simply exquisite.'

Jessica fussily checked the slightly strained zip on my dress and raised her eyebrows at my reflection in the mirror. I shrugged my shoulders in response but didn't say anything. I didn't know what to say; it was such a shock to hear Harriet, the least frilly, girlie girl we knew, spouting lyrical about flowers and bridal favours.

In fact, the shock was almost too much when we finally took in her transformation as she stepped shyly out from behind the decoupage screen and slipped her slender feet into her heels. Every time we'd visited the boutique in Norwich she'd refused to come out of the changing rooms and, beyond knowing that the dress fitted, even the bride was clueless as to how she really looked.

'But Harriet,' I teased, more used to seeing her caked in mud and sporting nothing more elegant than a pair of Hunter wellies, 'you really are a girl!'

'Shurrup,' she muttered, half flattered, half embarrassed.

The sound of voices and car doors slamming beneath the windows warned us it was almost time to leave and the three of us bustled about putting the finishing touches to our hair and our dresses. We didn't dare look at one another; there simply wasn't time to touch up our make-up again.

'Are you girls ready in there?'

Jessica's mother sounded as brisk and composed as ever. She had stayed out of the way while we dressed, opting instead to look after the little flower girl and keep Jessica's father out of the drinks cabinet and from changing his speech.

'The cars are here, Jessica!'

'You can come in, Mum!' Jessica shouted back. 'We're ready.'

'Oh my,' she sighed as she slipped into the room, 'don't you look beautiful. I admit I had my doubts about that dress, Jessica, but you were right.'

Harriet and I hid behind our posies as we registered the shock on Jessica's face.

'Now you girls,' the mother of the bride said addressing us, 'turn around so I can see the back. Mmm,' she frowned, her smile slipping slightly as she fiddled with her pearls, 'I still think backless was a racy choice. You don't want to be upstaged, Jessica!'

'It'll be fine, Mum,' Jessica tutted, ushering her mother back towards the door.

'Yes, well, too late to do anything about it now, I suppose.'

Harriet and I grinned at one another again but didn't say a word.

Chapter 47

The wedding service went without a hitch and it was a very happy party that walked down from Wynthorpe church to the marquee that afternoon ready to celebrate in style. Harriet, Jake and I opened the doors to let Jessica and Henry have the first look at the stunning interior and, seeing their reactions, I can safely say there was barely a dry eye amongst the guests.

After the meal and speeches the happy couple took to the floor for their first dance and I took the opportunity to make sure Annie was enjoying herself and congratulate her on her choice of hat.

'Do you like it?' she smiled broadly, giving it a little pat. 'I thought it was quite appropriate for the time of year.'

The decorated straw affair had definitely seen better days, but she was right: given that we were in the middle of fruit picking season the collection of silk and plastic fruit perched on top of her head was perfect.

'There's even a little sheaf of wheat tucked around the back,' she said, twisting round so I could see the full effect. 'If you hadn't have gone through the loft I would never have found it.'

I wasn't sure if that made me feel guilty or pleased. Judging by the way Jake was shaking his head across the other side of the dancefloor I guessed guilty was the way to go. As Jessica and Henry's song came to an end he made his way towards me, resplendent in a formal morning suit and looking far smarter and more dashing than I had ever seen him. The colour of his cravat I noticed matched the green of my dress and the pink rose in his button hole was the same as those Lizzie had used for the posies. I smiled and felt my face flush as I thought how we really did match each other in every possible way.

'May I have this dance?' he asked when he reached me, holding out his hand.

'Of course, dear boy,' beamed Annie, stepping forward, 'I thought you'd never ask!'

I giggled from the edge of the dancefloor as I watched Jake guide his auntie slowly round and round, his progress much impeded by a large bunch of cherries that seemed determined to poke him in the eye whenever he so much as glanced in my direction.

'Having fun?' said a voice close to my ear.

'Holly,' I smiled, 'hello. I didn't see you arrive.'

Surreptitiously we looked each other up and down. Personally I'd always thought it was bad form to wear white to a wedding if you weren't the bride, but perhaps I was wrong, and besides, given that she had such a glowing tan, I couldn't blame her for wanting to show it off. I was just about to compliment her on it, but she spoke up before I had a chance.

'Not everyone can carry that green off, can they?' she said, smiling sweetly. 'But with your dark hair and complexion it just about works.'

I pursed my lips and tried to think of something to say.

'Shame for Harriet, though,' she continued, wrinkling her nose and nodding to where my fellow bridesmaid and Rachel were sitting at a corner table working their way through a bowl of strawberries.

Bam, jellyfish by proxy! I definitely wouldn't be filling Harriet in on that one later.

'As I said, I didn't see you arrive,' I responded, deciding to talk about something else rather than get drawn in to a catty back and forth. 'Did you bring someone?'

'Oh yes,' she said, looking around her, 'he's here some-where. You'll see him later no doubt.'

'And did this mystery man,' I asked, remembering Harriet had mentioned that a man was probably involved in Holly's sudden disappearance, 'travel abroad with you?'

'Sort of,' she said, her feline eyes flicking back to me, 'he was abroad already. I just travelled out to spend some time with him.'

'Well, I'll look forward to meeting him later. Now if you'll excuse me,' I said as I spotted Jake settling Annie at a table and heading in my direction, 'I have a date with the dancefloor and my very handsome escort.'

'Save one for me!' Holly called coquettishly to Jake, before mingling amongst the other guests.

'Isn't it frowned upon to wear white to a wedding if you aren't the bride?' he said, watching her walk away.

'Hmm,' I said, slipping my arms around his neck. I had no desire to discuss his ex's choice of outfit. 'Now, are you going to dance with me or not?'

'I'd like to do *something* with you,' he said as he moved me gently closer. 'Have I told you how sublime you look in that dress?'

'No,' I said, pulling away slightly and pretending to play hard to get, 'you haven't.'

'Well, you do,' he whispered, drawing me back in and kissing my neck. 'In fact, I don't think I'm going to make it until we go to bed before I have to show you exactly how good I think you look.'

'At ease, soldier,' I smiled. 'If you meet me down at the river in an hour you won't have to wait until bedtime. There's something I have to tell you,' I added, just to make sure he didn't think the liaison was nothing more than a clandestine tryst.

'Oh,' he said softly, 'I like the sound of that.'

'Thought you might,' I said, moving so close that we were practically joined at the hip. 'Now come on. Just one more song and I'd better get back to my duties.'

The next hour seemed to take an age to pass but eventually it was time to slip out of the marquee, light the candles and run through what I intended to say again. My heart was beating to its own tune as I looked in wonder at the tiny lights that were beginning to twinkle in the trees and the pretty bunting swaying in the breeze. However, my steps faltered as I reached the river. The candles were already burning. I hoped Jake hadn't arrived early. I was determined to set the scene myself and didn't want anything to throw me off course. I was already feeling nervous, but I knew if I could just stick to my plan then I'd be fine.

A sudden movement next to one of the willow trees caught my attention and as my eyes adjusted to the change in light levels I could just about make out the tall silhouette of a man.

'Hello, Amber.'

'Dan?' I gasped, my heart beating a different tattoo in my chest. 'What on earth are you doing here?'

'I need to talk to you,' he shrugged as he settled himself on the blanket and patted the space next to him. 'Someone told me you had arranged a little seduction down here so I thought I'd make the most of it. Don't look so worried,' he laughed, 'I'm not gatecrashing the wedding. I was invited.'

'By who?' I frowned, my brain quickly scrolling through the guest list and trying to locate his name. 'Who invited you and who told you I was coming down here? I thought you were still abroad,' I added, my muddled thoughts spilling out in a clumsy rush.

I knew Jake would be arriving any second and I so wanted everything to be perfect and I also wanted us to be very much alone, but I could tell by Dan's demeanour that he was in no mood to be fobbed off.

'Holly,' he said simply. 'She invited me and she heard you whispering sweet nothings to Jake on the dancefloor about meeting him here.'

Holly. That one name sent a shiver down my spine and I was instantly filled with a horrible sense of foreboding.

'She came to see me in Dubai,' Dan continued, 'and asked if I fancied accompanying her tonight to keep her out of mischief.'

I didn't say anything.

'You know Holly, don't you?' Dan asked, looking up at me when I didn't comment. 'As I understand it the two of you are friends now.'

'I wouldn't go that far,' I croaked, my mind frantically searching for clues that might have forewarned me of this unexpected turn of events. 'Dan,' I asked, when I realised

419

Holly had been too clever to leave any, 'what are you *really* doing here?'

There was something unnerving about his sudden appearance. Surely if he was back in the country for the wedding he would have made the effort to catch up with his family at the house earlier in the day, rather than lurking in the shadows and turning up at my secret rendezvous spot. My heart sank further as I realised that his presence had nothing to do with keeping Holly out of mischief at all because he was clearly intent on making some himself.

'Actually,' he said with a twisted smile that made my stomach squirm, 'I've come to remind you that it's time to go back.'

'What do you mean, go back?'

'Simon's waiting for an answer,' he said. 'I've recently discovered that you've spent the last six months thinking about whether or not you want the Dubai job. You know, the job that I had assumed was mine. The job that you never mentioned you'd been offered and would be yours as soon as you snapped your fingers. You've just been playing at farms until I got everything up and running, haven't you?'

I felt my throat go dry and my heart began to beat faster again, but not out of excitement, rather a nauseating, all-consuming fear. I needed to get rid of him and explain everything to Jake before Dan relayed his own bitter and twisted version of events. He may have thought his anger was justified but I had only done what Simon had asked by keeping quiet.

'Amber?'

I almost jumped out of my skin as Jake called through the trees and I realised I was out of time.

'She's here!' Dan quickly called back, sabotaging my one and only chance to retrace my steps and steer Jake away.

'Dan?'

'Hello, brother,' said Dan, jumping up and amiably shaking Jake's hand. 'How's the farming life suiting you?'

'Great,' said Jake, looking confused, 'brilliant actually, but what are you doing here?' He turned to look at me and asked, 'Is this the surprise you were talking about?'

I shook my head but Dan didn't give me a chance to answer.

'As I understand it you've got some great plans for the place,' he continued. 'Letting out the cottage and putting some pigs in the orchard. That's right, isn't it?' he said, looking at me.

'How did you know about that?' said Jake.

He looked less than thrilled to see his sibling now and I knew Dan wasn't going to give me the opportunity to explain anything.

'Holly,' I croaked.

'What?'

'Holly,' I said again, clearing my throat and looking at Dan. 'She's switched allegiance. Dubai, that's where she got the tan.'

'Oh,' said Jake, 'right. I see. So you and Holly are an item now, are you?' he said to Dan. 'You're probably well suited actually. Both single-minded and headstrong, sounds like a match made in heaven.'

'Yes,' Dan smiled at Jake, 'single-minded and headstrong. But actually it's you who seems to have the knack for picking women like that, isn't it?'

'What do you mean?' Jake frowned.

'Don't,' I said, stepping forward and looking at Dan. 'Please.'

'Don't what?' pounced Jake.

'Amber here,' said Dan, nodding his head at me and carrying straight on despite my pleading, 'she's single-minded and headstrong, isn't she? I've come to tell her that Simon's waiting for an answer.'

'What do you mean?' said Jake, looking from his brother to me. 'An answer to what?'

'Whether she wants the job in Dubai he gave her six months to consider while I was out there doing the dirty work and setting everything up.'

'What?' said Jake, looking at me, his eyes narrowed to tiny slits.

I gasped for a lungful of air and felt the ground swaying beneath my feet. I couldn't believe Dan had said it any more than I could believe I'd put off dealing with it for so long.

'What?' he said again.

'Oh,' grinned Dan, 'oops, sorry, hadn't you told him?'

'Told me what?' Jake thundered.

'All yours,' said Dan, looking at me and taking a step back.

I swallowed hard and looked at Jake, my eyes begging him to understand what I was about to try to explain. What I should have explained before we even boarded the train to come to Skylark Farm.

'Before we left London,' I began, my voice catching and shaking in my throat, 'Simon told me that he was considering expanding the business. He said he was thinking about setting up an office in Dubai and asked if I was interested in managing it. I said no straightaway,' I quickly added, 'but he didn't want to lose me, so he offered me six months to think about it.'

Jake looked dumbstruck and I could see he didn't understand at all. I wasn't sure I did any more. I'd let my head and heart run away with life on the farm and put off sending that one simple 'thanks but no thanks' email that would have sorted it all out.

'So you came here with me,' said Jake, his voice unnervingly calm, 'what, on some sort of sabbatical? You came to the farm with a view to doing something different for a few months before you disappeared to Dubai?'

'No,' I said, 'no. It wasn't like that at all!'

'I fucking knew you weren't doing anything for Henry when you kept disappearing to check your emails. You were talking to Simon, weren't you? Is that what all this was about tonight?' he shouted. 'One last night together before you left for London?'

'No,' I sobbed, 'I never for one second had any intention of leaving. I knew right from the moment we arrived here that there was nowhere else in the world I would rather be. In fact I got so carried away with everything that I completely forgot about Simon and Dubai, and now he's turned up,' I said, pointing to Dan, 'and done this. I don't know why he's made me tell you but I promise I never wanted that job and I should never have left London without telling Simon once and for all. You do believe me, don't you?' I said, my eyes frantically searching Jake's for some clue, some hope.

'I don't know what I believe any more,' he said, his face unreadable as he ran his hands through his hair. 'This whole time we've been here feels like a sham now. All the time I thought you were committing to me and Annie and the farm and all the time you had this job offer in the background just in case things didn't work out.' He took a step back towards the orchards. 'Holly was right about you.'

'What?'

'She said you wouldn't settle here for long.'

'When,' I demanded, 'when did she say that?'

I couldn't believe he had been talking to her about me behind my back.

'Weeks ago,' Jake said nastily, 'she said you'd get bored here and go back at some point and she was right. And to think I tried to defend you to her.'

'But she couldn't be more wrong,' I sobbed, trying to push away the image of Holly and Jake alone together talking about what I did or didn't want. How many times had they met? Was it a one-off or was it a regular catch-up arrangement? 'She's wrong!' I said again, louder this time.

'I'm sorry, Amber,' said Jake, 'but even if she is, I don't think I know who you are any more.'

'I'm still me,' I pleaded, 'I just made a mistake, one silly mistake. Surely you can see that?'

'No,' he said, 'I can't.' He took another step away and shook his head. 'Why is it,' he shouted, 'that this place is never enough? I think you should just go.'

'What?'

'Leave!' he yelled.

I stood rooted to the spot too terrified to move and too shocked to speak. I watched through my tears as he turned and stumbled back towards the marquee and Dan began blowing out the candles and folding the rug as if nothing had happened.

'If I were you,' he said, passing me the blanket, 'I'd take his advice and get out of here as soon as possible.'

'What do you mean?' I sniffed, snatching the blanket from him. 'We'll get through this. You'll see. I'll go to Jake and explain everything properly.'

'No, no, no,' laughed Dan. 'It won't work like that around here, and besides, you heard him. He wants you to go.'

'Don't be so ridiculous,' I said bravely, 'that isn't what he meant.' I swallowed, feeling more unsure by the second. 'That was just heat of the moment stuff. This is my business, Dan, mine and Jake's. Not yours or Holly's or even Annie's. Jake and I will sort this out between us. You'll see.'

'And do you really think Annie will even want to look at you when she discovers what you've done? Do you think anyone will?'

'It's just a silly mistake,' I said forthrightly. 'Surely I'm allowed just one?'

'Oh, Amber!' Dan laughed. 'How can you not see?'

'See what?'

'As far as Jake's concerned,' he said bluntly, 'this is Holly all over again. You heard what he said: "why is this place never enough?" He thinks you're the same as her. Another woman he loved who found him and his beloved Skylark Farm wanting. Just another girl who couldn't be satisfied by him and this place!'

'Don't say that,' I sobbed, 'that's not how it is at all.'

426

'Well, that's what he thinks, and it's what Annie will think. To be honest,' he added cruelly, 'it's what everyone will think.'

I didn't say anything further but I could feel my anger giving way to fear. If my months on the farm had taught me anything it was that life here was visible and accountable, nothing like living in the city where you could just slip away, blend in and deal with your problems in peace. A giddy carousel of disapproving and disappointed faces swam before my eyes as I began to gauge how everyone would react to my apparent deception.

'As I said,' shrugged Dan, knowing he had made his point, 'the best thing you can do is exactly what my brother asked you to do: spare yourself and him the humiliation and catch a train back to where you belong.'

Chapter 48

I left Dan by the river and headed back towards the house. I had to get away to work out an explanation that would show Jake just how wrong he and Holly had been to judge me and question my commitment to life at Skylark Farm.

However, I wasn't only leaving the wedding party for my own sake; there was now the very real matter of the baby to consider as well. I still didn't know all that much about pregnancy but I couldn't imagine that adrenaline, fear and a racing heartbeat were the healthiest of cocktails for a developing foetus. Truth be told, I was scared. Not only had my revelatory moment been snatched from me, I was now in danger of losing the love of my life and my cherished home on top of everything else.

I had almost reached the house when I realised I wasn't alone.

'What are you doing here, Holly?' I seethed. 'What do you want?'

The she-devil herself stepped out of the shadows, her white dress glowing in the failing light.

'I just wanted to check you were OK,' she said smoothly. 'I thought I heard raised voices and Jake looked so upset when he passed me on the path.'

'You know I'm not all right,' I spat, 'you've engineered this whole situation to ensure I'm anything but.'

'But this isn't just about you, Amber, is it?' she smiled. 'And don't forget you were the one who lied about the Dubai job.'

'I didn't lie,' I shot back. 'I was only doing what Simon asked by not saying anything. I thought I was doing the right thing.'

'You only have to look at darling Jake to see how wrong you were.'

How dare she call him that?

'But don't worry,' she continued, 'you trot off back to London and I'll help him pick up the pieces. Give me a day or two and he won't even remember your name.'

'He doesn't want you!' I laughed.

'Doesn't he?' said Holly. 'Are you sure of that, Amber? If Jake doesn't want me, then why before I went to Dubai, did he keep in touch? Why did he keep seeking me out?'

'What are you talking about?'

'Everywhere I went he was there,' she told me. 'Every time I picked up my phone there was another text.'

'You're lying!' I shouted, feeling sick to my stomach.

'Why would I lie?' she shrugged, reaching for her phone. 'Here, see for yourself.'

'No!' I sobbed, turning away from the screen. 'I don't need to see. You're poison, Holly, do you know that?'

She opened her mouth to answer but I'd heard enough. Jake had already told me to leave and now Holly had confirmed that he still wanted her. She had the evidence to prove it stored in her phone. I rushed past her to the house, packed my bags and fled.

It wasn't until I was sitting on the train heading south to London that I realised I didn't have a clue what I was going to do when I got there. I had no job and no home to run back to. How was running away a healthier option for the baby than staying put, telling Jake I was pregnant and trying to sort the mess out?

But of course, that wasn't all there was to this situation now. Had it just been a case of crossed wires I would have gone to any lengths to unravel them, but the sudden, shocking inclusion of the Holly, Jake, Dan love triangle had complicated things beyond all reason. No matter what happened now, leaving Skylark Farm was the only sensible option, wasn't it?

Everywhere in the city felt cramped and claustrophobic, throbbing with people all living life at a frantic pace, and no matter how hard I tried I couldn't escape the noise and bustle. Being camped out in a busy Travelodge only compounded the problem along with my lack of sleep, but with a tenant in my flat and nowhere else to go, I simply had no other choice.

The first few days back passed in a daze and I only ventured out for the shortest amount of time possible. To be honest I was still feeling shaken that I had taken such drastic action and shocked by how quickly the situation had got out of hand. Had it just been nothing more than neighbours gossiping over my silly mistake I could have coped, but the addition of Jake's clandestine conversations with Holly meant that along with feeling stupid I was also feeling betrayed.

Coupled with the shock of knowing that I had left the farm behind and the fear that I could never summon the courage to see beyond what Jake had done behind my back, there was severe pain, an acute throbbing in my chest, and it didn't take a genius to work out that for the first time in my life I was experiencing genuine heartbreak. When I had watched films or read books about people describing themselves as heartbroken I had always believed it was more a state of mind, not something tangible that really touched the body, but it did. It literally felt as if my heart had ripped in two and I had no idea how to put it back together again, or even if I wanted to.

Had it not been for the baby I probably would have sunk far deeper than I'd care to admit but I never allowed myself to lose sight of the fact that I was responsible for the tiny life growing inside me. This baby, no matter how small and as yet unformed, had done nothing wrong. It deserved the best of me, not the worst, and it was these thoughts that finally pulled me out of my stupor and forced me to start thinking at least some way straight and consider how I was going to move forward.

My first port of call was the letting agency I had used to rent out my flat.

'Great timing,' said Annalise, the agent in charge, when I turned up unannounced and plonked myself on the chair opposite her desk, 'we've been planning to get in touch with you. Your tenant is rather hoping that you'll consider selling. She's totally in love with the place, especially that fabulous kitchen, and would be prepared to make a very generous offer, a good way above market value,' she added in a loaded whisper.

'Oh well,' I smiled weakly, 'wow. That's great news.'

The mention of my once treasured kitchen reminded me of the morning Jake had cooked the full English and I had gone into overdrive worrying about fat splashes and errant eggshells. How was it possible that so much had changed in such a short space of time and that just one silly misunderstanding could send it all free-falling out of control and beyond my reach?

'Can I tell her that you're at least open to the idea then?' said Annalise, her fingers already hovering over the phone.

'Yes,' I said, 'absolutely. Although I might need a couple of weeks to get myself organised enough to move the things out that I left behind. You see, I'm not exactly sure where I'm going to be living now.'

'Well, that doesn't matter,' she said briskly. 'The sale will take a little while to go through. I take it life in the country didn't suit after all then?' she added, her head sympathetically cocked to one side.

'Yes and no,' I said, gathering up my bag and phone before I made a complete fool of myself.

Pregnancy hormones I had learnt were very different to regular hormones. They were far harder to tame for a start. Recently I had found myself blubbing at cheesy adverts on TV and God help anyone who was nice to me. Suddenly there seemed to be nothing I could do to stem the flow and keep the ever ready tears in check.

'Keep me posted,' I said, swallowing hard and waving my phone in her direction, 'no problem with phone signal now.'

There was no problem with phone signal at all, but that didn't seem to matter to everyone I'd left behind. I hadn't heard a thing from anyone since I'd flung my bags in the taxi and made a beeline for the train station. I hadn't expected to hear from Jessica, of course. She and Henry were doubtless away enjoying the honeymoon in Vienna I had spent so long organising.

I wish I'd been there to see her reaction when Henry produced the two tickets to the Spanish Riding School in Vienna with its famous Lipizzaner ballet. I imagined her chattering excitedly about the baroque ambiance of the Imperial Palace, pirouettes, caprioles and gala performances, along with the extra-special tour it had been so difficult to organise.

No, no word from Jessica, but I had hoped that Harriet might have tried to get in touch.

Having escaped the letting agency without the embarrassment of traitorous tears, I hailed another taxi and set off to see Simon and find out just what had happened to send Dan ricocheting back into my life and so cruelly blowing it apart.

'Oh Amber,' said Simon, shaking his head when I relayed the horrid details of what had happened, 'I am so sorry. If I'd had any idea he was going to react like that I would have warned you.'

'I know,' I said, biting my lip to stop myself from crying, 'I know you would, but react to what exactly? Is it safe to assume that things didn't work out in Dubai?'

'No, the office out there is definitely happening,' he nodded, 'just not with Dan spearheading it. I'm guessing he didn't tell you that I've sacked him?'

'Sacked him?'

'Yep and I'm glad to see the back of him to be honest. He made a complete hash of the job, when he could be bothered to do it, that is. From what I can gather from the rest of the team and his expense account, he spent most of the time sunning himself and treating the experience as if it was nothing more than a glorified holiday!'

'Oh,' I said, 'I see.'

'The final straw came when he flew this woman out there to join him for a couple of weeks. Business class as well, no expense spared apparently! Well, I made him pay for his own flight back, and hers for that matter, and I know for a fact that he's now got no money to speak of and very few prospects.'

Suddenly everything began to slip into place. Dan, ably aided by titbits of gossip from Holly no doubt, had started to panic when he realised that in Jake's hands the farm had had a business makeover thus securing a potentially bright and profitable future. If everything was looking rosy at the farm and the place wasn't going to be sold then he wouldn't be getting his hands on a share of anything from Annie anytime soon. Not that he had any right to expect anything, of course, but I bet that hadn't stopped him hoping.

I had all my fingers crossed that Jake and Annie had seen through his sudden appearance and worked out his other motive for turning up and so viciously shovelling at least a dozen spanners into the works. I also hoped that my absence hadn't had an impact on their enthusiasm to secure the farm's future that we had all worked so hard together for. It was high time Skylark Farm thrived.

'I'm sorry he's spoilt everything for you, Amber,' Simon said as I stood up to leave. 'I really had no idea that he could be so spiteful.'

'Me neither.'

'So what are you going to do now?' he asked. 'If I can help in any way you know you only have to ask.'

I couldn't help thinking it was a shame there weren't a few more people like Simon in the world. 'No hard feelings,' he had said when I told him I didn't want the Dubai job and that I wouldn't be coming back to the office either. I wouldn't have been at all surprised if he didn't blame himself for some of what had happened because he refused to let me go in the first place.

If I could have just seen sense and walked away from the job before my move to the country then none of this confusion would have had the opportunity to arise, but it was too late to be thinking like that. The bomb had gone off and I had to salvage what I could and move on.

'I'm not sure what I'm going to do,' I shrugged, 'but there's no rush. I know the sale of the flat will make me a bit of money so I'll be OK for the time being.'

Of course I also had to factor into my equations and calculations the fact that the money would now have to stretch twice as far, as there was a baby on the horizon, but Simon didn't know that.

'Congratulations again on the twins,' I said, nodding at the plethora of photographs adorning his desk. 'What a lovely surprise.'

'Hmm, that's one way of putting it!' he said.

I left Simon proudly gazing at the photographs of his beloved babies, headed back to the Travelodge and made an appointment to go and see my doctor the very next day.

Chapter 49

'You know we don't really do this any more,' said Dr Green as she took the sample bottle from me and offered me a chair, 'especially when a patient is in the process of changing surgeries.'

'I know,' I said, 'and I appreciate that, it's just that given the circumstances I can't make any decisions about anything until I know that this is definitely happening and for that, I need your help.'

'And what makes you think the three tests you took at home could be wrong?'

'I don't know,' I shrugged, trying not to think of Skylark Farm as home. 'I guess I just won't really be able to believe it until I hear *you* say it.'

My doctor had been somewhat taken aback when I asked if she could confirm that I was pregnant, especially as she thought I had moved away for good, but when I explained some of what had happened and she took a long, hard look at the dark circles under my eyes and the brimming tears she agreed to do the test.

'Well, there you go,' she said, showing me the result, 'definitely pregnant.'

I wasn't expecting to feel shocked, but I did. Having her confirm it made me realise that my life really was no longer my own and no matter what I decided to do from now on, be it large or small, I was making choices for my baby, mine and Jake's baby, as well as for myself.

'Thank you,' I said, standing shakily back up, 'thanks.'

'Shall I make an appointment for you to see the nurse?'

'I don't know,' I said, 'I don't know where I'm going to be living. I might not be here,' I faltered. I didn't know anything.

'Well, have a think about it,' said Dr Green, 'and let me know, only don't leave it too long, OK?'

'OK,' I whispered, 'and thank you again.'

I headed back to my room in the Travelodge with a heavy heart and my life still in disarray. I might have sounded blasé about my prospects when I talked to Simon but actually, having now had my pregnancy confirmed, I couldn't help wondering if I would have been better off sticking to my original plan, brazening it out at Skylark Farm and waiting until Jake had calmed down enough to tell me exactly what had been going on between him and Holly. But it was too late to put things right. I would simply have to learn to live with my decision and move on with my life.

I was going to have to tell Jake about our baby at some point, of course, but I didn't know when. Perhaps it would be sensible not to reveal anything until I had a sizeable bump to show him. I couldn't blame him for not trusting me so there was no point telling him he was going to be a father until he could see the evidence for himself, but when was that going to be? I might know I was definitely pregnant but I had no idea how far along I was.

My phone vibrated in my bag and I pulled it out thinking it would be Annalise letting me know just how high above market value my tenant was prepared to go, but it wasn't. It was a text from Harriet.

'*Can you come?*' it read. '*Annie not well.*'

That was it. There were no details about what was wrong with her; whether she'd had another fall or if she was in hospital again; nor was there any mention of whether or not Jake had asked Harriet to send the text.

I banged out a short message in response and hit send.

No reply.

I waited almost an hour in my room with the arguments for and against jumping back on the train batting about in my head. In some ways even just the idea of it was ridiculous. I'd only been back in London for a few days. I still hadn't had enough time to clear my addled brain or make any real plans, let alone give the dust Dan and Holly had kicked up at the farm the opportunity to settle.

If I went back in this vulnerable state, with no emotional armour, no barrier or shield to protect me from Jake's disappointment or Annie's all-seeing gaze, I didn't know how I would cope. However, bottom line was that this wasn't about me, was it? There was something amiss with Annie and I knew I'd never forgive myself if anything happened to her and I wasn't there. Assuming, of course, she wanted me there.

The thought of what she must have been thinking about the situation had caused me just as much agony as what Jake had been going through (or not, depending on whether Holly had decided to stick around and console him), but as hard as I looked for it there didn't seem to be any way in the world to come up with a solution that would allow me to make it all better.

With confusion still running roughshod through my mind, I set about packing my bags for the return journey knowing I would just have to take my chances because life was too short for regrets. That was one lesson I had learnt.

Chapter 50

Even though I'd only been gone a few days, arriving back at the farm in the glow of the late afternoon and stepping into the porch felt like the best and worst kind of homecoming imaginable. It was the best because everything felt so right, and the worst because the farm was no longer my home. I swallowed away the lump in my throat, raised the knocker and waited for the dogs to begin barking, just like they had that cold, wet and windy night when Jake and I began our new lives together.

I gave it a few seconds then knocked again, but the only sound I could hear was my heart pulsing through my ears. Suddenly I felt beyond tired and couldn't even muster the energy to walk down to the orchards to see if Jake was there. Leaving my bags I went and sat on Annie's swinging seat in the little garden I had taken so much trouble over, and decided I would just wait until someone came along and found me . . .

I don't know how long I sat there, alternately swinging and dozing and thinking about how much I loved the farm and Jake and Annie, but it must have been quite some time because when I opened my eyes, roused by a gentle but insistent tap on my shoulder, the sun was setting and the intense heat had gone out of the day.

Apparently my eyes were playing tricks on me because the person tapping me on the shoulder was Annie herself and she looked in the rudest of health.

'Annie?'

'Are you all right?' she frowned, staring deep into my eyes. 'You gave me quite a turn, I've been trying to wake you for ages.'

Slowly I sat up straighter and felt the blood rushing through my body in all the wrong directions. I closed my eyes again and took a second to gather my thoughts.

'I'm fine,' I said eventually, my fear of feeling her disappointment temporarily forgotten, 'but how are you? I had a text from Harriet saying you weren't well. That's why I've come back.'

'I'm all right,' smiled Annie, 'nothing wrong with me, not now anyway.'

'So you have been poorly,' I said, feeling more confused by the second.

'Not poorly exactly,' she said, carefully lowering herself into a chair, 'more muddled. I had a bit of a turn, as my

443

mother used to say, but everything's almost sorted now. And,' she sighed, 'if Harriet's text hadn't have done the trick and got you back, then Jake was planning to drive to London tomorrow to try and find you himself.'

'I'm sorry, Annie,' I said, 'you're going to have to explain. Why was he going to look for me? After everything that happened at the wedding reception, I thought he would never want to speak to me again. Besides, he could have just called me if he really wanted to get in touch.'

'I don't know exactly what he planned to say, my dear, but I got the impression it wasn't going to be the kind of conversation you should have over the phone—'

She was just about to continue when the truck pulled into the yard and Jake jumped out. I bit down hard on my lip and furiously blinked away the tears that had sprung up as soon as I realised it was him. The dogs leapt out of the cab and came rushing through the garden gate when they spotted me. I stretched over to fuss them and kissed their silky heads, making the most of the time they gave me to try to compose myself.

'I'll go and make us some tea,' said Annie, tactfully disappearing round the side of the house.

Oh why had all this happened? Why hadn't I had the sense to talk to Jake about that stupid job offer six months ago? My heart was breaking all over again. I should never have come back.

'I had a text from Harriet,' I said when I eventually dared to look up. 'She said Annie wasn't well . . .'

I was desperate to explain what I was doing there but the words simply refused to come and I quickly looked back down at the dogs, my breath sharp in my chest and those damn tears stinging and threatening to fall all over again. A strangled sob escaped my throat and the next thing I knew Jake was through the gate, pulling me to my feet, kissing me roughly and holding me in his arms.

'I thought I'd lost you,' he said, his own tears mingling with mine, 'I thought you were never going to come back.'

'But I thought you wouldn't want me back,' I sobbed, 'you told me to leave. Even Dan said you wouldn't want me anywhere near here after what I'd done.'

'And he was right,' Jake admitted, pulling me back down on to the seat, 'but only for about five minutes! When I went back up to the marquee Henry was looking for you. He kept me talking for ages. He didn't notice the state I was in because he was too excited about the prospect of telling everyone about the honeymoon surprise he was about to reveal. He wanted to have you there so he could thank you for everything you'd done. I knew then that I'd got it all wrong and ran back up to the house to get you but you'd already left.'

'Because I thought you didn't want me,' I said, shaking my head. 'I thought you wanted Holly. She said you had been meeting and texting. She had messages on her phone.'

'And did you read them?' Jake quizzed. 'Did you actually see *anything* I'd sent her?'

'No,' I admitted, remembering how I had refused to look at the screen. 'No. But what about the job in Dubai?' I sniffed. 'I should have told you about that before we even left London.'

'Doesn't matter,' said Jake, shaking his head. 'Consider it forgotten.'

But it mattered to me and I owed it to him to be completely honest.

'It *does* matter,' I insisted, 'because to tell you the truth, in the beginning, I had thought I might consider it, but as soon as we got here everything just seemed to fall into place.'

'I know,' soothed Jake, 'I know. As soon as I'd calmed down I realised that I should never have listened to Holly's sly comments. You wouldn't have gone to all the trouble over the May Fair and the cottage if you were planning to leave, would you? I could see that you were really trying to establish a future here for us, for all of us,' he said, gently laying a hand on my stomach.

I looked from his face to his hand and back again.

'I know about the baby,' he whispered. 'That's why I didn't want to call you. I had to see you in person.'

'But how,' I gulped, 'how do you know?'

I hadn't breathed a word to anyone.

'When I saw your bags were missing I knew you hadn't just gone off somewhere for a think and I panicked. I went through everything you'd left behind to try and find out where you'd gone. I knew you couldn't go back to the flat because there's someone else living there, but other than thinking you'd head back to London I was clueless. Anyway, I was looking in the nightstand drawer and I found—'

'The pregnancy tests,' I gasped.

'Yes,' Jake smiled, 'all three of them. Why didn't you tell me?'

'I planned to at the wedding reception,' I whispered. 'Those candles and blankets weren't there for Dan's benefit.'

'I did wonder,' Jake smiled, pulling me to him.

While it wasn't quite how I'd imagined him finding out, at least now we could share the excitement, assuming, of course, he was excited.

'Well, thank you,' he said, kissing my hair, 'for the best present anyone has ever given me.'

'So you are pleased then?' I asked, pulling away to look at him again and suddenly aware that I had been holding my breath.

'No, I'm not pleased,' he laughed. 'I'm absolutely over the moon!'

'I've no idea when it happened,' I told him, relief coursing through my body and loosening my tongue. 'I don't even know how many weeks I am.'

'Well, there's plenty of time to think about all that,' he said, holding me tight. 'I'm not planning on going anywhere, are you?'

447

We sat for a few minutes listening to the farm's resident blackbird and the hens clucking companionably. I didn't try to stop the tears from falling; I just wanted them gone and this whole muddle to be behind us so we could focus once again on the bright and happy life we had been planning all along.

'Have you told Amber about the Patricia situation?' Annie asked Jake as she wove her wobbly way back from the house with the tea tray.

'Here, let me take that!' said Jake, jumping up. 'No, I haven't. Not yet.'

'She is all right, isn't she?' I sniffed, drying my eyes on the handkerchief Annie passed to me.

'Yes, dear girl,' she said as she stooped to kiss my head, 'she's fine.'

'Annie thinks she's finally worked out how she came to be in the yard the day the fox was around,' Jake said as he began laying out what looked like the best teacups and saucers.

'It was Holly!' she announced without any preamble.

'Holly?' I frowned.

As if by magic Holly's 4x4 pulled into the yard.

'Yes,' said Annie, twisting round and waving for her to join us. 'I didn't remember until I saw her at the wedding reception and then it came rushing back to me. And, with any luck, we're going to get to the bottom of it all right now.'

I had no idea what was going on but suddenly all my old fears and insecurities came floating back up. If Holly was still on the scene then I had no intention of sticking around and playing piggy in the middle.

'I don't know what she's doing here, Jake,' I said, standing up, 'but I'm not staying. I can't.'

'Sit down,' said Annie as Jake caught my hand. 'She's here because I just phoned her from the house and asked her to come. I want you to hear what she has to say for herself, Amber.'

Begrudgingly I sat back down and purposefully averted my gaze as Holly came rushing through the garden gate.

'Oh thank goodness,' she said in a rush, 'Amber, you're back!'

'I told you she was,' Annie tutted, 'that was why I called you.'

Shocked to hear what I thought was relief in Holly's tone I risked one quick glance up at her. I was surprised to discover that she appeared far from sleek and sophisticated and more like the upset and ashen version of herself who had turned up at the farm the day after Annie's fall.

'Amber,' she whispered, taking the seat opposite me, 'we've been so worried. The night you left—'

'No, no, no,' Annie cut in, 'let's start at the beginning, shall we?'

'Is there really any point to all this?' I said, looking at Annie.

'Yes,' she said, fixing me with her beadiest of stares, 'there is.'

I sat further back on the seat and sighed. Apparently I wasn't going anywhere until I'd heard what Holly had to say.

'Go on,' said Annie encouragingly. 'Let's get this done. Holly, I know you have a lot more to say than sorry for being such a spiteful cow at the wedding.'

Holly shook her head and took a deep breath, but didn't say anything.

'Oh for goodness' sake,' said Annie crossly. 'I'll start then, shall I?'

'No,' said Holly, clearing her throat. 'It's fine. I will. After all, I'm the one who messed everything up.'

'That's not entirely true, is it?' said Jake.

'Oh it is,' she said, biting her lip. 'Isn't it, Annie? The game's up. You know, don't you? You know I'm the one responsible for your accident.'

'*What?*' I shouted, annoyed that the shock of what she'd said had got the better of my determination to sit in stony silence.

'That day,' Holly continued, 'Annie and I argued when I came here looking for Jake and when I left,' she said, hanging her head, 'when I left, I unbolted the henhouse door, let Patricia out and closed it again.'

'What?' I gasped. 'Why?'

'Because I was angry,' she went on, 'and upset.'

'I can't believe you did that,' I said in amazement.

'I know,' she sobbed, 'neither can I. I did come back to try and make amends but it was too late. The ambulance was already here.'

I could hardly believe my ears. I knew everyone had always maintained that Holly had a mean streak but this was beyond *anything* I would have thought her capable of.

'So what happened?' I asked, turning to Annie. 'How have you worked all this out?'

'I'd almost got to the bottom of it at the wedding reception,' she explained. 'I had this kind of epiphany. I was watching Holly and Dan have this godawful row and the way she stomped off triggered my brain into remembering what I'd seen the day I hit my head. But this is the first time I've had my suspicions confirmed.' She turned to Holly. 'You knew I was on to you, didn't you?'

'Yes,' said Holly, looking mortified. 'I did.'

I thought back to how Holly had turned up the day after the accident to ask if Annie was all right, and although I was relieved to finally have the mystery solved and my guilt absolved it didn't do anything to quell the pain of still knowing that she and Jake had been secretly meeting and talking about me.

'I know you don't want to be sitting here listening to any of this, Amber,' said Holly, leaning forward in her seat and looking right at me, 'any more than I want to be admitting it, but I want you to know the whole truth and I want you to hear it from me.'

'But you told me the truth the night I left the farm, didn't you?' I reminded her. 'You told me that you'd be here to help Jake get over me, that he still wanted you and had been secretly messaging you.'

Jake shook his head.

'It was all crap,' Holly admitted, 'all of it. There never was anything on my phone, Amber. I'd made one dig about your commitment to this place when we were clearing the cottage, but that was all. There's been nothing going on between us, Amber, nothing. Please don't think that we've been seeing each other behind your back because we haven't.'

'So why did you make out that you had been?'

'Because I was jealous of you, Amber, jealous of what you and Jake have going on here.'

It felt good to hear her admit it but there was still more I needed to know before I could really understand everything that had been happening.

'So where does Dan come into this?'

'I thought,' Holly went on, blushing deeply, 'that when Dan got in touch with me again it was because he was in love with me and that I could enjoy for myself some of what you and Jake have, but I was wrong.' She reached into her pocket for a tissue and daintily dabbed her nose. 'I thought we were well suited and could be happy together, but it

turned out he was just using me. I realised the night of the
wedding that everything was unravelling and I just wanted to
hurt you while I had the chance. I was jealous that you were
making Skylark Farm work and that you were happy. I'm so
sorry.'

'And what does the man himself have to say about all
this?' I asked. 'I don't see him here taking any responsibility
for his behaviour.'

'I don't know,' she shrugged. 'Once he'd got what he
wanted he dropped me again and now no one knows where
he is.'

'What do you mean "dropped me again"?' I asked.

'We'd had a relationship before,' she confessed. 'Harriet
had her suspicions, but when Jake and I parted she promised
not to say anything. You can imagine what she thinks of me
now. No less than I probably deserve. I'm sorry, Jake.'

Jake shrugged. 'I kind of had my suspicions as well.'

'I'm sorry too,' I said, surprising myself as much as everyone else. 'I feel sorry for you all, especially you, Holly.'

'Thanks,' she smiled. 'I should have known it was all too
good to be true.'

'I still can't believe Dan would go to such lengths,' I said,
shaking my head. 'What happened the night of the wedding?'

'Our guess is he panicked,' said Jake, taking up the sordid
story. 'When he realised, courtesy of what Holly had told
him, that everything here was on the up his spitefulness got

the better of him and he decided to spill the beans about this Dubai debacle. In his desperation to get his hands on this place he thought, if he could get you out of the way, Amber, then everything would be ruined. He no doubt assumed we wouldn't want to carry on without you so we'd sell up and he would still be in with a chance of a share of the spoils.'

'But his nasty little plan hasn't worked, has it?' said Annie, fixing me with her trademark beady stare. 'You are coming back, aren't you?'

I looked from Annie to Jake and then finally to Holly. I couldn't help thinking that, even though she looked tired and unusually dishevelled, she also looked as if a weight had been lifted off her shoulders. For the first time since the wedding reception I could see my way ahead. I had finally heard the whole truth and could make up my mind once and for all.

'Oh yes,' I smiled, 'I don't have a choice. My heart won't seem to beat properly anywhere else.'

'And now it's beating for two,' said Jake wistfully, 'it simply has to stay here.'

'Two?' squawked Annie and Holly together.

'Yes,' Jake grinned, taking my hand and kissing it, 'Amber and I are going to have a baby!'

Epilogue

Even between the two of us Jake and I hadn't been able to pinpoint exactly when I fell pregnant but according to my new doctor at the Wynbridge surgery my due date was around Valentine's Day. It was incredible to think that in less than a year my life had changed beyond all recognition and was now poised for the biggest transformation of all.

When the sale of my flat in London was complete I had taken delivery of the few boxes I had packed away in the cupboard. Jake and I had looked through them together, and as I flicked through the pages of my old work diary I realised how much I'd needed my life to change. Well, I only had to look at myself in the bedroom mirror to know that, together with the help of Jake and Annie and Skylark Farm, life had indeed changed in ways I never would have thought possible!

Aside from some photographs, I kept nothing from those few boxes. Bonfire Night had offered up the perfect opportunity to finally purge myself of my old life, and along with the potatoes wrapped in foil, my diary, contacts book and files had fuelled the flames of the ginormous fire, while my mobile phone had been packed off to a far flung country to transform the life of someone who needed it far more than me.

The months had slipped steadily by and passed peacefully from the bumper apple harvest to the depths of winter and by the time the 17th of January rolled around I was beginning to wonder if my due date was not far nearer than first thought. I was literally the size of the cottage, to my mind at least, and had to be escorted down to the orchard to take part in the wassailing in case I slipped on the hard, frosty ground.

Before the New Year I hadn't even heard of wassailing but I was now fully clued up as to the importance of the annual ritual of blessing the trees and asking for a bountiful harvest. I was looking forward to seeing the apple tree man, the oldest and strongest tree in the orchard, having mulled cider poured around his roots and cider soaked toast hung in his branches.

Annie and I had been on our feet all day, rushing around getting everything ready for the evening's festivities and we all set off together down to the orchards under a starry sky and theatrically bright Wolf Moon.

I was amazed by the sheer number of people who had turned out on such a raw winter's night and knew that many of them would go on foot to neighbouring orchards to continue the important ritual as the evening wore on. I was more than grateful that Skylark Farm was first on the list because my back was aching and I was ready to put my feet up in front of the fire.

'Are you all right?' asked Harriet.

'Just a bit tired,' I told her.

'You probably shouldn't be out here at all,' said Jessica, fussily trying to button my coat and rearranging my scarf over my ample girth.

'That's what I've been telling her,' said Jake, taking over where the girls left off.

'Oh, I couldn't miss this,' I told them all. 'I've been looking forward to it for days!'

Harriet linked arms with Rachel, and Jessica took a sip of mulled cider from Henry's ancient battered tankard. I was surprised to see that lots of people had brought their own mugs and cups but apparently that was all part of the tradition.

'Are you cold?' said Jake, trying to wrap his arms around me. ''Cause I'm freezing.'

'What, with all this extra padding?' I laughed. 'No, I'm fine. Apart from my toes, of course.'

'I'll give you a foot massage when we get back to the house,' he whispered.

'Oh,' I laughed, 'you really do know the way to my heart, don't you?'

I hadn't been able to see my feet, let alone reach them, for weeks.

'Well, I hope so by now!' he said, giving me a quick squeeze.

We stood together looking at the ruddy faces of our neighbours and friends as they warmed themselves around the braziers and gratefully wrapped their hands around their mugs. The children ran through and between the trees gorging themselves on the sticky sweet toffee apples Annie and I had spent the day preparing.

The orchards had looked so pretty for Jess and Henry's wedding in the summer, but seeing them lit by fire and torch light and filled with the sound of laughter, while the darkness slunk around just out of reach, held a magic all of its own and I think I liked it even more.

Great things were in the offing for Skylark Farm and, despite Annie's protestations, some of my profit from the sale of the flat had made a marked difference in reducing the size of the overdraft. The baby's imminent arrival was now the biggest excitement, of course, but we were also expecting the pigs in a few weeks along with more chicks, and after last year's success we would be playing host to the May Fair again (where I would definitely not be taking a turn around the Maypole). Bookings for the cottage had been coming in thick and fast, and the demand for Jake's cider was also picking up.

The future at Skylark Farm was looking very bright indeed and as I spotted Annie passing around the jug of cider, the rest of my friends laughing in the glow from the flames, I couldn't help but feel delighted that I had swapped city living for my new life in the country.

THE END

Acknowledgements

As always there are so many people to thank for their love and encouragement in supporting my writing life and this time around the list has increased tenfold!

Firstly I would like to say thank you to my family, who are now playing their increasingly familiar parts with ever more confidence, competence and not so much as a hint of impatience. Paul is still supplying the time, love and under-standing, and Oliver and Amelia are enduring my incessant ramblings about character traits, plot twists and word counts with heroic stamina.

The fabulous Books and the City team continue to be an absolute dream to work with. My endless questions have been answered, advice has been freely given, emails and tele-phone calls responded to in a heartbeat, glorious covers designed, exquisite editing undertaken and the result . . . not one, but now two novels to be proud of!

Next I would like to wrap my arms around my fellow authors, the RNA and Book Bloggers the world over. I cannot emphasise strongly enough the gratitude I feel for the support I have received from you all. You have enthusiastically championed my work through social media and beyond and every tweet and recommendation is hugely appreciated!

I would also like to thank my wonderful friends and colleagues from St Mary's Junior School in Long Stratton. Your interest in my time at the keyboard and scribbling away in my car at lunchtimes is always welcome. Mr Dingle you will indeed find yourself in the plot one day so watch out and thank you Posh, (aka Mrs Daniels), for providing names for two of the Skylark Farm hens.

And finally, thank you dear readers. I have been simply overwhelmed by the love you have shown for *The Cherry Tree Café* and I hope you can find a space in your heart for *Summer at Skylark Farm*. May your bookshelves, be they virtual or real, always be filled with fabulous fiction.

H x

About the Author

Heidi Swain lives in Norfolk with her husband, two allegedly grown up children and a mischievous black cat called Storm. She is passionate about gardening, the countryside and collects vintage paraphernalia.

Her debut novel *The Cherry Tree Café* was published in July 2015.

You can follow Heidi on twitter @Heidi_Swain or visit her blog: http://www.heidiswain.blogspot.co.uk/

Apple and Berry Crumble

No trip to Skylark Farm would be complete without sampling a few of the wonderful apples from the orchards and a handful or two of the berries that grow in abundance in the surrounding hedgerows, so here is a simple crumble recipe that deliciously combines both.

Ingredients

For the filling
6 large cooking apples
A handful or two of blackberries

For the crumble
400g plain flour
100g oats
200g softened unsalted butter
150g sugar

Method
It takes a little while to peel, core and chop the apples so have a bowl of water to hand to pop them in to stop them turning brown.

Once they are prepared tip them into either a large pan (with 3 tablespoons of water), or a steamer, and heat gently for just a few minutes. Personally I prefer to use a steamer as the apples tend to keep their shape better. Once they have softened, turn off the heat and prepare the crumble.

Tip the flour into a large mixing bowl and rub in the butter until the texture resembles fine breadcrumbs.

Add the sugar and the oats to the mix and combine thoroughly using a knife.

Place the cooked apples into a large ovenproof dish and scatter the blackberries over the top. (Depending on the season you could swap the berries for blackcurrants, gooseberries or chopped plums).

Cover the filling with the crumble mix, place on a baking tray and cook for 20-30 mins at 180°C until golden brown.

Serve with lashings of cream or custard and enjoy a true taste of the countryside!

Elderflower Cordial

For a refreshing and thirst-quenching taste of summer you simply can't beat a dash of homemade elderflower cordial mixed with either sparkling water or wine to add fizz to a sunny picnic.

The season for picking the blousy heads is short (from late May onwards), and take care not to pick those growing along busy roads as they may be tainted with fumes. Also, if collecting from private land you must ask permission first. This recipe makes 1.5 litres.

Ingredients
30 freshly picked elderflower heads
1.7 litres of water
50g citric acid (readily available from chemists)
3 lemons (sliced and grated)

Method
Carefully shake the heads to give any lingering insects an opportunity to escape!

In a large pan slowly bring the water and sugar to a steady boil, stirring until the sugar is completely dissolved.

Remove from the heat and allow to cool.

Once cooled add the citric acid, sliced and grated lemon along with the flower heads and stir.

Cover and leave to infuse for 24 hours.

Strain and pour into sterilised bottles.

If stored in a cool, dark place the cordial will last a few weeks.

Once opened keep in the fridge.

Toffee Apples

Adults and children alike enjoy these sticky sweet treats which are quick and easy to make. They are a firm Hallowe'en favourite and proved popular at the Skylark Farm Fair and the wassailing.

They can be made two days in advance which is a great bonus when organising a party!

Ingredients
8 apples (any variety other than cookers)
400g golden caster sugar
4 tbsp golden syrup
100ml water
Also required
8 wooden skewers
Cooking thermometer

Method
Cover the apples with boiling water for a few seconds. This helps remove the waxy coating and although not strictly necessary I find it helps the syrupy solution stick.

Thoroughly dry the apples, remove the stalks and insert the skewers.

Line a baking tray with parchment, place the apples on it and set aside.

Slowly heat the water until the sugar has completely dissolved, then stir in the syrup and boil to 150 degrees.

Remove from the heat and dip, twist and roll each apple in the syrupy solution.

Set on the parchment after any excess has been allowed to drip back into the pan.

<u>A little extra</u>
If so desired before the syrups sets, the apples can be dipped in chopped nuts or hundreds and thousands for an extra flourish but this is entirely according to personal taste.

Enjoy!

Simple Makes for a Pretty Picnic

There's nothing nicer at the end of a long, hot day than a lazy picnic tea that stretches into the evening. These quick easy makes bring a sense of occasion and turn a simple mealtime into a memorable gathering.

<u>Bunting</u>
As you can see from my book covers and Instagram account I have a huge affection for bunting. It brings a sense of occasion and adds a decorative finishing touch to every room in the house as well as transforming a simple garden get-together.

The instructions below are for one-sided bunting which is quick to make and ideal for hanging against a fence or under the eaves of a summerhouse.

<u>You will need</u>

A selection of cotton fabrics to make the flags. 2-3 fat quarters will be enough and a mixture of plain and patterned pieces works best. Personally I love a floral, polka dot, striped combo, but each to their own!
Approximately 3 metres of 2.5cm wide colour-matched bias binding tape
Scissors and pinking shears
Pins and un-picker
Matching cotton thread
Sewing machine
A4 paper or thin card for the flag template

<u>To make</u>
Draw and cut out the triangle template
Pin the template to the fabric and carefully cut out the shape using pinking shears (as this avoids fraying and extra sewing). Repeat until you have enough flags to make your length of bunting.

Evenly space the flags along the bias binding tape (remembering to leave at least 40cm of tape at either end for hanging), then fold the shortest edge over. Secure with pins and tack so it is ready for the sewing machine.

Sew along the edge of the binding with a straight stitch and then remove tacking stiches.

Hang, stand back and admire!

Candle Jars

As the day finally begins to fade, lighting candles in the garden creates a magic all of its own and this next make is so quick, cheap and easy there really is no need to skimp on numbers!

You will need

A selection of glass jars of all shapes and sizes

Lengths of string, wire or prettily patterned ribbon (depending on the look you are going for)

Rock salt

Tea lights

To make

If the labels are pretty they can be left, otherwise soak until they are easy to scrub off.

Pick either the string, wire or ribbon to tie around the top.

Fill the bottom of the jar with a deep layer of rock salt and pop in a candle.

Dot the lit jars around the garden and between containers and enjoy the magic!

Curl up with Heidi Swain for cupcakes, crafting and love at The Cherry Tree Café.

Lizzie Dixon's life feels as though it's fallen apart. Instead of the marriage proposal she was hoping for from her boyfriend, she is unceremoniously dumped, and her job is about to go the same way. So, there's only one option: to go back home to the village she grew up in and to try to start again.

Her best friend Jemma is delighted Lizzie has come back home. She has just bought a little café and needs help in getting it ready for the grand opening. And Lizzie's sewing skills are just what she needs.

With a new venture and a new home, things are looking much brighter for Lizzie. But can she get over her broken heart, and will an old flame reignite a love from long ago...?

'Fans of Jenny Colgan and Carole Matthews will enjoy this warm and gently funny story of reinvention, romance, and second chances – you'll devour it in one sitting' Katie Oliver, author of the bestselling 'Marrying Mr Darcy' series

Available now in eBook

473